THE SAGA OF TANYA THE EVIL

Viribus Unitis

[10]

Carlo Zen

Illustration by Shinobu Shinotsuki

YEN ON
New York

The Saga of Tanya the Evil, Vol. 10

Carlo Zen

Translation by Richard Tobin
Cover art by Shinobu Shinotsuki

This book is a work of fiction. Names, characters, places, and incidents are the product of the author's imagination or are used fictitiously. Any resemblance to actual events, locales, or persons, living or dead, is coincidental.

YOJO SENKI Vol. 10 Viribus Unitis
©Carlo Zen 2018
First published in Japan in 2018 by KADOKAWA CORPORATION, Tokyo.
English translation rights arranged with KADOKAWA CORPORATION, Tokyo through TUTTLE-MORI AGENCY, INC., Tokyo.

English translation © 2022 by Yen Press, LLC

Yen On
150 West 30th Street, 19th Floor
New York, NY 10001

Visit us at yenpress.com
facebook.com/yenpress
twitter.com/yenpress
yenpress.tumblr.com
instagram.com/yenpress

First Yen On Edition: May 2022

Yen On is an imprint of Yen Press, LLC.
The Yen On name and logo are trademarks of Yen Press, LLC.

The publisher is not responsible for websites (or their content) that are not owned by the publisher.

Library of Congress Cataloging-in-Publication Data
Names: Zen, Carlo, author. | Shinotsuki, Shinobu, illustrator. | Balistrieri, Emily, translator. | Steinbach, Kevin, translator. | Tobin, Richard, translator.
Title: Saga of Tanya the evil / Carlo Zen ; illustration by Shinobu Shinotsuki ; translation by Emily Balistrieri, Kevin Steinbach
Other titles: Yōjo Senki. English
Description: First Yen On edition. | New York : Yen ON, 2017–
Identifiers: LCCN 2017044721 | ISBN 9780316512442 (v. 1 : pbk.) |
ISBN 9780316512466 (v. 2 : pbk.) | ISBN 9780316512480 (v. 3 : pbk.) |
ISBN 9780316560627 (v. 4 : pbk.) | ISBN 9780316560696 (v. 5 : pbk.) |
ISBN 9780316560719 (v. 6 : pbk.) | ISBN 9780316560740 (v. 7 : pbk.) |
ISBN 9781975310493 (v. 8 : pbk.) | ISBN 9781975310868 (v. 9 : pbk.) |
ISBN 9781975310523 (v. 10 : pbk.)
Classification: LCC PL878.E6 Y6513 2017 | DDC 895.63/6—dc23
LC record available at https://lccn.loc.gov/2017044721

ISBNs: 978-1-9753-1052-3 (paperback)
978-1-9753-1053-0 (ebook)

2 4 6 8 10 9 7 5 3 1

LSC-C

Printed in the United States of America

THE SAGA OF TANYA THE EVIL

Viribus Unitis

contents

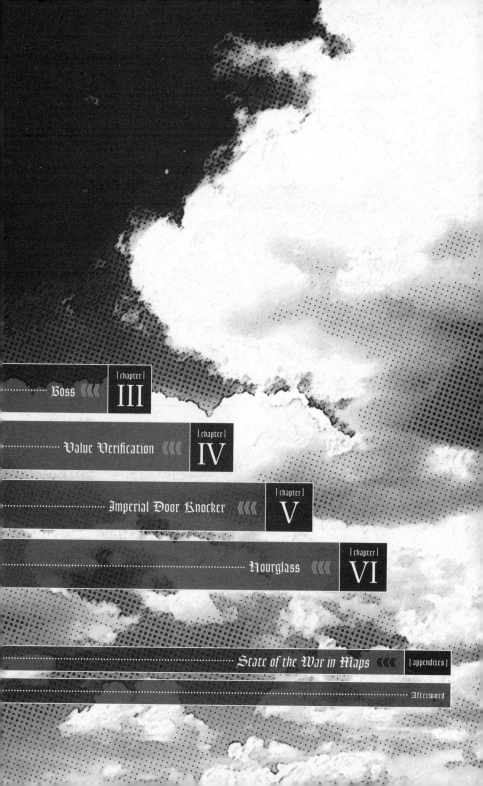

Prepared by the Commissariat for Internal Affairs

Federation

General Secretary (very respectful person)

Loria (very respectful person)

⌐[Multinational Unit]────────────

Colonel Mikel
(Federation, commander) ————— First Lieutenant Tanechka
(political officer)

Lieutenant Colonel Drake
(Commonwealth, second-in-command) ————— First Lieutenant Sue

Kingdom of Ildoa

General Gassman
(army administration) ————————————— Colonel Calandro
(intelligence)

The Free Republic

Commander de Lugo **(head of the Free Republic)**

Relationship Chart

Empire

【General Staff】

Lieutenant General Zettour
(Service Corps, inspector of the eastern front) ———— Lieutenant Colonel Uger
(Service Corps, Railroad)

Lieutenant General Rudersdorf ———————— Colonel Lergen
(Operations)

Salamander Kampfgruppe (aka Lergen Kampfgruppe)

203rd Aerial Mage Battalion

Lieutenant Colonel Tanya von Degurechaff

└ Major Weiss

——— First Lieutenant Serebryakov

——— First Lieutenant Grantz

(replacement)
First Lieutenant Wüstemann

Captain Ahrens (**Armored**)

Captain Meybert (**Artillery**)

First Lieutenant Tospan (**Infantry**)

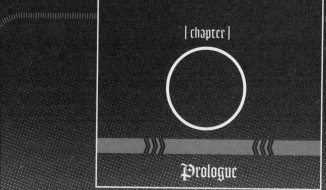

[chapter]

Prologue

Any era where heroes are needed is bound to be a time of misfortune.

Cao Cao, for example, is hailed by many as a brilliant leader who brought China out of troubled times. The legend of his triumphs is quite the story, to say the least.

But what happens when his legacy is examined from a different angle? Say, through the lens of a peasant who lived as a subject of the Han dynasty.

Given the choice, would they willingly choose to live through the tumultuous times that made it possible for Cao Cao to etch his name in the annals of history? Surely most people would much rather prefer the stable times he created for many who lived under the dominion of the Han dynasty after he rose to power.

In the absence of problems that require heroic intervention, there simply is no need for a hero. Naturally, the reverse is true as well. The only reason people scream is because there is something to scream about.

The same can be said for the Empire.

Its citizens banded together for a common cause—the Heimat.

The Empire sent each of its territories the call to arms.

In service of this unifying cause, there was no substituting the Empire's endless official propaganda, which caused its people to believe in more dangerous lies.

There was essentially no end to the war in sight without the Empire coming together.

Tanya von Degurechaff, lieutenant colonel for the Imperial Army, believes without a shadow of a doubt that there are far more calls for unity than could ever be supplied.

And what unity that could be found is far outstripped by how much is needed.

The delicate balance of supply and demand has been destroyed.

Any rational, logical person who believes in the market's integrity would be furious at the current state of its imbalance.

"…We're no longer in a position where we can let the free market determine what's right."

This sense of helplessness is met with a sigh Tanya can't keep to herself. A mutually exclusive contradiction is building up inside of her.

The ideal market is a rational one curated under the rational supervision of rational people. When it comes to capitalism, the market's integrity needs to be as absolute as one of the Ten Commandments.

I can understand the concept of bounded rationality.

I can also acknowledge that there are limits to rationality.

Even when taking this into account, one must respect the supremeness of rationality as a model.

But oh, how awesome the reality of this world!

Those who loudly claim they wish for peace have not the slightest idea of what they *actually want to buy.*

"The Empire is a chimera… The army desires peace, the government desires peace, the people wish for nothing but peace, and yet, the extent to which they're all seeing different dreams while lying in the same bed is unbelievable."

The mess that the Empire created for itself brings a wretched smile to Tanya's face.

The Imperial Army is an instrument of violence subordinate to the nation-state known as the Empire. Therefore, in terms of its principal-agent relationship, the Imperial Army merely has to fulfill the Empire's *version* of peace.

This issue is, the Empire doesn't want peace. What it wants is "victory."

Does it desire victory to draw peace out of the current armistice agreement? No.

A victory to create reconciliation as a pathway to peace? No.

A victory to satisfy the Empire? No.

The victory they desire is nothing more than winning for the sake of winning.

It no longer makes any sense. Using fire to fight fire can be logically sound depending on how the fire is used, but having the fire department dispatch a tank instead of a fire engine every single time is a colossal mistake.

It makes me want to scream. It's obvious they've completely lost sight of their goal.

And they call this a country? There was no strategy to any of it—the war machine simply careens toward its next battle!

While the Empire's utter lack of strategy should be the central focus of my concern, I'm completely taken aback by the straightforward manner in which we pitch ourselves toward more overt violence.

This may not make sense to those of you living in times of peace in the modern world. Let me explain.

Let's say that you were hired to run a storefront for a fast-food chain. Let's call it Reich's.

One day, for whatever reason, the owners of the chain and its shareholders come along and instruct you to "maximize profits as quickly as you can," without saying anything else. They have the utmost confidence that Reich's is going to take off but don't have any other information to offer: no plan, no goals, and no directions.

They also don't grant you any additional budget or authority over how the shop is run.

Should the operation fall through, it would be the employees who find themselves in trouble. How could they lay such a task on their employees without any guidance?!

No worker could bring success to their company under these impossible conditions.

To put it bluntly, this is precisely what the Empire's doing when it demands victory from its people.

Any employee at that fast-food place with even an inkling of common sense would immediately start looking for a new job.

It's not as if employees live for the corporation. They only work there to pay the bills.

Why should they pledge their allegiance to a restaurant chain? Who in their right mind would do such a thing?

Practically every human being with a brain can agree on the above.

However, some organizations operate on the premise that their members are inseparable from the group. This mirage of unity is the essence of what a nation is, and it is fully capable of deluding even the most intelligent, most civil, and most educated of citizens.

Love and hatred, good and evil. Or the greatest, most evil creation of the human race—the modern conception of the nation-state.

For Tanya, the mighty Leviathan from the parable would have been a cuter foe. It's tragic really. The Empire's version of the Leviathan is a chimera with three heads.

It's a system with three branches. The royal family and parliament dictate prestige and tradition, the bureaucrats ensure the nation continues to operate, and the Imperial Army firmly enforces the will of the other two branches.

The army, the bureaucrats, and the politicians form their own scrum.

This scrum acted as the word of God during the dawn of this nation. Despite this—nay, due to precisely this, the nation's founders eventually made a single, elementary mistake.

From the way Tanya sees it, her predecessors were wise and rational. This is what made their mistake inevitable.

Their mistake? Putting far too much in the hands of their successors. You see, intelligent people often operate on the simple premise that their successors will be just as wise and capable as they were.

The permanence of the system, in which its three heads work together to make it as robust as possible, is unconditionally defined by the Imperial system as "a given for excellent human resources."

Left to its own devices, a system that meets these requirements should grow into the most powerful nation in the world.

Fortunately and unfortunately for the later echelons of the Empire, the three heads indeed pursue their sole purpose during their "rapid rise to power." The knowledge and institutional traditions established by their predecessors were out of reach for the Empire, but the shackles that weighed it down were also light.

The chimera then sought to leapfrog its shortcomings with a system that relied on the talent and drive of individuals, who in turn—for better or worse—oversaw its rise to superpower.

As a result, the three heads each began to pursue their own goals. This can only end in one way: Each of the heads unconsciously believes that they are the "brains" that move the single shared body, and thus, each tries to pull it in their own direction.

It's a classic case of there being too many cooks in the kitchen.

What the country needs right now is unity.

The Empire cannot afford to waste even the slightest amount of time or resources on infighting with the number of fronts they are fighting wars on. Tanya isn't the only one who thinks this way, either. Any logical soldier fighting for the Imperial Army would have the same cold recognition of what is transpiring.

Tanya laments to herself the misfortune of the situation.

"The army is the only head that has unity... To be fair, this unity only extends to the realm of warfare."

Looking at it from a different angle, the army has maintained its sanctity by making itself an independent organization that exists within the Empire instead of acting as a *member* of the Empire.

What happens when each head of our chimera tries to assume absolute control over its own part of the body?

Each part will split up, break apart, and wander off on their own accord.

They each call for unity, but none of the heads show any intent of cooperating. The people may be united, but the beast surely isn't.

This may suffice during times of peace, but a country that can succeed under such governance in times of adversity does not exist anywhere.

This poses a dilemma for soldiers who are ardent patriots.

Foreign invaders need to be met with unity—that much is a given.

The question is, what constitutes unity?

There are too many heads on this chimera.

This sort of governance is something the army loathes. When it comes to thinking up strategies, the more heads the merrier. The issue is, once a singular goal is set, there can be only one head that commands the beast. The chain of command must be absolute to head off any confusion and eliminate all chaos.

This principle couldn't be more evident from a purely militaristic standpoint. It's imperative that battles are fought as one cohesive whole and not divided.

Chapter 0

A second chain of command is nothing more than fuel for confusion— let alone a third.

This should be painfully obvious to anyone who cares to study how the Empire has lasted this long in a war waged against the world. A mere glance at the grandiose treaty that binds the armies of the Federation and the Commonwealth is only further confirmation of this self-evident truth.

A divided army is little more than rabble. Even if there is a great horde of them, dealing them a crushing blow is a simple matter.

When one hundred soldiers must confront a force twice their number in battle, the chances of them winning despite the number disadvantage are slim to none. However, if those same one hundred fight twenty separate battles against ten soldiers at a time, then there is little doubt the force of one hundred will carry the day.

This common sense is drilled into every military commander at a very early stage. Nearly anyone who has stepped foot on the battlefield has learned these rules from firsthand experience.

This is the line of thought that brings Aerial Magic Lieutenant Colonel Tanya von Degurechaff to where she is now, as she haplessly stares at the ceiling in frustration.

"The army is unified. I only hope the same can be said for the nation."

So we have three heads on a single body.

Now here's a question:

What is the quickest way to break out of this chimera predicament?

"Are they trying to justify their actions on the basis of necessity...?"

The first solution that naturally comes to mind is a surgical one.

You could simply snip off the two extraneous heads.

Sadly, this way of thinking is far too simplistic. Even if the surgery could be completed successfully, it would be a terrible joke if the patient dies right afterward. Only a fool would try a stunt like this. Unfortunately, the Imperial Army is not for want of fools who have no idea what they're doing outside their realm of expertise.

What's more, these fools have only ever been taught how to perform surgery.

In fact, they've never learned how to find any other kind of solution.

The question *To snip or not to snip?* never occurs to them. If they encounter a problem, their natural reaction is to reach for their bayonets and perform surgery. It's simply a matter of when and where they operate, not if.

Perhaps worst of all, it's almost admirable how well they perform elective surgeries.

Take a high-ranking general like Lieutenant General Rudersdorf. There isn't a doubt in Tanya's mind that he is perfectly capable of such a thing. Though it's agonizing to criticize him and the rest of the brass as shortsighted, it's simply a fact that they are incredibly good at waging war. Too good.

It goes without saying that their intelligence isn't lacking.

The people who become staff officers all undergo a multitude of strict evaluations that scrutinize their ruthlessness, how calculating they are, and most importantly, how spiteful they can be—rigorous evaluations that Tanya has yet to undergo. It couldn't be clearer that the lieutenant general always keeps surgical removal as an option in the back of his mind.

The thought wouldn't crop up unless it was necessary.

But… Tanya shudders as a terrifying possibility crosses her mind.

People like the lieutenant general don't act according to their personal desires; they act to do whatever needs to be done.

To put it more clearly, the sort of screwups that put the final peg in their failing company's coffin tend to be made by exemplary employees who were most loyal to the company. What could possibly be more miserable than getting pulled down by the death throes of an organization's failed attempt to salvage itself?

Which brings us to the present. It's high time for Tanya von Degurechaff to take her patriotism and hurl it into the nearest rubbish bin.

It's clearly outlived its usefulness.

"This is ridiculous."

Is she getting paid enough for this?

Absolutely not.

Should she have to share her doomed country's miserable fate?

Even entertaining the idea is absurd.

There's no reason she should have to do work that's clearly above her rank and pay grade. Talk about labor standards.

Chapter O

Insufficiencies in the military system, structural failures of state institutions, and worst of all, the loss of any chance of salvaging the strategic situation. The only options left are hardly worth considering.

As it is now, the Empire is like a business barely scraping by from month to month, and Tanya is one of its loyal employees.

People who do good work need to be given commensurate rewards. Another way you could look at it is that money is the truest sign of faith and sincerity. As a concept or an ideology for structuring a society, it's perfectly reasonable. Tanya has no problem respecting her contract, either.

This social contract, however, is only legitimate if it can ensure stable employment and commensurate pay.

Now that it's plain to see that the Imperial Army's ship is in fact the *Titanic*, is there any reason she should have to stay aboard? If you want to live, then the only option is to run like mad for the lifeboats. This is the plank of Carneades in action.

In conclusion…

"I'm finished here… It looks like now is the time for a career change."

Tanya feels absolutely no remorse in leaving, even if it's considered defection. It's only natural to flee a sinking ship. And just as important is securing a path to retirement!

We are all nothing more than slaves to time.

Lieutenant General Rudersdorf, personal remarks

Human beings are creatures who are bound by their experiences and environment. No matter what knowledge they possess, no one can transcend this natural law. Take a beautiful sunny day, for example. Through the filter of war, even this beautiful sky could be reduced to *low cloud cover* and be a cause for concern.

It's impossible to take the world at face value. Humans are social animals; they have no choice but to close their eyes to embrace reality.

This is all the truer for members of a society with its own rules and regulations. Any person who is part of an organization will grow to personify that organization's culture.

Colonel Lergen was no exception to this rule.

He recognized this more than anybody. The man knew full well what being a senior staff officer for the General Staff meant.

Much to his chagrin, this awareness only deepened whenever he had to meet with someone from outside his bubble.

He walked down the familiar corridors of the General Staff Office as he made his way to the conference room, a wry smile coming unbidden at the thought of his upcoming meeting.

It was strange really.

It takes two to wage war, and when it comes to ending them, negotiating is an inevitable part of the program. It's not as if there was a way for the General Staff Office to bring an end to the war all on its lonesome.

Despite this fact, the Foreign Office and the General Staff Office were about to meet for the very first time.

The military and the Foreign Office had largely ignored each other up until this point. Their mutual tendency to avoid each other under the assumption that each branch should handle their own business had amounted to a colossal waste of precious time.

Time that had been bought with the bodies of young soldiers. The fact that years had gone by before this meeting was finally scheduled was nothing short of a sin.

For better or worse, the representative from the Foreign Office showed up on time and arrived before the very punctual Colonel Lergen.

"A pleasure to meet you, Colonel. I'm…"

"Your reputation precedes you, Counselor Conrad. I'm glad you made the trip here."

The suited man extended his hand to Lergen, who was mid-salute. He noticed the offer belatedly and gave a somewhat strained smile before lowering his hand to answer in kind.

They exchanged a handshake rather than salutes.

It was a simple social gesture, but it threw Lergen off. The man's grip was…so incredibly limp that he had to consciously avoid shuddering.

It wasn't the hand of a man who'd ever held a tool, much less a weapon.

This weak man was lucky to be born in the Empire of today—no, this was not the time to be having such idle thoughts. Lergen shook his head and set his eyes on the man across from him.

What he saw was a handsome, honest-looking man. At a glance, his counterpart seemed slightly older than himself…far too young to be a counselor for the imperial Foreign Office.

"I must apologize, as all my predecessors have been discharged."

"Oh… It is I who should apologize. Did my face give my thoughts away?"

"Yes, it did. Well, perhaps it's also because it's a bit of a sensitive topic for me." Counselor Conrad wore a slight grin on his face at this point. "I'm all too aware that I'm terribly young for my current position. I may be crossing a line by pointing this out, but are you not in a similar situation? You are awfully young to be a colonel in the General Staff Office, are you not?"

"You'd be surprised how quickly a man can climb the ranks during times of war… I'm not sure if you're aware of this, Counselor Conrad, but it isn't strange for recruits fresh out of the military academy to become lieutenants and lieutenant colonels as soon as they hit the battlefield."

"Fresh blood is a good thing to have in an organization." The counselor rubbed his chin playfully as he cracked wise. "We can leave the old bags to their card games."

He was clearly referring to his seniors at the Foreign Office.

By the sound of it, his workplace was a stressful environment for more junior members like himself. Colonel Lergen realized he was probably letting off some steam.

"Now then, Colonel, let's get down to business. We're both in the same boat. We need to clean up the mess our predecessors have saddled us with. I hope we can work well together."

Lergen was beginning to have hope that this counselor would pull his own weight after all. While he still had his reservations about whether the man truly grasped how much of a mess they were in, the fact that he didn't recite tired jargon like a broken record was a good sign.

"That's quite the scathing opinion you have there. Or…is it possible that's the reason you've blessed me with your presence today? You're getting my hopes up that changes may be on their way."

"Changes?"

"As a representative for the military, I would like nothing more than to work hand in hand with the Foreign Affairs Office."

Though the colonel wasn't honestly expecting much to change any time soon, he was met with a surprise.

The counselor nodded back with a look of indifference about him.

"Affirmative."

"What?"

"I'm saying you are correct, Colonel Lergen. We are but servants to the mighty Empire. We are but cogs in the machine that keeps the steel triad ticking. The government, the bureaucracy, and the army." An ever-so-slight smirk adorned his handsome face, and there was a stark fervor to the tone with which he spoke, hinting at the disdain lurking just beneath the surface. "The state of stagnation we find ourselves in today is the result of our isolation from each other. Now that we have realized our mistake, it's only natural we change course. Am I wrong?"

"No, I agree."

The counselor sitting before him began to display his animosity with a smile.

"It's quite simple, really, lest you be a fool. Unfortunately, our respective branches of the Empire think only the others are fools—a duet of obliv-iousness and ignorance." He scoffed, his tone growing angrier as if to emphasize just how disgraceful the situation had become. The man was unable to hide the sheer rage he felt. "We have fallen far from the sage tripartite that supposedly forms the basis of the Empire. Am I wrong?"

This was exactly what currently plagued the Empire.

Lergen couldn't help but agree with the man.

The Imperial Army espoused "military reasoning." That was the only language it knew. The imperial council, the imperial family, and the government cared about nothing besides public opinion. And as a result, the bureaucratic organization that kept the Empire running simply con-tinued to call for the preservation of the status quo.

The three gears no longer meshed.

To top it all off, each gear thought it bore the mission with the highest priority.

"The dysfunctional Supreme High Command is beyond salvation. Well, no one is innocent when it comes to our current predicament. In that regard, I should make it clear that I think the General Staff Office bears the largest responsibility."

Colonel Lergen sat at attention, acting as if he was taking the criticism to heart. The next thing the counselor would bring up, however, would shock him.

"Lieutenant General Zettour, in particular, has had an immense impact on the state of affairs with his rampant maverick behavior."

"The lieutenant general…? My apologies, but I'm afraid I cannot agree with that statement. The deputy director has been doing everything by the book. Could you elaborate?"

"During the battle with the François Republic, the leadership was kept in the dark about various military affairs. As a man of the military, Col-onel, you may not see the problem with this. From the perspective of this nation's people, we were all but ostracized. Moving forward, I'd like to request we share information equally."

"That's not our job."

This was all the General Staff officer, who had heard this complaint a million times before, could say in response. The counselor was upset about nothing more than a simple misunderstanding. From the General

Staff Office's perspective, the army wasn't being stingy with information at all.

"There seems to be some confusion. After all, we believe we are already sharing all information that needs to be shared."

"Of course you do. But, Colonel, a high-ranking officer such as yourself is surely aware of how Lieutenant General Zettour was involved with the arrangements that were made in the rear."

"...Are you implying he didn't share all the necessary information? The army shares what it knows and does its job. It's not like we're speaking in the presence of the emperor."

"Colonel... I must admit, I'm jealous of the General Staff Office."

"Come again?"

Counselor Conrad let out an exasperated sigh at Lergen, who was taken aback by the remark.

"I hear your operations are carried out brilliantly. The General Staff Office sounds like a phenomenal, intellectually stimulating work environment. I can only assume they recruited all the Empire's best and brightest."

"Forgive my arrogance, but it's only natural. A staff officer needs to be—"

Counselor Conrad cut off Lergen mid-sentence with more disparaging words.

"Thanks to you, us civilians have a hard time coming up with a satisfying explanation."

Lergen stared at him in open confusion, which was met with yet another deep sigh.

"You can't possibly think calling out morons for what they are suffices as an explanation, do you? You must be out of your right mind. Explanations need to be broken down. They need to be so easy to understand that even an idiot can understand them."

"And who exactly are the morons?"

"The common people you detest."

Lergen scowled at the counselor's scathing cynicism. He had gone too far. Lergen had never felt that way about the masses even once in his entire life.

"Well, Colonel. I'm assuming by the face you made that you disagree with my evaluation?"

"I don't feel like I've ever disrespected anybody based on class."

Counselor Conrad raised his hand to his chin and stroked it with a big grin on his face, openly skeptical.

"So you're the type who doesn't mind explaining the same thing over and over again. You'll go out of your way to help someone understand something they only comprehend a small fragment of, yes? What an excellent educator."

He had a point, and it genuinely rattled Lergen. He and most of the other staff officers were expected to comprehend and remember information after hearing it just once.

They were evaluated strictly on how efficiently they could handle their work.

It was the essence of a staff officer's duty. He couldn't deny that they were absorbed in trimming the fat wherever it could be found.

"It seems you understand at last what I'm talking about. Good. That will make this a quick conversation... After all is said and done, this is only a problem for you when dealing with outside organizations."

"As embarrassing as it is for me to admit, you've made me realize my coworkers are all highly capable communicators."

Lieutenant Colonel Degurechaff came to mind. She understood what needed to be said or done. This made her easy to work with. The same went for Colonel Calandro of Ildoa.

It went for his superiors, Lieutenant General Zettour and Lieutenant General Rudersdorf, too.

To put it bluntly, this applied to many people in Lergen's mind. This included those who worked under him as well. He never had to add any extraneous detail when he handed Lieutenant Colonel Uger an assignment.

Both his superiors and subordinates were quite responsive.

Their mutual military knowledge acted as a lingua franca, and they used shared tactics to complete their mission. What's more, they were all capable people who shared a common sense of pride in their duty.

When it came to communication, Counselor Conrad's grimace let Lergen know everything he needed to about the status quo.

"...So you're saying we haven't communicated enough?"

"To put it bluntly, yes. I believe it's worse than that. Of course, the

Foreign Office is not without faults of our own. Communication has been poor on all fronts."

Counselor Conrad took a moment to fish out a small case from his inner pocket before picking a cigar.

He cut it, then took out a match and—as if to show a sign of companionship—offered Lergen the case.

"Would you like one, Colonel?"

"If you're offering, I'd love to."

"Of course. These cigars are superb. They were a present for the vice-minister's office."

Lergen could tell their quality by the fragrance wafting around the counselor as he smoked. He could also tell by the seal that they had only been recently imported. They likely came through Ildoa... He was surprised the counselor was able to get a hold of them. Obtaining cigars like this was no easy task, even for the General Staff Office.

"I procured these to give as a gift, or at least that is what I told my irksome supervisor. Smoking one will make you an accomplice in my crime... There'll be no explaining this away when the ministry comes after us."

Counselor Conrad said this joke with the most serious of expressions.

It was hard to tell whether he was joking at all. Lergen let out an awkward laugh as he took a cigar.

"Never thought I'd see the day where I enjoyed meeting someone from the diplomatic corps."

Counselor Conrad brought his hands together in a gesture of wholehearted agreement, then put on a look of satisfaction.

"I'm glad you see it my way. You've guessed correctly—we both stand to gain something by working together. What's most important is your will to cooperate. Am I wrong, Colonel?"

"I agree with you, but wouldn't what we stand to gain be more important than our intent?"

"How very diplomatic of you, Colonel. Will does indeed come before ability. It's what drives all action. Ability without intent is worse than useless."

Counselor Conrad let out a quiet chuckle.

"You only need to look as far as my predecessors. On paper, they were all a competent bunch."

He held out his hand and began counting with his fingers as if he was naming the seven virtues.

"Multilingual, well connected, educated, sophisticated and cultured upbringing—they were all fine people with pleasant demeanors, and they each had a thorough understanding of the arts. Each of them a noble diplomat who has every confidence in the free market and the justice system. You couldn't ask for a better group of people."

He lowered all but one finger, which he used to poke his own head with the most serious of expressions.

"They all lacked drive. I assume your office is plagued with a similar problem?"

"I'll admit, mistakes were made during our initial confrontation with the Entente Alliance..."

"And now we're paying for those early stumbles. It's precisely the reason our branches have operated independently up until now. That needs to stop now. We need to start working together. I only hope we can start without delay. God forbid, we need to make *preparations*."

Regardless of how he felt on the inside, Lergen responded in a calm manner.

"Whether it be the army or the bureaucrats, I believe preparations for the worst must always be made."

It didn't matter what he felt. This was a sort of *political stance* Lergen had come to acquire as a staff officer—a military bureaucrat.

It was the exact sort of politics he loathed, but nevertheless, he was able to adapt to their way of thought with significant ease. He surprised even himself.

It was humiliating. He was also slowly but steadily becoming a political animal. As much as he loathed the idea, necessity is the mother of invention.

The same went for the counselor—it was the reason they were meeting in the first place.

After they calmly shared a brief stare down, the tension came to an abrupt end.

"You're absolutely right," Counselor Conrad said as he nonchalantly averted his gaze and gave a slight nod. "That being said, I don't see the need to dig new graves on the assumption of more failures. Rather than mourn our losses, why not work closely together to do what needs to be done?"

Lergen took a moment to think before he spoke.

What Conrad said undoubtedly sounded nice on paper, but Lergen didn't appreciate officials from other branches and their political games. There was no way for him to discern what hidden meanings might have been hiding behind the proposal. He tried to read between the lines. A moment of anguish passed as he pondered the bureaucrat's potential ulterior motives.

Unable to come up with anything, all he could do was agree with the premise.

"…You make a strong point."

"Excellent."

"What is it you find excellent, Counselor?"

"Oh," Counselor Conrad began to explain as if he was apologetic for not laying it out earlier. "I imagine the current stagnation occurring on both the eastern and western fronts is far from ideal. So I've come here to tell you how we view the current situation. We're deeply concerned about the situation and wish to figure out some sort of exit strategy."

"You're saying this as a Foreign Office official, I assume."

"But of course. As a member of my organization, it would be best for both of us if we could find a way to cooperate. This is why I think we should share the information at our disposal."

The way he speaks… He has no reservation about saying all this openly.

Conrad was remarkably easy to read for someone in charge of foreign affairs. This was likely why a strange feeling began welling up inside Lergen. He couldn't quite nail down the exact cause, but if he had to choose a word, the most accurate one was probably *jealousy*.

He was jealous of this man.

Given the current state of affairs in the Imperial Army, would it have even been possible for them to reach a consensus and propose something like this to another branch of government?

The ominous words *Plan B* flashed through Lergen's mind, but he brushed the thought away.

If everything went smoothly—if the army could fall in line with the Foreign Office—it would rid the Empire of its problems.

With a big smile on his face, Colonel Lergen extended his hand toward Counselor Conrad.

"It brings me the utmost happiness to be able to unify under the Empire flag."

"So you mean…?"

Lergen answered with a nod.

"There shouldn't be any objections from the army. If there's a way for us to end this war together, then they'll be open to it."

"…I must be honest, Colonel. This is a huge relief."

"May I ask the reason for that?"

"Of course," Counselor Conrad said as a puff of smoke escaped his mouth and billowed out past the cigar. "I was worried. Worried that there wouldn't be anyone in the General Staff Office that I could talk to in these troubled times."

The counselor's criticism was harsh, but Lergen was a staff officer. That didn't come as any surprise.

"I've come to realize the importance of maintaining a level of sobriety during these times of total war. War is nothing more than rationalized violence."

Lieutenant Colonel Degurechaff was a perfect example.

She didn't indiscriminately use violence as a means to an end.

She was an officer who had fully adapted to life during all-out war, though it would likely be for naught in the end. Lergen couldn't deny that she was a logical servant to the country, but there was something off about her.

At the same time, she wasn't like a runaway freight train. She could restrain herself when the situation called for it.

She was an officer through and through. She was measured, disciplined, and capable of taking the right action at the right time. It would be impossible to not hold her in high regard. One needed to look no further than her many accolades as a field officer—her record spoke for her. Lergen could only respect the young girl.

…In that regard, if that were the sort of field officer Counselor Conrad had in mind when he came to meet Lergen, it was perfectly understandable how he may have expected someone tougher.

After a brief self-reflection, Colonel Lergen realized that Counselor Conrad was standing up with a look of satisfaction about him.

"Colonel, thank you for today. I'm glad to have been able to meet you. I'd like to make the necessary arrangements to put things in motion. Is it okay for me to come by again tomorrow?"

"As they say, one must strike while the iron is hot. Let's get started right away."

 LATER THAT DAY AT THE OPERATIONS DIVISION AT THE GENERAL STAFF OFFICE—THE DIRECTOR'S OFFICE

"It's Colonel Lergen. I'm coming in."

"Hello, Colonel. What did the visitor from the Foreign Office have to say?"

"It appears they have also begun to fear for the worst. In that light, they have the same goals as we do. They know it's going to be a bumpy path to victory...but they believe that if we're able to work together, then there may still be a way out."

He glanced up at Lieutenant General Rudersdorf's face, which was deathly pale.

"That's good, assuming we can make it."

"Are we limited by time?"

"You'll need to ask the Ildoans about that. They'd tell you there's still some sand in our hourglass."

Lergen's brow creased at the blatant remark. He didn't need it spelled out for him that the Empire was in a bind.

"...I didn't think you were one for sarcasm, sir."

"Colonel, you're such a bumbling idiot."

Lergen let out a single small gasp. In all reality, Lergen recognized that he himself wasn't one for making jokes. Lieutenant General Rudersdorf was...probably just griping to let off some steam.

The remark certainly caught Lergen off guard, though.

The general was under immense pressure—tormented by the lack of hope in the war. Perhaps it was a coping mechanism that allowed him to carry on.

Chapter **I**

That said, Colonel Lergen, who had stood by his side all these years, had not failed to detect this change.

The Lieutenant General Rudersdorf from the past would've spoken much louder, with a firmer tone. *Could it be that he's on his last legs?*

"...It feels like everyone is running around without any idea of what to do. The turmoil of war is harsh. Fighting for all-out victory comes at a heavy price."

"We could use diplomacy to find an acceptable compromise. I believe it stands to reason that if we pour our resources into this, there may be a way to make it happen."

"Would you consider that a victory?"

Colonel Lergen answered the question with a firm tone.

"It is a victory."

Lieutenant General Rudersdorf gave him an intense, stern stare that said, *Go on.*

"I believe it's an ideal way for us to end the war. It would be a way for us to make the enemy accept our demands. Could it not be considered a different means to the same end?"

It wasn't a courageous victory. The war would effectively be ended by an armistice after so, so many had lost their lives.

An end to the fighting is still an end. It wasn't something to brag about, but sometimes the best medicines taste the most bitter. This was why Colonel Lergen remained steadfast about this proposal, even if he knew it was sugarcoated with hope.

"In terms of national defense, I believe this would be a clear victory."

"That only holds true if we can bring the war to an end on favorable terms. You and everyone else, you only talk about the future—about what you hope will happen. It's fine to talk about the harvest, but you need to sow the seeds and toil in the fields for there to be one."

"You're unmistakably correct, General. This is precisely why now is the time to prepare the soil, even if it costs us precious time."

"Oh?" Lieutenant General von Rudersdorf had a look of interest about him. "Are you unfamiliar with farming, Colonel? You need to have the soil ready by spring. By the looks of our calendar, we should be getting ready to start harvesting the crops by now."

He pointed out that it was already summer with a lighthearted laugh, but there was a flaw in his logic.

"If we're talking about oats, then you have a point... But timing depends on what you're trying to cultivate." Lergen was determined to stress that it was far from too late.

"What are you getting at?"

The glance aimed at Lergen was incredibly imposing, but Colonel Lergen kept his composure and continued his retort with a casual tone.

"I simply don't want any distractions. That's all. I want to have a clear mind when the time to harvest the homeland—the Heimat—comes around."

"I couldn't agree more, Colonel. As of late, there are too many trivial details that need to be hashed out despite the lack of 'time.' It's quite a shame."

He emphasized the word *time* as he shook his head with exhaustion.

"We are soldiers for the Heimat, for the Empire. We'll simply do whatever needs to be done. We can't hope for anything beyond that."

"I couldn't agree more."

"We need to try what we think is best. And hopefully, we choose the right way to go about it."

They both shared a sense of anguish at the notion that this was the best they could come up with. It was why Colonel Lergen decided to bet everything on making sure this new direction would bear fruit. Ignoring the call of duty was the last thing he'd ever do.

His love for the Heimat was more ardent than most.

"Colonel, work together closely with that...Counselor Conrad from the Foreign Office. No matter which path the Empire decides to take, we have to make do with whatever we've got."

"I'll see to it immediately. Would you mind if I borrow Lieutenant Colonel Uger?"

"...If you don't mind being met with the unbridled fury of the soldiers stationed on the eastern front—first and foremost, Zettour—when the trains stop running on time."

In these dire times, that was hardly enough reason to not secure Uger's help. Lergen knew what he needed to do, and he needed Uger to do it.

"I can endure that. This is for the Heimat."

"Perfect."

Lieutenant General Rudersdorf slowly rose from his chair. He gave a hearty chuckle as if a load had been lifted off his shoulders.

"If there's a way out of this with the limited time we have, then that's the best solution. I'm counting on you, Colonel."

"Of course, sir. You have my word."

"Now, I'll give you everything you need. You are acting on my authority. Do what you think is best."

Colonel Lergen thanked the general before giving a firm salute and taking his leave.

The colonel looked down at his watch. It seemed like there was a bit of time before his next appointment.

He took a moment to think about his day so far. His guard had been up from the moment he rose from bed.

The colonel had spent the morning meeting with Counselor Conrad, then Lieutenant General Rudersdorf.

Both these meetings were quite productive. But that progress came with a price... He found himself terribly tired. His body wanted a break to ease his mental fatigue. It didn't help that his less-than-stellar K-Brot breakfast only seemed to add to that fatigue.

At any rate, there was no escaping hunger.

Now that he had some time, Lergen figured he should grab something to eat...even if it meant dining at the General Staff Office's cafeteria.

Back in the olden days, he almost always would've eaten out instead. It was the obvious choice, considering the striking difference in quality and taste compared to the cafeteria fare. The war changed everything.

"It's more convenient if I eat in... To think the day would come where that argument would be enough for me to put up with that terrible taste."

Without the war, this probably would've never happened. After all, this was about the only place that could make eating out every single day a reasonable proposition. For everyday use, the banquet room at the General Staff Office was now a more logical choice.

Lergen was all too familiar with how total war had a funny way of making the impossible possible.

With that in mind, he made his way to the extravagant banquet room, where he would down some criminally bland food before grabbing some hot water and drinking cheap tea in his office before it was time for his next meeting.

At the exact same moment he reached the door, he heard a sound coming from the other side.

"It's Lieutenant Colonel Degurechaff, sir."

It was an elegant knock. Degurechaff had made some incredible accomplishments as a field officer. Even the stricter officers from before the war would have nothing to say about her greeting. There weren't many soldiers who carried themselves as she did. All officers were meant to be examples for the rank and file, but Degurechaff was likely the pride and joy of the military academy and the General Staff Office.

It was regrettable that they couldn't make more like her. But not too many. Too many Degurechaffs on the battlefield could very well lead to the apocalypse.

Either way, Lergen admired her.

"You're right on time. Punctual, as always."

The aerial magic lieutenant colonel stared blankly in response. Lergen had no doubt it was because she never would've guessed in a million years that she'd be complimented for showing up on time. Being punctual was an essential part of life, but to Colonel Lergen—however fundamental it may be—it was important and praiseworthy.

He was pressed for time. All the problems of the Empire were related to timing.

Colonel Lergen thought for a moment... The aerial magic officer who stood before him, Degurechaff, had never let him down. She had gone too far on more than a few occasions, though. That said...Lergen knew that sometimes desperate times called for desperate measures. He appreciated her decisiveness, especially now, when time was in such incredibly short supply.

"Thank you for the kind words, Colonel. I've come prepared for whatever suitably unreasonable orders you might have for me."

"How keen of you. We'll be sending you to the west in the coming days."

"The west?"

Colonel Lergen began to share the details with her.

"You heard correctly. We're going to give Lieutenant General Romel a single pawn. Think of it as a symbol of the General Staff Office's affection for him. I realize this is sudden and unexpected in the middle of a raging war...but I hope you'll produce results."

Abrupt, unofficial transfers such as this usually required haste, but the fact that they went to the trouble of keeping it discreet like this meant there was still a bit of time. Lergen recognized that this was a strange contradiction, but the Imperial Army was an organization that lived by the words *Eile mit Weile*. Slow is smooth, and smooth is fast.

This was especially true for colonels and lieutenant colonels.

"Yes, sir. I'll gather my things and head west. The General Staff Office has been quite considerate lately... How nice of you."

"Lieutenant General Rudersdorf is a compassionate man."

"Understood. Shall I deploy my Kampfgruppe?"

"No, we only need your aerial magic battalion. We want the other troops to focus on recuperating."

The calm lieutenant colonel saluted to show she knew her orders and would carry them out to the letter. How Lergen wished he could show her response to every imperial soldier.

Her conduct was exemplary. Her silence was impeccable. And yet, there was something about her stare that he couldn't ignore.

...Considering the Empire's current state, Lergen felt he should probably elaborate on what he meant by the General Staff Office's affection for Romel.

"There's something else I'd like to mention, Lieutenant Colonel."

"Sir?"

"The time has come for us to prepare for the worst. I want you to do your best to keep us from slipping over the brink. Please keep the bold and rash decisions to a minimum."

"Colonel, I'm a soldier—a simple officer who follows orders. I'll plan for the worst, and then I'll carry out my mission to the best of my abilities within the realm of my jurisdiction."

This was another formality. It was the exact response Lergen had wanted to hear, but she was no longer an officer who needed to assure anyone that she would carry out her duty.

Her textbook response was almost painful to watch. She was clearly trying her best to draw a line in the sand and emphasize that she was a soldier and nothing more. Lergen used to be that way, too. He hated politics.

"Lieutenant Colonel Tanya von Degurechaff, I feel like I'm getting to know you better as of late. I'm just curious as to where on earth you picked up that remarkable nose of yours."

"What do you mean, Colonel?"

He knew the answer to his own question. It was only natural for a hunting dog to have the nose of a hunting dog.

She had most likely already caught on to their Plan B.

It also made a strange kind of sense why Lergen thought he was getting worse at explaining things to people. He had spent too much time working with someone like her. Counselor Conrad was right—he needed to relearn how to break things down into laymen's terms.

He stifled a self-deprecating laugh to focus on the task at hand. Colonel Lergen jumped back into the moment and began telling Degurechaff what she needed to know.

"On that note...there's something I want you to do while strictly adhering to a schedule."

"Yes, sir. What is the schedule?"

"I need you to head to the eastern front on some official business. You're going to deliver a secret letter to General Zettour on behalf of General Rudersdorf. After that, I've arranged for you to spend some time preparing in the east. When that is finished, you'll return to the imperial capital. You'll head west after that."

》》》　　LATER, AT THE GENERAL STAFF OFFICE BANQUET HALL　　《《《

The banquet hall at the General Staff Office was always filled with officers who had just finished their lunches. This tendency was quickly becoming a routine.

People who thought this was how it always was didn't know the times before the war.

It may have been hard to believe, but as far as General Romel knew, the General Staff Office banquet room was merely for show. Taste wasn't a factor in the equation. In fact, this venue was famous for serving the world's worst-tasting meals.

But look at it now—it was packed full of officers. Even if the most alluring delicacies from around the globe were waiting outside, the ever-shifting war situation kept the senior staff officers too busy to eat anything besides the bare minimum.

This was why most of the officers at the banquet hall could be seen inhaling their food as quickly as they could to avoid tasting it. After this, they would smoke whatever cheap military tobacco they had on hand to wash the taste out of their mouths. For what it was worth, the officers refrained from tossing their cigarette butts to prevent the building from becoming a complete mess. Nevertheless, it was a far cry from what most people imagined when they thought of the prestigious General Staff Office.

In fact, most visitors who saw the scene in the past few days would have a hard time believing this was the center of military operations. This was all the truer for someone like Lieutenant General Romel, who hadn't been there in a while.

His disgruntlement with the vain olive wreath that had been placed over his head kept him from noticing right after his return, but...he found the state of the General Staff Office so disconcerting that it now seemed impossible to ignore.

From victory on the Rhine front to the struggling expedition in the southern continent...the drastic changes that had occurred in between made him feel like Rip van Winkle or Urashima Taro.

He had heard rumors, of course, but it was still a shocking sight to see for himself.

"...Not all old habits are bad. Maybe I didn't need to eat before coming to the General Staff Office."

He scoffed to himself as he walked down the same carpet that hadn't changed his entire tenure there. There were far more people here now than he could ever remember.

The halls were abuzz with activity.

Though it felt calm from the perspective of a field officer... This was the General Staff Office. Not too long ago, anyone who made noise for no good reason would have gotten an immediate tongue-lashing.

But look at this place now!

It was like he had wandered into a completely different building. The first thing he noticed was how the place was in total disarray. Romel was a firm believer in squaring away this sort of chaos with planning and order!

The sanctity of the General Staff Office had been lost. It was like a drunk, tottering man now.

This was supposed to be a place where soldiers marched in unison, a symbol of order, the temple of war. Has the death of thousands stripped something important from these sacred halls?

The lieutenant general shook his head and continued down the hall.

He headed deep into the General Staff Office building to a room that hadn't changed much despite the current state of the facility...and Lieutenant General Rudersdorf appeared exactly on time to welcome him in.

They exchanged salutes and jumped right into the thick of things.

The meeting was about the fortification of the defensive line as well as the establishment of a command-and-control framework on the western front. Frankly speaking, the orders to establish a command center there weren't coming from the General Staff Office directly, and it was still unclear whether or not a coup d'état was in the works.

Well, something along those lines was bound to happen out of necessity. He wasn't so old and senile that he didn't have some idea of what the head of the General Staff Office was thinking.

Nevertheless, out of all the infinite possible scenarios, he knew only one future awaited him. Their contingency plan was, as the name suggested, a mere contingency.

He didn't know Lieutenant General Rudersdorf's true intentions. This whole Plan B could be a feint of some sort. Regardless, General Romel's job wasn't to trick his comrades. He was a soldier, and his job was to fight wars. He would simply focus on gaining momentum on the western front.

There wasn't a doubt in his mind that the General Staff Office would use his excellent military service to their own advantage. He knew he should just focus on the war; there was no time for him to get caught up in petty games and politics.

This is why he had nothing but gratitude when he received his orders that explicitly told him to head west.

"I must extend my thanks for deploying White Silver with me to the front. It'll make things much easier."

Degurechaff was a talented aerial magic officer and an excellent staff officer. She was a rare diamond born in a generation of so many lumps of coal. An officer capable of handling the workload of two or three, maybe even four officers.

She was also a hunting dog he could discuss the contingency plan with.

It was no mystery why Romel was grateful to have her under his command. Unfortunately, there's usually a rain cloud waiting to rain on every parade.

"I must apologize—it will take some time before she's able to deploy. Know that Lieutenant Colonel Degurechaff won't be there as soon as you'd like her to be."

"May I ask why?"

Romel's expression tightened up a bit, though not enough to say that he was in a bad mood. The reaction was perfectly understandable.

…He liked to think of soldiers he was promised as checks. They couldn't be considered proper currency until he cashed them in. The reason for this was because reinforcements sent from the top usually ended up being fake checks.

He wanted cash in hand as soon as he could get it.

So he fixed the general with an intense stare and asked him why directly, but the answer he'd get was an unexpected one.

"Personnel has been riding me about getting her to spend both her summer vacation and the vacation time she has yet to use. Her summer vacation only just began as of today."

Lieutenant General Romel unconsciously—no, quite consciously—raised his voice.

"A vacation? Did you say vacation?!"

There had to have been a better excuse than that! The thought of a veteran aerial mage taking some time to relax and enjoy their summer during wartime was preposterous.

"My apologies, sir. But I must ask… Are you… Is the General Staff Office going to allow this?"

Romel thought of strategists as priests for the merciless god of necessity. They were fully capable of sacrificing their subordinates' vacation time for the sake of advancing war goals. Should the need arise, they were even willing to revoke already promised leave.

It went without saying that it's vital for the human mind to rest from time to time. But at the end of the day, farmers in the field of strategy were slaves to necessity. Not only that, but the person standing before Romel could easily cancel the aerial magic officer's vacation with a single phone call.

Stifling a chuckle, Lieutenant General Rudersdorf clasped his hands together while giving a slight shrug.

"Taking time off is important, no? It's simply a breather for Lieutenant Colonel Degurechaff while she runs a small errand for us in the east. We're having her deliver a secret document for us."

"Oh? And Lieutenant Colonel Degurechaff has to be the one to deliver this particular document?"

She was an aerial magic officer and an exceptionally skilled one with ample experience. Whatever she was delivering, it must've been a crucial set of papers.

General Romel had a good guess as to what the all-important package might be—a message regarding Plan B. Most likely a direct line of communication to General Zettour.

"Let's not get ahead of ourselves. It is a simple mission for her so she can take her vacation time. Think of it as a treat for her. She'll be able to do some sightseeing in the east and meet with Lieutenant General Zettour."

"Hopefully, heading to the eastern front will actually be relaxing for her."

"Yes. Let's pray that it will be."

Lieutenant General Rudersdorf casually muttered this to himself. It was evident to Romel that he didn't want to discuss the subject any further.

Romel almost felt bad for the tiny lieutenant colonel. She could never catch a break. He could only hope that she would get some real time off in the east before she came to the west, where he fully intended to work her to the bone.

"Well, if that's the case, then I understand."

"Good."

Lieutenant General Rudersdorf let out a single pointedly deliberate cough before getting back on track.

"Then it's decided. I look forward to your performance on the western front."

"You'll appreciate the results of our time in the south."

Lieutenant General Romel gave a salute before leaving the room. Once he was in the hallway, he heaved a leaden sigh.

The path back was a dim one as well. The halls he passed through might as well have been one long, decrepit rathole.

Even a cat wouldn't have wanted any part of this place. Romel was becoming afraid of the godforsaken General Staff Office.

It was scarier than the battlefield in its own way. He wanted to get out as soon as he could. The man who had endured hard fighting in both extreme cold and heat knew he would never get used to the doublespeak he encountered in his own country.

The same country that he was duty bound to protect from foreign threats as a soldier.

...He just couldn't shake the feeling that he was getting into something that went well beyond his duty. It was far too difficult for him to fully grasp the mess that was Plan B.

Things were getting too complicated.

If he were to liken the situation to a battle, it was as if his troops were strewn all over the place. It flew in the face of the tried-and-true principle of focusing the troops on a single target. Was he expected to pull off a miracle in this thick fog of war?

It was fodder for disaster.

"General Rudersdorf might be too far gone."

He couldn't help but feel the general was in over his head.

Something about the whole thing just didn't add up.

[chapter]

II

Con Artist

I'm not a talented man.
I simply do what needs to be done.

—— **Lieutenant General Zettour** ——

To sum up enemy General Zettour, he is a con artist.
He relies on deception to fight his battles and gambles
with his army during decisive battles.

—— **Federation Adversary Assessment Team** ——

A familiar scene was playing out on the eastern front.

"So we're being transferred? I had a feeling we would be, but…"

The assembled Imperial Army officers shared a looked of puzzlement after receiving their latest orders.

The eastern front was large beyond belief, so being transferred didn't seem very out of the ordinary. Despite this, or maybe precisely because of this, the men grumbled as they began filtering back to their respective battalions.

They were on the move again, marching through the vast tracts of land that characterized the eastern front as they made the journey west.

"Heading west again, eh? It feels like we've been heading west a lot lately."

There was a reason for their grumbling.

They were keeping an eye out for roaming partisans as they traveled with the assistance and guidance of the Council for Self-Government. The army was slowly going back from whence it came.

It was a slow withdrawal as they steadily contracted the front line. From the average soldier's point of view, it felt eerily like committing suicide by letting an open wound slowly bleed out.

After receiving the orders to pull back time and time again, the officers started to think the same way. They were bound to let out a grumble or two after pulling back so many times.

July had seen the Imperial Army perform a series of measured retreats. This change in Lieutenant General Zettour's tune was stark after the large-scale maneuver warfare he conducted back in June. It felt an awful lot like they were being pushed back by an advancing enemy.

Chapter **II**

Do we still hold the initiative? The soldiers were beginning to have their doubts.

"…Not again. They want us to pull back even more."

It wasn't just one or two soldiers who made small remarks like this.

There was a dangerous edge to their voices. They collectively gritted their teeth as they—yet again—packed up their gear. They often stayed only a single night before they got new orders to move out, crawling ever westward. Most of these soldiers weren't the type to go charging ahead without thinking.

From a military standpoint, the general withdrawal was essentially inevitable.

Graduates from the academy and the rare, well-seasoned soldier understood this implicitly.

That the endless shuffling of soldiers… That was something that always happened before a large-scale battle. Consequently, in the beginning at least, most of troops in the ranks were hopeful this was the case.

And so they obediently took up their new positions where they would wait for their next orders, only to be disappointed over and over.

Being known for his aggression and decisiveness on the battlefield, the famous strategist Lieutenant General Zettour's orders were exceedingly simple.

As far as anyone could remember in recent memory, the only command he gave was *fall back, fall back.*

Thus, officers on the front could only raise idle complaints as they fell in line. They told themselves that higher up, there must be some sort of secret intent behind the orders that they couldn't grasp.

Their superior officers, however, didn't have this question to fall back on.

They were confused about the orders they were giving their men. *Why are we acting so cautiously?*

One glance at the map was all they needed to begin thinking, *There's something wrong with these orders.* The more time that passed, the more this incomprehensible feeling reared its ugly head.

Had the orders been *fall back and hold the line* instead, it would've made a little more sense. Enough for the commanding officers to rationalize the orders, at least. But it felt like they were continuing to retreat without any perceivable strategy. It was difficult to process.

At first, they thought it could be an attempt to establish a new defensive line, but their movements weren't conducive to fortifying any positions. All Lieutenant General Zettour's orders had them deployed with an emphasis on mobility. Again, the commanding officers chalked it up as preparation for their next strike…but the retreats didn't stop.

The general was known for using aggressive maneuver warfare to encircle his enemies. This made it exceedingly difficult for the commanding officers to reason out why he would give orders that had them going backward rather than forward. It would be a different story if they were shifting the line back to conserve resources for a major operation. That was textbook military strategy. Unfortunately, there was a major problem with that conclusion.

Such a strategy would have involved retreating, regrouping, then preparing for an eventual counterattack.

Had they been following these three steps, not a single soldier would have questioned their movements even once. The issue was, they weren't regrouping.

As far as they could tell, the entire front was steadily ceding ground.

They couldn't shake the feeling that they were yielding to enemy pressure on the front line. That possibility felt all too real.

If they knew what their ultimate goal was, they would quietly listen. Nonetheless, falling back in the face of mounting enemy pressure was beyond their comprehension.

It was enough to make some soldiers furious, and for those tormented by their suspicions—they'd convinced themselves that there must be some grander, well-thought-out scheme. In that sense, the Imperial Army was an organization that didn't accept silence. Everything started with obedience.

Offering a dissenting opinion was a right and a duty for anyone who had one.

And so the commanding officers raised their concerns with the General Staff Office.

Each time they were met with the same answer: *It's all part of the plan.*

Chapter **II**

They would accept that explanation once.

They would grudgingly go along with it a second time.

But the third time was where they drew the line.

As time passed, their suspicions only deepened. By that point, the field officers had joined their enlisted troops in openly doubting the current strategy.

No one knew what Lieutenant General Zettour had in mind for the eastern front. Quietly questioning his intentions became something of a greeting among the soldiers.

"What do you think the general's trying to do?"

"We're probably just going to draw the enemy in. Then we'll surround them like we always do." The cautiously optimistic crowd hoped this was the case even as they assured their comrades.

In the end, skeptics and believers alike went quiet and followed their orders.

》》》　　THE SAME DAY, INSPECTION OFFICE ON THE EASTERN FRONT　　**《《《**

The man standing at the center of the quagmire—that was how Lieutenant General Zettour viewed himself.

Friend and foe were desperately trying to figure out his true intentions. The man chuckled bitterly to himself.

"How delightful. I wonder if this is a vice of mine?"

He stretched before relaxing his shoulders for the first time in quite a while. He wasn't afraid to admit it. On some level, he was enjoying himself as a military man.

His current situation could almost be described as pleasurable.

"What a terrible habit to develop… I've been on the battlefield for too long."

Lieutenant General Zettour continued to chuckle to himself in the corner of his command office. The command center was considerably less busy these days as their bread and butter had become retrograde operations.

The general even had time to enjoy a cigar while he let his mind wander. He scanned the large map spread out before him as he paced around the room in thought.

It was the perfect environment for thinking.

...He paced around the same way he always did at his deputy director's office when he strategized. The general puffed one of his favorite cigars while he analyzed various war scenarios.

It went without saying that he never forgot the burden he shouldered—not once. He had to fulfill his duty as a general. *Having said that...* He laughed quietly to himself with that private thought. Lieutenant General Zettour was merely human. When humans realize the true nature of their work, they can only lean into it.

"...I can't fight against my inner strategist."

While he was an operations man, he was specialized in a different field compared to his peers. His responsibility included virtually all aspects of the war. That was why he no longer considered operations to be supreme...or so he thought.

"Look at me now."

A puff of smoke escaped past the cigar in his mouth as he lamented with a mixture of self-deprecation, surprise, and nostalgia.

"Seems there's still a part of me that sees operations as the deciding factor of warfare."

Should we focus our efforts and ensure victory in the east?

That was what he thought, though it wasn't long before he began to feel ire toward the politics, advising, and logistical juggling he was forced to handle.

Naturally, these feelings were wholly unjustified.

"I thought I had separated myself from the church of necessity. Rather surprising that I'm still bound by its precepts deep down inside. I suppose forgetting where we come from is harder than I realized."

Lieutenant General Zettour's official title was the deputy director in charge of combat support services for the entire Imperial Army; the idea of prioritizing combat operations over all else should be anathema to him. From that perspective, what he was doing was clearly a huge mistake. If his plan caved in on itself, he would be incredibly hard-pressed to justify the unjustifiable.

But changing one's position also sometimes offers a new perspective.

Looking at the problem through the eyes of an operational planner flipped the entire war front on its head for Lieutenant General Zettour. There were too many external factors that restricted all activities on the eastern front. This not only put constraints on how they strategized but also made it difficult to pursue a purely military plan of action.

To start off, he needed to take into consideration how they governed their territories similar to the Council for Self-Government. This was a precarious problem seeing as it easily could have knock-on effects for army logistics.

The general questioned whether or not civil administration and military command could be handled simultaneously on the battlefield. Were he to pull it off, it would go down in history as an incredible strategic feat. But he was barely getting started.

The next problem was the troublesome orders coming from the homeland. While it was showing signs of decreasing, the Empire was a classic example of a nation that was addicted to winning. Even the mere idea of retreating provoked reactions of contempt... Whether or not there was precedence for retreating from a military standpoint, the masses had no appreciation for that kind of logical reasoning. Even the more liberal camps in the war college were unwilling to entertain such ideas.

But Zettour's greatest fear was something else entirely.

The third problem was the quality of his soldiers. What hurt him the most was the severe lack of soldiers who could competently conduct mobile warfare. There simply weren't enough soldiers to cover the sprawling eastern front, and what soldiers he did have were replacements who were practically children. Who could have possibly foreseen this Great War or whatever they've taken to calling it?

"Nobody except for Degurechaff, I suppose. Her sensibilities and perspective on the war are so different from any of the other officers. It's as if she's standing on the shoulder of a giant. I have no words."

He wondered if it was because children lacked a certain level of common sense, which inversely gave them the ability to think more freely than those burdened by the passage of years. Though it did feel strange to lump Magic Lieutenant Colonel Tanya von Degurechaff together with other children.

Lieutenant General Zettour flashed another wry smile as he sat down.

The same old map laid out before him. It had become a habit for him to read the map, make a note of his forces' positions, and run through potential scenarios in his mind. Being able to put together the entire picture with a single glance at these maps was something of a talent of his—a point of pride for him.

And yet, compared to the past...the situation was incredibly depressing. The disposition of the battalions told the story. They weren't under his command in the official order of battle. Even the three big restrictions he mentally listed earlier paled in comparison to the greatest systematic flaw facing Zettour.

"I doubt even God...could have predicted this outcome."

Zettour's position as the inspector on the eastern front was honorary. His orders had no command authority in his current position; they were considered a form of strategic guidance and were followed thanks to his reputation and insight that stretched over multiple theaters.

In other words, his orders weren't really orders.

They were nothing more than professional advice. Although he technically had the eastern army's endorsement, it was hardly proper protocol.

Zettour's supremely limited ability to issue orders was officially supposed to be something like a precautionary measure that could be temporarily considered should an emergency arise. Or perhaps it could justify him taking charge of a snap evacuation if it became necessary. It may ultimately just have been a means to draw attention away from the commotion that took place before the summer festivities.

Either way, the reality was completely different. The current system had been put into place upon his arrival and had remained in effect for quite some time now. The Imperial Army's officers were the kind of soldiers who valued substance over form and would rather circumvent the rules than disregard what they considered legitimate command authority.

What resulted was an unofficial chain of command that allowed greater individual freedom.

"...We're a hop and a skip away from forming a military clique."

And yet, Zettour found himself enjoying all this.

It was interesting. This strange dynamic only served to rile up his inner-operations officer.

He had an urge to use his dormant skills—and what an incredible urge it was. These three restrictions only added spice to the scenarios as he enthusiastically played them out in his mind.

"This really is such a poor habit of mine. If you want your man to be a gentleman, don't send him to staff officer training."

Rubbing his chin in thought, Lieutenant General Zettour chuckled to himself. His habit was neither here nor there, so long as they won the battle. He looked down at the map again. They were one step away from ending this long backward trek.

It was all going according to plan. The final moves were so well executed, he felt somewhat validated.

"This is more alluring than a game of chess, more challenging than a hunting trip. I may end up getting addicted."

It almost felt like it made his cigar better. He had outwitted his enemies and even kept his allies guessing as he prepared his masterstroke. This was his chance to implement all those theoretical tactics and strategy he had ever studied in the war college... For a commander—especially one who stood on the battlefield like Zettour did now—this was a dream come true.

"Winning this will be the ultimate prize. I yearn for the taste of victory... And wine always tastes the best when you're already thirsty."

Delectable wine. The nectar of the gods. An ambrosia so enticing, a single taste would be enough to enthrall you.

To the newly conscripted soldiers who had been sent to the east, it would be like poison.

A way to give them hope and rally them—but should they taste victory here, they would surely ache for it for the rest of their lives, no matter the cost.

It would drown out the voices within the Council for Self-Government who questioned the Empire's chances of victory.

In other words, it was the spark they needed to set the army ablaze.

"I'm worse than the devil himself."

If he could win this fight, it meant there was another waiting for him. There was hope for another day.

The only issue was he needed to get his country addicted to the venomous wine he had brewed… It was, unfortunately, the only course of action he could take. What more could he hope for?

"It's why I must dare to try."

He knew it was an incorrigible habit.

He also realized that deep down inside, he no longer desired to change his ways. This was a sort of desperation born of the dire situation that he had been placed in by circumstance. It was a catch-22 really, as there was nothing else he could do. It was hard to describe how it felt to know that the fate of his country rested on his ability to salvage the war.

A heavy burden had been laid on his back, though he learned to bear it with composure… He had to be this way if he was going to shoulder this national crisis for as long as he did.

"Hesitation, eh? Maybe I'd be more reluctant if I were a simpleton, like that dolt Rudersdorf who slams windows and screams at the drop of a hat. It seems I can't afford to be as simpleminded."

This was why Lieutenant General Zettour was always accused of being too academic in his assessments. He felt a sense of nostalgia well up inside, though such emotions were useless to him now. He turned his attention back to the war plan. He repeatedly tapped his finger on each of the points on the map.

The salient, their base, and their communication lines in the rear.

He painstakingly reorganized his troops and arrayed them carefully against the emboldened enemy, camouflaging their deployments so well that even his own troops were complaining about their seemingly mindless series of retreats.

The Federation was…without a doubt, still cautious. With great chagrin, he needed to acknowledge his formidable opponent. It was likely that they were already aware of his habits and methods.

This meant they had a dedicated strategy to combat his maneuver warfare tactics. It was only natural that they would—it was how he preferred to wage war.

And yet… Lieutenant General Zettour puffed his cigar as he confirmed his suspicions by reviewing the enemy's positions.

"The enemy is wary, just as I had hoped…or at least it seems that way."

He had laid the simplest of traps, clear as day—teaching the enemy to be wary of his habits. This was the core of his art. With the way it seemed like they weren't luring the enemy…his plan was plausible.

Plausible being the key word.

Certainty was like a bluebird of happiness. This was the only certain thing in a terribly uncertain world.

In any case, Zettour had planted his seeds and painstakingly tended to the field. The only thing left now was the harvest.

Harvests are by no means guaranteed—not until the crops are already safely in hand.

"…It depends on if we have enough sickles. Finding out we have too few could be very painful."

Even the best farmers can't do good work with rusty tools. To keep their sickles sharp, they needed time, which was hard to come by even in the best of times.

A shortage might not stop the harvest entirely, but it was a sharp thorn in his side nonetheless.

Just the thought of how much wheat he stood to lose from this simple fact was enough to make Zettour's head spin. All he could do was stare up at the same old, stained ceiling above him with his hands idly laced together.

"…I feel like I have an idea as to why palaces and churches around the world paint their ceilings."

His predecessors were surely troubled the same way he was. The purpose of ceiling murals was empirical knowledge that could be gleaned only through intense mental anguish.

"Now…what to do, what to do."

His goal was to show the fresh recruits a ray of hope through victory. The problem was, he didn't have the budget for it. Taking the safer route should still net them a harvest but most likely a minimal one.

To start off with, centralization is a core tenant of strategy. The worst strategy is one that's weak because you split your assets between too many goals.

It's imperative to keep your forces together.

"It'll be a gamble."

Zettour knew he could only stare at the map for so long before it became pointless. What were the consequences should he fail? Getting panned by history teachers looking back on this moment?

The need for him to make a decision was lying on his map, staring at him.

"This reminds me of the Rhine. It's hard to call this the right way to draft an operation... But at the end of the day, an operation plan isn't something you can create with only a level head."

No matter what kind of strategy you scheme up, it's nothing but theory until it hits the battlefield. Plans always have a way of blowing up in your face once the shooting starts. Zettour knew this for a fact, but it was still tough for him to swallow nevertheless. To think that after he risked everything to concentrate his forces only to find their numbers still lacking!

He brushed his hand across the map. There was an ambiguous grin sliding onto his face.

"What would've happened if necessity wasn't driving us forward, whip in hand?"

Necessity is the mother of invention and innovation. If he thought he could have afforded it, Zettour likely would've opted for a safer option. Chances were he may have even left the planning to a subordinate under different circumstances.

That was the kind of man he was.

In comparison, he found it much simpler to go out on the front line where danger could be found wherever he looked. Were he to die, it would only be his life that was lost. Commanding an army was completely different. The lives of thousands rested in his hands.

"Now, when to start... Yes, that is the million Reichsmark question... Hmm?"

Just then, there was a firm knock at the door. Zettour had been so absorbed in his planning that he didn't hear his visitor approaching. The general shook his head to clear his mind and let the young commanding officer in. A nervous-looking fellow entered.

He looked so anxious that it almost made the general worry about his country's future.

"Is there a problem?"

Preparing for the worst was another habit of his. His tone always tensed at moments like these.

"W-well...sir. There's someone here to see you from the capital."

Lieutenant General Zettour laughed a little awkwardly; he wondered if it was his harsh tone that made the young officer nervous.

"Ah, my apologies. I'm not one to kill the messenger. Please show our guest in."

Had there not been a messenger outside, the general may have very well scoffed… But he wasn't one to pick on the younger officers.

He needed to make his final decision. It was the worst possible time for some official to pay a visit, but such was the life of an operations man.

He swallowed his frustration and waited for his guest's arrival. To his surprise, he was quite pleased to see them. A small figure walked down the hall and turned into his office… He lowered his line of sight to better see them.

The short officer was young enough to make the nervous wreck from before seem like a veteran… The Imperial Army was large, but there wasn't a single soldier shorter than the magic lieutenant colonel standing before him.

"Oh, it's you. Lieutenant Colonel Degurechaff. Had I known you were the official being sent, I'd have prepared some coffee."

The general smiled warmly. When lost during a hunt, who better to consult than a hunting dog?

"Yes, sir. I've come to deliver these to you."

"Seems that stubborn old man is considerate enough to lend someone of your caliber to the eastern front. I guess you can teach an old dog new tricks. At least this gruesome war has served some purpose."

"Could you please confirm the messages?"

Tanya overtly shrugged off his jest and, with her tiny hands, held out two sealed envelopes. Degurechaff stood at attention in silence. Her duty was to deliver a message.

"Let's have a look."

Lieutenant General Zettour broke the seals and scanned each of the letters before letting out a hearty laugh.

"I don't have time for either of these. A boring message and a worthless congratulations. It's an extreme waste of personnel to have someone with your skills delivering these. I take it skies in the homeland are as cloudy as always."

The first envelope contained a letter from human resources. The second was a political message.

"I thought this would happen, for the most part."

Zettour reached for the cigar resting on his ashtray, then took out a match to light it. He rubbed his chin as he took a drag.

Though politics in the homeland always moved at a snail's pace, this was a good sign.

The news wasn't exactly bad. If the Foreign Office had a newfound recollection of what the words *foreign diplomacy* meant, there might be a different way to end the war after all. As far as Zettour could tell, this was the best way out for the Empire. Should their fatherland decide to take the right path, he could find a way to hang on.

He was perfectly willing to hold out for the best outcome if it meant getting rid of the army's need for a Plan B, which might as well have been synonymous with complete and utter destruction. As his friend once said, "*Time is limited,*" but Zettour wasn't particularly interested in making a suicidal decision based purely on their lack of time.

All he could do was fight for the sake of the future. This was precisely why it was worth considering his gamble on the eastern front.

"The letters are top secret, but both contain good news in a way. You have my thanks, Colonel. By the way…were you informed about their contents?"

"No, sir. I was only ordered to deliver them to you."

"Very good. I'd like to celebrate this bright moment with you before the hardships that lie ahead are upon us. It appears the shot callers have recognized my contributions to the war effort. I'm being promoted."

"So you will be a full general soon? That is great news, sir."

It wasn't easy for the general to stifle a chuckle when he thanked Degurechaff for her congratulations. To Lieutenant General Zettour, it was nothing short of irony that he would be promoted to General Zettour right before launching his offensive.

"This is actually Rudersdorf taking a jab at me. That idiot. He sure has learned some useless political techniques. The man might as well become a bureaucrat himself."

He knew Rudersdorf wanted to leave the eastern front entirely in his control—an unreasonable request for a mere lieutenant general. Though they were late, he finally had the suitable credentials to justify what he was already doing. It was a considerate move as an operational planner but could only be described as insufficient as a General Staff officer.

Chapter **II**

He had wanted this title when he *arrived* at the eastern front. Either that or *some* sort of clear-cut authority to go along with the promotion to general.

The title of general was a major milestone for any career military personnel... But it didn't excite Zettour.

"...The other message is just as pointless as my promotion. It's a regular letter. There's nothing worth noting other than the fact that Rudersdorf is coming dangerously close to doing something drastic."

"As it was my duty to deliver the messages with the utmost discretion, I can't speak for the contents."

"How bureaucratic of you to answer that way, Colonel."

Or perhaps this was just how they always handled things at the General Staff Office. Zettour never paid mind to such petty politics while he was there, but now that he was on the outside looking in, it struck a different chord. Documents that pertained to political affairs were always considered top secret within the Empire. As a man fighting on the front lines of the war, however, its contents amounted to nothing more than a mental note.

The nature of what was an urgent matter was different for a high-ranking officer standing on the battlefield.

They cared about where the battle would be heading in three weeks or three months from where they were now... Not whatever politics were the flavor of the day.

"I need you to deliver a verbal message for me. Right now I'm an operations man. I'd rather talk about plans than politics."

"I never would've guessed someone as high ranking as you would ignore politics, sir."

"I don't ignore them entirely, of course. Politics are a critical part of grand strategy, and strategy is what gives operations meaning. That said, it's important for those of us fighting on the eastern front to not lose sight of what's in front of us. For someone like me, there are too many soldiers I need to keep alive to be worried about political maneuvering." Lieutenant General Zettour rubbed his chin as he continued to speak. "Well, it seems like we're moving in the right direction, so now I can conduct operations in peace. I'll let him be the one to fill you in on the details."

Considering the sensitive nature of the letters she delivered to him, dispatching the magic officer as a courier was a legitimate choice, bureaucratically speaking. Setting aside what Zettour viewed as important information for the moment...these documents spelled out details about the inner workings of the Empire. It would be catastrophic if they ever fell in the hands of their enemies.

In that regard, nobody would second-guess Rudersdorf's decision to have Lieutenant Colonel Degurechaff, the famed White Silver—now known as Rusted Silver—in charge of their delivery.

Zettour had something else in mind for his messenger, though.

"That was a good read," the general said as he lit the two letters on fire with a match. As their ashes drifted into the ashtray below, he jumped to what he really wanted to speak with her about.

"Colonel Degurechaff, I too have the authority to give you orders. How about it? Would you like to do a little job for me?"

"Sir?"

"I have high hopes that you will go down in history as the embodiment of the ideal aerial mage. Do you have objections to how I feel? I want to hear what you think."

"No, sir."

She nodded, but there was something about her expression that showed her bafflement at the words *little job*. The same expression also showed her strong sense of obligation to follow orders. It was quite the facial expression to see, Zettour thought. He needed more boots, though. So he asked her despite knowing his imposition.

He did this because he knew he could trust the magic lieutenant colonel to do the job right.

"Good. Very good. I'm glad you haven't forgotten to take some time to enjoy yourself in the east. Let's start by having a short chat about the war."

The small soldier held the clue he had been searching for all this time... A highly skilled field aerial magic officer he could trust was more precious than gold on the eastern front.

He wouldn't let this chance slip by him.

The general always assigns the toughest jobs with a friendly expression—it's a talent of his. In other words, he knows how to wrap up a burden like a present. This is an important skill for a talented manager, but Tanya cannot help but stand in awe at the way General Zettour has perfected it.

I know how to wiggle out of bothersome work like this from my days as an office worker, but there's no way out for Tanya when the orders come straight from the dragon's mouth like this. In other words, General Zettour is skilled at cornering talent. He may even be the best in the game. There's no choice but to go along with his request.

I'm going to need to be very careful with any attempts to transfer away from a superior like this.

All bosses hate losing people. It makes sense. As they say in Japan, a bird who leaves the nest should leave it clean. Birds don't need to worry about this, though, until they can actually fly. Tanya should— No, her response needs to be genuine *precisely because* she's trying to leave. Not to mention, the more inside information she has, the more likely she'll be accepted with open arms wherever she goes.

Above all else, while Tanya currently enjoys a certain level of fame within the Imperial Army, that may not hold true when it comes to the surrounding countries. Depending on how much they personally know or how much propaganda they're subject to—due to their lack of relations with the Empire—talking about Tanya's stellar military credentials to officials in other countries could be worse than worthless.

Tanya's name needs to be known in all the countries she could potentially defect to, and she needs to be the one to visit them. To do this, she needs to be sent out into the field more to secure even more accolades.

This is why I meet Zettour's request with an earnest response.

"At your discretion, sir."

"Excellent. Take a look at the map. This is the current state of the war."

He points at the desk, which has a large map spread across it.

Tanya's eyes, guided by his finger, scan the extensive notes on all eastern front dispositions. These are military secrets worth drooling over. Any career soldier told they were allowed to look would realize in an instant that the Imperial Army is being pushed back. Their entire front is slowly retracting. And with hardly any reinforcements trickling in and a dire lack of firepower on their defensive line, it's bad enough to be worth crying over.

There are far too many glaring weak points...but for some reason, it isn't the map of a defeated army.

"It looks bad, but there's something about the map that doesn't show signs of collapse."

"Do you think so? Even though we're being pushed back this far?"

Lieutenant General Zettour sounds like he's enjoying this. As he says, the glaring matter of fact is that the Empire has been forced to cede a great deal of ground. Our enemies are hammering a weak defensive line. In that sense, the map is displaying the Empire's weakness.

And yet, there is one other difference from when Tanya was last deployed to the east—all the fatal choke points are perfectly guarded. A direct result of the continuous contraction of the front is that all the holes in their line have been effectively filled.

To put it nicely, the front line has been completely reorganized. Phrased less charitably, General Zettour has adjusted the line by completely abandoning all positions that seemed difficult to hold.

Setting such details aside, the map paints a picture of an extremely radical strategic redeployment.

"The slow and steady retrograde operation...looks too clean."

"Regardless of how it looks to the other imperial officers, I'm sure the Federation would agree with your statement. Assuming, of course, that they are as clever as you."

What do you think? the general asks Tanya with his eyes. I'm still baffled.

Could it be that he picked up on the fact that I've been entertaining the idea of relocating? It can't be. I'm thinking too much. But if not, then he is asking Tanya to think from the perspective of their enemies.

"...I'd like to see their sullen faces. They must think they've been had, sir."

"Without a doubt. Look at how cleanly we've pulled back. When they draw it out on the map, they should be able to guess what my decision was. I'd imagine their war planners are livid right now."

He grins. I can almost make out the outlines of the vicious fangs he's trying to hide. Lieutenant General Zettour boasts to Tanya, "I believe they've made a miscalculation about our plan."

"That the Imperial Army is primarily focused on fortifying its gains?"

"Yes... It appears they've forgotten that dominance on the battlefield is and always has been my true goal. I'll give them all the land they want. The price they'll have to pay for it is control."

This was something only a general who pulled this off on the Rhine front could say. A lesser general would never have even attempted such an extreme reshuffling of their forces. This general can, though. He's a man capable of commanding his army to fall back when he sees the need to. His reasoning is sound, but it's incredible that he can pull it off so perfectly without compromise.

Most people would hesitate in his position or cave in to the pressure of naysayers. It's impossible for a strategic retreat as exemplary as this to be pulled off by any ordinary commanding officer.

...I really don't want to leave a superior this capable. Even if I do intend on changing jobs, I hope I can do so on good terms, with the backing and recommendation from a man as competent as this. The only problem is that not only is Tanya limited in places she can go but also anyone who might be a reference for her would likely fall alongside the Empire should they lose the war.

That's a huge problem.

But it isn't something I can figure out right here, right now. I shake my head and focus on the task at hand.

Changing jobs is important, but it's just as important that Tanya doesn't fail at her current one. If she's going to change jobs, it's imperative that she demonstrate her capableness here until the very end. Only those who are capable and have drive are ever headhunted. What nation wants to recruit someone who makes basic mistakes?

Time to focus on everything I've learned as a soldier.

This is also the perfect moment to call upon what I remember of history and two lives' worth of experience. I scan the map several times before offering some thoughts on the operation unfolding...and then happen upon a stunning realization.

"Allow me to be straightforward with you. I believe you've made a bold decision."

The plan is excellent; I can't believe he's gone this far.

It's harder for most people to let go than it is for them to acquire things. There are many fools who are so fixated on keeping what they have that they eventually lose it all.

This is why it's important to know when you should cut your losses.

In order to salvage the entire war effort, the general has lured the enemy forces in while discarding territory that couldn't be held anyway in order to prepare for what's coming next.

The precision of his calculations makes me want to sing his praises from the rooftops. Using the same reasoning that has led me to the decision to pursue a new employer, Lieutenant General Zettour understands that he needs to cut his losses.

This man absolutely deserves to be promoted to full general.

That might also explain why a thorough analysis of the entire map reveals an unnatural formation. There was a notable swelling at one point in the front line.

Every time my eyes pass over it, I can't help but notice that specific point. It sticks out like a sore thumb.

In that spot, a salient was forming.

The Empire's front line had been broken all too easily, and this salient seemed like the beginning of a deadly cancer that threatened to eat away at the Imperial Army's entire front. And yet...how could there only be one visible tumor? There should be limits on how deliberate you can be with these kinds of things.

"What do you think?"

Tanya answers her superior's question with a genuine compliment.

"This can only be described as art, sir."

No one else in this war could possibly pull off a stunt like this. It's nothing less than the product of expert craftsmanship. Honestly, the Imperial Army should offer the deputy director a bonus.

It's important that talent and labor are met with commensurate rewards.

"Oh? I'm glad you like it. So you're one for the finer arts, Colonel?"

"No... I have no confidence in my aesthetic sensibilities. I'm just an officer who likes to move her body, not her paintbrush. But even I can recognize the appeal of something this beautifully orchestrated."

Any senior officer who uses their head for something other than a hatstand would agree with Tanya's comment after gazing upon this map. Is Lieutenant General Zettour some sort of con artist?

Whether it's deviously cunning or terrifyingly brilliant is a matter of semantics. Either way, I'm glad that this strategist on our side is far more talented than those of our enemies. I definitely want to stay on good terms with this man, if at all possible, even if I stay the course and really do end up changing careers.

"Are you planning to cut off this salient, sir?"

"What makes you think that, Colonel?"

He sounded surprised. Tanya answered him without hesitation.

"Their salient is too *well-placed.*"

"...Look at the map. There's a hole in our front line where we don't have the strength to oppose the enemy forces."

"I see. So the salient seems legitimate to a certain extent. That said, I can tell that it's artificial. Excuse me for saying this...but I know how you hunt, sir. This is as excellent a trap as I've ever seen."

"Good eyes, Colonel."

Tanya hit the nail on the head. Or at least she nods as if to make it seem like she did. These are really the only times when Tanya acts her age.

"Does that mean what I think it means, sir?"

"I have indeed lured the enemy army into a trap. It was hard work."

"Drawing in the enemy all while conducting a careful organized retreat? That's history book material, sir."

Draw out the enemy and destroy them—far easier said than done. In fact, the scale of what General Zettour's trying to do makes it seem virtually impossible. He's masterfully ceding ground to bait the enemy with the ultimate goal of annihilating their field army. Should this plan succeed, it'll be studied for years to come.

I quite honestly can't believe that he's pulled this off.

"It's a bit too early for praise, Colonel. No matter how much you plan, it's nothing more than an assortment of scribbles on paper until you actually pull it off."

"But, sir, your plan is unfolding exactly the way you want it to, is it not?"

"Our enemies come from the same stock as the soldiers of the Russy empire. As imperfect as they may be, it's too soon to assume they've forgotten how to do ballet. Hopefully, this old bag of bones is worthy of a dance or two."

Could their enemies really see what was coming? I can't reject the notion flat out, but it seems highly unlikely...

But then again, there's always a chance.

"So what do you think they'll do next, Colonel?"

"May I have some time to think, sir?"

Staff officers are constantly thinking about how they can outwit, out-think, and outmaneuver their enemies. Based on that...

Tanya shakes her head.

The problem is...I don't have a single clue what the right answer is.

"Colonel, time's up. This is war. I can't give you all day."

"...Then I'll go with the aggressive option. Despite realizing it's what we want them to do, they will knowingly play into our hands to force us to show that very hand. It's not exactly the same as the revolving door operation on the Rhine front, but I believe this is a good opportunity to encircle them."

"How would you make that happen?"

Tanya answers the moment Lieutenant General Zettour finishes his friendly question.

"A pincer movement targeting the salient's base would be the textbook approach. Once we cut the fools off from their country, we can close ranks and achieve local superiority..."

It was hard to describe how fulfilling it felt to hear her say that. The best example Zettour could come up with was having a large stag right where you wanted it during a hunt. Was there a greater joy than lying in wait while aiming down your sights at big game before making the perfect shot?

He had managed to dupe even the magic lieutenant colonel who stood before him. This was a senior officer, someone who knew the way he planned. Well, to a certain extent, at least. Still, he had been able to fool her!

"I would've marked that answer *correct* back when I was teaching at the war college."

"What?"

By the blank look on her face, he could tell she had been taken by

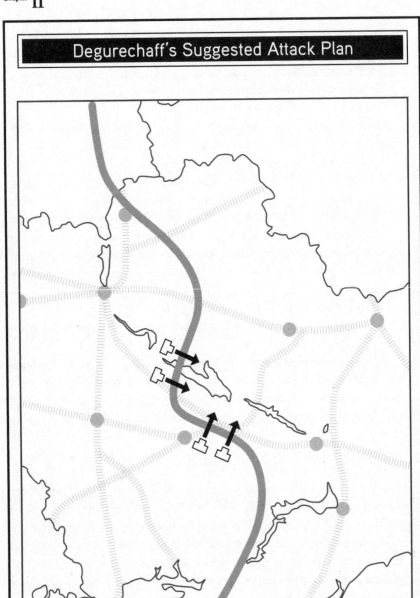

Degurechaff's Suggested Attack Plan

surprise. His strategic ambush had fooled Degurechaff, one of history's greatest magic lieutenant colonels. The feeling of satisfaction was indescribable.

"Things are dire on the eastern front. Drastic times call for drastic measures."

With a bit of a chuckle, Zettour grabbed a cigarette instead of his cigar. He lit it and took a drag. Even his cheap military tobacco tasted incredible after this small victory he had earned.

He had thought that Lieutenant Colonel Degurechaff might be able to see through his ploy. If that were the case, then wouldn't it stand to reason that his enemies would be able to do the same? ...Except she hadn't. His plan had passed this impromptu litmus test with flying colors.

"So even a field officer as formidable as yourself can't detect my trap. If that's the case, then we may be able to stay in the game longer than I'd first assumed."

"Sir? I'm having a hard time following you…"

"Lieutenant Colonel, I'd like you to go on a recon-in-force mission for me."

"Yes, sir. I'll get right to it," Lieutenant Colonel Degurechaff said before cushioning her objection politely as she continued. "However, are you sure it's a good time for such a mission? I feel a probing attack now would be…somewhat provocative. It could end up giving away your plan, sir. This is even more so the case if you intend to encircle the enemy forces, though it looks like there will need to be a proviso added."

"Your point?"

"I wish to hear what your intentions are."

He could hear the bewilderment in her voice. Anybody can wrongly interpret a map. Lieutenant Colonel Degurechaff was no exception. He recalled his college days, back when he was busy trying to be a good student. The moment of nostalgia put a slight smile on his face.

He thought about how simple things were back then. The reality now was much more complicated. One thing stayed the same. Something that people learned the hard way once they stepped onto the battlefield.

"Lieutenant Colonel, let me tell you one thing." It was obvious he was speaking from experience. He took a deep breath before he continued. "The rules of war never change."

"Do you mean that the side lacking in numbers will inevitably have to think up a strategy?"

The general wanted to nod affirmatively at her instant reply. His expression loosened slightly. An officer who knew what they were talking about was always an incredible thing to behold.

Her ability to follow along allowed the general to keep his own answer short and simple.

"Exactly. That is why we'll use our mobility. An encirclement will work perfectly!"

"But earlier, you said…"

"It's a matter of where you look. Lieutenant Colonel, perhaps I should resolve some of the contradictions as well."

The lieutenant colonel wore a dubious expression that screamed, *What is he getting at?* while she thought as hard as she could. Evidently, he couldn't be outdone by even the younger officers when it came to creating bold strategies.

"I'll let you in on the secret, Colonel." With an ever-so-slight skip to his step, Lieutenant General Zettour continued his explanation. "Just like on the Rhine front, we're only allowed to retreat a distance that will enable us to conduct a counterattack. These are the orders from the homeland. Assuming this is the case, then we can't simply encircle the enemy while we retreat. There has to be more to it than that. It's simple, don't you think, Colonel?"

The orders to attempt a counterattack were purely political posturing by people in the capital. They were a joke, thought up by somebody in Berun who was too busying polishing their chair with their ass to know what it was like on the front line. Even so, many soldiers would pay the ultimate price if this joke was issued as an official order on the battlefield. Just thinking of the collapse such a pitiful command would result in was enough to evoke a dry laugh or two.

But fret not, for we're senior officers. There's nothing to fear.

An impossible mission or two wouldn't be enough to break them. He was going to push aside logic with the art of war to catch the Goddess of Fate from behind by grabbing her hair.

"We have no choice but to follow orders."

"…A frontal assault? If we use the soldiers as human bullets, wouldn't it simply devolve into trench warfare and stop us in our tracks after a few meters?"

"That's absolutely right, assuming we play it by the book. However, we don't have the time nor the obligation to mount a frontal assault. Thus, we'll have to take a more deceptive approach. What do you think about this?"

He tapped a spot on the map. Lieutenant Colonel Degurechaff's eyes widened when she realized what she was looking at. A simple tap of the finger was enough for her to discern his true intentions.

"Sir, this is..."

The small senior officer couldn't hide the astonishment in her voice, a clear sign she fully understood his plan.

"I had no idea you had ambitions to become a field marshal, sir."

Though she must have been exaggerating...it showed that it only took her an instant to get on the same page as him. Her perceptiveness was so incredible it made him laugh, though he hid it with a small puff of cigarette smoke.

"It's too early to tell if we'll be able to move quickly enough to take over an enemy base. If the enemy reacts poorly, though, I may very well become a marshal."

Obviously, they were both joking. Should their troops advance that far into enemy territory, their already pitifully overstretched supply line wouldn't be able to support them. Not only that, but they would need to move much quicker than they did when they trapped the François army in the revolving door.

At most, they would be able to pull off a strategic victory on the battlefield.

Either way, he was impressed that the young lieutenant colonel comprehended the ambitiousness of his plan. The magic lieutenant colonel already knew what Zettour wanted her to do.

"Will I be the diversion, sir? Similar to what we did on the Rhine front."

"Yes, I need you to seize their attention."

He had forced the enemy to bring their supply hub forward.

Before, he had put his odds of success at fifty-fifty...but now he had the perfect bait to lure them into his trap. He had everything he needed to win. There was nothing left to worry about. It was time to start the operation.

"With all due respect, you would make an incredible con artist, sir. You're something of a trickster."

"That has a nice ring to it, Colonel. General Trickster, soon-to-be Field Marshal Trickster. I'll make sure to reserve a seat for you on my board of trickery."

With a big smile, Zettour took out another cigarette.

Just as he was about to give the final order, he realized there was one flaw he had overlooked.

Zettour was a fan of smoking when he planned, and it only just occurred to him that he couldn't share this with the small lieutenant colonel who had never smoked before. Judging by her stiff expression, Zettour thought there was a good chance she was personally against smoking as well.

That was fine. If Lieutenant Colonel Degurechaff had been smoking at her age, he would've been obligated to alert the military police. They were a strict bunch. He put on a wry grin at his tactless thought before turning his focus back on the war planning.

"I want you to act as bait, Colonel. I'll hit the enemy with the main forces while you have their attention. It'll be a simple but highly effective assault."

"But, sir, I'm a bit worried about the main troops."

"What do you mean?"

He shot the lieutenant colonel a look, asking her for elaboration.

"It's about where they're currently deployed."

Her tiny hands pointed out a few numbers on the map, which indicated the Empire's divisions, with a confused look about her.

"As far as I can tell...some of the forces on the front line are units I've *never even heard of before*. Why have we positioned the newer divisions here for such an important assault?"

"To give them hope, Colonel. It is an investment for the future."

He looked over at the ace mage. It was very evident that she had no idea what he was talking about. It made sense that an officer with troops as elite as hers would feel this way.

"Did you know, Colonel? Hope is what gives people the will to fight."

Hope was like a deadly poison, but depending on the dose, it could be used as a miracle drug. It was something only older officers would be able to understand.

"Sir, I'm not quite sure I follow you... Is that some sort of code word above my authority...?"

She was an excellent officer and soldier, but she was still young. Her limited experiences didn't allow her to notice the subtleties of the human spirit. Zettour thought that was the most likely reason the small child was unable to grasp the core of the issue at hand.

"Lieutenant Colonel Degurechaff, I know this is sudden...but could you tell me about your decorations?"

"Of course, sir. Are you referring to my accolades?"

The lieutenant general answered her question with a look, and—still confused—she answered him back.

"In addition to the Silver Wings Assault Badge, I have received the General Assault Badge, a war merit medal, a special skill badge, as well as various other distinguished service awards and campaign medals..."

"I believe the 203rd and the Lergen Kampfgruppe have also both received unit citations, correct?"

"Yes, my subordinates do incredible work."

The lieutenant colonel seemed proud of herself and the men and women she worked with. It was another one of those moments where she showed her age. Of course, there weren't many schoolgirls who boasted about their friends' achievements on a battlefield.

What strange times they lived in.

Zettour felt the need to stifle another sardonic smile when he thought about just how twisted the world could be.

Of course, he had nothing but applause and praise for the young soldier standing before him.

"Superb. Absolutely outstanding, Lieutenant Colonel. You and your subordinates are the cream of the crop and make no mistake: That's something to be proud of."

"I believe it's all thanks to our education and training, along with our unbridled warrior spirit on the battlefield."

It's likely that she was proud because she was capable. It was sad, though there was also a strange humorousness to it.

"Let's have a friendly debate for future reference. What do you think the core of your success is? What was important for elevating your troops to such a level?"

"I believe it's our training. My battalion prides itself on the blood and sweat we put into our training."

Success and effort. He figured that she would say something like that. The subordinates who worked for her would likely say the same thing.

They were a group that had experienced significant success, and it was a core part of their identity now.

"Ah…is that so."

"Sir?"

Lieutenant General Zettour sighed as he spoke with an inquisitive voice.

"Forget about the illusion of success."

"…What?"

"Do you need me to lay it out for you? I can't hold it against you, though… You need to understand what it's like for people who lose battles, Colonel."

The young officer was visibly confused by his words.

It was rare for her to lose track of a superior's train of thought… Was it because she was still a child even with her outstanding battle record, impressive accolades, and an incredible battalion? Or perhaps it was because she was too outstanding and simply couldn't understand those who were not.

He remembered the day he told her not to choose her subordinates. Hopefully, her terrific prowess wouldn't lead to measuring her peers by impossibly high standards.

"Remember this, Colonel. These are trying times we live in, and there aren't many who are stoic enough to train as hard as your troops."

"Insufficient training will kill a soldier on the battlefield as surely as any bullet. Training to the death is the only hope they have of staying alive." There was a tone of indignation to her voice as she continued, "It's important to take the state of the war into consideration. Everyone knows there isn't much time, and what little we do have is tremendously precious. Wouldn't anyone who wants to survive devote themselves to training body and mind, sir?"

"Ha-ha-ha, that way of thinking would have been just the thing we needed *before* the war started, Colonel. Our current recruits don't think that way."

"Is it a lack of competence causing that? Either way, I believe true soldiers are forged with time and training, then blood and fire…"

"The will to fight is derived directly from victory on the battlefield," Zettour declared in a firm voice. "For someone like you, whose troops know no defeat, it's impossible to comprehend this feeling. Fighting a losing war will turn even the finest soldiers into worthless dogs."

"I'm failing to follow you."

"See for yourself. Pessimism about our victory quietly plagues the eastern front, even at the higher levels of command."

"It's my opinion that people with middling levels of intelligence will inevitably think that way."

"Colonel, your insight for total war is second to none. I'd venture to say your perception is on a level of its own. That said, you have a tendency to use yourself as an objective measure to evaluate those around you. You've placed your own experiences above those of others, which is admittedly quite interesting, considering you're still a child."

Would some experience off the battlefield give her a different perspective? Zettour wore a sullen grin when he entertained the idea. Funnily enough, he was the same. The majority of his life had been spent in the service of the military. He supposed that what wisdom he could lay claim to had come with age.

That train of thought was cut short when he suddenly realized something. What about that idiot, Rudersdorf? He was living proof that wisdom wasn't a matter of age… Zettour then considered whether it was perhaps the degree of hardships he had endured.

"Hmm, I wonder which it is…?"

"Sir? Is something the matter?"

"Oh, it's nothing. I was just thinking about the importance of education. Let's get back on topic. This is a secret report on the morale of our soldiers on the front line… I want you to read through it, Colonel."

Zettour pulled out a folder from his desk and set it in front of Tanya while he fiddled with his tobacco in his other hand.

"Wait, have you been conducting a covert investigation on morale?"

"It's important that we know how the soldiers truly feel. The results were that forty percent of our soldiers still believed that the Empire could win this war. Considering the situation of the war, does forty percent not seem surprisingly high?"

I quickly read through the papers in the folder as requested; the contents are indescribably bad.

Though uneasy, Tanya announces her objection. "Sir, there's no way to interpret these numbers as good."

If someone asked me right now whether the Empire can win, I would simply say the answer is self-evident. I know for a fact that we can't. The most we can hope for is fighting to a *draw*. If we work incredibly hard to spin that as a victory...there's a chance the masses might consider it one...but a clear-cut, total victory is the stuff of dreams.

And yet, if the soldiers on the front line don't believe it's possible, then who would have the will to fight on? It's possible that there are officers similar to Tanya who willingly go into battle purely out of a sense of duty.

But could the same be said for the rank and file? Back in my old world, even the holdouts on Saipan believed reinforcements would come for them until the very end!

If the enlisted no longer believe in eventual victory...then our country is in dire straits on the psychological warfare front.

"That's right, Colonel. Sixty percent of our troops believe the war is already a lost cause. The numbers among the new recruits are even worse."

"...I would have thought that only the battered and worn down would feel that way."

"Not too long ago, that would have been the case. It's incredible when you think about it, but most of the pessimistic veterans have already gone ahead to Valhalla. The ones who remain know exactly what's at stake and are putting everything on the line for our victory. This has actually inoculated them against the rampant defeatism that currently plagues us."

While I can understand what the general's trying to get at on multiple levels, there seems to be a few contradictions.

"Creating a struggle for hegemony in the east, dividing the enemy with the establishment of the Council for Self-Government, and deciphering the nationalist code—are these strategic victories not enough to boost the morale of the troops?"

"The new recruits lack the perspective to see it that way. Besides, if they had that much experience, they'd also be able to recognize the predicament we've gotten ourselves into. They need a taste of real victory to rally themselves."

"What about all the propaganda they gobbled up in the homeland before they made their way here? I've always thought they were a naive bunch, but have they really lost their nerve that easily?"

"The propaganda has had the opposite effect. It's worked too well. They arrive thinking the Empire is due for certain victory. The moment they realize that couldn't be further from the truth, they fall apart. Frankly speaking, most of the new recruits are shocked by the reality of the eastern front."

I see. I'm starting to understand what he's getting at. When the new recruits come here under the impression that our forces are dominating in the east, it must be devastating to learn firsthand what's really happening around these parts.

That's how exploitative corporations in my old world worked. The more a company boasts about its ideals and vision, the more shocking it is when new hires realize how rotten it is on the inside. Fortunately, the last firm I worked at was an upstanding company. We performed so well that we could actually afford to lay off all the slackers and underperformers. We did everything by the book and followed all the relevant laws, of course... The Imperial Army, however, is not so kind.

Ah, damn it. Memories of my previous life as an HR manager remind me of how much I miss peace. My desire to find a better working environment has only gotten stronger.

"This is why we need to give them a taste of victory, even if it means asking them to do something slightly unreasonable. In other words, all that nonsense about needing to win is actually right for once."

While what the general had said sounded nice, the true meaning behind his words makes me want to sigh. This is no different from a company with toxic work culture that tries to convince its employees their work is super important!

Chapter **II**

Tanya's gaze shoots up as the sinister scheme comes to light.

"…They didn't teach us this at the war college."

"Think of it as learning on the job, Colonel. You should be happy. Like you said, we'll be walking the path of a great trickster together."

From the bottom of my heart, I want to scream *No!*

Tanya von Degurechaff's military career is steadily growing. I want absolutely nothing to do with this exploitative promotion of artificial job satisfaction. If I could refuse, I would.

If this was a regular company, I'd already have my resignation letter in hand. Tragically, there's no *transferring* or *resignation* for a field officer during a war. The only way to transfer out is defecting. Oh, how I miss Japan. At least then I'd have the freedom to choose my job.

At the end of the day, Tanya is just a humble white-collar worker. I can entertain the idea of leaving all I want, but there's no way I can change the system from the inside. Not that I would even if I could—I'm not that altruistic.

Therefore, for the sake of my conscience, I decide to confirm one important detail.

"If we can be partners in crime, then make this my first honorable step in joining you. To start off with, it's important that I fully understand the nature of our con. So please enlighten me, sir. What is the trick you have hidden up your sleeve?"

"You've really perfected roundabout speech as an art, Colonel. If you're asking about my confidence in the Empire's victory, then there's only one answer."

All capable leaders have a firm grasp on what their subordinates are thinking. I'm not sure if I should be glad or if I should be more careful about what I let come out of my mouth.

All I can do now is wait silently for Lieutenant General Zettour's answer.

"Victory is no longer achievable. Our only option is, just as you pointed out, to continue holding on while preventing total collapse. Even that will prove to be difficult, I'm sure."

"So you'll be providing the soldiers with the opium of hope in order to keep them from losing? You're going to create an army of addicts?"

"While that's not a great way of putting it, you're not wrong. I'll bestow them with hope and confidence by giving them a victory. At this point, the thought that this is what my job has become is enough to bring tears to my eyes."

He's not wrong. I can feel something welling up in the corner of my eye as well.

"I see you're prepared for what will come next, sir."

Unable to choose where his career leads him, Zettour is just like Tanya.

Not even the amount of authority and experience that comes with his positions as deputy director and inspector are enough to free him from the twisted system. I can only hope that I'll never find myself in his shoes.

The inability to escape one's fate is a nasty business. They say that you don't realize how precious freedom is until you lose it... As obvious as it sounds, it truly is a sad thing.

Also, judging by the nod he just gave me, it seems that while I was pondering the importance of the freedom to change jobs, General Zettour likely mistook it as me understanding his sentiment.

"Good. Very good. Now then, Colonel. Give them the hope and dreams they need. Give the Federation the nightmare they deserve. And give our army the foundation it needs to stay in the fight. I'm counting on you."

"I hadn't realized that I've been transferred to the circus to become a clown." Ultimately, Tanya can't refuse to do her duty. It'll be tough, but I'll do my job with my head held high. "It's not what I'm used to, but I'll do my best, sir. Please enjoy the show."

"I look forward to it, Colonel."

**≫≫ JULY 31, UNIFIED YEAR 1927, THE MULTINATIONAL VOLUNTEER ≪≪
UNIT GARRISON IN THE FEDERATION**

The volunteer troops who had traveled far to aid the Federation came from a variety of backgrounds and were a brave lot, every one. Commanding this band was practically an adventure in and of itself. Every day was filled with exciting episodes born from the unexpected and heartwarming ways that very different yet like-minded people came together for a common cause.

For Lieutenant Colonel Drake, things always got poetic at the end of the month, whether he liked it or not. He even requested a collection of famous comedic poems from his homeland to stimulate what he felt might be a new side of himself.

The reports he wrote about the garrison were filled with nice words to take his mind away from reality.

"...There's so much to think about and no end in sight."

This was what it meant to be at war. It felt rather similar to unrequited love. As most could guess, one reason was because it involved a lot of wondering about the intentions of that one person you couldn't stop thinking about. It also involved a lot of bumbling about, wandering in complete darkness, hoping to find a hint of their shadow.

At this particular moment, however, Drake was reading an old newspaper in a field tent while he thought about how to fix his teakettle. He swallowed the fact that the order for his favorite jam never found its way to his camp while he spent his time thinking about his enemies.

Whether they be asleep or awake, it was sort of an instinctive impulse for officers to think about enemy movements.

"I can't help but feel impressed by the Federation's reach..."

Just earlier, the political officer attached to Colonel Mikel visited him to deliver a plethora of top-secret files. The diligently translated documents described the inner workings of the Imperial Army with surprising detail.

The office that provided him with all this information was known as the Commissariat for Internal Affairs at the Federation... It was infamous for a whole slew of reasons, but the documents were also undoubtedly valuable.

They were so thorough that even the specific brands of cigars and tea the imperial officers favored was listed. Lieutenant General Zettour, for example, evidently preferred coffee over tea. It would seem he liked his coffee black, the same color as his heart. At the same time, Drake had to admit the level of detail the Federation put into these briefs was almost obscene.

What other nuggets of information were they keeping hidden away? Drake grimaced when he saw that the file after Zettour's was for the infamous Devil of the Rhine. According to the reports, the two were close.

The Federation's Commissariat for Internal Affairs reports stated that the Devil of the Rhine *also* preferred coffee and made a special note that the two shared similar tastes. Drake felt compelled to ask the question of whether beverages had the power to bring people together... In any case, he was in awe at the level of information he had on his enemies.

At the same time, it made him feel a bit greedy. It was only natural that he would wonder how the Federation was able to attain such information.

"I'm curious. I'd love to know more about this."

His whisper to himself could be heard throughout the tent, though Drake knew well that such information was well beyond his reach.

Their source was the most heavily guarded of secrets.

Whoever it was, likely few in the internal affairs office even knew, let alone their foreign allies. It wasn't something they'd tell him even if he ever had the chance to ask. Approaching them alone was enough to put a dent in their already fragile relationship.

"They do say that all's fair in the name of love and war... But it's probably best I keep my nose out of this one."

He was honestly surprised that those secretive Federation agents were willing to share this much with him. The *Federation* provided him—a citizen of the *Commonwealth*—with this level of information before he even requested it.

"Could this be the work of God? I suppose only the impossible is impossible."

Perhaps the Federation had finally picked up on the fact that they were technically allies.

That was a good thing in and of itself. It was a good sign for the future.

As someone who wanted to pull off a counterstrike against the damned Imperial Army, he felt grateful to the Federation for once.

It's what convinced Drake to swallow his woes from that day on. He started by mobilizing those who were willing to fight.

His first step was to put on a show for those annoying journalists he detested so much. He sang high praises for the multinational unit in front of the press corps from around the world. He put forward a positive message, painting their collaboration with the Federation Army in the best light possible.

He didn't enjoy having a picture of him shaking hands with the Communists plastered all over the international news... Nevertheless, he made peace with it by simply considering it part of the job.

He forced himself to shake their hands and smile.

His country was happy with his work.

Drake caught wind of First Lieutenant Sue talking behind his back about how he *was so eager to take pictures*, but what did he care about the grumblings of a little girl who didn't know the first thing about politics? He decided to take out his frustration on his journalist friend Andrew anyway.

In the end, Lieutenant Colonel Drake's guardian angel appeared to approve of his hard work. The multinational volunteer unit was better prepared than ever in anticipation of an imperial counteroffensive meant to blunt their advance west.

Colonel Mikel and Lieutenant Colonel Drake were working even closer together than before on behalf of their Federation-Commonwealth alliance. The Commonwealth even made an effort to accommodate the infuriating political officer corps whenever the opportunity presented itself.

What's more important was the sheer amount of information he had access to. The Federation Army had almost analyzed the entire plan created by the Imperial Army. The Imperial Army intended on using Lieutenant General Zettour's preferred tactics of luring out the enemy before encircling and annihilating them. The Federation's intelligence analysis seemed right on the money.

Ascertaining his enemy's intent to this extent was enough to make him want to jump for joy. In actuality, their information was almost perfect…like an exposed magic trick. He could see certain victory on the horizon along with his enemy's defeat. There was a skip in his step as he spent his days preparing for his enemies to taste bitter defeat.

Doing so led him to the very next day when Lieutenant Colonel Drake would come into contact with his enemy, just as he predicted.

》》》 AUGUST 1, UNIFIED YEAR 1927, EASTERN FRONT, MULTINATIONAL 《《《
UNIT GARRISON PROTECTED AIRSPACE

"Bogeys identified. I can't believe it… It's just as the reports said. It's the Devil of the Rhine!"

One of the soldiers Drake had assigned to monitor their airspace called out in surprise.

It was exactly as the Federation Army's analysis stated—Lieutenant General Zettour had a tendency to use his little apprentice when it counted most.

It seems like his protégé—the Devil of the Rhine—had finally decided to show up.

The enemy's goal must have been the salient's supply line. To be honest, when he first read that the Empire was going to use one of Lieutenant General Zettour's favorite tricks—a surprise attack—he had his doubts, but...

"Are you sure?! How many are there?"

"It's a two-man cell! Maybe they're here for recon?"

"That's what they want us to think. At first glance, it'll look like nothing more than an imperial scouting mission. But if these documents are correct, then they're here for more than just information. They'll either conduct a recon-in-force or try to take out an officer. Either way, we're not going to make it easy for them."

Drake could feel it; he had successfully seen through his enemy's plan. There was a solid chance they would win this fight. This was the good sign Lieutenant Colonel Drake could feel confident in for once.

"We saw right through them... We owe the Federation Army for their expert analysis."

Yes, this was a diversion. The pair of mages looked like nothing more than a scouting unit. Normally, they would never pay any mind to a pair like them.

The two mages were attempting to present themselves as a simple reconnaissance team, but it wasn't going to work this time.

"We know all about your little tricks. You're not going to have your way anymore."

The salient was crafted by Lieutenant General Zettour.

The whole thing reeked of a blatant trap. After studying what happened on the Rhine front, it was plain as day that their general had an addiction to encircling his enemies. The way Drake saw it, the imperial General Staff Office was full of officers who believed in surrounding their enemies.

He knew that they generally started their attacks by targeting their enemy's weak points, often aiming for their supply lines.

Chapter **II**

It was no longer a question about what hand they were going to play. Formulating a plan is the easy part of the job once you know what you need to do. However, the battle-hardened soldier who stood next to Drake didn't share the same optimism.

"There's something off about all this…"

"What's that, Colonel Mikel?"

Mikel was one of Drake's closest companions, and he wouldn't openly share his reservations without a good reason.

Unable to take this lightly, Drake questioned his comrade. He was met, however, with a look of doubt.

"It's just a feeling… Don't you think there's something strange about those two?"

Something strange? That was hard to answer.

The enemy had come in a flight of two—standard procedure for a reconnaissance mission. There wasn't anything particularly unusual about their enemies surveying the battlefield…

Drake was more surprised that he was able to predict their appearance… The rest seemed remarkably run-of-the-mill.

"My apologies, but I don't notice anything out of the ordinary about their movements. That's not to say I'm underestimating them. We're dealing with a Named mage. We'll hit the bastards with everything we've got."

"Please do. I just can't shake the feeling that there must be more to all this… Something feels off about their appearance here."

Before Drake could ask his partner what he meant, his subordinate called his attention back to the enemy duo.

"The enemy has increased their altitude to eight thousand! They're moving fast!"

Drake looked out at the pair of hostiles. They shot up into the sky with incredible speed. They were moving with such unbelievable speed that it was literally sickening. Just seeing the state-of-the-art Imperial Army magic technology was enough to make Drake's stomach turn.

It was absolutely infuriating. They were going to take full advantage of their aerial superiority.

"Damn it. Well, the fact that their recon was just a ruse isn't news for us. They sure didn't waste any time making their move, though."

The fact that they treated climbing to eight thousand like it was nothing pissed him off more than anything. Those bastards fully intended on watching his troops struggle for air at six thousand.

But their plan wasn't going to work this time.

Little do they know that the multinational unit has figured out a way to breach the eight thousand flight ceiling. He had his soldiers condition their lungs at that altitude and reevaluated their flight formula. The sky no longer belonged to only the imperial mages.

"I'll head out first. We'll show them what we've got."

"Good luck."

Drake thanked his friend before speeding off to muster his volunteers.

On short notice, he managed to ready a single battalion for battle. The Devil of the Rhine was a tough opponent, but with these numbers, they should be able to come out on top.

Or so they thought. Once Drake's unit was up in the air, the two imperial mages gracefully foiled all their attempts to catch up. But why? They had reached the appropriate altitude, and yet they couldn't quite keep pace.

"Th-they've reached ten thousand!"

His subordinate practically screamed that report. Drake didn't even need the report to know—he could see with his own two eyes.

While he did manage to keep that snide remark from slipping out, he couldn't stop himself from swearing.

"I thought their Type 97s could only go up to eight thousand? Damn it! Those sons of bitches…!"

There was nothing more aggravating than being at an altitude disadvantage due to inferior hardware. It wasn't fair… They were being forced to fight a skilled hunter with a collection of rinky-dink weapons.

Would it hurt those nitwits back home to send us some proper equipment for once?

He cursed whoever was in charge of their supplies from a continent away while he commanded the flights in his battalion to take up positions. While each individual soldier still had a long way to go, as long as they stuck with their wingmates and worked together, they'd probably make it through this.

There was just one soldier who didn't follow suit… She seemed to lack the awareness that teamwork was their only way to fill the technological gap.

"Cover me…! I'll bring them back down!"

"Lieutenant Sue?!"

Drake hesitated for a split second. *Should I stop her?* He shook his head. *Fucking hell.*

He had to let her do it.

Their altitude difference was far too great. He needed a way to close the distance. Even if it meant relying on First Lieutenant Sue's suicidal rush into battle.

To his chagrin, Lieutenant Colonel Drake changed the way he thought about it.

He wanted to face the enemy as a cohesive unit as much as possible, but this wasn't the time to be inflexible.

If Sue wanted to be a wild card, then he was going to use her as just that.

"Cover First Lieutenant Sue! Ready your weapons! Optical sniper formulas! Pay attention to the altitude difference! Fuck the imperials! Aim like they're four thousand out!"

Things are looking impressive from Tanya's high perch in the sky.

The enemy commander is doing a bang-up job.

Not only does he have an entire battalion operating at an altitude of eight thousand feet, but he's even staying on our tail. At the start of the war, six thousand feet was considered a sort of soft altitude ceiling that older orbs had a hard time overcoming. The fact that the enemy unit can blow past this hurdle is a testament to the amount of work he put into training his aerial mages.

Judging by the flight skills of his individual mages, which are dismal at best, this can't have been easy to accomplish. They're keeping up reasonably well despite us pushing our dual-core Type 97 computation orbs to their limits. Impressive for their single-core models. There must be some trick to how they're using them.

What's worse is they're already putting suppressing fire on us. It's a good strategy. They're even adding optical and guided formulas into the mix. They're forcing us to choose between throwing up our defensive shells and maintaining our protective films against withering fire or taking evasive maneuvers to avoid getting hit. This makes it slightly harder to act freely.

As someone who works in a similar position, I have to pay them respect where it's due. Unfortunately, for our enemies, the world is dictated by physical laws.

Some things just can't be done.

It's a simple, undeniable truth. To circumvent this natural law—to make the impossible possible—sometimes requires overcoming limits. Limits are still limits, though, and tricks can only get you so far.

It's time, Tanya gestures to First Lieutenant Serebryakov, who is flying with her.

"02, time to fight back."

"02 copies."

Her adjutant responds with just two short words and a wave of her gun. This brings a smile to Tanya's face.

The enemy forces are completely focused on climbing—something their gear isn't made for at these altitudes. If we were to say, nosedive right into them... I'm sure they'll show us some worthwhile reactions.

"The moment they're unable to climb any farther..."

"That's when we'll strike," she begins to say, but can't finish her sentence before noticing a *small speck* rapidly approaching them.

"Hmm? There's a wild boar flying toward us."

"You're right, Colonel. I'm surprised... Are they flying solo? At this altitude?"

Tanya scorns her enemy in response to her adjutant's admiration.

"More like they've abandoned all logic and decided to act recklessly."

"I feel like the fact that they're still breathing at this altitude is proof they're a cut above their peers."

Tanya's adjutant isn't wrong. Compared to the run-of-the-mill aerial mage, this *speck* is on a level of their own. Regardless, the decision to charge us is a rash one. If they had happened upon us all alone, it could be considered the logical thing to do, but this mage has completely left the rest of their formation behind.

Chapter **II**

War needs to be fought in an organized manner. This isn't the Stone Age—it's not about how strong any individual is. I'm glad this lone mage is our enemy. I'd rather die than work with someone that incompetent.

"I recognize the mana signal. This is one tough customer. I'd rather not deal with them if we can help it... Then again, it might actually play to our advantage having them around this time."

My adjutant knows exactly who I'm talking about.

"A tough customer...? Ah, of course."

Their tank is rushing forward, leaving behind all the soft targets. Though not necessarily role theory, we're extremely lucky that our opponents have decided to break formation despite having total numerical advantage.

"You know what to do, right, 02?"

"02 to 01, your face is scaring me."

"What, should I be smiling as we charge into the enemy? I'm an upstanding person, you know?"

Laughter fills the air as we dodge our enemies' lackluster optical sniping formulas with ease. It's important to keep your spirits up. There's no room for negativity in a dogfight if you want to win.

Staying calm and collected is also a core part of being a civilized human being—something our opponent evidently isn't.

The confidence this dignified bearing grants is truly great. It's what makes us proper human beings. This is where a person's decisiveness and courage stems from when duty calls.

"All right, watch the timing. On my mark."

"Copy."

Utilizing our altitude advantage to its fullest extent, I watch for the perfect moment to get the drop on our enemies.

It'll be the moment the multinational volunteer unit stops to cover the *wild card* they've deployed forward. Two imperial mages aren't going to let that chance pass them by.

"Enemy salvo! Three rounds incoming!"

Tanya's wingmate deserves praise for being able to identify the attack before the formulas have even been completed. Our enemies should also be lauded for presenting us the perfect opportunity with their blunder. It's time for Tanya to give the order.

"Fools! That's what we were waiting for!"

For even the most skilled mages, firing in unison means one thing... Their movement is restricted. This holds even more true for mages with little training.

They'll pay for their foolishness.

"It's time. We're going in."

I begin my nosedive with a grin.

We're going to utilize our height advantage to drop down and close in on them fast. It's time to convert our altitude into pure speed. Feeling the air pressure build as wind whips past our protective film, two human bullets are nose-diving toward the poor multinational unit.

For the mages below, who can't do much more than focus on maintaining their altitude, the two mages descend on them like a literal bolt from the blue.

They can't respond fast enough to the two imperial monsters that are hurtling toward them at terminal velocity.

Lieutenant Colonel Drake was familiar with the excruciating gap between his enemy's technological and technical skills compared to his own battalion's—a feeling that was uncommon for a marine mage officer. Adding in a great deal of strange political idiosyncrasies that he had to deal with during his time abroad, his experience was truly unprecedented.

These unique experiences gave him the perspective he needed to understand the almost depressing importance of mastering the basics. Hunting was a numbers game. Whoever held the numerical advantage and didn't squander it would almost always come out on top.

Anyone who couldn't maintain numerical superiority could forget about hunting. They were more likely to become the hunted.

Unfortunately, the multinational volunteer unit he commanded was made up of soldiers who couldn't even speak the same language; it was nigh impossible to move as a unit with less than a moment's notice.

What's worse was that Colonel Mikel and Lieutenant Colonel Drake's forces were run by two commanders. Having two possibly conflicting chains of command was disastrous. No matter how clear their commands were, they could never shake the looming anxiety that was inherent in such a system.

While their formation was able to function more or less, that was all for show, at the end of the day. Drake watched as his units opened fire in unison with the most pitiful aim.

"The enemies are evading our fire. Shit, their mobility is too much for us."

He stopped himself from commenting on their superior coordination as well.

Their opponents flew in a way that made it clear they knew where their wingmate was at all times, and yet they were able to move in tandem and keep each other covered. Though it looked simple at a glance, Drake could only gulp at the amount of technical skill that went into making such flight possible.

Their situational and spatial awareness was unparalleled—and they flew with virtually superhuman coordination!

"From that altitude, at that speed…"

It couldn't get any worse than this. Drake realized that the infamous Named mage had earned that title for a reason. His unit was shooting to support First Lieutenant Sue, who charged without a single thought for safety, but it could hardly be called cover fire. Drake knew this wouldn't be enough to land a hit on their enemies.

He had trained his troops to the point where they could be considered decent, but against an outstanding opponent like this, things weren't looking good. First Lieutenant Sue charging in certainly didn't help. He needed to work the discipline and cooperation kinks out of her… *Putting it off until later has come back to bite me in the ass*, Lieutenant Colonel Drake thought as he looked up to the sky above.

"Lieutenant Sue should be making contact soon… Hold on."

It started out with a ringing in his ears. The moment he recognized this battle was three-dimensional, something about it stuck out to him. Drake of course knew how to keep track of their movements in the air, and something about their current position seemed off.

He had a feeling that something terrible was about to happen. He felt a chill run down his spine despite his defensive shell being up.

"What—what am I…?"

Before he could get the *missing* out, he realized the oddity.

Why did it feel like First Lieutenant Sue was too close to the enemies? True, she was charging them…but had enough time passed for her to make contact?

Lieutenant Colonel Drake's senses were screaming back at him—*NO!* That couldn't be right. As the question flashed in his mind, he suddenly realized what was happening.

The enemy was ignoring First Lieutenant Sue. But why?

"How can they ignore her…? Wait, are they coming toward us?"

Their real target is…us! Shit!

"S-spread out! Scatter! Don't bunch up!!!"

A moment earlier and he might have made it in time—but it was too late. Even as he called out, the enemy pair had already reached maximum speed in their descent. They slipped right by First Lieutenant Sue without paying her any mind.

There was nothing she could do to change course as they whizzed by her. Without a doubt, the younger members of his unit had nothing but offensive maneuvers on their minds. The lion's share of them weren't capable of turning on a dime the moment they heard their commander's unexpected orders.

The few who managed to disperse were the more battle-hardened Federation Army soldiers. They were the only ones who attempted evasive maneuvers… Everyone else suffered a pitiful fate.

Their formation, a line meant for concentrated, disciplined fire, was what did them in. Caught out in a vulnerable formation, the multinational volunteer unit never had a chance.

Having their comrades close by dulled their senses.

The negative effect this had on their reaction times proved to be fatal.

The two imperial mages took advantage of their proximity and unleashed three explosion formulas each just before they made contact.

There couldn't have possibly been a better target for their attack than the tightly packed multinational unit. Their enemy was sharp and knew exactly what would hurt them the most. They chose explosion formulas for their large area of effect.

The strength of the attack wasn't extraordinary. Under normal circumstances, even if the explosions penetrated their defensive shells, the mages should've been able to protect themselves with their trusty protective films.

These weren't normal circumstances, though. Drake's troops were struggling to fly at an altitude of eight thousand. That had major consequences.

Even the most experienced aerial mages tended to operate within the limits of their gear. It should have been obvious that they weren't well adapted to severe environments.

The attack was one they should've emerged from relatively unscathed, but the lack of oxygen and the freezing temperatures at these altitudes made them sluggish and distracted. It was a matter of seconds before the entire battalion was overcome with panic. The majority of them followed their instincts and dropped their altitudes. This was a sinister trap.

The line fell apart as many of the soldiers, unable to breathe, focused on air-purification formulas. This was when the imperials struck.

Yes—the enemy had attacked with three waves of formulas. The first was to cause panic. The second was to break their line. And the third was to massacre the routing soldiers.

Anyone caught by the three-pronged bombardment—save for the more experienced soldiers—was doomed. The damage suffered by the first two companies, which suffered direct hits, was nothing short of catastrophic.

Bodies were raining from the sky wherever the explosions occurred... If those mages couldn't regain consciousness before hitting the ground, they were goners. If the superheated air reached their lungs, the agony would be indescribable.

But now wasn't the time to be worrying about others. Drake would have to come back to them later.

"Enemies approaching fast! Prepare for close combat!"

The imperialists were using gravity to dive at the multinationals at unbelievable speed.

He could see the reapers had their scythes in hand. The magically enhanced blades, held at the ready, shined ominously as the two demons plunged toward their ranks.

Drake felt fortunate that he had any time to gauge their trajectory at all. Or maybe it would only be enough time for him to learn how it felt to be a prisoner who knew they were only moments away from being executed by guillotine...

Ah crap. In no time at all, the enemies had split up and one was coming straight for him.

His opponent's murderous tenacity was so palpable that he swore he could feel it through both his protective film and defensive shell. Drake cursed as he kept the human missile in his sights. And that was the exact moment he realized what the enemy was really after.

He wasn't the only target... They wanted to wipe out the entire chain of command! They were here to kill the commanders. With just two mages? No, two was more than enough for them!

The moment Lieutenant Colonel Drake came to this realization, he called out to his troops.

"They're going for the officers! It's a decapitation strike! That's what they're here for!"

The Devil of the Rhine was apt for the job.

The enemy had come to take out the two commanders of the multinational volunteer unit by themselves. It was absolutely reckless. Drake would normally laugh at the idea if he wasn't literally dealing with a devil. He barked out his warning to his troops while the two monsters came flying toward them like comets. Lieutenant Colonel Drake cast an explosion formula with everything he had.

The air around his formula warped as an explosion screeched across the sky ahead of him, but it barely fazed the imperial mages, let alone stop them.

"You're charging me?!"

The two mages continued their advance despite the detonation that had just rocked the skies. *Fire should strike fear into the hearts of all!* The mental fortitude of these imperial mages was beyond comprehension.

Drake cursed again while he prepared an optical camouflage formula. Then he finally understood why they were so focused on him.

His support fire was almost nonexistent. *What in the hell is going on?* Due to their insufficient training, they were not only slow to react but the multinational troops were also *waiting for orders*.

New recruits didn't know what to do during a battle without orders!

"I need suppressing fire! Hit them with everything you've got!"

He commanded the battalion to open fire. A single order was all they needed to start shooting immediately... They really didn't do anything until they were told. Not only that but their aim was all over the place.

You call that marksmanship? Lieutenant Colonel Drake held in his impulse to swear as he caught on to another enemy trick.

"Watch out for decoys! Shit, is this optical?!"

They had used an optical camouflage formula to create a convincing decoy. He had read about this in the reports more times than he wished to. Projecting illusions had been a common tactic for these mages back on the Rhine front.

It was a simple trick but terribly effective. It was harder than it seemed to distinguish what is real in the chaos of battle—especially if you were panicking.

"There's no point if you aren't concentrating your fire! Calm down and aim!"

His orders went unheard. Not only were his troops unnerved but they were also wholly unable to lay a significant amount of firepower on their targets.

The situation was an absolute mess. To make matters worse, the suppressing fire had seemingly no effect on the enemy's freedom of movement.

Their shots were undoubtedly landing. However, simply hitting the imperial mages with several rounds wouldn't be enough to penetrate their protective films. This was something he could've guessed...but how were they still charging forward?!

Drake then caught sight of a short imperial mage. He didn't want to imagine the power of the magic blade in their grip. One slash was surely more than enough to end his life, and the enemy was moving far too fast for him to have any chance of stopping the blade.

"They're here! Cover me!" Drake shouted as he instinctively sped up. Ideally, he would've used his reach advantage to land the first blow, but the small imperial mage was already too close. This wasn't a friendly fencing match... There wasn't enough time to parry.

He drew his own magic blade to try and mount at least some sort of defense.

"Guh?!"

It felt like he had slammed into a boulder. He couldn't get the leverage he needed in midair. Unable to maintain his form, he was getting pushed back. The worst part was how small his opponent was. *Am I really going to be overpowered by this mouse of a mage?! Don't make me laugh!* He wished he could wake up from his nightmare. Unfortunately, this was reality. *Oh, Lord.* He tried to gather his wits and recover after being flung wide, only to find two cold eyes staring at him, like a predator watching its prey.

"Goddamnit!"

There was nothing he could do to stop the magic blade from flying toward him once again. There was a moment of desperation before Lieutenant Colonel Drake accepted his fate.

They were close enough for a knife fight.

With their size differences and positioning, the short imperial mage had the advantage. Conversely, so little distance separated them that there was no way for him to miss, either.

He let the imperial mage's blade pierce his shoulder. At the same time, he began to cast an optical sniping formula. Drake ignored all safety guidelines for casting speeds and worked as fast as possible. Low on air and running out of blood, his brain was sounding the alarm as he manifested his final explosion.

The light from his formula shined, giving Drake a brief glimpse of hope.

"?!!!"

The enemy mage screamed and let go of the blade that should have impaled his shoulder. A moment later, Drake felt something rock-hard—probably a gunstock—hit him in the gut.

An indescribable agony welled up in his stomach, and his formula fell apart, causing his last-ditch effort to fail milliseconds before it was about to go off.

The enemy mage then looked at the groaning Drake and, with perfect command of the Commonwealth language, swore at him as he writhed in pain.

"Stay out of my way, you bastard."

"Damn...you..."

"Good-bye, Limey."

With those parting words, a leather boot unceremoniously kicked Drake away.

Lieutenant Colonel Drake came to a realization as he just barely managed to make out what seemed to be his enemy pulling out a submachine gun and aiming it at him while he continued to fall.

Ah, damn it. I'm not going down without a fight. In a fit of desperation, he reflexively converted his failing formula into an explosion formula.

He had pushed his body past its limits long ago, but he forced himself to finish one last formula.

It felt like his brain was going to melt. Despite that, he was still conscious. He knew what he needed to do.

Lieutenant Colonel Drake prepared his formula just before his vision faded to black. On the very edge of consciousness, he managed to spot his enemy gracefully circling in the air.

He knew he couldn't win, but he wanted to at least burn that damned devil's tail off.

"Ha-ha-ha! Take this, fucker!"

Unbelievable. This must be what people mean when they say *boiling with rage*. I'm livid. There's no way to remain the usual calm Tanya after witnessing such irrational recklessness.

It happened right as I struck one of the enemy unit's commanding officers.

The attack was surgically executed, keeping unnecessary damage to a minimum. It was the most peaceful and humane assault anyone could perform in a war zone.

A small sacrifice to ensure the safety of the Imperial Army—and myself, of course.

If anything, these emergency evasive maneuvers are about as fair as they could be.

The response I was met with is what's unbelievable.

That officer tried to use an optical illusion at ultra-close range—an act that could already be considered suicidal—and then decided to follow up with a full-blown explosion formula, guaranteeing he'd be caught in the blast.

To think that these people consider suicide bombing an option. This is war—it's not like this fight is personal. As a means to an end, I can understand viewing soldiers as weapons but to willingly become one is a crime against humanity.

Ah…what a shitty world this is.

It's not like I'm demanding that people become uppity snobs. This is war, and it's going to get dirty. I don't need you to play by the rules. But please, let's at least try to maintain our humanity.

"So this is what happens to people when they fight war all their lives."

How repellent. Could anything be more unpleasant?

I pour my frustrations and stress into a formula. Let's see how they like an explosion formula behind their lines.

I'll drop a few more wherever they start spreading out.

There's some incoming fire, but that's easily countered with an optical decoy. Our enemies are always so easy to deal with when they panic. Most of them would focus solely on the decoy. This is ignoring the large bulk of them who just fly in random directions. Aerial combat is three-dimensional. This is something that soldiers stuck in the realm of two dimensions will never understand.

Speaking of, I still need to keep my guard up.

Stray bullets are a thing, after all.

But, well…I can't help but snicker as the sky around me fills with screams and explosions. Altitude control is my forte at this point. For a while now, I've been able to rely purely on inertia when it comes to achieving air superiority. Most attacks never get past my defensive shell and protective film.

Shoot, evade, then penetrate their line at maximum velocity.

I watch as the distance between me and my enemies widens. There's no need to worry about their numbers with this much space between them. The multinational army isn't suited for chaotic combat.

That said, I do believe they're truly mad in the head.

"…They're wearing the Commonwealth uniforms, but as far as I can tell, these are no Commonwealth soldiers. They're nowhere near as tough as the people I fought during the Western Air Battle."

Even during the fiercest moments at the Rhine front, I never saw a cornered Republic aerial mage choose suicide. Needless to say, there wasn't a single mage who took such drastic measures during the dogfights over the Commonwealth homeland, either, as far as I can recall.

It's as if they've lost their pride as knights, or perhaps maybe it's their common sense that has been abandoned.

...There's something twisted about the eastern front.

Imitate not evil men, lest you yourself become evil. Conversely, any horse can become a stallion if only it takes after a stallion, and any man can be wise, so long as he mirrors the actions of the wise.

I remember learning these old adages back in Japanese class while studying for my college entrance exams... Maybe I should've paid closer attention to the snippets of truth my ancestors left behind.

"Even if only in form, it is wise to imitate the wise."

Hmm. I want to give that old adage a bit more thought.

Unfortunately, the battlefield isn't a great place for reminiscing about my studies. Is that not the reason why they get so chaotic? If that's the case, a war is nothing more than a helpless downward spiral.

There's no stopping it as it falls.

War is uncontained entropy and chaos.

Even though in modern times, people have put tremendous effort into making violence an unusual occurrence, our enemies have made it commonplace because of this total war. *Order* and *disorder* have completely swapped places. These soldiers take a daily stroll through hell like it's a walk in the park. It disgusts me to my core.

It's normal for the enemy to see Tanya as an object of hatred.

A sad thing, really. All she's doing is earnestly devoting herself to her job. This is war, after all. A great deal of people will hate her for it.

But really, this isn't the time for that. I focus on my flight trajectory.

Getting too hung up on negative thoughts will only make Tanya's already dark life darker. A healthy mind is the key to a healthy body, for the most part.

I've finished my withdrawal. Tanya is officially outside enemy lines. The only noteworthy thing is a half-hearted amount of harassing fire coming from behind. They're not really shots that the enemy is capable of landing; it's more or less random bullets that just happen to be traveling in the right direction. Nothing to worry about.

I'm effectively out of their range now.

"02 to 01, I see you've made it out."

"01, affirmative. Report, 02."

Did you down the target? Tanya's adjutant emits an uncharacteristic sigh in response to the unspoken question. Does this mean she failed?

"I reached the target but failed to shoot down the commanding officer."

I let out a disappointed chuckle. We've both come back empty-handed, so clearly there's no reason to berate her.

"Same here. They were tough after all."

"Was it someone that we should've taken out while we had the chance?"

Tanya's partner sounds surprised. I begrudgingly pay our opponents the respect they're due. Though my response is not without its fair share of snideness.

"They were too much for a sensible mage such as myself. And insane enough to resort to suicide bombing. That said, it is an effective tactic for fending off a decapitation strike."

Our enemies are like antibiotic-resistant bacteria. The more we kill them, the more they build up an immunity to our tactics.

Whether or not a suicide attack should be considered an actual countermeasure or just plain insanity aside...I can't deny that our foes are steadily getting better. It's more clear than ever how important it is to finish off your opponents before they can ever get to this level. But even though I fully understand that...it won't be possible on the eastern front. That is the inconvenient truth.

"But this should be enough to satisfy the general's demands..."

Looking at it another way, we've successfully created a major distraction, as per the orders Tanya received...

Just as I think that, I notice something strange happening around us.

"Huh?"

There's a slight burning sensation building up in the air. I can feel it through my defensive shell...an unpleasant stream of magic. I look behind me and see nothing but ants where our enemies should be... And yet, a chill shoots through me as if someone's pressed a gun against my head.

"Is this radiation?! At this distance?!"

I swallow the rest of my disbelief. Now isn't the time to talk. We need to move. Both Tanya and Visha immediately begin evasive maneuvers.

We push our dual cores to the limit and make sudden changes in trajectory. We speed up, flying in a serpentine path to throw off the enemy's aim. This kind of mobility is only possible thanks to our Type 97 computation orbs.

Just barely possible, I should note. As a result, we avoid the blast by the skin of our teeth.

I audibly scoff as the large-scale, long-range optical formula blasts right by me. I quickly cast an optical observation formula to identify the source of the attack.

In the distance is a lone, awfully small figure. It's giving off the same annoying mana signal I know all too well at this point.

It's the same wild boar from before. And to top things off, the freak of nature is already in the midst of charging up her second long-range blast.

Wait, is that charge for two blasts? One for First Lieutenant Serebryakov and one for myself? I double-check to be sure, but the computation orbs used by the multinational volunteers are nowhere near ours in specs.

"Isn't that far too much magic for any single person to use? Damn monster."

To my disbelief, it isn't a special technique or advanced technology that made this possible. It's simply that boar's raw power.

I can't help but feel jealous. Tanya was born with an average pool of mana. As someone who needs to carefully watch how I use my precious stores of magical energy, it almost makes me want to cry. This disparity in magic levels can only be described as outrageous. It was called a miracle when I figured out a way to save up my mana in that accursed Type 95, but look at this idiot come blasting without a second thought. Is this what it's like to have more mana than you know what to do with…?

This monster already defies all logic with that ridiculous amount of magic but then actually takes that power and pours it into a formula that literally alters the world. This convenient, self-serving circumvention of natural law reminds me of Being X.

I shake my head with a groan. There isn't anything more to it. Why am I, an ace aerial mage, getting upset about someone who has a little extra magic? Let's look at the facts: Tanya and First Lieutenant Serebryakov are two veteran mages who braved and survived the Rhine campaign.

Experience is the world's greatest teacher, though the tuition is usually extremely expensive... However, once you've paid your dues, experience becomes your permanent ally.

Learning makes it possible to handle anything. And I've learned a great deal. I have options.

That boar's formula was powerful...and accurate to boot. Nevertheless, it's still a long-range attack formula. An attack like that is merely for show in a fight between mages. That much should be obvious at a glance. There's ample time to prepare between shots. While there are some practical applications in area denial, it isn't great for frontal assaults. Especially at this range, where evading such an attack is a simple matter. Frankly speaking, I'd have to be an idiot to get hit by it. Even a sneak attack that doesn't give itself away with radiation can be avoided if you know what's coming.

There are times where high speed is a better defense than thick armor.

"Hmph, I guess all the magic in the world is worthless if you can't land a hit."

The enemy mage could've launched another attack, too, if it weren't for that one little... What's more troubling is that she'll probably fire more of those until we completely leave her range of fire.

Though it would be a pain, there isn't much cover along our exfiltration path. It's time to get out of here. Dealing with idiots only makes me tired... But then I realize something peculiar.

"Hmm?"

There is ample distance between us and the enemy, so much that I can barely see them... So what is this tingle? Is it more pre-radiation like before?

That's when it dawns on me that the enemy is in the process of weaving a ridiculously large formula. It looks like an explosion formula, but considering the range...

"Is that for predesignated fire?! Shit! They can't hit us, so they're just going to blow us to pieces?!"

Still in disbelief, I take evasive maneuvers and descend at high speed.

Glancing back, I can see that First Lieutenant Serebryakov has made the same decision.

Very good. And then it happens.

I click my tongue as a heavy *fwoom* whips out past me. The air above begins to coil and twist. It's an explosion. The sky-warping formula has sent shock waves far enough that I can feel them from here.

"You have to be kidding me... This is supposed to be maneuver warfare. What the hell are you thinking, using this kind of formula?"

To think I'd have to deal with an attack that's effective at such an extreme range... It can't get any worse. Terrifying images of the near future bring an abrupt end to the joy I'd been feeling while savoring our small victory up until that moment.

How annoying. This monster is just like Being X.

Then again, if this boar is just like Being X, that means they're also dim-witted.

I mentally snap my fingers. That's it—this mage is an idiot. I won't underestimate their ability, but I won't overestimate their intelligence, either. After seeing us dodge the big beam, their first thought was to blow us out of the sky... That's just too trigger-happy.

I mean, it's not the worst decision...but I highly doubt any of that was part of a coordinated plan. There's an even better chance of this being the case if this volunteer mage is angry.

Hopefully, angry enough to forget about how high the misfire rates are for explosion formulas. Which gives me an idea.

I quickly calculate my coordinates and change position slightly. Now I just need to lower myself a bit. This should bring the enemy mage's allies on the ground into the line of fire. With my adjutant close by, we pick out the perfect spot. And then...there, that should do it.

I know my guess pays off the moment I feel the telltale radiation from our enemy mage taking aim. Any decent aerial mage always keeps in mind what's *behind* whatever you're shooting at.

The fact that this mage is still trying to target us means...all logic has flown out the window for our attacker...

"Looks like the fact that we're flying directly over the Federation Army is completely eluding them. They must be frantic."

Tanya is wearing a wicked smile as she turns to her adjutant.

"First Lieutenant Serebryakov. What do you think about sharing these fireworks with our friends on the ground?"

"You want to bait the enemy into causing friendly fire...? What another ghastly idea you've come up with."

"Magic needs to be used wisely. It's called being *eco-friendly*."

"As in, good for the economy?"

This is both ecological and economical. That makes it doubly eco-friendly. Good for the environment, bad for Commies. I'm not a huge fan of the idea of getting shot at...but I'll chalk it up as part of the job. This is war, after all.

》》》   **THE SAME DAY, FEDERATION ARMY ENCAMPMENT**   **《《《**
ON THE EASTERN FRONT

Federation generals were pragmatists and placed reality above politics.

They knew that reality could be harsh, but it was politics that destroyed people. The more manipulated they were at the beginning of a conflict, the more likely high-level commanding officers would develop a realistic outlook of the world. This was because fame and power were a type of poison that could end people. Those who served spent their days in the harsh reality that was the war; they had no choice but to wade through a bloody, cursed world in their military-issued boots.

They were in a constant struggle to find out whatever they could on their enemies. The sacrifices they'd made at the start of the war forged them into the officers they were today. They scoured the world for intel, which they analyzed to the fullest extent.

In other words, the Federation Army evolved into one of the world's most pragmatic organizations. And they continued to evolve in a unique way to excel on the battlefield.

They were professionals. Diligent specialists who both feared and respected their enemies, the Federation generals gave their all to find out everything about those they had to defeat.

Needless to say, they knew a lot about the Imperial Army. In that light, their intelligence gathering even encompassed knowing how the Empire understood itself. As a part of this, they included research on the backgrounds and tendencies of high-ranking military officials for the Imperial Army on an individual level.

Naturally, this was only made possible thanks to the powerful backing of the Commissariat for Internal Affairs... For the greater good, the army was willing to shake hands with the devil. It wasn't long before objections from the army's trusted inner circle vanished like smoke. Objections and pushback were to be expected. However, the naysayers swallowed their reluctance. They were forced to comply in the all-powerful name of necessity.

And this deal with the devil bore tremendous fruit. Their folders on the enemy commanders steadily grew thicker with increasingly useful information.

Lieutenant General Zettour was a good example.

They conducted a thorough investigation of his background and military records, gathering all classified information on the man that they could find. The more dangerous the target, the more the analysts pored over their file.

What stood out in General Zettour's summary was his unrivaled cunning. To put it simply, the Federation Army analysts accurately depicted Lieutenant General Zettour as a con artist on the battlefield.

As far as they could tell, he loved using tricks and deception while conducting maneuver warfare. To be specific, he was an ardent believer in encircling his enemies with his superior strategic mobility, even if it meant risking everything to do so. People who analyzed his tactics revered his ability to consistently pull them off, even when it was evident that they were the best course of action.

His most notable operations always included bold reorganization of his troops with a sharp focus on annihilating the opposing field army over seizing territory, all without exceeding the theoretical limits of logistics. And he would always top off these tactics with what seemed like a sleight of hand.

The bottom line being that he was a nasty man—the nastiest sort one could imagine. His ruthlessness rivaled the Communist Party's secret police in the eyes of not only those who researched him closely but those close to him as well.

Considering this, there weren't many analysts who thought he could be defeated in any straightforward manner. He was the type who pulled his troops back to deliberately create salients that could be exploited by flanking attacks, with the ultimate aim of cutting off his enemies from their supply lines.

This was a scenario that even a new student at the war academy could grasp. If the enemy sets a trap, then just destroy them along with their trap.

The Federation Army had been duped far too many times—their chance at revenge was drawing near.

All they needed to do was come up with a plan to neutralize Lieutenant General Zettour's mobility. Predicting that he would send his most mobile forces there, the Federation Army placed the bulk of their reserves right at the base of their salient.

They even mustered their newest recruits for the large-scale ambush they had planned. And so they made ready to use the trickster's trick against him and destroy the core of the Empire's military might.

It eventually seemed like the enemy had fallen for this trap.

They had found what appeared to be aerial mages who belonged to a Kampfgruppe scouting their supply lines on the eastern front. The multinational volunteer unit stationed nearby attempted to intercept. They had been waiting for the imperial mages.

And while they succeeded in driving them back…the multinational forces lost two companies to Lieutenant General Zettour's deadly fangs in the process. This was a tremendous loss for the Federation.

But it was the final confirmation they needed.

"…He always starts his operations with a big attack."

As much as it made them want to swear, the Federation Army command knew the presence of highly skilled aerial mages was the signal they had been waiting for. The fact that he was using Named mages revealed the area where he would focus his attack.

"It's about to begin."

Multiple people in command expressed this sentiment. An imperial attack had occurred exactly where the Federation Army had predicted a full-scale frontal assault would eventually come. The first shot was fired with a large-scale artillery barrage.

They were inundated with a hail of shells like it was the opening salvo of an all-out attack. It wasn't the sort of bombardment an enemy could execute if they were on the run. This was what made the Federation commanders believe they had successfully read his intent. The Federation Army was growing confident in their information.

"Seems like our intel about their lack of ammunition was another one of his tricks."

The same voices expressed another sentiment.

"We'll get him this time!"

Had they failed to predict his movements, the attack would've thrown their troops into a panic. Fortunately, the Federation Army saw this coming and took appropriate precautionary measures.

They deployed their units in the lulls of artillery fire. They set up a tight perimeter and even conducted counter-battery fire.

"Everything is moving as we predicted... We have him right where we want him."

The commanding officers knew they were ready—this was their chance for revenge.

This time, for sure, they would catch that damn Lieutenant General Zettour. That was the very moment when the Federation Army command had quietly convinced themselves of their impending success.

It was the same moment when the con artist across the table, who they expected to show his hand at any moment, kicked the entire table out from in front of them.

>>> **THE SAME DAY, THE IMPERIAL ARMY'S PROVISIONAL COMMAND** <<<
CENTER ON THE EASTERN FRONT

The senior officers had assembled in the command center. They had been summoned there on short notice, only being informed of Lieutenant General Zettour's plan moments ahead of time. His orders: Prepare for imminent battle.

They collectively nodded when they saw their target was the enemy salient.

Practically everyone had guessed that would be their goal, after all.

Not only had the front line been reorganized, but most of their firepower was also quietly concentrated around the salient in a way that didn't immediately stand out. Most of the battalions were comprised of new recruits, but this was the norm for keeping their numbers up on the eastern front. With this in consideration, their current formation was designed for mobile warfare.

Most of them believed this signaled that the master of maneuver warfare, Lieutenant General Zettour, was preparing his counteroffensive.

That was...until they saw their target.

"W-we're going to advance directly toward their main forces?! We're not hitting their supply line?!"

The room was immediately filled with astonished cries and dubious gazes. Lieutenant General Zettour quickly blew away their doubts with a laugh as he introduced his plan: Operation Mini–Revolving Door. His goal was the enemy's field army. It was a bold plan. He wanted to bypass their supply line entirely and punch deep into enemy lines.

Should they succeed, it would without a doubt go down in history as a legendary victory.

Emphasis on the *should*, as this was all contingent on them not failing. The officers were realists to a man. They all had the same word flash through their minds: *reckless*. It was a leap of faith that assumed their army could seize the initiative and penetrate deep into enemy territory, achieving total surprise.

It almost felt like a freshly minted lieutenant, straight out of the war academy, had come up with a too-ambitious plan after getting drunk off his ass.

"Sir, are we...really going to attempt this...?"

In an attempt to change the general's mind, a handful of officers approached their superior with sullen looks about them. Lieutenant General Zettour remained firm as he bluntly cut them off.

"I've committed myself to this plan. This is our chance to act, and we need to do so with a steel resolve!"

He slammed his desk with his fist. The officers stared at one another in disbelief as Lieutenant General Zettour began speaking in a delighted tone.

"Think of it less as a strategy and more as a tactical ambush. We stand to gain a lot from this."

His subordinates timidly listened to his confident words before finally

building up the courage to speak. A single officer stepped forward and raised a concrete objection.

"Sir, please reconsider a frontal attack."

Spare me the excuses, the general's eyes seemed to say, but the dissenting officer boldly pressed on.

"This is a prime chance to strike the enemy's supply line! Please reconsider, sir!"

"Let me ask you this… Are you fond of poker?"

"What?"

"Try your hand at playing cards. It's even more interesting if you bet your cigars. You see, people can really learn a thing or two about over- and underestimating their hand when they have something to lose."

Card games are good because you have to hide your facial expression, and your opponent hides theirs. A game of bluffing, reading each other, and tricking each other.

Not only that but there was an element of luck to it, too.

Playing cards was like a strategic battle with your opponents, so much so that it was considered a reliable barometer for judging capable General Staff officers.

"Your suggestion is exactly what the Federation Army is waiting for. This is them we're talking about. You'd be out of your minds to think they don't have a welcome party waiting for us. Which is why…I'm going with an ambush. We're going to flank them so hard they fall into the seventh circle of hell."

When it came to reading their enemy's movements, the Federation analysts knew what they were doing. The enemy forces had predicted the Imperial Army's movements, just as Lieutenant Colonel Degurechaff had.

This is perfect, Lieutenant General Zettour thought with a smile.

It was easier for him to abuse enemies who knew what they were doing. The most diligent commanders tended to be the easiest to trick. He planned on hunting them, hanging them, draining their blood, and cooking them up nice and juicy.

"You're at your most vulnerable when you think you have the enemy right where you want them. Convincing your enemy they have you caught in a trap is also the best way to trick them."

Chapter **II**

"You mean to tell us, sir, that the Federation Army's salient is something that we lured them into, and they are already certain that we are going to attack their supply line?"

The officer's question had a tone of overt suspicion to it...leaving a bad stench in the air.

It reeked of arrogance and underestimation. His contempt for the Federation Army made him biased. There were limits to how much pride one should show in their own ability.

"Are you insinuating the Federation Army doesn't have the ability to do that?"

"...I find it hard to believe they would. Surely they'll learn our ways at some point...but would it really happen so soon?"

"They have a good teacher."

The officer seemed confused. Lieutenant General Zettour puffed some smoke from his cigar. As unfortunate as it was, the Empire wasn't the only entity capable of research.

War forces its combatants to always continue learning.

Forgoing the slow accumulation of new tactics was the same as waiting for defeat. Relying too heavily on prior experience and habits was another deadly pitfall. He had to prevent these soldiers, who were accustomed to the eastern front, from developing misconceptions.

"It's all about experience, men. You need to learn from it. As unpleasant as it may be for us, the Federation Army has paid their entrance fee into the university of experience with blood. They should have something to show for it by now."

While the Federation Army was an extension of the rigid Federation, the same logic couldn't be applied on the battlefield.

This was when a lone, tense-looking command officer showed up. He was only there to do his job, but with this many higher-ups assembled, he found it hard to jump in.

Lieutenant General Zettour tactfully addressed the poor man.

"You, what is it?"

"Y-yes, sir. I have a message. A message from Lieutenant Colonel Degurechaff."

"Good. Calm down and read it to us."

"'The sun has cleared the fog.' I repeat, 'The sun has cleared the fog'…
She's succeeded in drawing out the enemy, sir."

"Excellent." Zettour nodded with the biggest of smiles on his face.
The colonel always accomplished the most with the least.

"Th-there's also…"

What is it now? All eyes in the room rest on the messenger, who
continued.

"Sh-she's left a complaint."

"A complaint?"

He didn't expect to hear that. For once, Zettour found himself on the
receiving end of an ambush. He reflexively raised a questioning eyebrow.
His surprised expression urged the young officer to continue.

"'I'd like to request for this to be the last time you send me on a mission this reckless,' she says."

"I can make that promise. This will be the last time I give such ambi-
tious orders for this endeavor."

"Will there be a next time?"

That poor lieutenant colonel. That thought was plastered all over the
young officer's face. Lieutenant General Zettour answered in an easy
tone.

"There's no need to worry about that now. Worry about the next time
when there is a next time."

Lieutenant General Zettour thanked the young officer before turning his scowl back onto his subordinates. He didn't have time for petty
debates.

"Now, gentlemen. It's time to get to work. Let the Federation know
what defeat tastes like."

And so the mobile forces under the command of Lieutenant General
Zettour began to carry out their plan to encircle and annihilate the
enemy, just as the Federation Army predicted they would.

The only difference was their true target lay east of the front line. It
was an attack the Federation Army would never even dream of.

The Federation Army was ready to withstand a general imperial counteroffensive. It was what they had prepared for. But their experience was
what would do them in.

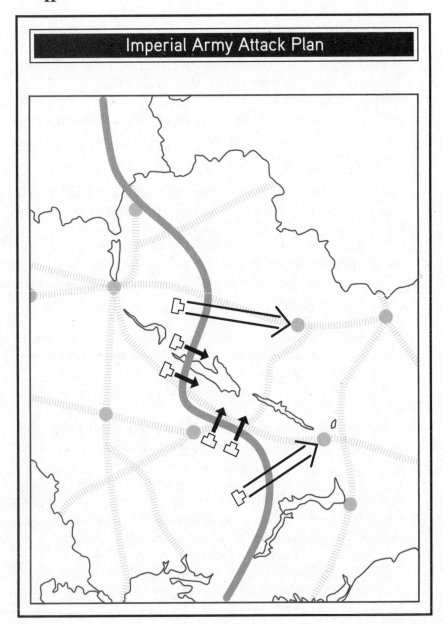

…Knowledge can be a scary thing.

Those who were on the receiving end of the Imperial Army maneuvers would learn a new lesson this day. They had previously learned that the Imperial Army encircles their enemies and cuts them off by pinching a salient at its base.

This was why they had an idea where the Imperial Army would show up when they caught word of them mobilizing for a counteroffensive.

It was a pitfall of the mind. They were too sure of their insight on how the enemy moved.

They're coming for the supply line was all they could think about. It created a blind spot that allowed Zettour and his troops to lay a relatively basic ambush.

They would feint attacking their supply line when, in fact, they were using the salient as a revolving door. They would be conducting a full frontal assault against now-defenseless enemy positions. The surer of their predictions they were, the harder it would be for the Federation Army to right themselves.

And Lieutenant General Zettour had moved his troops without delay. After all, it was just the other day he had his troops *retreating* back the way they came in order to lure the enemies out. Despite being in Federation territory, he had created a rare spot where the Imperial Army's knowledge of the land could more than compete with the Federation Army's.

It was also a spot the Federation Army hadn't surveyed yet. Being thrust into the morass of battle there would cause problems for them. Their generals wouldn't be able to make the snap decisions on how to deploy their reserves. They would know they needed to fill the hole in their defense. They would know they needed to send soldiers there to do it. But they wouldn't know exactly where they should place them.

They would frantically research the spot they should've already had covered, but by the time they came up with an answer, it would already be too late.

It was the newly established supply hubs that were key.

The Imperial Army pushed deep into the Federation Army's front line to strike at these all-important bases. This spoke volumes about something Lieutenant General Zettour had learned from the Federation. He had also thoroughly studied his enemy—except he hadn't focused on his counterpart but the idiosyncrasies of how the Federation Army set up its supply lines.

It had become standardized, which, for better or for worse, made it easier to predict. It was simple for Zettour to guess where the Federation supply bases were located when he knew the local geography.

Securing these supply depots certainly did clear logistical hurdles for bringing their troops provisions. He abandoned various precautions and ordered his tanks to accomplish the difficult job of overrunning these bases.

Without enough time to decide on what to do, the enemy would ultimately abandon around half their depots with the supplies intact. The Imperial Army could use what they left behind to fuel the tanks that had led the charge. Even better than this was...the seizure of their field artillery and supply of ammunition.

The heavy guns and shells were a godsend for Zettour's forces after they had used up what few shells they had held in reserve for their diversion. *These are the supplies I needed*, a delighted Lieutenant General Zettour thought as he immediately began reorganizing his field artillery.

Imperial artillery corps would finish their battle with Federation artillery pieces.

This was the eastern front, after all. They needed to make use of whatever they could get their hands on. The gunners they managed to scrounge up were already used to operating Federation weapons, so they were more than ready to light up enemy territory with their own equipment.

Unfortunately, the Federation Army command had a very accurate picture of the Imperial Army's troop strength, thanks to their incredibly thorough research. According to their predictions, the Imperial Army didn't have enough gunners to be able to spare any for a mission deep behind enemy lines.

That's why if they were suddenly hit with artillery from a place they deemed impossible, it was guaranteed to throw them into chaos.

Not only would it hit them in their blind spot but reports of enemy artillery behind their defensive line and the chaos that was coming would also muddle their intel on where the Empire's forces had procured the ammunition.

And after that…well, hitting the enemy where they were weakest was Lieutenant General Zettour's forte.

You think the bureaucracy will end over something as minor as a war?

——— Unknown, scribbled note from the war ———

To celebrate Lieutenant General Zettour's promotion, Tanya generously gave him an early gift—a nice friendly outing with the Commies on the eastern front. However loathsome it may be, it was a fittingly good day for battle. Almost ironically so.

For the soon-to-be general was far from a kind man. After penetrating enemy lines, his drive into Federation territory was as brilliant as it was destructive. Tanya, however, was nowhere to be seen. Unfortunately, during this key moment of the war, the official was...out of commission.

She had been ordered back to the capital with her adjutant as they were no longer needed in the east. At the end of the day, she was a General Staff officer. The army couldn't borrow her for too long, so she was sent back, just like that.

She was sent back empty-handed as well. The only thing she got out of the excursion were a few more kills to add to her score.

When it came to her job hunt, there wasn't much she could do with these.

I was a part of that operation! You know, the big one! Yeah, that won't get Tanya very far in an interview. She could be lying for all they know. What Tanya really needs is a concrete demonstration of her talents. Running small errands for generals isn't going to cut it. I'm not exactly surprised, but the government-run corporation that is the Imperial Army is as shady a business as they come.

This is but part of a long chain of events that have hindered my plans to get out of here.

I haven't even left the imperial capital, and I'm already fed up with the general sense of overflowing optimism here... It feels even worse after getting back from the eastern front. Despite knowing how fruitless it is to get emotional over things like these, I can't hide my disappointment in my employer's lack of insight into their employee's desires.

"What am I even working for...?"

My desire to serve is beginning to wear thin. I've been pissed off ever since I got back to the homeland.

It doesn't help that Tanya isn't old enough to drink away this stress. On the way to my next mission, I can feel my fatigue beginning to get to me.

To my surprise, I even find myself playing with the totally twisted notion that I'd rather be on the battlefield. Maybe it's my lack of sleep, or it could be that I've been overworking myself.

Either way, I'm clearly approaching my limits. It's moments like these that make me remember how important it is for a person to get the rest they need.

As sad as it may be, what waited for Tanya on the western front...is the type of general who says stuff like, *You can get some rest after you die.* This is General Romel we're talking about. He himself is the epitome of a hardworking man, making him the worst kind of person to serve under.

Tanya arrives at the western front command post. As per protocol, she makes her way to the command center to report to her superior, only to find that he's away.

To my incredible surprise, everyone from the high-ranking staff officers on down are away on a trip. The official reason is that they're conducting an inspection.

The only officer left behind is a captain who seems to be the general's adjutant. According to him, General Romel and his staff are out in the field observing from a tank and communicating via radio.

So he's out and about checking the front line and his troops on wheels—or I guess it'd technically be on tracks—instead of on foot. It sounds like a loud way to conduct an inspection. However, such activities are completely normal for a newly assigned general.

Visiting the front line directly is quite routine and even encouraged for officers.

"So they've been out on inspection for days now? Must be tough for the field units and officers alike."

Slightly intrigued, I prod the duty officer. Though expected, he answers with his agreement.

"Well, you know how the general can be."

"I learned all about his habit of randomly disappearing down south. Active as always, I see. It certainly keeps his allies on their toes as much as his enemies."

"It's the same deal as always. He blows right past the walls that normally separate the military branches to make his rounds with the navy, army, and air units."

"Oh? You don't say...? How admirable of him."

I nod and thank the officer for handling the formalities before immediately deciding my next course of action.

You see, this is General Romel we're dealing with. I know how he is— he's insufferable. He's also unstoppable, like a runaway freight train.

I know this better than most, since he ran Tanya ragged down south.

The man is brimming with vitality. He's the sort to start a maneuver campaign the moment he hits his new post. He practically personifies diligence and aggression. As a devoted employee myself, I can attest that he's essentially the ideal worker.

In this same light...he hates anything he views as wasteful. My guess is his life revolves around his work.

This normally wouldn't be a problem, but something about hearing a man like this overcoming the walls between military branches leaves a bad taste in my mouth. He's the type of commander who wouldn't hesitate to use necromancy to revive the dead and use them in a fight if he could... This set off more than a few alarms in my mind, not unlike when I'm bathed in radiation from enemy targeting.

Hearing about him approaching the army and navy in particular raises a few flags.

"Why go there?"

The current issue on the western front revolves around *air superiority*.

I can see the utility of bringing more anti–aircraft artillery to bear, but would something like that require going out of his way to visit other branches of the military? Contacting the army makes some sense, for the most part. General Romel is a lieutenant general for the Imperial

Army, after all. It stands to reason that he would have a good amount of contacts there.

But what business did he have with the navy?

It's not as if the relationship between the Imperial Army and Imperial Navy is especially poor—it's actually quite good. That said…it certainly isn't so good that they're liable to go on fun little excursions or the like. It goes without saying that he has contact with the naval armada stationed in the west, so it's fair to assume that they hold meetings on occasion, but…

Such meetings would be regular affairs, would they not? Would a general like Romel attend a meeting when he could just *have someone go for him*? The answer is—there's no way in hell.

Tanya has a few contacts in Fleet Command. Though less periodic than ideal, we do meet and exchange information, not to mention the occasional formality. These meetings are purely social in essence.

I can't think of a single reason a high-ranking army officer would go there for an inspection of all things. There must be…a deeper reason other than simple communication for what he's doing.

Something is off about this. Could it be related to Plan B?

"…That would explain why he's meeting the army. But why the navy?"

Setting aside its maritime prowess, the navy isn't particularly impressive when it comes to troop strength on land.

First off, foot soldiers are the natural choice for storming the capital. Perhaps military rationale isn't the right way to approach this problem, though. Whatever the contents of this fabled *Plan B*, it's a product of politics. In this regard, Tanya is nothing more than a pawn in the game, as is General Romel. This begs the question: Would that man willingly and proactively participate in such a plan?

But we're getting off topic. I turn my attention back to the military.

"…So let's say he's away on legitimate business. The question still stands: Why the navy?"

The first possibility that comes to mind is a plan to raid enemy commerce. I've heard that our submarines have put considerable pressure on the Commonwealth in the west. Would this warrant a visit from my commander?

While that's certainly possible, it still doesn't seem like a compelling reason for General Romel to go in person.

Considering the movement of our naval fleet in the west... Ah, none of this makes any sense. I cover my eyes with my hand just as I run out of time. Moments ago, the duty officer who I'd become acquainted with—General Romel's adjutant—brought Tanya a summons order from the general.

It's a telegram flown in from his mobile command center ordering her to report to his position.

I snatch it away from the man and give it a quick read...or more like a single glance. The paper literally just says, "Come." Nothing more, nothing less.

No room for refusal. Boss's orders. How arrogant.

I get myself ready as I make my way to the location of the mobile command center I've been provided.

I'm ready for the next unreasonable demand to be laid on me. It's funny how unrewarding it is to be correct about these sorts of things.

Tanya arrives on the scene and is welcomed by her boss's smiling face. Or perhaps more aptly described as a devilish grin. I wish it could end here. This is already scary enough.

But alas, it gets even more frightening when he opens his mouth.

"I've been waiting for you, Colonel. I have the perfect job for you."

Could this get any worse? Woe to General Romel. I look at the plan laid out before me. It's absolutely terrifying.

The gist of it is a full-scale assault on the Commonwealth—from the sea.

My first impression is that I must be seeing things.

An instant later, my hand makes its way to my eyes. I give them a rub because this can't be real. It must be some sort of joke. My brain is racked with a permeating, senseless doubt.

"What do you think, Colonel?"

When the general poses the question, I come to my senses, though my thoughts are still in complete disarray. Put bluntly, this plan is essentially a gamble. One that Tanya can't professionally condone.

Let's start with the most basic of premises. As unfortunate as it may be, we've effectively lost our air superiority. It's taking everything we've got to prevent disaster over the industrial area in the François Low Lands, and the situation there is growing direr by the day.

The Western Army Group that oversees the area is currently on the back foot. The situation is unfavorable, and there's no practical way for us to reach the Commonwealth homeland, where the enemy's base of operations sits. Despite there being no chances for us to destroy, occupy, or incapacitate the Commonwealth, General Romel is proposing a plan that would require his fellow officer's full compliance.

Does he want to go to their island? From the front?

"It says we'd pose a full-scale attack on the C-Commonwealth... Is this accurate...?"

"That's their base of operations, isn't it? This is basic stuff here."

"The definition of *basic* depends on the circumstances, sir. Are the orders from the General Staff Office not to fortify our defenses on the western front?"

"That is correct."

Tanya quietly shakes her head.

Fortifying a line's defenses in this context usually means *reorganizing its air defenses*. I'd assumed the mission I would receive from General Romel involved something like that.

So what is all this ...?

This is a leap in logic that almost reminds me of Being X. Has the war finally gotten to General Romel?

To my great misfortune, General Romel is Tanya's superior, and his operations always emphasize aggression.

"Your orders are written right there, Colonel, clear as day."

"In that case, I may need your help. My eyes seem to be acting up." I protest my assignment with a barely permissible rebuttal. There is a hint of angry disbelief in my tone. "This is supposed to be a defensive strategy, right? I seem physically unable to read this correctly. Is it all right for me to call a doctor?"

"Fret not, Colonel. Your eyes do not deceive you. I can guarantee you that the plan you hold in your hands outlines a fine defensive strategy."

"So it's a *defensive* full-scale assault on the enemy base."

The name of the plan challenges my command of the Empire's language in a way I've never experienced before.

It says we're going to outflank the enemy's Home Fleet, the unmatched naval force that rules the seas, and attack their homeland. Not only is it not defensive but it's also recklessly aggressive.

The plan is thoroughly and patently insane. But Tanya is a mature member of an organization. Her words need to be chosen carefully.

Taking a moment to think before I speak, I fold my arms and look up at the ceiling.

"I'm not sure what to say..."

Though I've decided to change jobs, it's not like I have an offer lined up or anything. It's important to always keep a foot in the door of your original company until you're ready to move on to your next job. Quitting before your career move is decided is a big no-no. That means I need to fulfill my duty as best I can until my next gig comes along.

"Sir, if you'll allow me to be frank, I can't get behind this. This is beyond the realm of acting within your power. It feels as if you've redefined the terms of the mission."

"It's an aggressively defensive strategy."

"Sir... This is a full-scale assault."

"In the military, the best defense is a great offense. An extreme way of putting it is that a spirit of aggression and a hunger for military dominance are more important than the attack itself."

The implicit *you should know this already* couched into General Romel's comment made it hard for me to refute that.

There is a certain logic to his thinking. The decision of where to apply their power, the appropriate deployment of reserves, and achieving a strategic goal.

It's essentially the same as changing one's job.

Those who are proactive and prudent about creating a better future for themselves are the ones who build strong careers. Thus, the decision to take a big risk isn't *always* bad.

"Lieutenant Colonel Degurechaff, we don't have time to be cordial about this. I don't plan on letting you fail to comprehend this plan. It strikes me as odd that a mage boasting the name White Silver would rather embrace detestable fear over a chance to bleed her enemies. Perhaps your silver has rusted?"

At this point, I almost wish that were the case.

But I can't say that. Tanya needs to be mature about this. As a member of society, I can't raise my voice while objecting if I want to maintain my position.

I let out a deep sigh before staring right at General Romel.

"Heroes know how to wait patiently, sir. Recklessness is not the same as bravery. I also don't want to uncritically consider biding one's time as being feeble in spirit."

"Yes. But one must forge their chance. Am I wrong?"

Tanya had no other option than to nod in agreement.

"Of course, I don't mean to say that a certain level of aggression isn't needed to mount a good defense. The issue here is what's at stake!"

"Tactics are a game of all or nothing. We concentrate our forces and point them all at one spot. The same can be said for defensive tactics."

He's right about this, too. Oda Nobunaga is lauded for the revolution he brought about, but his revolutionary military tactics shouldn't be overlooked. His formidable defense literally went down in Japanese history.

As far as I know, even Japanese children know about Oda Nobunaga. A significant event for him was the Battle of Okehazama at Dengakuhazama. But since too many people fail to ever call upon the knowledge they have…they never truly understand what defense actually means.

There aren't many terms as misunderstood as *defense* is. Defense can include offense at times. Unless you're trying to bide time, a defense that doesn't take care of the enemy's offense is a stringent strategy.

What did the Oda clan do before Imagawa Yoshimoto invaded Owari Province? Did they *wait* for the attack with a strong defense and bring the battle to their castle?

One only needs to read a Japanese history textbook to learn the answer.

The Oda clan went on the *defensive* by sending their samurai to behead Imagawa Yoshimoto and then intercepted their invaders. This was how the Oda clan successfully defended their castle.

And what if the shogun Nobunaga had just sat idle in his castle waiting for the enemy to make the first move? His life would've ended with a valiant defense, and his legacy would have been relegated to a footnote in history, only noticed by the odd history buff.

"Sir, I won't deny that aggression is vital to a strong defense. Decapitation strikes and General Zettour's maneuver warfare in the east are both testaments to this fact."

As a skilled field officer, I know how to use taking the initiative and knowledge to get the upper hand defensively all too well.

Chapter **III**

"So what's the problem? This is an extremely defensive plan."

"It is extremely defensive on a national level. However, I find it hard to call this plan defensive-minded."

There is a limit to everything, and I can't accept General Romel's extremely liberal definition as to what constitutes a good defense.

"This is the equivalent of mixing up a horse for a deer. It should be more than self-evident that it can hardly be called a strategic defense."

"We have a difference in opinions, Colonel. I also can't help but notice that your lack of desire to charge into battle as a field officer…"

Tanya's expression twisted at her superior's absurd comment. For better or for worse, I never dealt with bosses of this caliber in my previous world…though it was a daily occurrence in the exploitative job environment created by times of war. It's precisely why I'm considering getting out of here.

But right now, I need to protect my current position.

"With all due respect, a hunting dog…needs to remain calm until its prey is just within reach."

I straighten my posture and look directly at the general.

"Only a mutt would run around doing what it wants without orders. No matter what happens, that's not an appropriate way for an imperial soldier to conduct themselves."

"Your point being? Let's not get too caught up in metaphors, Colonel."

"Your *reinterpretation* of our mission strays far too much from the homeland's orders."

General Romel's jovial expression doesn't budge even the slightest bit when I give him my honest opinion. The dignified look in his eyes that urges me to go on couldn't be any worse.

"We could mobilize our boats. Not to intercept but to charge enemy territory! I believe this is more than aggressive enough for where we stand."

An attack on Commonwealth waters. We're effectively going to go right up to the world's maritime superpower and punch them in the face… How could this be considered defensive in any shape or form?

Setting aside the fact that it's insane, it's nothing more than a rash attack.

"We're not of the same opinion on this matter. The way I see it is that getting rid of the enemy is the best defense. Tell me what you think.

Considering where we stand on the subject matter, I want to hear what you have to say."

"Are you really going to assert that an attack behind enemy lines could be considered a defensive strategy?"

My superior quietly nods, forcing me to point out what I thought was obvious from the start.

"No matter how you look at it, this strays a great deal from what we were sent here to do. A coordinated naval strike using both mages and naval infantry…"

"This is well within my discretion as a means of protecting the integrity of the western front."

Does your discretion cover getting into a fistfight with the enemy *on their turf* in the name of defense?

This man is sick in the head. Even Shimazu, one of Japan's most infamously insane warlords, limited his defensive actions to his sphere of influence.

"…I simply cannot get behind this decision. To call this a defense erases the concept of offense in the first place."

"Colonel, I'm hoping to fundamentally improve our defensive posture in the west. As you know from the other day, there are plenty of circumstances at play here."

"No matter what is fueling this decision of yours, sir, I'm a soldier. Therefore, it's my duty to strive for the best defense possible here in the west."

"White Silver, you sound like a rusty old politician."

General Romel shakes his head in disbelief.

"The air in the Federation must be riddled with miasma."

Though he sounds astonished, he speaks the truth. I can attest to this, of course, having just come from the eastern front; things are beyond dismal there.

"The east is a quagmire, full of bodies that will never see a proper burial. The Federation is like a two-headed beast, with one looming head representing Communism and the other nationalism. It's entertaining in a way. I'd like to take you there with me if we ever get the chance."

"Sounds like quite the playground. Unfortunately…I'm getting a bit too old to play in the mud."

"You must be joking! I'll have you know that General Zettour waded his way through sludge in the east with my company."

"I see—so it's a place where that general can spread his wings. You've given me an idea of how truly terrible a place it must be. I owe you my thanks, Colonel."

Considering what I saw while I was there, I must admit that the east is the worst of all worlds when it comes to battlefields.

It's hard to romanticize what happens there as a clean, ideal version of war. In terms of how harsh an environment it is, it's similar to the southern front, but...other than the intense changes in temperature, that was a relatively easygoing battlefield.

The southern front is unique in its own way. It's a bit strange, considering how things started there, but winning or losing the battles down south isn't considered all that important for determining the outcome of the war on either side. This in turn has resulted in a level of mutual civility born from the relatively low-pressure environment you can find on the southern battlefields.

However...the same can't be said for battles on which the fate of an entire country rests. Countries place their raison d'état in winning these battles, no matter what the cost.

Well, then... General Romel folds his arms and begins to speak.

"Let's cut to the chase, Colonel. My mission for you is similar to what you did while you were spending time in the Federation."

"Sir, these eastern and western fronts are entirely different environments. With all due respect..."

"Wait," he says.

I am about to object but stop when I pick up on his displeased tone.

"Cut it out with your 'all due respect' crap. I'm not some bureaucrat."

"...Maybe I've been in the capital for too long. I think that all the red tape is starting to get to me."

"If a line officer such as yourself has problems with that, then the General Staff Office and the bureaucrats are all screwed."

"Ha-ha-ha."

General Romel gives a hearty laugh. Something about what he says causes my expression to twist.

The excesses of bureaucracy run rampant even during a time of unprecedented war. I can feel it affecting even me. Though frightening, there's something to be said about it. Setting aside Parkinson's bitter law, I never dreamed that the bureaucrats would ever be able to make this much work for themselves.

"Colonel, my plan is based on what I see as a reality. I'd like for you to directly threaten their capital. See? I've learned my lesson."

"You want me to bomb fog city?"

"Don't you think I've done some growing of my own since our time in the south?"

"That's an interesting turn of phrase. Would you mind if I borrow your dictionary so I can brush up on my vocabulary?"

"That's strange to hear you say, White Silver. This is the Empire, and you're an imperial soldier. We're both using the same dictionary obviously. Forget what others think and say what's on your mind in your own words."

This has to be on purpose. He's playing dumb.

This isn't someone I can keep in check by being indirect and nuanced. As cheerful as his demeanor may be, it looks like General Romel learned well during his stint as an Imperial Army staff officer.

Argh. This is why I can't stand General Staff officers who wind up becoming generals.

"On that note, I actually wanted to ask you something, Colonel. How about you share some of your wisdom with me. Is there any other way to fortify the west? Do you have a better plan than this one?"

His tone indicates his doubt in Tanya's ability to give a compelling answer, making it a form of penance given the fact that Tanya cannot refuse. I find myself wondering if the army will ever compensate Tanya for all her work-related stress. Back in the here and now, I entertain a few different ways I could reply to the question before choosing to be a professional as I politely begin to completely deconstruct my superior's supposition.

"I have confidence in myself. What I know, I know well. And speaking from experience, most aerial combat comes down to a battle of efficiency. If we're going to fortify our line, we need to organize our anti–air defenses to make them efficient as possible."

Chapter **III**

"That would be a good answer if we had the resources for that. But tell me, do they have anything in the textbooks on what to do when you're on the losing side?"

They don't, I wanted to say with a private laugh.

Toxic companies seek out innovative ways to create hype and move up in the market, but the desire to use innovation in such an oblique way speaks volumes for their failing strategy. Innovation isn't something born from having your employees chant stupid slogans. Conversely, freedom and creativity must be utilized to their maximum potential.

As sad as it may be to think about…poor working environments aren't generally conducive to fostering an environment where creativity thrives.

"It's a struggle of life or death for our AA gunners as the enemy pays us nightly visits with their bombers. It would take massive reinforcements to make the current system efficient. That's not something we have access to right now."

This is true, the three words carelessly make their way to the tip of her tongue.

I understand where the general is coming from, but to agree with General Romel would be to agree with this ridiculous gamble he's currently proposing. The saddest part is Tanya has to pretend she wants to be in the vanguard unit that would be tasked with attacking the enemy capital. Tanya loves herself. She wants to take care of herself, from the bottom of her heart.

Born from this deep-seated desire, I try to put forth a new proposal.

"There is a way for us to fight with our current numbers. This is particularly true for my aerial magic battalion. I'm confident we can produce the results of more than the few we have. We're the oldest members of the group. The enemy is nothing more than hatchlings when you compare our flight times."

Aerial mages are hardly optimal for intercepting high-altitude bombers…but they could easily handle a small portion of them. This is especially true for my battalion, which is the strongest of them all.

I intended for this to seem like a competitively aggressive plan, but as one might expect…my superior's expression doesn't even budge.

"Lieutenant Colonel Degurechaff, that amounts to nothing more than a painkiller, a palliative measure at best."

"Dulling the pain will buy us the time we need to think of a better plan."

"There's some truth to that, but you've made it a habit to procrastinate when it comes to defense. Biding time will only delay our defeat if there is still no path to victory. We perish either way."

I understand the logic behind what the general hopes to accomplish. It's similar to what Nobunaga did when he was surrounded. The Oda clan chose to target the weakest links—the Asai and Asakura clans—in the chain that bound him to win his freedom.

This could be considered a textbook example of an aggressive defense that followed the doctrine of interior lines. I'd venture to say, though, that the only reason it made it into textbooks was because it was successful. In most cases, people like to focus on *the management* when looking at companies that were run into the ground. It's rarely taken into consideration how poorly people in the field are treated while things are falling apart.

As much as I try to quell the doubt inside of me, it continues to grow.

"So we need to act for things to change?"

"It's the opposite, Colonel. I don't see how you can't understand this. If we don't act now, it is only prolonging our inevitable death."

While he has a point, the chances of success are still worrying.

Even if Nobunaga proved this could work in theory, what proof is there that General Romel can secure the same success? The answer is there isn't any!

To start off with, there are too many differences between the Empire and the Oda clan. True, the Oda clan was surrounded. Just like the Empire is right now. That's essentially it. That's the only similarity. The Oda clan had something behind those who surrounded them. They had relationships all over Japan with people who were willing to help them.

What about us? Does the Empire also have allies waiting just beyond our hostile neighbors? Nope. Not a single one. I think and think and think, but still can't come up with a single one.

This brings me to my conclusion.

Contributing any more is pointless. More worthless than unpaid overtime. There is absolutely no reason why I should have to suffer the same fate as the Empire, and it's high time I focus on self-preservation.

In other words, it's time to devote my energy to changing my occupation. And what's the most important thing for job hunting…? A shining performance record.

Tanya needs achievements prominently attached to her name. Her reputation within the Imperial Army is beyond stellar, but sadly I know from experience that this won't count for much with any potential employer I'm interested in.

I can say with confidence as an ex–HR representative that people tend to overestimate their own market value. Everyone believes they're an above-average performer.

This phenomenon is known as the Lake Wobegon effect, and—to someone as highly objective as myself—it is an unbelievably fatal mistake to make.

I'm perfectly aware that I am average and that only through hard work and determination have I just barely managed to pull ahead of the pack. I'm always strict with myself to make sure I never get too optimistic about my career prospects, as that could easily throw a massive wrench in my plan to transfer.

This is why I know that even if I have a few accolades to my name, I'm still nothing more than a mere lieutenant colonel for the Empire. Even if I want to defect, who's going to pay any mind to a random mid-level officer?

I could talk all I want about how I was awarded the Silver Wings Assault Badge…but it wouldn't mean much outside of the Empire. I know better than anyone that I can't afford to get full of myself.

I am well aware of the asymmetry in information between any two given companies.

In fact, it's a simple concept. How well is your own company's star employee known at other companies? To make matters direr, this is most definitely not Japan. There's no Internet here, and Tanya is attempting to change her national allegiance, which is quite a bit harder than changing the company you work at.

I definitely don't want to bet everything on how well-known Tanya is in the other countries—that would be a reckless gamble.

"I need an extremely prestigious accolade, or…"

I could potentially leverage being a part of an operation where the

Commonwealth could see me pull off something big. I need to get close so that they could see my face. It's hardly what I'd call the perfect market, but this could be a chance to raise my stock value on the international stage.

Let's view it as a PR move. Nothing wrong with doing a little PR to make the world realize how much Tanya's really worth. Her advertisement needs to be strategic. Thus, with a tinge of self-admonition, I quietly speak up.

"To think I would let the direness of the situation get to me this much…"

After that wilting comment, I feel a hand pat me on the shoulder. General Romel is wearing a beaming expression on his face.

I had been worried about how he would react to my pretending to have come around to his way of thinking…but I didn't expect this reaction.

"Now you're getting it, Colonel. Strong results on the battlefield are our only way out of this. That's some splendid insight you have there."

"If there's no other way out of this bind, all I can do is my best."

I quickly recompose myself, and the general starts laughing as if there's been a strange misunderstanding.

"It's a lonely road. Let's walk down it together."

I stare blankly at him. *Together?* Is he saying he wants to defect as well? No, that'd be too much of a stretch.

"Sir, do you intend on accompanying me?"

"It's a play on words. I don't think a man of the army can cross the sea."

Oh, he's talking about the upcoming mission.

It's just the general's way of wishing Tanya good luck. In that case, I have just the response for him.

"Sir, I am indeed a soldier who belongs to the magic branch of the military, but the war college was also a part of the army. If you're going to treat me like an outsider at times like these…I can't help but feel like a terrible rift has come between us."

"Don't worry, Colonel. You'll always have a seat next to me with your name on it at the army banquets whenever you wish."

Using food as an example made it hard for her to press him any further. What an ordeal this has been. I shake my head in relief as the end of our conversation comes into sight…but, well, you know what they say about assumptions.

Enemies aren't the only ones who can catch you by surprise when you let your guard down. Unfortunately, I failed to foresee that there might still be danger lurking about.

"Oh, Colonel. I almost forgot."

Wait, what? I have a bad feeling about this. My superiors rarely save the best for last.

I'm reflexively on my toes at this point, but the fact that I have no idea what's coming suggests it's already too late.

"What's that, sir?"

I do my best to hide the fear in my heart.

"There's something I need permission for from the homeland."

"Right…"

This sets off an alarm in my head. That ominous feeling is welling up inside. I'll try to sidestep it by adopting a vague tone of voice and expression.

This calls for immediate emergency evasive maneuvers.

Look to the side, steady your breathing, and remain calm. Avoid eye contact as much as possible and speak as little as possible. Now, activate the troubled look, maximum power. Remember, you have no idea what he's talking about—why are we even here…? That little farce buys Tanya a scant few seconds at most.

The enemy is far too powerful.

"You know what I'm getting at. I want you to go get the permission I need."

It goes without saying that I would love it if I didn't understand what he's implying, but there's no way to escape an order this plain… Just my luck. First, General Zettour, now General Romel. It seems like the Empire's high-ranking officers all really know how to work their subordinates to the bone.

Tanya might be an aerial mage, but flying back and forth between the Empire and the far extent of their war fronts is no easy task!

"Sir, considering the importance of the matter, would it not be better for you…?"

"A commander can't leave his post so easily."

Oh, *now* he's logical. Even the mildest of objections for a principle as obvious as this could have a drastic impact on a soldier's career.

As a senior member of an organization, I have no choice but to swallow my tears. There's no way out of this one.

"Convince higher-ups at the General Staff Office for me. I'm sorry I can't go with you. Let's make this happen together."

"...I'll do what I can, sir. I'll proceed with the utmost secrecy to see to it that the plan makes its way to the battlefield."

What else could she say to the man?

>>> **AUGUST 14, UNIFIED YEAR 1927, COMMONWEALTH SUBURBS** <<<

It was a regular suburban house like any other.

A typical country home for a noble. The house's design, the attached facilities, and the general accommodations suggested a certain level of status and means for the many people who stayed there. It was the perfect place for the military and other officials to use as a temporary residence...or at least, that was how it appeared on the outside.

Everything changed the moment one set foot in the building.

The guards, most of whom were familiar faces, feigned a sense of boredom and unimportance... They were recognizably naval mages. During wartime, they were the type of veterans desired more than anything else on the front lines.

There wasn't much an officer wouldn't do to get their hands on even one of them, and here they were pretending to be foot soldiers.

The only other group that might use elites like these as bodyguards... was the Imperial Guard in the fog city.

But they fit in here as well because this was the headquarters for the Commonwealth's Intelligence Service. And yet, one can only let out a dry chuckle when every time they visit here, a new set of eccentric security protocols have been put into place.

"I must admit, these protocols are prudent."

Decapitation strikes had become commonplace ever since the Rhine campaign. The owner of this establishment knew how troublesome such tactics could be more than most.

Chapter III

Whether hailing from east or west, the head of any intelligence agency was always vigilant. This was a good thing. It was important to be cautious.

…It would've been better, though, if he wasn't the one you had to report to directly.

"The injury that Devil of the Rhine gave me is beginning to hurt. What a pain. I have nothing but bad feelings about this."

They say that scars are like medals, but they can feel more like canaries sometimes. Scars might even give you warnings if you're the type of person who thinks too much.

Sadly for Lieutenant Colonel Drake, he was a social animal. His logical mind wouldn't allow his instincts to take over and up and run no matter what kind of premonition he had.

He briskly walked beside another soldier through the halls.

Well, more like he was led by the soldier. The lack of freedom given to visitors, no matter their rank or status, said everything he needed to know about the building's stringent security.

That said, even if the soldier leading him to his destination was strict… He was not a wall but a boat mage. He was there to bring Drake to where he needed to be. Drake mused that the man was like Charon. Following the soldier closely, he eventually reached the promised gates of hell. There would be no running or hiding now.

He took a deep breath.

He then gave his guide a brief bow as per military etiquette before entering the room, where a man with a domineering expression was waiting.

"Hello, Colonel. It seems your injury is healing well. Now, let's hear your report."

Drake thought briefly about his preferences when it came to people… and how he rarely got along with older chaps who didn't speak much. It was even worse when they were wise enough to understand the gist of things but also short-tempered enough to explode at any excuses he would give. He could already feel a headache coming on.

"Yes, sir. Where shall I start?"

"Let's start with the accidental shooting. What actually happened?"

Their first order of business already had his stomach churning and his head thumping. A strange constricted feeling was coiling up inside him. Though in name only, the incident had been caused by a junior officer under his command. While he didn't have complete authority over her, he still bore some responsibility.

This was unavoidable as someone who served the crown.

Drake handed over his report. It detailed his professional opinion as the person in charge at the time of the incident. He did everything he could to maintain a calm voice as he began to speak.

"Officially, it's been reported as collateral damage that is a by-product of the chaos during the battle, but the reality is a volunteer mage ignored my orders and acted on their own."

"As unfortunate as it may be, collateral damage is a part of war. How bad was it…for the Federation to make such a fuss about it?"

"Regretfully, the formula was too powerful."

Not only did Drake have to offer his mea culpa to the political officers but also Lieutenant Sue—who caused this whole mess—had a friendly chat with them afterward. It was difficult to comprehend how any of it made sense. In all actuality, Drake was mere seconds away from blowing a fuse right then and there, but…the Federation report Colonel Mikel got his hands on matched their own, so the buck stopped with him.

"I heard…there were Federation field officers who got caught up in the explosion and died. Though unofficial, this is coming from a reliable source of mine."

The scale of the damage was immense, and it came at the worst possible time. Enough to chill his boiling blood in an instant. It was another nasty example of how Lieutenant General Zettour toyed with them on the battlefield. It was a miracle that after everything was said and done, Drake was still in command.

The matter was handed over to the Foreign Office, which bore the brunt of the fallout.

Drake was still wondering deep down inside if there would be any repercussions for him…

"How unfortunate. We can't issue them a formal apology, either… We'll just have our prime minister apologize to the Communists in private. That wraps up that conversation. Good work."

There wasn't a hint of blame or chiding in his final remark.

Chapter **III**

"What?"

"Colonel, I have no interest in meaninglessly reprimanding my subordinates. We're at the mercy of the politicians, and I'm not so incompetent as to push their unreasonable demands onto the men and women in the field. I may be old, but I intend to age with grace and avoid picking up as many bad habits as I have years under my belt."

Drake appreciated his thoughtfulness. As heartless as it may have seemed to an outsider, he almost felt exempt from any responsibility for the matter. Almost... While the incident was officially resolved, he felt like he couldn't let himself go unpunished.

This was the exact reason he had produced his own report, despite knowing it would be disrespectful.

"By the way, why did you go out of your way to attach a withdrawal appeal to your report? I understand you had the authority to access the backgrounds of the multinational volunteer unit, including First Lieutenant Sue."

Drake was being scolded by the man, and he understood the political nature of his appeal. The ever-so-slight hint of irritation that could be detected in his superior's gaze was awfully frightening.

Nevertheless, Drake felt compelled to speak his mind.

Even if the brass were intent on including a *former Entente Alliance army orphan* in their ranks, it was his sworn duty as an officer to give his superior an honest report.

"General Habergram, with all due respect, I included it due to my fear of a repeat."

"What? They're only Commies, Colonel. You needn't worry about whatever losses they sustain."

"I'd agree with you if I didn't know the truth. But...as someone who was on the scene when it happened, I can't allow myself to do that."

In the next moment, the uninterested, almost casual demeanor of his superior changed slightly. The head of Intelligence, who had treated Drake like a gentleman of the navy, now looked at him like a soldier.

"Lieutenant Colonel Drake, I may be misunderstanding you, but..." He studied Drake with slow, observant eyes and hit him with a sharp inquisition. "I had always pegged you as a man who hated the Federation."

"Allow me to correct you, sir—I absolutely abhor Communism with every fiber of my being. And to be frank with you, sir, I don't think I could ever come to like the Federation."

For Drake, there was a big difference between the people of the Federation and the ideology of Communism.

This difference was impossible to ignore when he stood alongside them on the battlefield.

He believed that while many of the Federation's people were genuine dyed-in-the-wool Communists, assuming every citizen of the Federation was the same couldn't be considered anything but incredibly shortsighted.

"Most of their military are members of the Federation before they're Communists. They're driven by their nationalism, not Communism. I'd go as far as saying we're in the same line of business considering we're all soldiers."

Drake knew this assertion could very well end his career. He had come prepared for that.

This was the Intelligence branch of the Commonwealth Army, and they despised Communism with unmatched fury. In their eyes, to even reference an ideology as destructive as Communism was grounds to ruin an officer's future.

Despite this, Drake remained steadfast.

"I hate their system, but I question whether or not we should hate their people."

Without responding, his superior reached for a cigar and wedged it between his teeth. There was a viciousness to him for someone who had just declared his desire to be a kind, old man. He held a match as it burned slowly, but Lieutenant Colonel Drake found himself feeling an unintended familiarity with that match.

Standing at attention, Drake waited for his superior to say his first words. The silence was incredibly uncomfortable.

He found himself indifferent about the ultimate outcome. He just wanted to hear his superior's thoughts on the matter. It almost felt like he was a defendant about to receive their final judgment.

His superior, on the other hand, leisurely smoked his cigar before abruptly placing it on an ashtray and beginning to speak in a blunt tone.

"So you're a humanist. Affection for others is a good thing off the battlefield. However, we're at war, Colonel. Sentimentality like that will get you killed."

"My apologies, General... But I'm not some monster when I step onto the battlefield—even then, I'm still human. This is a matter of having a good conscience. My advice is to remove a handful of members, starting with First Lieutenant Sue."

"Not only do you lack appreciation for being abdicated of blame, but now you deign to give advice? You're more arrogant than I thought. You're killing me here, Colonel."

Though he made a point not to hide his displeasure, his superior was willing to listen to him.

"Fine, let's hear what you have to say. So, Colonel...are you saying this wasn't an accident?"

"When you consider the problems with our positioning during the battle, it could be considered accidental. However, that poor positioning was a result of the enemy deliberately luring the novice members of our multinational unit. This is what makes it human error."

General Habergram listened to a brief explanation of what happened before raising his old cheeks for a scornful sneer. It was evident that he now understood the enemy had baited them.

His evaluation of the unshapely front line was simple.

"...I see. So they pulled one over on us."

"Yes, sir. One can only wonder if the Imperial Army's senior mages all have tails."

"Like devils, you mean. In any case, we have to face reality. Is it difficult to make sure something like this won't happen again?"

In response, Drake simply shook his head shamefully.

"Considering our soldier's backgrounds...I'd say it's impossible."

"How about teaching them not to fall for provocation? Is that too much to ask for?"

"...Sir, I'll do everything in my capability to train them, but this is the Devil of the Rhine we're dealing with here. That mage's deviousness and trickery is second to none."

Lieutenant Colonel Drake let out a sigh to muffle his annoyance.

"That damn ghost is the worst sort of human."

Cunning beyond a doubt—and a powerful Named mage to boot. The devil had even earned the new title Rusted Silver, referring to all the blood of the mage's countless victims. Having to fight a foe like that repeatedly on the battlefield was truly concerning.

"The Devil of the Rhine? I've heard that name before."

"Yes, it's a cheeky little…"

"Hold on. The Devil of the Rhine… Isn't that the Named mage known for decapitation strikes? They're one and the same?"

The general was intrigued. Drake wasn't sure what had struck a chord within his superior, but he answered the questions.

"I made contact and visual confirmation. If it were just a mana reading, there are ways to fake it, but honestly…there is no mistaking that devil on the battlefield."

Drake was sure of it.

"In fact, we had ourselves a brief cuddle session at extremely close range. The devil stabbed me with an enchanted blade, and I returned the favor with an optical sniping formula and an explosive one."

"Your injury is from your fight with the Named?"

"Correct. Had it not been for the urgent care and magical therapy, I'd either be in early retirement or a body bag right about now."

Returning at all from an encounter with a decapitation specialist could be considered an accomplishment all on its own. It appeared Drake's emotional words now had his superior's full attention.

While the slightly graying general seemed calm, Drake could tell there was something on his mind.

"Yes… I'd like to ask you a bit more about your encounter."

Sharing information about the front lines was one of the reasons he had been called back to the homeland. So, for Lieutenant Colonel Drake, there was nothing out of the ordinary about his superior's interest.

"I find it interesting that the Devil of the Rhine was seen in Federation territory. Start by telling me about what happened in more detail."

He began going into detail about what had happened, as requested.

"When my troop saw the Named mage, the ex–Entente Alliance aerial mages were especially riled up. The same went for those from the Unified States who had run-ins with her before. Their emotional state made it easy for her to provoke them—"

"That's not what I want to hear, Lieutenant Colonel."

The general waved his hand as he interrupted.

He shot Drake a look as if to say, *You know what I mean*, but how was Drake supposed to respond?

As regrettable as it was, Drake rarely found himself in an office, so he had no idea how to interpret General Habergram's mood or tone.

He merely detailed what he was asked to explain… A moment passed before his superior shook his tired head and gave him some more details.

"I'm not asking what you thought about the devil. I want more details about your encounter with the Devil of the Rhine. Is there a chance it may have been a mistake? Tell me what happened during the fight."

"The devil was one of two hostiles initially thought to be an enemy recon flight."

"Have you fought before?"

"We have clashed a few times, but this was the first sighting in a while."

His superior nodded, then shot him a look, demanding he give more details.

"We determined the two mages were conducting a recon-in-force and mobilized our entire unit for battle. Regrettably, the battle ended before we could take them out. The pair managed to down six of ours. If you include the heavily injured, the total losses amount to a full company."

"…All this and there were only two of them?"

Lieutenant Colonel Drake's expression remained unchanged while his superior scowled. Deep down inside, Drake also had qualms regarding the matter.

"It's another case of Lieutenant General Zettour toying with us."

"Yes."

Though he concurred with his superior, his clenched fists and intense expression showed how agonizing it was to think about. Even the most well-trained officers are still flesh and blood, still human. They can't make their emotions disappear completely.

"So you believe the trickster and the devil teamed up?"

"Yes, sir, very much so. That's certainly what my sighting suggests. Those bastards are as cunning as ever."

"Really, now. It's an interesting story you have there, but…"

"Sir?"

The general shoots him a single glare.

"I find it hard to believe the Devil of the Rhine was actually on the eastern front. Even with your report, I can't be certain. It clashes with the information we have on our side."

"Is there doubt about my visual confirmation? Sir, I…"

"Our latest report shows that the devil and that famous battalion are both in the west."

It sounded like a bad joke. Drake could feel his shoulders slump. This wasn't something he wanted to hear from the intelligence community, especially its head.

"I've only stated what I saw. If you need me to comment on it, all I can say is that there may be errors in your latest information."

Drake had fought in hand-to-hand combat and even sustained an injury. He had come face-to-face with the Devil of the Rhine. It couldn't have been anyone else.

"Colonel, I'm not doubting you."

The general said this, but his eyes told a different story. Drake idly thought about how eyes could be more honest than words while he politely listened to his superior elaborate.

"At the same time, we're talking about combat. You know how easy it can be to make mistakes in the chaos of a battle. Am I wrong?"

"I can't argue with that, sir. But I'd like you to take into consideration my tenure as an officer and my performance record."

"I believe…what you saw may have been a mirage or an illusion."

"Sir, with all due respect, I—"

"That's enough."

Habergram shook his head and held his hand up to forestall Drake's retort. He kept his irritation from showing in his expression and dismissed the colonel.

"Mr. Johnson will take your report on the state of the eastern front. Feel free to tell him any details that might get removed from the report. I think that's enough for one day."

"Thank you for your time, sir. I could also prepare something in writing for Mr. Johnson instead of an oral report."

"Like me, he's an old man. I don't think he has the patience for a letter. Give it to him quick and straight… And make sure to tell him about that illusion you saw."

With a quick thank-you, Drake was shooed out of the room where the man who led him there was waiting. Guided with a quick "This way, sir," Drake realized there was no use pressing the issue any further.

That was probably for the better.

"…An illusion…?"

Lieutenant Colonel Drake mumbled to himself as he walked down the hall. He felt like someone had just told him a terrible joke. Had General Habergram breathed in a bit too much of this country's moldering air?

"Is this the fabled *fog of war* everyone always talks about?"

His wounded shoulder began to throb. Maybe this was an illusion, too.

The medical treatment he received in the homeland was performed magically, and his shoulder had already fully healed. There was no reason for it to hurt any longer, but the injury screamed at him all the same.

"I know what I saw."

The little devil who wreaked havoc on the battlefield.

That unmistakable thirst for blood and that expert formula control told him everything he needed to know. He had gotten so close he had to resort to a suicidal attack to finally break free, and the general thinks he's seeing things? Even an optical deception formula wouldn't be able to trick him at that distance.

That infuriating *voice* was what really gave it away!

He would never forget it for as long as he lived. There was no way to mistake it for someone else.

"…Seems like the information coming from up top can't be trusted. As they say, seeing is believing. I trust my own two eyes."

He didn't know who the devil was. He probably never would. But all he knew was that the intel they had on the Devil of the Rhine was absolutely full of shit.

"This is going to drive me insane… I'd better head to the pub and knock back a few to get this off my mind."

The person leading him through the hall stayed silent as Drake's mood grew worse and worse.

It was at that exact moment when a man in a nice suit at the end of the hall noticed him and called out his name in surprise.

"Oh, if it isn't Drake! I didn't know you were back in the homeland. Why the long face? Did something happen?"

"Kim? Ah, just some business in the east. I'd rather not talk about it."

"Sounds rough. I'll buy you a drink. I bet you haven't been to a proper pub in a while now, have you?"

The friendly offer made Drake happy. He was in a genuinely tough spot. All he wanted to do was coop up in a pub with a pint in hand and talk about all the garbage he was dealing with.

The sad truth was he still had some work to do. His night would be spent filling out mandatory forms before he could enjoy the sweet release of booze.

"Thanks, but I'm not free just yet. Sorry, but I'll be on my way."

"Be careful now, you hear? You can always drop me a line if there's anything wrong!"

Drake appreciated the homeland for its friendly hospitality... But he didn't think that really extended to venting about the intelligence agency *to* one of its agents.

Drake said his thanks before following his guide to Mr. Johnson's office.

All he wanted to do was up and run to a pub at this point. He shook his head.

"No, I'll just grab a drink when this is all finished."

Though there was no way for him to know this, Drake's abilities as an aerial magic officer were held in extremely high regard. So much so that the Commonwealth intelligence agency valued him higher than he did himself.

It went without saying that those at the Commonwealth Intelligence Service Headquarters weren't the types to openly tell him this, though. But the general consensus was that he was the real deal.

He was as loyal to the Royal Army and the crown as any naval mage. His pedigree was impeccable as well. He came from a long line of military men, and there were no problems with the way he thought or his personality. From an intelligence perspective, he was a reliable asset—something that was both rare and extremely valuable.

This was part of the reason he had been the officer chosen to go straight into the rotten nest that was the Federation. The Commonwealth used those it trusted first and foremost.

If he says he saw *that mage*, then it was more than worth considering the plausibility. Enough for Habergram to seriously consider doing so, at least.

Though he shot the man down during his debriefing…it was actually quite difficult for him not to show his shock. If it had been anybody else, the general would've kicked them out of the room without a second thought. But it had come from a man he trusted.

That was what caused him to groan.

"The Devil of the Rhine? In the east?"

He didn't want to admit it was the same mage. But he also couldn't prove that the devil hadn't been there.

The source that told him the Devil of the Rhine was in the west was proven. There were also many reports coming from the defensive line set up along the channel that corroborated the claim.

That said, Lieutenant Colonel Drake was fresh back from the east; his information was still new. What's more, he insisted that he saw the devil in the flesh. Was the imperial ace there just to help Zettour go on the offensive? This wouldn't explain the infamous battalion's whereabouts, though. They had them perfectly marked.

The Devil of the Rhine's battalion was unmistakably stationed in the west… So why would their commander be seen in the east? Well, it wasn't unheard of for commanders to occasionally move on their own. There were certainly cases where they would go on leave or move around for communication purposes.

If that were the case, though, then what circumstances would lead the devil to participate in a battle? That was unheard of. Why leave your battalion in the west only to go fight in the east? Habergram couldn't think of a reason why.

Not a single conceivable reason. He could only see it as a complete and utter contradiction.

"…What the hell is going on?"

He had in his hands Ultra's intel—decoded Imperial Army transmissions.

These described the Devil of the Rhine's and the mage battalion's movements in great detail. Every last one said they were heading west. They were stationed there as a part of the Lergen Kampfgruppe. The devil would be reporting directly to Lieutenant General Romel. Looking at the pair's service records, they were such a good match that it made the analysts sick to their stomachs.

These two were like demons who could consistently come out on top of nearly every hand in this shitty card game called war.

Evidently, they were in the middle of planning a commando strike on the Commonwealth homeland. Sending the Devil of the Rhine in first…made sense, to say the least. Leading the assault with aerial mages was perfectly logical in military terms.

There was no reason to not believe it until word came from a soldier trusted as much as Ultra that he had *seen the devil in the east*. As inconceivable as it sounded, Habergram couldn't simply brush the report aside.

"Lieutenant Colonel Drake says he saw the devil in the east… What a pain in my ass. Does this mean the Devil of the Rhine has relocated?"

He wanted to reject the notion, but he couldn't flat out discard the possibility. So what was the correct response to all this?

He thought of the worst-case scenario—endless possibilities began flooding his mind. But he had to figure out which of them would be the most catastrophic. Would it be the scenario where the enemy figured out radio codes had been deciphered and were actively using this against them by sowing counterintelligence?

That was certainly a possibility, except for the fact that they had been confirming every last thing they gleaned from the intercepted messages. They knew that imperial ships were covertly assembling in a single location thanks to their SIGINT work and sources in the resistance.

The danger of intercepting fake messages was ever present…but the Empire had a tendency to put too much stock in their encryptions.

The biggest giveaway was how unsettling the channel had become. Considering the number of friendly mages who had been taken out as of late, the Commonwealth intelligence community felt a pressing need to remain wary of a powerhouse with the ability to change the game.

Chapter III

"I'd hate for this to be a ruse…"

Habergram stopped, then knocked himself in the head with his knuckles. Cruel logic and reality dictated the course of intel battles. There was no point in him hoping for one outcome over another.

"I have to let go of my desires…and think purely about the possibilities."

Was the enemy on to them deciphering their codes? If that were the case, then Ultra would be in trouble. However, there wasn't any other evidence that Ultra's intel had been compromised.

"What if they've picked up on Ultra's identity and are laying an elaborate trap?"

Doubt and suspicion were couched in every thought, and his mind was tormented by his inability to trust anything.

Was this the fate of those who handle information? General Habergram rubbed his temple while he smoked his cigar. He then helped himself to some of the brandy hidden under his desk before letting out another groan.

He didn't know. He couldn't be sure of anything.

"Which one could it be?"

Was the enemy playing a trick on them, or were they still in the clear?

"No… There's no feasible way for them to know about our source. It just doesn't add up. Let's think this through. If they were going to use Ultra to entrap us, they would have reacted in some noticeable way from an intelligence and military perspective."

If the Empire even suspected that their codes were no longer safe, they would have almost certainly changed up as a matter of security. Considering that all the SIGINT coming in and out of the Imperial Army had remained the same, it was hard to believe they were aware of Ultra.

"…But then again, what if it's part of a wider scheme?"

There wasn't enough time in the world for him to worry about every single possibility.

As much as he wanted to put his mind at ease, the amount of stress this was causing seemed liable to give him PTSD.

Habergram continued to sigh and sigh until he poured himself some tea. He found himself cursing the trade route—both its general complications and how it had led to his ignominious fall in the ranks.

It's not as if he lacked for results. Using Ultra's info, he knew where each of the enemy submarines was stationed. He had managed to pull the channel shipping back from the brink by grouping their merchant marine ships into armed convoys to protect them from imperial U-boats.

This strongly suggested that Ultra's information was still reliable. But the fact that it was merely a suggestion was frightening.

Was Ultra right?

Were they wrong?

Not knowing the truth was a terrible feeling. The general noticed a peculiar side effect of staring at his office's ceiling too much in consternation. He had memorized the pattern of his ceiling.

"I know it's ridiculous, but I'm really starting to hate this ceiling. Damn it—if I knew I'd be staring at it this much, I'd have painted a picture or something."

Every stain he saw reminded him of something he'd worried about in the past... It was incredibly annoying. It felt like he'd spend the rest of his day grumbling to his ceiling.

He played with the idea of hanging his own pictures.

He added this thought to a list of things to do, and in an attempt to figure things out, Habergram picked up the black receiver of a phone on his desk and dialed a number.

"You've reached Section B."

The voice that answered his call was a frail, lifeless one—as if their poor soul was in charge of patrolling the seventh circle of hell.

"It's Habergram."

"...General? Do you need something?"

"I need to talk to you about the strength of our encryptions. Now. Send me the officer in charge," he demanded.

A few hours later, there was a knock on his office door. An officer who looked exhausted after working for days on end let himself in.

The bags under his eyes proved that he suffered from a clear lack of sleep. His unkempt stubble also stood out. This happened to even the fittest of officers who spent too much time in the decoding department, which considered nothing but talent when recruiting.

As for his uniform, well, at least he remembered to wear his hat. But... his appearance was more than enough to put Habergram in a bad mood. He expected his subordinates to dress and act like gentlemen.

"Hello, Colonel. Looking mighty dapper today, aren't we?"

"Forgive me, sir. We're just so short on staff, and…well, we're short on everything these days."

The man buckled a bit at his superior's sarcastic comment, a sign that he hadn't completely lost his humanity. One look at his tired eyes was enough for the general to understand just how worn down the decoding officer was.

Unfortunately, he had called him there to question the fruits of the man's labor.

"There are worrying signs we may not be accurately decoding the Empire's messages. I want you to go back and look through them, taking into account that counterintelligence may have been planted in the intercepts. We need to find out if anything's not adding up and fast."

Were their readings accurate? Or were they being tricked?

This was a question that could determine the outcome of the war. The decoding officer, utterly unfazed by the question, confidently answered his superior.

"If that's the issue, then let me reassure you."

"About what?"

"That we've cracked the Empire's codes without a doubt. I believe there have yet to be any discrepancies with the magic intel we've provided."

The man spoke with confidence. This colonel oversaw the department that stood on the front lines of a cryptological battle unfolding between the Commonwealth and the Empire. He had absolute faith in his department's work.

"We have a strong grasp on their coding patterns and the communication habits of their individual officers. We've conducted cross-examinations of multiple codes. We've even been able to reduce our deciphering times to the point where we can almost crack their messages in real time."

"That's true…for now…," Habergram said before pointing out a possibility they needed to be aware of. "The issue is whether or not they've picked up on our ability to decipher their messages."

Even if they knew exactly what the Empire was saying, whether that information was real and actionable was another story entirely.

It was fully within the realm of possibility that they were sending out false information to throw off complacent code crackers. Lacing such counterintelligence with tidbits of truth was the best way to trip up your enemies.

"Do you think there's a possibility they're on to us? Or that there's a possibility of them using dummy codes to throw us off?"

"We haven't seen any signs of that happening..."

"I want you to make absolutely sure."

This was easy to say but incredibly difficult to do. The cryptography department was already using all their resources to decipher encoded messages; asking them to analyze the message's accuracy would grind their staff into dust.

The colonel's already lifeless face seemed to wither even more as he grimaced. Habergram didn't fail to notice his reaction, but he remained steadfast about his orders.

"We need to examine these codes. There's no time to waste."

The colonel obeyed, and after having the entire Intelligence branch go through every message they'd deciphered, the result of their audit was delivered with a simple report.

No abnormalities detected.

The Commonwealth Intelligence Service could still read the Empire's encrypted messages like an open book.

Bad tea is a sure sign the country is doomed.

Lieutenant Colonel Drake, a joke made at a pub

I like to think of Tanya as an upstanding modern citizen who understands commonly accepted ethics and social norms. To word it differently, while I am a social animal, I am also fully aware of the precariousness that comes with being a part of society.

Instead of a suit, I don my uniform, and instead of a project proposal, I bring a battle plan. Today I won't be presenting at the headquarters of my old company but at the nerve center of Tanya's current employers—the General Staff Office. I accent my outfit not with a necktie but with a variety of medals and badges.

When all is said and done, the essence of my work isn't all that different from my old job.

I still need to head to the main office to request permission for the implementation of a new project. In terms of power balance, I'm still on the side that has to bow down. As if this wasn't unpleasant enough already... And to make things worse, I'm here selling a plan I don't actually want to be a part of to superiors who don't want to hear about it.

One may wonder why it has to be this way. And to that, I say: It's rather simple. Unfortunately, for all parties involved, the market has stopped functioning properly, forcing workers to perform meaningless tasks for miserable wages.

Be that as it may, I still have a job to do. It's important to do your work, after all.

I swallow a sigh and don my cap as I get ready. The written report I'm carrying needs to be signed by the commander of the Kampfgruppe, Colonel Lergen, so I knock on his door.

"It's Lieutenant Colonel Degurechaff. I have an appointment with the..."

Chapter IV

Before I can get out *colonel*, the door opens. A group of clerks comes pouring out. They grab the report out of my hands as they tell Colonel Lergen and me to come along.

We follow the group to a military vehicle sitting outside the General Staff Office. Without any idea of what's happening...we pile inside and are promptly whisked off to an unfamiliar government building.

If I was feeling generous, I'd describe the structure as avant-garde. The reality is that it's basically a concrete building that was designed to be easy to construct first and everything else second—a gem of modern architecture.

In the capital, this building is known as none other than the Foreign Office, the agency tasked with the handling of all foreign affairs.

Or—as all other agencies view it—a cozy nest of deadbeats. No one really knows what the people inside have been up to ever since the war broke out.

While soldiers are doing far more work than their salaries can justify, I feel compelled to ask what on earth are these freeloaders doing?

I almost want to scream, *Do your damn jobs!* at the top of my lungs in frustration, but I digress.

This is the Foreign Office we're dealing with here. Had they been engaging in diplomacy like they were supposed to, our country probably wouldn't be on the verge of collapse after such a prolonged war.

The lion's share of the responsibility for this mess falls on their shoulders. And that's putting it lightly; their negligence is on the level of war crimes at this point. If I were in charge of this country's HR, let's just say they would be on an actual chopping block. What a nightmare it is when the wrong people are doing the wrong jobs!

Diplomacy is all about people.

If there was even a single Bismarck in today's Empire, I'd probably be sitting happily in my office right now, enjoying military benefits for the rest of my peaceful life.

At the very least, we wouldn't be stuck in an unwinnable war.

In the sacred privacy of my mind, I complain about the state of my nation's diplomacy before something dawns on me.

It seems obvious now that I think about it. An Empire that has no Bismarck and no idea how to conduct diplomacy competently is doomed. There was no chance of them winning this war from the very beginning.

As I pass through empty halls of the Foreign Office building with Colonel Lergen, I can't ignore the ostentatious paintings that line its walls.

They're a series of works that tell the story of the Empire's illustrious past. The paintings depict the nation's founding, famous victories, and acts of heroism, whether it be the charge of a knight or a score of private citizens who banded together to drive away foreign invaders. It frightens me to think someone went out of their way to hang these oil paintings, each a crystallization of the nation's pride. It bears noting that this is the Empire's *Foreign* Office.

…Sadness wells up in my chest.

If this were an army building, it would be a different story. For the military, taking pride in historic triumphs and extoling the nation's strength is a way to maintain morale. Not that there would ever be a need for such a thing—the members of the General Staff Office are ardent realists.

"Sir."

"Yes, Colonel?"

Without putting too much thought into it, I grab my superior's attention.

"The Foreign Office sure seems proud of our nation's martial prowess. Almost to the point that they want to show it off to visitors more than we do."

I'm looking at a painting of a girl, who represents the Empire, vigorously striking down the other nations of the world in a piece that's supposed to depict our nation's founding.

The young maiden towers over her enemies, sword in hand. It's a mighty fine work of art—if they're doing their damnedest to intimidate any foreign dignitaries.

If that's deliberate, then it could just be an entertaining part of gunboat diplomacy.

But the situation is beyond dire if the Foreign Office is hanging these without any thought. It suggests that they don't understand the point of decorating their building in the first place. I don't know how much the painting is worth, but as someone who doesn't subscribe to the romanticism behind the foundation of the Empire, it's a hard piece to swallow.

"About that, Colonel…"

"Don't worry, sir. I'll watch my tongue in front of the diplomats."

I know what is and isn't appropriate in social settings. But just as I grimace internally, my superior says something surprising as a grimace also appears on his face.

"Actually, Colonel, we're about to meet with a counselor named Conrad. I think you should be up front with him about an opinion like that."

"So you want me to let him have it with some army logic?"

"It's the opposite. He sees things the way we do. Unlike his predecessors...I wager he'd be delighted to hear what you have to say about the state of things."

"Well, well."

This diplomat sounds like an intelligent man who can handle some healthy criticism. He must have a good head on his shoulders. To think there's still some sane people left in the capital! As jealous as I am that he gets to work in the rear where it's nice and safe, there's a part of me that also feels for the man. It must be difficult working in this strange place.

What's it like to be a rational foreign diplomat for a country that may or may not win a war? It is rare for me to feel sorry for others. Colonel Lergen and I continue down the hall until we reach Counselor Conrad's office.

The first thing I see can only be described as culture.

The counselor had gone out of his way to pour us tea with his own two hands. How polite of him. Or maybe it's just a way for him to mask the lackluster taste of their cheap tea... Suspicions aside, I'm in a decent mood—that is, until we sit down at the meeting table.

The first words that escape Counselor Conrad's lips as my superior and I take our seats cut like a dagger.

"Can we win this war? I want to hear your thoughts on the matter. I'm asking you frankly, so I hope you can be frank with me as well."

His question floors us. The moment he brings up the Empire's war prospects, both Tanya's and Colonel Lergen's faces become sullen enough for their entire Kampfgruppe.

Victory. What a loaded word. I can't help but wonder just how many people out there in the world know its meaning and yet ponder its definition.

Victory is like an illusion. The Empire is trapped in a dream where the promise of victory must be kept at all costs.

It's like a curse. Nothing is crueler than a dream that will never come true.

That one word is enough to get a groan from anyone in the military who knows the state of the Empire's war front. To their great frustration, even entertaining the idea of defeat is inconceivable.

The Imperial Army is but one part of the nation-state known as the Empire. Its collective memory and culture are rooted in the shared experiences of the greater whole.

In other words, the Imperial Army is an organization forged from victory and valor. While the military may suffer the off defeat here and there on the battlefield, their collective memory is dominated by the glorious myth that the Empire was always destined to *win in the end*. This has been both a blessing and a curse.

Victory is seen as a *result* for the Empire and its army. It's simply considered the result of their military initiatives *always* coming to fruition.

How can a nation fight a war for this long if they don't believe they will win? That's doubly true for an army that has never lost a war!

Even the majority of officers are still convinced that they'll win eventually. They believe in the ultimate victory because it justifies all the losses they've suffered so far.

It is the simplicity of Counselor Conrad's question that makes it so difficult for Colonel Lergen to answer.

A patriot like him could never admit that the resources we've poured into this war are *all for naught*.

He hasn't been inoculated against defeat. But how many could claim they had? Everyone tells themselves that it's impossible for the foundation of the Empire to crumble in a single night. What's the alternative when ever-present fear is suffocating and the consequences of failure are so dire?

It's a nice white lie to avoid total collapse. Or perhaps it's simply to hide from the truth. It doesn't matter in the end. What does matter is that when asked whether the Empire can win, there's only one answer Colonel Lergen can give. And that answer is *Yes, we can*.

"Is something wrong, Colonel? I'd like to hear your honest opinion."

The counselor stares at Lergen. The fact that the man is questioning the reality of the situation makes it hard for the colonel to answer.

Chapter **IV**

As a man of the military, it's unusual for him to beat around the bush. This is what makes it impossible for him to put together a coherent response. *Defeat* is a forbidden word. It's not something he can bring up so easily. It's clearly causing him a tremendous amount of distress.

He just can't say it—he can't even open his mouth. Tanya, on the other hand…is completely unaware of the silent mental anguish of the man next to her. For Tanya, it's a question that she would politely answer simply because she was asked. Maybe her willingness to do so was simply in the spirit of service.

Without putting too much thought into it, she formally answers the man's question in what she considers to be good faith.

"Counselor Conrad, is this something you truly need to know?"

"Lieutenant Colonel Degurechaff?"

The counselor makes a strange face at her, but for Tanya, this is all just a part of dealing with clients. It's important to make sure people really want to hear the truth of how dire a given situation is before you give them your honest opinion.

"Could you ask us one more time? The question, I mean."

"Okay, I'll say it again. Can we win this war? I, a diplomat, would like to hear your professional opinions as people who work directly with and within the General Staff Office. Please let me know what you think."

Counselor Conrad's confirmation couldn't be any clearer. That was all Tanya needed.

She wouldn't have answered the man's question until it was put in such undeniable terms.

With a twisted smile, Tanya finally felt free to give her scathing analysis on the matter.

"It's impossible. I can say without a doubt that we will not win."

"Wh-what are you…?"

"I'm being straight with you. You're barking up the wrong tree if you're expecting a win from the military. This war is out of our hands."

It's important to be up front about products your company doesn't carry. That's the basics of business.

She knows not having what people ask for can be…disappointing, but you don't have what you don't have, and no amount of wishful thinking can change that.

Nevertheless, she keeps her tone and demeanor calm. Smiling is the first and most important part of dealing with clients.

Follow-through is also crucial. Taking the time to explain your professional opinion when someone asks for it is the best foundation for building trust.

This is why Tanya embodied a straight-shooting specialist to answer the counselor's question.

"You can believe what the con artists and zealots are saying in the newspapers if you wish. But if you want me, a logical soldier, to tell you we can achieve a complete victory, then you're dreaming."

If they could win this war, the idea of a *job change* would've never even crossed Tanya's mind. Sadly, not unlike Japan during World War II, the Empire is a sinking ship.

Anyone with the slightest aptitude for analysis could only tell you the glaring truth—that the country is on its last legs.

"…Have you lost your mind?"

"No, Counselor."

Tanya remains calm and lets him in on the terrible news.

"I'm simply providing you truthful advice."

"Truthful? So, what, is that supposed to make you an honest broker or something?"

"If you need me to be."

Counselor Conrad shakes his head.

"This is ridiculous. A mere lieutenant colonel thinks they're qualified to predict the outcome of the war? And a child at that? I would think twice before speaking so boldly."

The first one to respond to Counselor Conrad's words wasn't Tanya but the man sitting next to her, Colonel Lergen.

As a fellow serviceman, he felt compelled to interject.

"Counselor, let's not forget that looks can be deceiving. I know she is young, but Lieutenant Colonel Degurechaff is one of our most decorated soldiers. Until just recently, she was a force to be reckoned with on the front lines. I will admit she can have an extreme way of wording things…"

"That seems a bit over-the-top, no?"

The urge to correct the man's rather rude assessment came over Tanya.

It appeared the problem was that he didn't know *who* was offering him a frank opinion.

Obviously, that would be resolved if she took a moment to let him know who he was dealing with. While the fact that her record didn't speak for itself outside of her country was unfortunate...the medals that lined her collar did all the talking she needed within the Empire's borders.

"Silver Wings Assault Badge, Field Assault Badge, Wound Badge, Trench Action Badge First Class, Close Combat Clasp Special Class, Iron Cross First Class..."

Tap, tap, tap... Tanya points to all her medals, one by one.

Awards carry weight at a company. They mean even more in the army. They're certainly more than enough to earn the respect of a fellow countryman.

"Do these look over-the-top to you? I'm also a Named. I feel I'm at least as qualified as the next person to talk about the state of the war."

Confident in her prowess on the battlefield, Tanya had no reservations in using her accolades to win the man over.

I'm not the type to let organization choose me—I'll be the one doing the choosing. A lack of presentable achievements would only force Tanya to make unpleasant comprises down the line. Who would voluntarily do something so idiotic? It's a simple matter of letting the man know her true worth.

The last thing I want is for the market to evaluate Tanya as some nobody who can't pull her weight.

"My first battles were in Norden. I then became a platoon leader on the Rhine front. After a brief stint in the war college, my next stop was Dacia, where I was placed in charge of an aerial magic battalion. After that, I returned to the Rhine, where I took part in Operation Revolving Door. Then I saw some action in the south before being rapidly rede- ployed for a key assault on the Federation front..."

Diligence, integrity, and an impeccable record.

These were what made Tanya von Degurechaff who she was, and she had done more than enough to prove her worth on the battlefield.

It's certainly more than enough to get an accurate market valuation. This is something to be proud of.

"If you have an issue with my record, feel free to take it up with the General Staff Office. They should be able to provide you with a more thorough record that will prove beyond a doubt that I'm not some random little girl who's never stepped foot on the battlefield."

A bit overwhelmed, Counselor Conrad backs down a bit before Colonel Lergen takes the reins on the conversation.

"...As you can see, looks aren't everything. As I'm sure you can understand now, while Lieutenant Colonel Degurechaff may seem young, her fangs are among the sharpest in the army." Colonel Lergen adopts a reserved tone as he continues, "Regarding youth, you're in a rather similar situation yourself, aren't you, Counselor? And I mean that with the utmost respect."

Though a disrespectful notion to point out, the man sitting across from them laughs.

"This is war. I know how it is. Anything goes. Sometimes it can be hard to keep that in mind."

The tension visibly drains from his shoulders as he brings one hand to his head and reaches for a cigarette with the other before quietly lighting up. It's clear he can tell when he's been beaten.

"By the way, Lieutenant Colonel, I must ask. Is there a trick to being able to muster up the courage to say such bold things? Something to stop yourself from worrying about the criticism you may face afterward?"

Tanya laughs off Counselor Conrad's legitimate question with a light no. The counselor seemed shocked by her response, but was there really anything so bewildering about it?

"I've always thought of humans as the type of creatures that will look for any excuse to criticize one another."

"Counselor, it's simple, really. I don't need words to prove my bravery. I've already done that on the battlefield."

For Tanya, military exploits are a wonderful thing. No one can dispute them, and simply pointing at them can silence quite a lot of criticism. In other words, success on the battlefield earns you the right to speak back in the homeland.

This was the same for sales. No one would bat an eye at the top salesperson clocking out early.

"I still haven't met anyone who dared to call me a coward or question my sense of duty."

"So the brave have the right to speak their minds... I see. You're an interesting person, Lieutenant Colonel. So give it to me straight. Do you really think that the war is a lost cause?"

"I do. I'm sure of it."

Colonel Lergen slumps a bit in his seat as he hears his subordinate announce their country's inevitable fate.

On the other side of the table, though, Counselor Conrad flashes a big grin. Not only is he smiling but the man is practically at the edge of his seat. He stares at Tanya with bright eyes almost to the point that it's disturbing.

"What's your reasoning?"

"Can the Empire take on the entire world and win? The Federation, the Commonwealth, and now the Unified States are joining forces against us. We also can't ignore Ildoa. Oh, and let's not forget the far-away land of Akitsushima. They may jump in at some point as well."

We're dealing with all the world powers and possibly even more.

When all is said and done, even if the Empire wields a mighty sword known as the Imperial Army, it isn't as if the rest of the world is unarmed. Tanya doesn't need to wait and see to know which side will emerge victorious.

"Forget looking at a map. It's a numbers game at this point. There are too many enemies for us to handle."

Tanya continues as Counselor Conrad nods with delight.

"This is beyond the realm of military theory... It's all about leveling out the playing field. We weren't diligent enough early on when it came to limiting the number of counties we're fighting."

It's important to speak theoretically. Treating personal conclusions and conjecture as fact is for cultists and con artists. In the real world, the most important thing to consider is universal laws. I consider it unpatriotic for a rational, upstanding citizen such as myself to not back up my assertions with rigorous theory.

"You shouldn't even need to look at the balance of power in numerical terms. It should be obvious at a glance. A single country is fighting on four different fronts."

It was indeed unheard of.

"I see. So that's why our predecessors favored the interior lines doctrine in the hopes of defeating our enemies in detail."

Tanya shakes her head as she emits an overt sigh.

"Unfortunately, that strategy was originally set in motion with the goal of amassing a great army to speedily and efficiently win a select few decisive battles. It was never meant to be used against the entire world."

The generals at the start of the war found a small path forward they could follow to do the impossible, but it was more or less an insurance policy in case they lost strategically. Why was this strategy being used to defend the country on the whole? The answer is quite simple: The strategy had been created under the assumption we would be attacked; the planners never dreamed that it would be used *outside* the Empire's borders.

"The interior lines strategy is like an insurance policy for if we're ever attacked. Insurance is exactly that—insurance. It's something you pay for but hope you never have to use."

Do people who pay for life insurance do so in hopes that they'll die? What kind of idiot sits there and thinks, *Oh, I'd better get cancer so I can capitalize on my health insurance?*

For anything less than insurance fraud, it makes absolutely no sense.

"The Empire has made a mistake. We've been thinking about this all wrong. It's like losing a healthy fear of death because you have great life insurance. Not only that, the insurance policy isn't even that good to begin with, considering how much we're paying for it."

"Wait, Lieutenant Colonel." With a curious expression about him, Counselor Conrad voices his doubt about one thing. "Are you insinuating that we've wasted our resources? We've accomplished quite a lot as a nation."

"Since the onset of the war, we've repeatedly won key battles against enemy forces, but none of them were decisive enough to bring an end to the war. Even our stunning victory on the Rhine went to waste because we didn't know what to do with it…"

Operation Revolving Door created François Republic refugees and solidified the endless nature of the current war. I'm confident this can't be considered an effective use of resources. Money that has been spent on life insurance is more or less pissed away. It won't be long before the Empire doesn't have enough money to pay for its basic necessities.

"To make matters even worse, it's becoming more and more difficult to maintain our dominance and force concentration. In the most extreme cases, we have lost the ability to reliably secure local superiority for even brief periods of time."

Tanya slaps her hand down on the desk between them as she continues to spell out the terrible truth.

"Even *if* Ildoa remains neutral, we simply have too many enemies."

The country is barely scraping by and has been in this quagmire for far too long. It's only a matter of time before time runs out.

If Tanya was the Empire's lender, she would have cut them off without a second thought. Any hope for them to come out on top is virtually nonexistent. The country's plummeting at terminal velocity, and I would bet that there'll be more than a few defectors in the coming days.

The things that decide the fate of a country were not all that dissimilar to what decide the fate of a company.

Time and money are everything.

If one of the two dries up, then the endeavor is brought to a screeching halt.

"Once we start falling down the hill…all that's left to do is continue falling. If we press on with this war like we have been, we'll only create more enemies for ourselves."

Opportunists won't make their move until they're sure the time is right.

In this regard, Ildoa has taken one of the wiser positions in the world. They're willing to maintain relations with the Empire despite its unfavorable position in the war. It guarantees their sales of war matériel, fuel, and other highly demanded resources—not to mention the occasional wine or coffee bean.

This friendly relationship won't last long once the Empire's impending defeat becomes readily apparent.

Anyone who thinks the Ildoans would even *hesitate* when the time comes to turn on the Empire are the same sort of people who believe their company will remain unchanged after it's been sold to new management.

The new reality will destroy the old world. This leaves the Empire in a position where it needs to be prepared for anything that might happen.

Trying to be ready for literally every possibility is the same as trying to be perfect—impossible. Even trying would simply result in an inability to prepare for a single thing. Claiming you can do anything is the same as saying you can't do anything well.

"The result? Our country has its hands full just keeping itself stable and lacks a concrete plan to get out of this war. It has been a long time since victory on the battlefield has held any real strategic meaning. At this rate, it's all but impossible."

"Can I ask a question, Lieutenant Colonel? What makes our victory impossible? With the correct strategy, could a series of decisive victories not potentially lead to winning the war?"

The counselor's asking a loaded question. He may be smart...but it's obvious that he doesn't know the current state of the front lines. Almost makes me want to laugh at the picture propaganda had painted in this country.

"Sadly, I believe we're out of time."

The counselor tilts his head in confusion, clearly thinking, *What do you mean?* He needs it spelled out for him. Colonel Lergen quietly grows more agitated. He's obviously wondering how much clearer it could be that the Empire already doesn't have a moment to spare...

"Do you need me to be more straightforward? Our country is on the verge of bankruptcy. Nothing we do on the battlefield will buy us an extension."

"And?"

"Winning battles only prolongs our inevitable defeat due to our strategic disadvantage."

"I'm asking what your point is, Lieutenant Colonel."

What's not to get? This man is dense to the extent where it's borderline ridiculous. Tanya hesitates for a moment as she starts to feel suspicious. It's obvious that the counselor is an intelligent man given the conversation leading up to this moment.

So why is he being so...elusive about coming to this conclusion?

"Counselor, I don't know how you couldn't know this already, but allow me to inform you...we're already losing the war on the strategic front."

"What I'm asking is why you don't try and figure out a way to overturn said disadvantage."

Strategy must defeat strategy. It makes sense to focus on strategy when it comes to breaking free from this bind.

The reality is that the current situation is very much like trying to put water back in a cup after it's already been spilled.

"Do you think we're in a position to even try?"

"Is that a reason not to try nonetheless, Lieutenant Colonel?"

"That's unreasonable. We have already tried, and we couldn't think of anything. Did you think otherwise?"

No, wait... Could it be that he's rejecting his nation's defeat with his heart and not his mind? Searching for some way to win must be his way of escaping reality. So even someone as intelligent as this man refuses to face reality despite having played this game for so long!

Upon coming to this chilling realization, Tanya takes the conversation a step further.

"It's true that a comeback would require a strategic victory, but—as unfortunate as it may be—the military is putting all its resources into merely staying afloat on multiple fronts. Counselor, we must prepare for the worst."

"And by that you mean...?"

"You'll be hard-pressed to find an officer who, with confidence, claims we'll win the war. The military should either line their academic advisors up in front of a firing squad or praise them for the boundless fighting spirit they've instilled in their officers." Tanya then adds her two cents as well. The man asked for *her* professional opinion, after all. Think of it as a form of customer support. "If it's a matter of my own opinion, I believe officers need to be intellectual. Therefore, a firing squad seems like the apt choice to make here."

I can feel two pairs of nihilistic eyes honing in on me. Even Colonel Lergen is staring after that remark.

Though the counselor is at a loss for words for a moment, he eventually speaks up.

"The desire to use such draconian measures must be due to your youth, Lieutenant Colonel."

"Well, no, Counselor. It's simply born from my desire to fulfill my duty in preventing an epidemic."

"An epidemic, you say?"

"The inability for soldiers to face reality on the battlefield is a form of incompetence. Is there anything more dangerous than an officer who isn't fit for their position? Fear is an ally to the incompetent. It's something more frightening than even the most formidable enemies."

These words are what eventually set him off.

"So we need to face reality, eh... Ha-ha-ha-ha-ha-ha-ha! Yes, that's it! It's about time we woke up from our little daydream!"

His laugh, which starts scornfully, begins to take on a hysteric tone. Lergen and Tanya stare, startled by the man who's raking both his hands through his now disheveled hair, laughing all the while like a maniac.

A strange sight to behold.

Well, strange to see *off* the battlefield, at least. Based on personal experience, I figure this is the result of too much stress. Breakdowns are fairly common on the front lines, where soldiers become worn down both physically and mentally.

It's always a difficult thing to watch—someone losing their composure and showing the dark emotions they bottled up inside...

I feel for the counselor. The illogical event known as war has evidently eaten away at Counselor Conrad's reasoning.

In any case, it's awkward to be in the same room as someone suffering a mental breakdown. Thankfully, this isn't a trench and the counselor doesn't have a weapon, or else Tanya would have shot him right then and there... Hopefully there's no need to subdue the man.

It wouldn't look good on paper, considering their respective positions. Albeit an imperial soldier, Tanya is still an outsider to the Foreign Office, so there would be hell to pay if she had to get physical. If push came to shove, there was no way for it to end well. It would undoubtedly have an immense negative impact on her reputation. Liability is definitely a concern of hers, so it's worth war-gaming. Would it be better to just grab Colonel Lergen and make a beeline for the door? Definitely not out of the question when considering the potential repercussions.

She glances at the door. It seems like it would give under pressure. All I'd need to do next is fireman carry Colonel Lergen out of here... No, better create optical dummies to confuse the counselor first. Tanya almost imperceptibly sits forward in her seat so she can make her move at any moment as several scenarios play out in her mind.

This series of calculations ends up being for naught.

With a loud curse, Counselor Conrad sits back in his chair and crosses his legs while looking tiredly at the ceiling above.

Pressing his fingers against the corners of his eyes, he asks Tanya and Lergen a question.

"Colonel Lergen, Lieutenant Colonel Degurechaff. Please forgive me. That was embarrassing." The counselor lowers his head and pointedly turns to Colonel Lergen. "Now that we've got that out of the way, there's something I want you to tell me... How in the hell did you raise *this*?"

Tanya pauses, as being called *this* doesn't sit entirely well with her. Colonel Lergen has a different reaction, however. He gives a deep nod as if to show the depth of his agreement with the counselor.

"She was born this way. If we could mass-produce Degurechaffs, the Empire would have blown Moskva and Londinium off the map with a single aerial magic battalion long ago."

That's a compliment, right? I think so...? Let's interpret the comment as flattery and a bit of an overstatement.

"I think I see what you mean. But the thought doesn't sit very well with me. Such a warlike notion is lost on civilians such as myself."

The counselor stares at the ceiling with tired eyes. This is the moment Colonel Lergen decides to say something unexpected.

"My apologies, Counselor Conrad. Considering your career, would I be wrong in assuming you have experience as a second lieutenant?"

A year of conscription service is considered a fundamental part of learning about the world. In the Empire, this is especially common for children brought up in higher-class families. Had Tanya not been born an orphan, it's the career path she would have expected and wanted.

This was the basis of Colonel Lergen's question, but it's met with a wry laugh.

"I was a second lieutenant in name only. I never saw the Rhine or the eastern front. I spent the year studying military etiquette in the barracks."

A lieutenant in name only—his service as an officer was nothing more than a rite of passage for a young man about to become a formal member of society.

In other words, he's your typical Junker.

Someone Tanya was jealous of—someone who left the service while there was still peace.

"It's probably better if you didn't have so much faith in me. I'm humble enough to not pretend I know what I'm talking about."

The two military personnel both fought the urge to express their desire for the leadership to have the same humility.

Had he a single iota of this, the war would've played out much differently.

From an expert's perspective, there's nothing worse than a person of middling intelligence who thinks they know everything about any given subject.

Tanya peruses the catacombs of her mind for the right words. She throws out a phrase a diplomat would use.

"Reconciliation is our only way out of this. And it needs to happen fast."

She looks Counselor Conrad in the eyes.

His blue eyes stare straight back, and it seems like her words are effective. Tanya's resolve was clear in her suggestion, and they share a brief but intense gaze before the diplomat lets up.

He sighs and peers back up at the ceiling.

It's possible he didn't realize it, but he's been shaking his leg.

"Reconciliation, reconciliation, reconciliation…"

He repeats the word three times before lighting a cigar. With the same blank gaze, he scratches his head while he takes a drag.

A thick plume of smoke streams from his mouth.

Just as the smoke starts to bother Tanya, Counselor Conrad finally speaks up again.

"If a field officer feels this strongly about it, then it must be true."

"Meaning…?"

"I understand the army's desire to resolve the war with reconciliation. Considering the current circumstances…it's a prudent idea. That's precisely what we should do."

It's hard to understand these diplomats at the best of times.

They're always so vague and obscure, always beating around the bush, always taking care with their words but never saying anything of substance. Clarity and conciseness—you can't be a soldier without either.

Colonel Lergen shakes his head next to a bewildered Tanya.

"Counselor, the key issue here is our enemies. How will they receive such a proposal?"

"What makes you ask that?"

The counselor stares in confusion with a blank look on his face.

Colonel Lergen hesitatingly answers, "Because we're not in a position to make demands?"

"Colonel, that's what I'm not understanding. Is that not why we need to reconcile?"

"That's correct. But this is where your people come in, after all…"

Counselor Conrad brings his hands together with a clap, interrupting Colonel Lergen. He readjusts his cigar and, after taking a few puffs, begins to speak again.

"Colonel Lergen, you need to be more consistent with communication within the military. The way I see it… No, wait."

"And by this, you mean?"

Counselor Conrad looks past a perplexed Colonel Lergen at Tanya, who has remained silent up until that very moment.

He's wearing a roguish grin.

Tanya couldn't miss it. The diplomat must've picked up on the discrepancy. The difference between the *conditional reconciliation* proposed by Colonel Lergen and the *white flag* proposed by Tanya.

"The little devil next to you to is suggesting we beg for peace. Am I wrong?"

Aware of the fact that she's being scrutinized, I bark a sharp laugh on the inside. If Tanya weren't a soldier, she would've screamed, *You're damn right!*

But I am a professional. I understand perfectly what the diplomat was getting at. And moreover, I feel calm.

I almost admire the diplomat Conrad. How did the Empire ever get itself into such dire straits with a diplomat this capable?

As I mentally pay him my respects, I address the elephant in the room.

"I'm in no position to gainsay how this fine Foreign Office wishes to label its diplomacy."

Tanya has no authority here. Which means she doesn't have any responsibility, either. That goes without saying. As a soldier, Tanya could only hope and pray that the bureaucrats would use their competence—the very criteria set by their supposed meritocracy.

And the same could be said about Tanya, as the diplomat's eyes made it clear that he had reached the same conclusion as she had.

"Incredible. Truly impressive, Colonel Lergen."

Things like this always came down to being able to understand the same language—a lingua franca.

How delightful it is to be able to treasure the same things.

Even more delightful is the fact that he has an invitation ready. Counselor Conrad is staring at Tanya with eyes so full of enthusiasm that it would have made even the most seasoned HR rep jealous.

"What do you think about working at the Foreign Office after you leave the military? I know it's looked down upon, but I'm ready to write a recommendation letter to vouch for you." An accurate evaluation, a courteous attitude, and a proper request. Invitations don't get much better than this! Counselor Conrad could see that Tanya's cheeks are ready to burst at their seams and turns up the heat to seal the deal. "If that's the case, I believe I can push this through. What do you say, Lieutenant Colonel Degurechaff? It's your decision to make…"

"It's an honor to receive such a generous offer."

Tanya bows her head as a gesture of genuine gratitude. This is the moment Colonel Lergen, who looks like he just swallowed a stink bug, decides to interject.

"Counselor, please stop headhunting General Staff Office personnel."

"There's always a demand for capable workers. Especially during a war like this. Do you find it strange we both desire the same things?"

It's a somewhat bitter exchange, but Counselor Conrad relents with a smile and a lighthearted chuckle.

"Anyway, enough with the banter. Let's get back on topic. What are the army's desired terms for a reconciliation? Where do you want the Empire to stand when the dust has settled?"

"We don't know."

Colonel Lergen's curt response wipes the smile right off Counselor Conrad's face. He furrows his brow slightly while clutching his cigar in his mouth in a way to make his dissatisfaction and displeasure apparent.

"Let's stop with the jokes, Colonel."

"Trust me, Counselor—this is no joke."

"Colonel Lergen, while it isn't my style, let me be very frank with you. Though I'm a counselor, I'm also a member of Supreme High Command. I have the authority to access any military secrets pertaining to the matter."

Listening from the sidelines, it seems to me that everything the counselor said checks out. He should have access to any and all classified information. Though diplomats are technically civilians, there is a clear need for him to know what the military's ultimate intentions are, considering his position. Though the military does operate on a strict need-to-know basis when it comes to information sharing, the counselor is well within his bounds to make his request.

That's when it suddenly dawns on me.

Oh, is *that* what's going on? The counselor isn't the problem here—it's *me*.

Though I'm technically a member of the staff, the nation's geopolitical interests are a bit above the pay grade of a magic lieutenant colonel. Perhaps the way my superiors treated me had finally gone to my head.

Having realized the mistake, I embarrassingly interject.

"Colonel, my apologies. It seems I don't have the authority to listen in on the conversation from this point onward. Shall I remove myself from this meeting?"

I can only hope my boss doesn't think that I'm some clueless officer after such a blunder. All that time I spent on the front lines must have dulled my senses. To think I'd ever make such a mindless mistake! Quietly excusing yourself is one of the most basic techniques a good worker should know how to do…

Perhaps I've lost my edge after all these years.

I hurriedly rise from my seat when the colonel abruptly says, "No, you're fine where you are."

Chapter **IV**

Caught off guard by Colonel Lergen's comment, I freeze while half-way out of my seat.

Turning to my superior, I give him a blank look.

Did I make a mistake...? I can't come up with a single reason to explain why Tanya should be allowed to sit in on this conversation. Colonel Lergen certainly wouldn't jeopardize his access to such information by sharing it with her.

What's going on?

"Lieutenant Colonel, this is something...you would probably rather not know."

I still have no idea what he's alluding to and have little choice but to wait as my superior begins speaking with a solemn tone.

"Let's see. Where should I begin? Counselor, what I'm about to tell you is by no means a secret. Therefore, please understand that, in a way, it's far more serious."

Well, that definitely doesn't sound good.

I have a terrible feeling about what I'm about to hear. Now I almost want to leave, but I fight back that urge with the understanding that this is probably something I should hear.

"Listen with caution."

After one look at Counselor Conrad, who has his chin drawn slightly back, I adjust my posture as I brace myself.

Little did Colonel Lergen know that what he was about to say was almost as explosive a bomb as the one Tanya had dropped on the counselor only moments earlier.

"It wouldn't be much of an exaggeration to say that, in a certain sense, the General Staff Office, Supreme High Command, and the government are all of the same opinion."

"What? That's an awfully strange disclaimer. If it's such common knowledge, then one can't help but wonder how we don't know about it yet."

"Counselor, it's the opposite. It's the complete and utter opposite."

His strange wording strikes me as odd, and this is when I first notice something. This is Colonel Lergen's way of avoiding an issue. He seems calm on the surface, but there's no missing the hesitation and inner turmoil lurking just behind his words. This isn't likely something Counselor Conrad would have been able to pick up on. After all, *why would he?* On the surface, even to Tanya, who has spent so much time at Colonel Lergen's side, the man seems to be his usual self.

That's quite the mask he has on. Is this the fortitude you need to work in the homeland?

If I didn't know how much the General Staff officers stressed keeping things concise...I probably never would've been able to recognize this ironclad poker face of his for what it is.

"Colonel Lergen, I must request that you explain yourself."

Counselor Conrad makes his demand as he fishes out another cigar. This time, the colonel finally acquiesces.

"Do you really want to know?"

"Of course I do, Colonel. Please indulge me."

"Very well." There's a strange sense of peace about Colonel Lergen as he takes out a cigarette and puts it in his mouth. He smokes for a short while; then along with a puff of cigarette smoke, he hit them with a nasty revelation.

"There is no consensus. The only thing everyone can agree on is that there is a complete lack of consensus between the General Staff, Supreme High Command, and the government."

The only consensus is that there is no consensus.

Oh, the irony!

Colonel Lergen continues spitting out this awful joke while Tanya and the counselor listen in mute shock.

"You want to know the nation's consensus in regard to a reconciliation? You won't find a single person who could possibly answer you. You'd be lucky to find someone who's even thought about it."

Tanya finally raises her voice.

"But that shouldn't be possible. Does the army not even have guidelines in situations like this? They haven't considered it as an organization at all?!"

With a solemn face, Colonel Lergen shakes his head. For Tanya, who's learning of this for the first time, the fact that he could sit there so calmly is beyond comprehension.

Chapter **IV**

"What is the General Staff Office even doing?!"

"Lieutenant Colonel, I've explained this to you before. We are soldiers, and thus, as soldiers, we—"

Tanya cuts him off, rejecting her superior outright.

"With all due respect sir, soldiers may be just that—mere soldiers—but even so, this is ludicrous! I can't see how we wouldn't at least consider the idea?!"

This isn't a conversation that needs to be had multiple times. It's something Tanya had been pointing out for a while now.

Something that she'd tried to communicate to the other General Staff officers in every conceivable way possible.

And yet, she had to say it again.

"Why don't my words reach anyone? Why doesn't anything ever change?"

It appeared, though, that Colonel Lergen had his own thoughts about Tanya's display of apprehension. He ostentatiously blew a big billowing puff of nicotine and tar, then replied with a distant look on his face.

"Lieutenant Colonel, as someone in the same organization…let me tell you what you're doing wrong."

"Please."

"You need to coat the bitterest of pills with sugar. And you can't be stingy with it, either."

"That doesn't make sense during wartime. We converted all our sugar beet fields into potato fields long ago. Where am I supposed to get all the sugar I'd need?"

"There aren't many like you who can swallow the bitter pill that is reality. This is especially true during a war, where people throw common sense out the window. Unfortunately…this is reality."

Tanya finds herself staring at the ceiling as she listens to a tired colonel give her tired words of advice.

I'm frankly at my wit's end. It's a trial to learn your country's deepest, darkest secrets. I'm really beginning to regret staying in the room.

"Just incredible!" I exclaim as it dawns on me that my career meant nothing from the start. Who can blame me for grumbling a bit?

The fact of the matter is that the Empire isn't even functioning properly at this point. Their checks could bounce at any moment. It's baffling. My country is essentially dipping into revolving credit because they lack the cash to settle their debts.

This is absurd. You don't take a loan out to buy groceries. Rights are rights, even if it's the right to be negligent. But that principle goes right out the window when your country is trying to fight a war on advance loans.

I want to vomit. The sheer incompetence, stupidity, and pointlessness—it's hard to describe how revolting this all is. The foolishness of individuals is part and parcel of having freedom. Idiocy is allowable in the name of diversity.

But stupidity at the national level? Unforgivable. A nation—nay, an organization—needs to be an institution founded on and grounded in logic. If the brains up top are rotten to the core, then there's no hope of saving the body.

"We can't win this war without diplomacy! How do you expect to reconcile with the state we're in now?!"

What do the people in the field want?

There's no way to know. The Empire could win ninety-nine times, but it would all be washed away by a single defeat in the hundredth battle. I don't want to end up like Xiang Yu. I don't want to serve Liu Bang, but I want to stay aboard a sinking ship even less.

"We're running out of manpower on the front lines. The societal foundation upon which the Empire's limitless potential was based has been all but pissed away, and there isn't a single sign of it being built back up! To think the military would use our future as fuel for today's fire. It seems the sun is moments from setting on the Empire."

To be honest, it isn't a problem for a company to lose its incapable employees. There's always more where they came from. But speaking from experience as an HR rep, I know that one of the biggest problems for any organization is that talent tends to leave, starting with the people you want to keep the most.

S-rank employees are usually the first to go, followed closely by the members of the A-rank, which eventually leaves the B-rankers in control. At this point, the company would be running on pure inertia from having *once* been a strong player.

Tanya needs to get out as soon as the chance presents itself. Unfortunately, her success within the Imperial Army is only recognized internally.

This makes it difficult for any of her country's *competitors* to judge her accurately. As a result of the war, talented labor cannot freely move from workplace to workplace. This is the worst sort of failure a market can suffer. This is why nothing good could ever be born from dictatorships.

By this point, Tanya is finding it hard to keep her nausea at bay. This whole thing is absurd. Just like that damned Being X. Unlike a world that rests in the invisible hands of a higher being, the most this world has is the dirty paws of Being X. Truly, what a nightmare.

Unable to contain that anger, Tanya began to speak out again.

"This is supposed to be our nation's raison d'état? It must be some sort of terrible joke—!"

With an expression that contains both sympathy and disapproval, Counselor Conrad cuts off Tanya's grumbling.

"Calm yourself, Lieutenant Colonel. Have you forgotten your manners...?"

The ruthless way he spoke made him seem more reliable in my eyes. I smile in grim approval.

He admonished Tanya, completely forgetting his own episode from earlier. This is the sign of a man who could separate his work from his emotions. What's more, he has the intelligence to argue his points logically. This is the most important thing I look for in a coworker. It's a sign that I could work without worrying about extra stress.

I'm sure I'd enjoy working under this man as much as I do under Lieutenant General Zettour. Gritting my teeth, I hope the conversation will take a turn for the good as I fix my gaze on the counselor and sit back down.

His eyes are cold and calculating.

Behind a curtain of formality and etiquette, there is a levelheaded intelligence. That is all I can ask for. Those are the eyes of someone I can do business with.

"Counselor, I need you to understand the price the army, my subordinates, and I have paid during this war."

"Say no more. How about it, Lieutenant Colonel Degurechaff? I feel like now that we're quite familiar with each other—" Counselor Conrad slowly leans forward in a way that suggests he has no intention of letting Tanya elude his question and continues with a grin, saying, "—I think it's about time you start telling me how you really feel."

He doesn't care for being roundabout and oblique. It's clear he wants to do away with the smoke and mirrors and hear what Tanya really has to say.

That makes this the perfect chance for Tanya to take the initiative and ask him what she really wants to know.

"We'll do whatever we can. We'll pay the price that will get the best possible result. So there is one thing I want to know—what do you want from us?"

This is the question on everybody's mind that no one is willing to answer. What do the shot callers want from the people on the front lines? How could anything get done if they didn't know the answer to this? How much more explicit could we be?

"There needs to be a reason for negotiations to start. After all, even the best diplomacy can go south if the timing isn't just right."

I almost slap my knee in agreement—I'm impressed. Running a country is no different from running a company. Different challenges call for different solutions.

Everything needs to be stated in clear and simple terms.

"…So you want us to decide the timing?"

"How is General Zettour's maneuver warfare holding up in the east? I hear he's fared well against the Federation's unrelenting onslaught."

That much is true—the work of the soon-to-be general is nothing short of a miracle. General Zettour, the con artist, is currently leading the Federation into traps up and down the entire theater of war.

"I'll be the first to admit that the Federation is very good at learning. It's almost frightening how fast they pick things up. Nevertheless, General Zettour is a ruthless instructor. Their textbooks will be marred with tears for a bit longer."

This probably seems like a bold statement coming from a mere lieutenant colonel, but for a General Staff officer, being called ruthless is a sort of compliment. It's what most General Staff officers strive for.

"The Federation must be racking up heavy tuition fees considering how much they're learning through both experience and General

Zettour's lessons. Though it may not be enough to salvage the Empire's economy, I believe it could still be useful as investment for a new venture."

"You'll need to tack on a few more digits for any hope of that, Lieutenant Colonel."

The counselor waves his hand in the air with a sad look about him.

"We don't need a minor victory in the east. Not to discount the work of our soldiers over there, but simply winning battles isn't going to get us out of this. Victories can't be used in negotiations..."

I can't even begin to express my gratitude to the man before telling him how I really feel.

"Then we need to take it one step further." The two listen to Tanya's words and watch in silence as she presses on. Colonel Lergen still has a sense of detachment about him, and Counselor Conrad seems... uncomfortable? Tanya shakes her head. Everything that needs to be confirmed has been confirmed. At this point, it's a lot like deploying the battalion. Once the important decisions have been made, all there's left to do is follow through.

It's time to fire my shot.

"If we must accept our dire circumstances, then why not embrace them fully? How about getting down on our hands and knees and pleading for an armistice?"

"...That's impossible, Lieutenant Colonel. As a diplomat, I know this for a fact. That's something we'll never be able to do."

"Why?"

Tanya's question is muffled by an exasperated sigh from Counselor Conrad.

"The nation wouldn't survive it."

"Any missteps after we lose could lead to the country imploding regardless. Instead of waiting idly for our eventual destruction...a truce is the safer option for our people, even if it means bankruptcy."

"This isn't a question of logic, Lieutenant Colonel. It's about the Reich. The Reich doesn't know defeat."

The counselor sounded both proud and depressed as he explained. I can't help but agree. I think of the Reich as a deadly illness—its symptoms could be seen even in the hallways of the Foreign Office, in those paintings that detailed the Empire's glorious past.

The Empire is grand and powerful... The idea that our nation always marches while hoisting the flag of victory is too set in stone.

"The Reich...has built its society on the institution of victory."

Counselor Conrad squeezes out another sigh; his mental anguish has apparently found its way to his lungs.

"A defeat would completely obliterate this foundation of eternal victory. It would cut the country down at the knees."

The reasoning he expresses with his strained voice isn't something I can accept without a fight. Not only that, but from the perspective of a soldier like Tanya, the very idea is utterly disgusting.

"It's as if the Reich is a child who thinks they're invincible. Probably one close to my age."

"That's hard to hear coming from you. However, I also feel fear and revulsion, not to mention an instinctual rejection toward the notion that there's absolutely no way for the Empire to come out of this victoriously."

"...That's honest of you, Counselor. Your bravery deserves respect."

In response to Tanya's argument, a troubled Counselor Conrad turns his attention to the ceiling again.

"Colonel Lergen, I'm truly astounded. I must pay my respects to the military. As surprising as it is, this lieutenant colonel has a clear view of reality."

Why is Tanya being complimented all of a sudden?

Changing your perception of reality has no effect on actual reality.

In a similar vein, using a magical formula allows you to manipulate natural phenomenon and thus influence reality, but is still a far cry from bending the world to your will.

The world is the world. Making do with what you have is an important part of living in it.

"Hesitation is useless when it comes to facing the real world. Does anyone still feel there's a need for me to apologize for not packing it in a nice sugarcoated pill?"

"No."

"No."

Counselor Conrad and Colonel Lergen both deny the need for such an apology.

Watching their reactions inspires another realization. The two of them are speaking in tandem, like there's a mirror sitting right between them. A good sign that these two would probably work well together.

Even more noteworthy is how Counselor Conrad's expression relaxes as he gives a satisfactory nod. His mood seems to have improved slightly. I can sense genuine joy and relief welling up inside him.

"Then it's simple. In order to save the Empire—and for the sake of our own happiness—I'd like for the army to start fighting while keeping rapprochement in mind and in a way that will satisfy our people."

I consider the diplomat's proposal for a moment.

"That's a massive contradiction."

He wants to carry on with the war to end the war? It sounds completely ridiculous, though the true absurdity is how the country ended up in this position in the first place.

"It's better than simply chasing victory, Lieutenant Colonel."

"I guess war is, after all, an extension of politics…"

Tanya shakes her head and sighs.

If it wasn't for the harshness of the reality we're dealing with, this conversation would have been rather enjoyable! But there's no sugarcoating a terminal illness!

The intellectual elite of the Empire have to be convinced to accept the ultimate contradiction!

It smacks of taking out a loan for a get-rich-quick scheme despite being deep in debt. Why does it seem like we're trying to pay our debts by winning the lottery?

Is it just me or is the world around me getting darker?

If nothing else, this conversation with Colonel Lergen and Counselor Conrad has convinced me of one thing: *This ship is already sinking.*

I almost feel sad. Who knew it was this difficult to suppress the urge to retch… Everything Tanya has done up until this point is going to waste. Her career, her hard work, all the extra overtime, all those cases where she went above and beyond the call of duty—it's all going to disappear in the ether.

Though she isn't here by choice, Tanya has always fulfilled her duties with her future in mind.

And look at where that got me! What reason or need could there possibly be for ordinary people to accept a fate like this?

It's impossible.

I've done more than her fair share to keep this leaky boat afloat. More than enough to earn my spot on a lifeboat out of here.

I just need a connection to the outside.

Where are the recruiters in this world?

I want to get out of this insane world as soon as possible. It's time to find a way to defect.

On the car ride back, I push the little package I brought with me from the west onto the man sitting next to me. General Romel's plan, to be more precise.

I was prepared for the worst, but what happened was completely unexpected. Evidently, the man charged with defending the western front had the complete trust of the bigwigs. Personally, I had high hopes that the plan would get shot down.

…Not only was it passed, but it was done with full backing. It wasn't just any old superior who spoke in support of the plan, either. It was the General Staff Office's very own Colonel Lergen. He was an extremely powerful backer when it came to obtaining consent from the higher-ups.

I'm fairly well versed when it comes to working the lower rungs of military administration and various middle managers. I've done it many times before when I fought for supplies, railway allocations, and struck hard bargains with quartermasters. For a soldier who stands on the battlefield, it's all in a day's work.

Convincing upper management, however… That's a different story. The weight of personal connections and experience plays a much bigger part here. This is something that Colonel Lergen is an expert at. Immediately after I finished reading him the documents on our car ride back, we were able to clear the process in one fell swoop.

What would've been a monumental task for Tanya to handle alone… was stamped and ready to go by the next day, thanks to Colonel Lergen.

He's a man who's capable of getting both the army and navy to agree on and approve such a reckless plan. His ability to navigate the system is frankly unbelievable. The colonel knows exactly what buttons to press to make things happen. That's how the paperwork was wrapped up in the blink of an eye. It may seem simple at a glance, but anyone who's ever worked with a government office knows that this is nothing short of a miracle.

After that hurdle was cleared, events transpired so quickly that it actually threw a wrench in my original plan to gather information on the fabled *Plan B* under the pretext of doing so for the sake of General Romel's proposal.

As much as I wanted to do some digging, there was absolutely no time.

Colonel Lergen immediately asked for various details about the condition of the western front like the weather, the state of the water, and the units stationed there. Once all the information was squared up, we presented the proposal to Lieutenant General Rudersdorf, who gave his stamp of approval on the spot.

Mind you, Tanya won't get compensated for any of this. Some office coffee is all there is to look forward to. Talk about unpaid overtime. After finishing the proposal, the only information I gleaned about Plan B was that it wasn't going to start anytime soon and that I should continue monitoring the situation. Absolutely nothing concrete.

All I could get out of Colonel Lergen was that he was hashing out a plan with the Foreign Office.

That's great and all, but I can't help but sigh loudly on the inside.

I wish he'd consider the burden placed on the frontline troops. In light of this, no one can blame me for letting out a complaint or two. My superiors' collective optimism is the ultimate source of the swears and curses streaming from my mouth as I roam the halls of the General Staff Office.

This is so absurd.

"Part of me wants to hope that it all ends in disaster, but that wouldn't be good for me, either."

I shake my head and try to calm down by taking a deep breath in the hallway.

Fresh air is just what an overheated mind needs. Grumbling is good and all, but if I don't want to spontaneously combust, I need to remember to breathe no matter how heated I get.

That said, this is absolutely a crisis.

But for what it's worth, there is still a bit of time before the situation becomes unsalvageable.

Using the *Titanic* as an example, it's like we've just hit the iceberg and are starting to sink. The ship will eventually go down. We might be starting to list to one side, but we're mostly level for the moment. The rest of the passengers aren't sure what to do and are hesitating—I need to run for the lifeboat while I still can.

I have a little bit of time; not many people have thought about heading for the lifeboats yet.

There's still one thing I need to decide before making my escape, though... *How* exactly am I going to jump into a lifeboat? The next couple steps need to be taken with the utmost caution. Contacting someone abroad during a war could be like poking a beehive with a stick. I'll need to prepare a nice gift if I want to survive the initial greeting.

Look no further than defectors who succeeded in my old world.

The fact that they've gone down in history at all means they had something valuable to trade for their lives. I'm going to need to figure out the rules of defection and go about it intelligently if I don't want to end up in a shallow grave.

It's not too different from a career change. Everything has to be done right unless you want to be stuck unemployed, forever looking for your next job.

The most important decision I need to make right now is figuring out what my chosen asylum country wants most. If possible, it'd be best to keep Tanya's reputation intact. It would be terrible optics if people interpret her leaving as abandoning her soldiers...

More importantly, I'm going to have to hit the ground running if I want to join a new employer as a mid-career hire. Having the right credentials is just the bare minimum. No matter where I end up, I need to ascertain my new employer's standards and change tack in a way that puts me in the best light possible.

Chapter IV

It also doesn't help that job hunting is like wearing two pairs of sandals at once... I still need to maintain my foothold in the Empire while doing all this.

It's a simple concept, but people who look for jobs with only their own interests in mind never get the best positions. You're not going to find a job that both pays well and is stable from the very start.

The worst possible outcome would be being labeled a *traitor*.

Take industrial espionage, for example. Anyone who betrays their company is bound to be heaved overboard with great abandon wherever they go next. People who have the capacity to stab their first employer in the back won't be trusted by their next one.

Tanya's resignation needs to be on amicable terms, and her transfer needs to be smooth—or as we say in Japan, Don't wreck the nest as you leave it.

This is how you change your job in an ever-changing society.

It'll be difficult—that's for sure.

Ideally, I'll be playing a major role in overcoming the dire circumstances of my current posting. There isn't a great chance I'll be able to pull this off without a hitch, so I'd like some insurance. Even if it's a fixed-term plan, insurance is still insurance.

》》》 AUGUST 14, UNIFIED YEAR 1927, WESTERN COMMAND CENTER 《《《
FOR THE IMPERIAL ARMY

As soon as I enter the office, its owner is already sizing me up. Those eyes are demanding a report. I start with the requisite formalities.

"I've returned, General Romel."

"Welcome back, Colonel. Did you get any information on Plan B from the General Staff Office?"

He cuts straight to the point. Without offering so much as a thank-you, General Romel asks about the state of the homeland.

"I didn't get anything worth your time. It looks like they're keeping it under wraps for now."

"So Plan B is being kept as a contingency? Are there other plans in the works?"

I nod before saying, "Counselor Conrad from the Foreign Office is making a move. It looks like their days of stealing a government pay-check have come to an end as our diplomatic corps begin to mobilize."

"They're too damn late. They should've started working three years ago. We've lost far too much time already." There's a strong tone of resentment in his words. "...Just how many had to die because of their do-nothing policy."

The general is right, for the most part. The Foreign Office's idle approach to foreign policy can be directly tied to a staggering number of deaths.

I even feel compelled to add, "If we're being honest, even three years ago wouldn't have been fast enough. We needed to kick them into high gear back in Norden. Had we done so, we could have shaved a digit or two off the death toll."

"...So you think starting the war at all was a mistake."

"I don't like the idea of disparaging my predecessors...but it is a fact that the Empire has put too much stock in its military."

A quick read through a history textbook is enough to know that, at its onset, diplomacy and military action went hand in hand for the Empire. But today, the Imperial Army and the Empire's diplomats have grown into separate heads. Was it negligent of our predecessors to not formally institutionalize cooperation between them?

Of course not.

High performers tend to make simple errors in calculation due to their inability to predict the incompetence of others.

"I'd wager that the founders of the Empire never dreamed in a million years that their progeny would be this incompetent. They'd most likely laugh in your face if you told them the soldiers on the war front aren't coordinating with planners back in the homeland."

"You're not wrong, Colonel." The general takes out some military tobacco and begins to smoke. I want to ask him to stop but can't for obvious reasons, and it pains me.

All I can do is stew in the secondhand smoke.

General Romel lets out a sigh mixed together with a puff of smoke before he speaks up again.

"Well, that's why it's our job to show the world where the Empire stands."

Chapter **IV**

"So that we don't embarrass our predecessors? As one of their disappointing grandchildren, I only hope my shoulders can help carry the burden."

"Fear not, Colonel. You of all people will be able to shoulder it."

He hands over a folder labeled with a simple title.

"Operation Door Knocker?"

I flip through the packet of papers that have the words *top secret* stamped on the top-right corner of every page. It details every aspect of the upcoming operation. This isn't the first time I've laid eyes on a secret document, but for me to be able to read all this...it's an honor. Though it would've been nice if I had a chance to read through it before everything was already set in stone.

"Two battlecruisers, three light cruisers, and three assault destroyers packed with marines."

As I finish reading the summary, I comment on the forces allocated for the operation with a doubtful expression. Prioritizing speed to capitalize on the surprise aspect of the plan is a good choice. Still, it begs the question: Why do we need surface ships?

"Sir, if the whole point is to move with the element of surprise...I feel like it would be more prudent to send in commandos from a submarine."

That way, our forces would be able to sidle up to the Commonwealth mainland with submarines and slip in undetected. To put it simply, it would be a proper sneak attack. It would also more than accomplish the goal of striking the enemy right in their homeland.

My ultimate goal is to mitigate any unnecessary risk the proposal might pose to me personally, but General Romel barks a boisterous laugh.

"There are political reasons for this strategy, Colonel."

Oh, I see.

"So these politics supersede the necessity for superior tactics? Even so...I think there's still precedence to attack from the sea."

Correct, her superior nods.

"We're going to pierce those wooden walls of theirs. An attack from the sea is what we need, but it has to come from above the water. Our underwater assaults just don't strike fear into their hearts."

The general isn't wrong.

If that's what we're after, then I see how an attack executed by a high-speed assault squadron would have the best chance of pulling it off. It doesn't change the fact that this mission is going to come with a lot of risk. Even the fastest ships are slow compared to anything that can fly.

There's also the need to weigh anchor when disembarking soldiers. The whole time they're conducting amphibious operations, the ships will have to remain stationary, no matter how fast they can move on the go.

Though…it appears the general has already thought of a way to mitigate that disadvantage.

There's a word in the plan that I've never seen before—an *assault destroyer*. It says here the ships will steam at thirty knots directly onto enemy shores before unloading landing parties? It sounds like we took a page out of the Commonwealth's book.

"We'll scuttle the destroyers if it comes to that. I'm sure the navy won't be happy about it, but what needs to be done needs to be done."

"We're going in on the assumption that we won't be taking all our ships home?"

The general's comment is shocking. And yet, the general said it so casually… The navy would have a fit if they heard him say this.

Though a difficult notion for me to swallow, it shows the conviction General Romel has in the plan.

He knows there's no going back.

"Necessity demands it. We need to physically get our soldiers onto Commonwealth shores."

"What if we used aerial mages to provide air support? It would help split up the enemy's focus, increasing our chances of victory."

"That would be a good idea if we're thinking in purely military terms. It's not something in the cards this time, though. We need to defeat their navy with ours and show them that the sea isn't theirs alone. If we use mages, it will dilute the impact of a purely naval victory."

"So we need to rely mainly on ships? Would keeping the theater of operations overseas not serve the same purpose?"

General Romel gives a deep, silent nod before he answers.

"We have to decimate the Commonwealth's confidence that they have in their navy before we can start diplomatic negotiations with them.

Their faith in their prowess at sea currently knows no bounds. We need to show them where those bounds really lie."

"So our aim is to destroy their maritime confidence? Strangely enough, it sounds quite rousing when you put it that way."

Though not in the same vein as my ongoing battle with Being X… it's human nature for people to try and find purpose in the meaningless work they're required to do.

Work is work, but you get more out of it if you enjoy what you're doing. This assumes you're getting paid properly, of course. No one wants to work for free. That said, people are generally more eager to do jobs they enjoy. Forward thinking and positivity produce innovation.

I clap my hands.

"Now would be a great time to break out our heavy siege artillery. Instead of knocking on their wooden walls, wouldn't it be better if we just blew them to smithereens?"

"We don't have what it takes to crack them open. If the most we can do is knock, then it's best we do it properly."

"That's incredibly unfortunate. I was hoping we could bring along a few long-range railway guns."

It would have been spectacular. The commandos would've made landfall with naval support at the same time the high-caliber artillery rounds did. No amount of censorship would be enough to keep the news from spreading far and wide in the Commonwealth.

"When it comes to maritime warfare, we only get one chance. I hope that you aren't thinking about holding back now, of all times, sir."

"My wallet is empty. I could turn it upside down, but all that would fall out is receipts."

"Even so, we'll need to knock as many aircraft out of the sky as we can… Our ships will be sitting ducks without air support, even if it is limited."

Those who control the skies control the war. At the very least, this theory has been proven true time and time again during the course of the current war. Even the mightiest ships don't amount to much more than floating targets to the air force. Take a look at the history of the Pacific War. Without air cover, battlecruisers aren't going anywhere besides the bottom of the ocean.

That's why I have to doubt my ears.

"—Sorry, but it's not going to happen."

"What?"

"The best we can do is deploy units who have experience with setting up anti–air defenses. Air assets have long since been diverted to support other campaigns far from home. Even our most prized squadrons are in the process of being reorganized."

The Empire is the world's strongest military superpower. And yet, the Western Army Group can't get what it needs to fight at full strength?

I've been sighing more and more recently, but for once, I have to speak my mind.

"If that's the case, General, then the premise doesn't stand."

If we're going to attack by sea, then it's imperative to ensure the skies are safe. The two battlecruisers and three light cruisers are going to need serious air cover. Even if the operation is conducted under the cover of darkness, we need to take care of enemy night patrols at the bare minimum.

"If possible, I'd like to at least aim for limited air superiority. If this is a problem, then we should at least cover the choke points. Anything else would only result in the total loss of important warships."

"You're right, Colonel, and that's why I'm counting on you."

"…What?"

"Lieutenant Colonel Degurechaff… You and your battalion should be able to achieve limited air superiority over those key points. You only have to hold these points for the night. I'm counting on you."

There it is. Tanya's orders. He seems serious, too.

First General Zettour, now General Romel… The Imperial Army leadership really knows how to work their soldiers to the bone.

"General, my unit is only a battalion. Not a regiment or a brigade."

"The enemy's night patrol isn't that large. While they'll have the numbers advantage, I'm sure you can secure our safety for a few hours."

"Are you saying our battalion will be able to pull it off alone?"

I say this in an attempt to point out that it would be too difficult a task for them. However…

"…Colonel, if you and your battalion can't pull this off, then no one in the Empire can. I'm putting my trust into the 203rd Aerial Mage Battalion."

Well, shit.

While I curse on the inside, I respond with a perfect smile, a gracious compliment, and an excellent salute.

"If those are your orders, sir, then I shall see to it they're carried out."

»»»   0100 HOURS AUGUST 17, UNIFIED YEAR 1927, 203RD AERIAL   **«««**
MAGE BATTALION ENCAMPMENT

The battalion received word that they were shipping out. Frankly speaking, it's business as usual for the troops. Whenever someone wanted something done, they inevitably came to the 203rd.

After they finish lining up perfectly, I address them.

"Attention!"

The entire battalion snaps to attention the moment they hear. The way they can respond at the drop of a hat is a testament to their excellence as a part of the war machine. These soldiers are the cream of the crop that I raised by my hand.

They'd be able to make it through this unreasonable mission. I know that there isn't anyone in the business better than my battalion. They're tough as nails, and I'm proud of them.

"Here we are, back on the western front. The last time we flew these skies, we scored a big victory in Operation Revolving Door. Today, my comrades, we're about to embark for the homeland of the Commonwealth, an enemy that has been a thorn in our side in the skies from time to time."

We're about to attack a land we've visited before. It's time for us to say hello to the Commonwealth again. Of course, we're mages. We need boots on the ground, and mages can't hold territory. We aren't foot soldiers, after all.

That's why...we need to bring the foot soldiers with us.

I know how difficult a task this will be, so I'll do everything in my power to try and inspire the troops.

"Why?"

I stare out at my subordinates, looking at the faces of each and every one of them as I continue with the patriotic and passionate speech.

"Why? Why are we here?"

The General Staff Office always prefers going on the attack and the 203rd Aerial Mage Battalion is their ace in the hole. To say each of these elites is enough to match a thousand soldiers might be an overstatement, but they can certainly take out a company of nobodies.

Now it's time to tell them their mission, roles, and objective.

"The answer to this is simple. We're here to win. We're here to dominate the skies with our power alone."

Defeat may be bitter, but victory is ever so sweet.

Unfortunately, the Empire that employs them has a chronic case of *insufficient funds*. It doesn't have the money needed to put toward its victory. To my great annoyance, I'm beginning to get used to working under such dismal circumstances. It's incredible what war can do to a person.

While it's something to be feared, I also need my soldiers to maintain their calm.

"Comrades, the enemy will probably laugh when they see us. *Look at how few of them there are,* they'll say. And they'll be right. We are but a lone mage battalion. We're reinforcements. If they laugh, we may as well congratulate them on their ability to do basic math."

That was just the truth. Our enemies are going to have the advantage. I'm simply trying to be up front. It's imperative to objectively lay out the circumstances so my subordinates fully understand the situation.

Once they know what they're getting into, I'll let them in on the fact I do have a plan. Though this doesn't address the meat of the problem, it's justified by my need to keep morale up.

Necessity is like an iron fist of its own—it dictates all.

"You are the members of my battalion. I believe you're elites who have been forged with blood and iron. We're on a different level than mages still in their diapers. This is why we're called to the battlefield."

I'll instill a strong sense of purpose in them.

Willpower is a convenient thing. It allows people to cover their eyes when they're left with no other options and put away their convictions with their inability. For fuck's sake… It's important to never lose a sense of self-loathing. Losing the ability to tell when something is wrong is the path to true incompetence.

So, without giving them any time to do so, I jump right to our objective for the coming mission.

"I'll give you a summary of the operation we'll be performing over the next two weeks."

As this is a briefing for the whole battalion, and due to the secretive nature of the operation, better to keep the explanation short and simple. That said, they should get the gist of things as they've been at this for quite a while now.

"We'll start with recon-in-force. Each squadron will split up and infiltrate the Commonwealth under cover of night. The goal is to test the enemy's nighttime anti–air defenses."

It's going to be a sort of stress test—a reconnaissance-in-force mission to find the enemy's weak points. It's not something veteran mages would consider particularly dangerous.

Relieved to see a look of confidence in my subordinates' eyes, I mention another detail.

"We'll simultaneously be conducting counterintelligence with 'rotten eggs.' Should you fall into enemy hands, you'll give them a story about rotten eggs."

I can feel a glance coming from my first officer. He takes the initiative to ask the question on the rest of the battalion's minds.

"I have a question about these rotten eggs, ma'am. What kind of script will we be using?"

"Good question, Major Weiss. To put it simply, we're going to make it look like the main goal of our attacks is to harass their night patrol. In response to this, the enemy will hopefully pull some of their troops away from the Western Air Battle to fortify the defensive line on their home front."

They'll need more troops to help defend against aerial mages who attack at night.

Just like the plan says.

"As a result, rotten eggs will likely weaken their air campaign against the Empire. We need them to *think* that's our plan."

The Empire is going to trick the Commonwealth into thinking they're trying to force troops off from the front lines.

"This is the script we'll be following for the entire two weeks. We'll conduct nightly operations, and once we've established air superiority somewhere along their defensive line, we'll enter phase two."

My subordinate flashes a grin as he suppresses a laugh. I quickly wave a hand to let them know I won't be taking any more questions.

"The specifics will be announced at a later date. Let's show them what we're made of."

After the troops are dismissed, I notice a group of officers approaching me. The group, headed by Major Weiss, includes the lieutenants and other officers. First Lieutenant Serebryakov is among them; this should make things easy. I already have an idea of what Major Weiss wants to know.

"Are you working overtime, Major? How diligent of you."

"There's something I wanted to ask… Can I have some of your time?"

Though he asks his question politely, his expression is very intense.

"Enthusiasm is admirable. Is it about the second phase?"

"Yes. What do the higher-ups…have in mind?"

I nod in approval.

"I'll tell everyone who's here."

While paying special attention to my surroundings, I cut right to the heart of the matter.

"…The plan is for the navy and the army to work together and storm the shores of the Commonwealth before day breaks."

"We're going to conduct a surprise invasion of the Commonwealth?!"

"Keep it down." I glare at him with a sharp look before continuing. To be clear, I do get a good laugh out of it on the inside.

I can tell by the shock on my subordinates' faces that this plan will work.

Forget Major Weiss—even Visha can't hide her surprise. So not even these war hounds saw this coming… I can't wait to see the faces our enemies are going to make.

The Empire is going to shake the Commonwealth to its core when those leather boots hit the ground. Our objective is purely political. I get it now. This ploy seemed reckless and pointless on the surface, but apparently there's more to General Romel's plan than meets the eye.

Bringing the war to the *Commonwealth homeland* will have a profound effect on how its citizens perceive the Empire as a threat.

Chapter **IV**

"What's wrong, comrades? You look like pigeons that just got shot by a kid with a popgun."

My first officer responds to my joke with a doubtful expression.

"It's just...such a bold move."

"How can you win a war without being bold?"

My astonished adjutant also decides to chime in.

"I...never thought war could be fought like this."

Well, this is surprising. I expected Major Weiss and the others would respond like this, but Visha's response catches me off guard. You all do realize that this is total war, right?

"If they think they're safe on that little island of theirs, wouldn't correcting their little mistake be the humane thing for us to do?"

"Oh, I..."

"Lieutenant Serebryakov? Is there something else you'd like to say?"

I give my adjutant a look, but she quiets down. What was she going to say? I regard the line of officers with confusion. Why is there so much tension on all their faces?

This is quite troubling. Communication is important, after all.

"This is total war, comrades. We can't discriminate."

"...Is this a question of discrimination?"

Though timid, my adjutant poses a legitimate question that causes my expression to twist up—well, on the inside at least.

That's right! They don't know about human rights! I can't believe they haven't learned anything about discrimination!

Evidently, coming from another world makes me fundamentally different from those born only to this world. My shoulders slump a bit, and I decide to change the subject. It's important to respect the culture and customs of the world I find myself in.

"Back to the original question... This is a commando mission where we'll be storming the enemy's beaches. It will be an extremely precarious and risky operation. Our job is to protect the commandos, but I also want you to study the enemy."

I give them a stern look to confirm whether they understand, and my officers give their affirmatives. To my surprise, the air of uncertainty has all but cleared with this simple comment.

Not only that, but my first officer also comes forward with a constructive proposal.

"Shall I collect information from Meybert and Tospan?"

The mere mention of military affairs, and she brings them up. My subordinates' areas of expertise are still extremely specialized. To my chagrin, however, it isn't a bad idea. The two of them are experienced with harbors now, after all. Seeing as how their ability to protect one of the Empire's ports was tested under fire, they may have some useful insights.

"Good idea. But stay vigilant."

"Colonel? By vigilant, you mean…?"

"Don't use your radios. No matter what. If you need to send a message, use anything but your radio. I need you to keep this mission top secret. If you must, set a meeting and gather the entire Kampfgruppe's officers. This goes for everyone."

While I agree with seeking advice from specialists, I also make sure to stress the importance of secrecy.

If Weiss is going to speak with those two, they need to make it look like a meeting for the Kampfgruppe.

"Should I call Captain Ahrens as well?"

"Of course you should, XO. By everybody, I mean everybody."

"But he's…"

I already know what he's going to say and cut Weiss off. Ahrens is of course currently off having fun rebuilding the Kampfgruppe's tank unit back in the homeland.

I'm going to need to prepare for the captain to hold a grudge against me for pulling him away from his enviable life on the training grounds. But it needs to be done.

"The enemy resistance is always watching and listening in on everything we say. They keep track of every time we move and what units we send where. You can never be too cautious when it comes to things like this. First Lieutenant Serebryakov, I'll allow you to buy some wine with battalion funds. Hold a small party for the Kampfgruppe."

"Are you sure it's okay for us to do that?"

I give her a firm nod.

"Just make sure nothing leaves the party. We need to be vigilant with how we proceed from here on out."

"Understood."

Excellent. I cross my arms as I turn to my deputy.

"You heard that, right? Don't screw this up. We're throwing a party, got it?"

Major Weiss offers a vague nod. How much of this is he following? He may be a serious officer with a good head on his shoulders, but he's also a bloodthirsty war hound.

"Major Weiss, is the western front too peaceful for you? This is effectively one of our territories now."

"With all due respect, ma'am…it doesn't feel that way."

"In that case, feel free to act as if this were the eastern front. Understood?"

The major gives me a look that makes it clear something's finally clicked for him, and inner Tanya lets out a wry laugh. This is what he knows best! Seeing it is worth more than a million words. These soldiers have been living with war for too long.

After giving their salutes, my troops take their leave. Once I return to my own room, the grumbling begins.

"What am I even doing here?"

I'm about to take on the unreasonable challenges thrown down by the military like some kind of ardent patriot. It is a worthless act in the most literal sense.

The Empire is doomed, and I want nothing more than to get out of here.

Nothing more, nothing less. And yet, here I am, bound by the shackles of my position and sense of duty, unable to set myself free.

This is why I hate government authority.

If the market wasn't such an absolute mess, I could promote myself as valuable human capital to other employers at a fair price! Damn that Being X to hell. That's the cause of all this.

If it weren't for that bastard, I could have lived a life with basic human rights!

"I want happiness. I want to live a life with bare-minimum cultural standards."

What's more, I don't want to have to stay aboard a sinking ship. The fate of a sunken ship is a miserable one. There isn't a great chance of escape once the vessel has capsized. I want to get off this boat as soon as possible. As much as I want to, though, not only is going on a job hunt virtually impossible but I'm about to attack a potential employer.

Of course, it's only out of obligation to my current job.

Nevertheless, the fact of the matter is that I can't deny that I've grown very subjective to the whole thing. If this is out of necessity, then why is Tanya now a slave to necessity?

"War... What an insane enterprise."

How could anyone stomach this massive waste of money?

Never mind the fact that it's completely derailed my career plan.

Tanya von Degurechaff is a firm believer that every human being should have the right to the pursuit of happiness. It's self-evident. It's one of our natural-born rights.

"Damn that Being X. How can he call himself a god when he doesn't even know this?"

Thus, a logical inconsistency is born.

I can't let anyone get in the way of my happiness.

I shouldn't have to let them, and it would be completely irrational to do so.

"If they're wrong, I simply need to correct them."

I need to win.

For a bit of peace, for a humble future, and for my own career.

And I need to do it as a human being.

 THE SAME DAY, IN THE SKIES ABOVE THE CHANNEL

That night, the troops in charge of patrolling the channel were completely abandoned by Lady Luck.

They were outstanding soldiers.

Outstanding, yes—but from another perspective, they could be considered slaves to their skills.

Had the outcome of the Western Air Battle tilted in favor of the Commonwealth, their countermeasures for the sporadic appearances of the Empire's reconnaissance aircraft and harassment night bombing would have fallen into the category of *high-stress routine work*—a sort of oxymoron.

It was the same old thing every day, where they balanced a level of caution with relaxing their nerves.

Unfortunately for the air defense department, this rhythm was thrown awry when a ferociously violent change caught them unawares.

One of the survivors from that night would live to tell their tale.

A tale about *a ghost who descended upon the channel.*

"Fairy 01 to all units. Commence attack."

The simple orders given in standard imperial dialect fade away into the night sky shortly before a horde of monsters made their appearance.

The first one to pick up on their presence was a man at air traffic control. The Commonwealth air traffic controllers who were on watch that night pried their sleepy eyes wide open when their machines detected an immense magical signal.

It had been some time since they'd seen anything like this. But not so long that they forgot what it meant: The enemy was here.

There was no time to put the kettle on. Instead, they were now running on pure adrenaline. The people stationed at the southern interception control area were met by a sight they could have never imagined.

"The mana signals are rapidly increasing! What the hell?! They aren't even hiding it?"

Despite attacking at night, the enemy had lit themselves up like beacons. It completely went against the norm of aerial mage doctrine to always stay hidden.

Though it was strange beyond belief, one thing was still certain—they were enemies. The Commonwealth soldiers knew what that meant. It was time to welcome their guests.

"Sound the alarm! Prepare for battle!"

The duty officers moved with great haste.

"Prepare to intercept enemy air units! Get the quick response team ready, ASAP! Contact the other units as well! Get the reserves up in the air, too! We're throwing everything at 'em!"

If the enemy was going to waltz into their front yard, the Commonwealth troops would use all available resources to crush them.

As alarms blared, all aerial mages on duty were ordered to take to the skies. For good measure, they also scrambled their reserve units. They woke up the Third Regiment as well and lined them up on the runway, ready to deploy at any time just in case.

As the officers in charge began to feel a sense of relief in their seemingly overwhelming response as well as a tinge of excitement at the idea of performing well, a scream could be heard shattering the night.

"What the—?! It's that monster!"

The person in charge of checking the enemy's mana signal had positively identified the enemy and shouted in dismay.

When the chief air traffic controller turned to see the results, the first thing he noticed was the terrified, colorless face of the operator.

"According to our database...it's the D-Devil of the Rhine!"

"The Devil of the Rhine?"

They didn't know if they were lucky or unlucky. While those in the control room who'd yet to *directly* encounter the Named mage could only stare at the chief air traffic controller, he and the other duty officers practically kicked their chairs over in unison as they rushed to their radios.

"Warning! Warning! Emergency alert to all units in the AO!"

There was a chill running down their collective spines. The chill was like a polite sign that they were about to be visited by the grim reaper. They needed to be on their toes, or a lot of people were about to die.

"Identity of incoming hostiles confirmed! It's the Devil of the Rhine! I repeat, it's the Devil of the Rhine! We've got Named mages! One of the deadliest Named units is heading our way!"

The man frantically shouted into his radio. He sent out his message across the airwaves, but it was already too late. The screams of the air patrol were already ringing out in the black sky.

"Intercept control, intercept control! We need reinforcements! We need them now! Shit! Our formation leader..."

Chapter **IV**

"One company of aerial mages is trying to force their way through! They've downed everyone they've come into contact with so far! They're Named! We can't hold them off!"

"Commander down! Commander do—"

It was chaos.

To say the channel was thrown into turmoil that night would be putting it lightly. Even in the control room—where things were generally kept calm and professional as a rule—spittle flew through the air as the commanding officer shouted his orders into the maelstrom of confusion. This kind of thing never happened. Something strange was going on. Everyone there knew it—they couldn't handle what had come.

"Two aerial mage companies have been dispatched... Engaging the enemy... They're *engaged*?! Already?!"

"Both squads Argyle and Carbene have made unexpected contact with the enemy! Shifting to battle mode!"

"Quick response team two has finished mobilization on the ground."

The officer received glances of doubt but didn't hesitate even for a moment.

"Shit! It's going to be a long night! Call up all the reinforcements we have! Including the reserves!"

Their orders were to mount a full-scale counterattack.

We need to stop them. Just when the command center was regaining its calm, it received another report.

"Warning! New Imperial Army air units sighted in air zone twelve! And also sixteen! They're all Named?!"

Impossible. Several people uttered the same phrase. It wasn't just the battalion headed by the Devil of the Rhine. Multiple Named units from the Rhine front had appeared.

It was like they were at the Rhine Air Battle. No, the living hell that was the Rhine campaign had come back to haunt them.

"Emergency alert to integrated control center! Multiple powerful imperial air units closing fast! Damn those imperial dogs! Do they want a second Rhine?!"

The duty officers did everything they could to ascertain the situation despite all the confusion. The ones in charge of the southern interception control area sent updates to command while they gathered as much information as they could.

"Calm yourselves! Prepare for electronic warfare! Find their guidance signals. The Empire should be providing navigation support electronically. Find their signals! That should give us an idea of what they're after."

"…? It's not working… I'm not picking up anything."

"Don't fall for their dummies. Just narrow down the potential sources."

"Th-that's not the problem. There are no signals coming from line control…"

"What do you mean there are no signals? Are they using some sort of new technology?!"

More bad news? The officers collectively rubbed their temples… Bad news had a way of coming all at once.

"Th-the enemies fighting Argyle have taken out their commanding officer! Carbene's commander is also requesting immediate reinforcements!"

"What? Damn it all to hell! Get the rest of the quick response teams ready! I want anyone who can fly in the sky right now!"

"A-Argyle's been wiped out! It's just been confirmed! Carbene's reporting that Argyle has been annihilated!"

It'd only been a few minutes, and their elite quick response force had already been taken out. It was like taking a bite out of a sour apple. The officer in charge couldn't control himself as he shouted out:

"How could it be over that quickly?! They only just made contact!"

He thought he knew. No, he did know. He didn't want to forget the *Devil of the Rhine.* The *nightmare* the François Republic saw was no fantasy.

They knew that monster was real, and this was why they were prepared to hit the invaders with everything available.

But why? Why was it turning out this way?

These were the best of the best they had for night air defense. Why couldn't they stop the enemy? How were they able to tear apart their defenses with such ease?

"Hostile mages have penetrated air zone twelve! Whiskey Battalion is on their way to intercept line two."

"The enemies in air zone twelve are turning around!"

"What?! No! They're trying to regroup with the enemies in zone sixteen! Damn it, their target must be… Whiskey?!"

Chapter **IV**

The officers moved as quickly as humanly possible.

"Alert, Whiskey Battalion! The enemy mages are regrouping and heading straight for your position!"

The man prayed that they'd be able to avoid the danger as he sent the warning across the airwaves. At the same time, a different Commonwealth battalion did their duty to protect their country.

"Scotch Battalion is taking off to meet up with Whiskey Battalion! ETA, four hundred seconds! No, they're moving faster! They'll be there in 360!"

"They're pushing their limits. But that's what we need right now. It'll be close…but it looks like the reinforcements will make it in time."

Walking on a tightrope like this was incredibly draining.

As of late, the Commonwealth enjoyed the upper hand in the war, so things hadn't gotten this hectic for a long while now. It seemed war was a monster that could never be trusted.

What a terrible thing it was.

That was as true for an officer as it was for anyone else. The air traffic controllers could hear the endless mix of screams and harried reports coming in over the radio. They'd probably need to drink themselves to sleep for the rest of their lives.

"Damn it, it's been a long while since we've seen anything like this…"

Agonizing messages about shorn arms, dead friends, and comrades bursting into flames came flying in, all cutting off with bloodcurdling screams.

All the radio operators could do was sit and listen. It had an immense impact on their minds. Even so, they needed to listen. Cursing the stroke of fate that had saddled them with watch duty on this of all nights, they continued listening to and reporting the messages they never wanted to hear.

Suppressing the collective nausea permeating the control room, they each pushed thoughts of their comrades who likely wouldn't return out of their minds and latched onto their transceivers.

They didn't know if it would be worth the sacrifice. That was exactly why they didn't want to miss a single message.

"Warning! Warning! It can't be?! Emergency report from Scotch Battalion!

Th-they've encountered aerial mages who snuck past our perimeter at low altitude!"

This warning to southern interception control, unfortunately, wouldn't make it in time.

"What?! The enemy! The enemy!"

"The enemy what?!"

In response to the horrified voice, there was a request for details, but their comrades on the other end were out of time.

"They're here! The enemy is here!"

The command center's operators shouted into their radios, asking for a status update. These would be the last messages that came through that night—the last messages southern interception control would ever receive.

Static filled the airwaves before a large explosion rang out. Then everything went silent.

For the Commonwealth mages in the sky that night, it was more than evident what this meant.

They got southern interception control.

They listened closely to their radios for their next orders but picked up something else.

"Veni, vidi, vici."

It was a victory message.

No, it was more like they were boasting. The imperial mages shared this terrible joke on all frequencies.

"I came, I saw, I conquered...? Bollocks!"

As angry as they were, the soldiers knew that the night wasn't over yet.

"Scotch Leader to integrated control center. Emergency. It's urgent! Southern interception control has been taken out! I say again, southern interception control has been taken out!"

The man shouting this had seen the terrors of the Rhine front firsthand.

Wreak havoc, spread chaos, and eventually cause a total collapse.

This was the Empire's way of doing things. He and anyone else who saw them operate knew this all too well. These men had trained hard to make sure it never happened on their turf.

And yet, despite their best efforts, these were the miserable results. What the hell was happening?

"They're coming for us. This is bad… Those imperial bastards were quiet for a time, but it looks like they're back in action!"

"Commander! We're ready for battle!"

"We're not going to let them have their way any longer!"

With their weapons armed and ready, Scotch Leader's battalion was prepared to jump in the fray. He was proud of how capable his troops were.

Though he also found himself questioning whether his unit's bullets would ever strike home.

The enemy was the Imperial Army's meat grinder that first appeared on the Rhine front. They were supposed to somehow fight monsters that had been racking up kills ever since. The battalion leader directed every swear in the Commonwealth dictionary at God in heaven for this cursed fate.

His doubts and fears, however, would never be tested that night.

"Wha—?! They're retreating?!"

To everyone's surprise, the enemies began withdrawing from the southern interception control center after razing it to the ground. In what could only be described as gorgeous maneuvers, the enemy swiftly turned on a dime and rapidly left the area.

"Th-the enemy is retreating?"

The battalion that had been ready to mount a counterattack was left in the dust as the imperial soldiers left them behind.

Time to go after them was the first thought that popped into their collective minds. But anyone who had spent any significant amount of time on the battlefield knew this was the forbidden fruit.

"…Gather the troops! Don't follow them!"

The devil was trying to seduce them.

The only thing that awaited in that direction was living hell.

For the careful soldiers, it was nothing but a pointless risk. And unlike Scotch Leader, the only one who came out lucky that night, ground control came forward with a thoughtless question.

"Integrated control center to all units. Integrated control center to all

units. We have confirmation of enemy retreat. Scotch Leader, is pursuit possible?"

"The bloody hell?! You're asking us to chase after them?!"

He promptly rejected the request.

"No can do! Pursuit is impossible. They pulled one over us. We need to land and reorganize before we attempt to attack unless you want us to get annihilated as well!"

Scotch Leader swore and cursed some more before finally landing at a different base. He shook his head and grumbled while being handed a glass of alcohol by the ground personnel.

"They got us... Shit, and this is probably just the beginning!"

Beware of leaks.

Unknown

If there was a secret to ruling the world, then it was definitely in tea.

Lieutenant Colonel Drake believed this to be an immutable truth. It was self-evident to any member of the Commonwealth military.

This cup of tea was the starting point of his nation's bid to build a global empire.

It seemed a little silly, but anyone who laughed at the thought lacked an understanding of the way the world worked. After all, the Commonwealth ruled the planet through its control over the distribution of goods.

They created and controlled the market for tea, then supplied it to the rest of the world.

In order for this to be possible, they needed a strong navy to protect the waterways they used for shipping, which was the foundation of their industry.

The tea leaves were produced in a faraway land before eventually reaching their destinations via ship.

The shipping began with tea clippers, but these would later be replaced by steamboats. The sun never set on the shipping lanes owned by this great power. Their dominance in maritime shipping was what guaranteed their superiority over the continental nations limited by their reliance on land-based transportation. The people of the Commonwealth traversed the sea shrouded with the fragrance of tea leaves.

To have a strong navy was to gain control over a free and open sea. In other words, a maritime nation was worthy of claiming hegemony over the world.

This was why, after such a long absence from the homeland, what Lieutenant Colonel Drake experienced in the hotel's tea lounge that day shook him to his very core.

Chapter V

Teatime in the Commonwealth was the essence of what it meant to be home.

The gentleman intended to sit down at his table—a heritage piece of furniture in this magnificent historic hotel—and enjoy a cup of tea served in the finest porcelain.

But he didn't even need to take a sip before his plan fell apart.

As every Commonwealth citizen knew, the smell of tea was like the fragrance of a blossoming flower.

It was the smell of culture.

However, the aroma that normally evoked joy and excitement wasn't what emanated from his teacup. While its color somewhat resembled that of tea, it only made the experience all the more miserable.

It was almost comparable to—no, it was objectively worse than the cheap tea served in the Federation military camps.

They were served tea produced in the neutral Unified States there. Tea that was mass-produced and sold in cans. Drake was absolutely baffled that such a tea could taste better than what one of the finest tea lounges in his home country could muster.

This is unbelievable.

A waitress seemed to notice Drake shaking his head in disbelief and walked over with a tray of scones for him.

"Is there a problem, Lieutenant Colonel?" the waitress asked with a smiling face, forcing him to share his thoughts.

"As much as it pains me to say this, the tea here tastes absolutely horrendous. Were this my first time here, I'd ask to see the manager." He knew this hotel and its quality. Had he not, though, he may have thought they were playing some kind of joke on him at first. "I can't believe you're serving this... I don't believe I've seen you here before, either. What happened to all the waiters?"

"They're either in the trenches or at sea or friends of yours. If you have an issue with our tea, you can take it up with the Imperial Navy."

"Things are tough here, too, then, eh? Bother... Well, I'll help myself to one of those."

He made some small talk with the waitress while reaching for one of the scones she had brought over on a tray.

It was dry, and the taste didn't even resemble wheat.

He swallowed his sigh and reached for some butter, which he could also tell was a substitute. He added some jam in hopes of salvaging the taste, but that was stale as well. It lacked sugar, and the quality of the fruit wasn't great, either. It almost looked like a fruit compote...

"...Well, the jam and butter aren't much better, either. They're both cheap knockoffs."

This was the one thing I had looked forward to. Drake held back his complaints and washed down the scone with the lukewarm drink they called tea.

It was teatime only in appearance.

Which perfectly explained why there weren't many patrons despite it being the best time of the day for tea. He tried not to disparage everything, though. It was wartime, and the hotel was doing its best with what it had.

That said, no one enjoyed filling themselves up with fake goods.

Drake tried to take his mind off things by reading the newspaper. Right as he worked up the courage to try and finish the rest of his scone, an old man walked up to him.

"Mr. Johnson?"

"Hello, Lieutenant Colonel Drake. How's your recovery coming along?"

"Almost as good as new, as you can see. And thankfully so. How else would I enjoy everything the home country has to offer without the use of my arm? This sure tastes good."

The old man nodded in understanding while staring at Drake. It had occurred to Drake once before when he met Mr. Johnson on the eastern front, but he could never really tell what this man was thinking.

It was as if he was always using an abacus in his mind, making calculations while he made unreasonable demands with a big smile.

"I'm assuming...you have some free time, Lieutenant Colonel. If you have a moment to spare, would you mind entertaining me for a bit?"

"Excuse me?"

"Are you one for exorcising ghosts?"

"I used to pretend to do that all the time when I was a child. Well, it was mostly just fooling around."

He felt nostalgic as he remembered the good old days when he used to swing a branch to fight fairies and goblins.

It was all pretend, but it seemed so real to him when he was younger.

It was just the sort of thing people did in their youth. As embarrassing as it was to think about, these memories warmed Drake's heart. He found himself wondering if perhaps he had forgotten about these memories in the confines of his military dorm.

"That's good to hear. In that case, I'd like for you to bring out your inner child again. Do you think you could do that for me?"

"This is an order we're talking about. I'm going to have to do it either way, aren't I? So let's hear it. You need me to kill a ghost for you?"

"It's the Devil of the Rhine."

The old man's casual response made Lieutenant Colonel Drake choke on the tealike substance he had been drinking.

"What?"

He immediately responded with a mix of surprise and coughing before the man struck him with another bomb.

"The little phantom you saw on the eastern front. A little birdie in the Empire tells me...that ghost will be visiting us soon."

"Mr. Johnson, I'm sorry to ask, but is this true?"

"It is, I assure you." With a smile on his face but no joy in his eyes, the intelligence agent began to speak with a jovial tone. "We have complete trust in our sources. We're still doing background... The ghosts that have been showing up at night the past few days and attacking the channel are reported to be the Devil of the Rhine."

Intelligence believed that the attacks were so the Krauts could break through the Commonwealth's palisades. That they had crossed the wide sea for a surprise attack.

"You can't be serious?"

Though a casual-sounding response, there was real anger hidden within his words. The old man seemed to be in a very bad mood. However, as a military officer, Lieutenant Colonel Drake had a few choice words for an old man who talked about secrets in such a place.

"You mean to tell me those damn Krauts will put down even a single leather boot on Commonwealth land? That's some shocking news to take in, especially in a hotel lounge like this."

"Well, this is *our* land."

The old man chuckled. He was hinting at something by mentioning land.

"Looks like you've learned a thing or two during your time in the Federation. Being cautious of your surroundings is a good thing. I'm glad you were able to learn something from those Commies. Here's a little more advice for you."

Mr. Johnson flashed a dastardly grin. It contained all the backhanded nastiness of the John Bull spirit.

"Scarcity and war go hand in hand. And yet, take a look at this hotel. As imperfect as it may be, it's still operating. Always remember that there are strings attached to the intelligence we provide."

He gave Drake a small wink, telling him that this was the area that had been "cleaned up," so to speak.

"...You're making me worried about the Intelligence Service's future. I thought the scotch you prepared for me as payment for fighting in a faraway land was fairly decent, but have you considered using some of that budget here at home?"

"Even if His Majesty or the Lord himself were to allow such a thing, the bureaucrats never would. They're as strict as they come."

This was another contradiction. A career bureaucrat of the treasury, someone thoroughly loyal to His Majesty, would frown when they asked, *Why is the cost of the department that serves only to issue foreign visas costing the country so much money during a time of war when people aren't entering the country?*

It should be evident to them as well that this was the budget allocated to the Intelligence Service. They likely knew that the visa department of the Foreign Office was only there for this purpose. Still, this didn't change the fact that the treasury officials worked for the treasury and that sadly they still required a justification for expenditures.

Specifically, it needs to be a justification that could be explained to opposing members of parliament loyal to His Majesty.

"The patriotic members of parliament we're so blessed to have... They just love to bandy about phrases like *wasteful bureaucracy* and *sabotaging wartime efforts.*"

Their patriotism was what made them denounce waste. Denouncing waste and the laziness of the bureaucratic organization was likely the pride and joy of the members of parliament. This was fine for the Commonwealth as a nation…but was a big problem for the Intelligence Service to get caught up in the cross fire.

As ridiculous as it seemed, the Commonwealth Intelligence Service was in the middle of a purely political fight with the treasury. While the agency technically didn't exist…the money it spent was still procured and budgeted through public channels…which meant they got to enjoy the luxury of dealing with public officials.

It was also why Mr. Johnson emitted another large sigh before continuing.

"This is the information we managed to obtain with what little budget we have. I want you to use it and knock that little devil out of the sky before the Empire kicks our country to the curb with their military-issue boots."

"Excuse me, but do you have a timetable of when the Devil of the Rhine will make another appearance?"

"General Habergram believes so. I know you're taking a break before you head back to the east, but such is the nature of war. Between you and me, I haven't been able to take time off in for as long as I can remember."

The old man grumbled in a bid for sympathy. Though it was likely just a part of his act as an intelligence agent, there was a hint of genuine grief behind his request for Drake to do this for him.

"The higher-ups are growing impatient, and we want to offer them something concrete. I hope you can produce results."

"Of course, sir. Orders are orders."

"Good. You'll be sent out to protect a brigade that will intercept the devil's battalion."

Lieutenant Colonel Drake's expression tightened a bit. *He says that like it's easy…* They were orders, so he'd follow them, but he couldn't help but question their significance.

"Pardon me, but will I be acting alone?"

"No, no. Of course not. Considering the objective, you'll be sent with some of the more powerful members of your old marine mage unit."

Knowing a strong company was prepared for him, Drake was now sure that this job was one he couldn't fail.

"They're the best of the best, so I think you'll do well."

"I'll do what I can. Just make sure the devil shows up."

"Of course! I promise we won't hold it against you if it doesn't."

 AUGUST 16, UNIFIED YEAR 1927, COMMONWEALTH MAINLAND

Things moved very quickly after that meeting. A sign that the Intelligence Service was very serious about this. Bureaucratic organizations were ruled by inertia. For them to act this quickly meant that there was immense pressure building behind the scenes.

"...Who knew they could be this diligent."

Things happened so quickly that Lieutenant Colonel Drake expressed his surprise out loud without realizing it.

The gears on the war machine moved quickly once they'd been given a bit of oil, and Drake's orders, along with his temporary assignment, fell right to his feet. As difficult as it should have been for them to give orders to the command officer of the multinational volunteer unit, the Intelligence Service was able to part the seas and move mountains to make it happen.

Just one day after his teatime with Mr. Johnson, Drake was picked up by a car and brought to meet the commanding officer of the interception brigade he would be joining.

Evidently, they were planning an ambush that would involve the Home Fleet. It was a bold move that risked blowing the anonymity of their contact in the Empire, but numbers were a good thing to have in battle.

The same went for Drake; he was going to be attached to a company of familiar marine mages. Although Brigade Commander Ballmer would go on to tell him a tidbit of less-than-ideal information about his brigade over a cup of tea.

Apparently, it was mostly made up of fresh recruits. They were still fledglings when it came to the sea.

"Seems we're both at the mercy of the politicians. I'll tell you what, Lieutenant Colonel, they're not too different from the multinational volunteer unit. I felt sorry for you when I heard what you were dealing with, only to suddenly find myself in the same position."

"It must be tough working for the palace, sir."

"I suppose it's the price I must pay to be called general. The day will come when it happens to you as well if you stay in the armed forces long enough."

They indulged in some witty banter to make sure that they were both gentlemen who shared the John Bull spirit. It was best to learn about a person's character before going into combat with them.

There definitely could be worse places to be stationed, Drake thought.

Speaking the same language always made things move faster, especially for specialists. The commander's summation of his brigade's strength gave Drake a newfound sense of danger.

These were new recruits he would be dealing with, after all. Sure, there were a lot of them, but he had serious doubts about their quality.

Then again, with a unit of this size, it was possible quantity could make up for quality. As long as the Home Fleet kept the enemy's naval forces in check, it should be more than enough for them to scatter enemy air support.

The problem was *who* would be supporting their enemy from the sky. Both Commander Ballmer and Drake feared the Named unit more than anything else

"I want to hear what you think about the Devil of the Rhine. Is that mage really as strong as they say?"

"Well, they don't call that monster Rusted Silver for nothing. I'm grateful to the gods that I came away alive, but I also curse them for sending me back into that devil's reach."

"…That's no good. If what you say is true, this might be too much for us to handle. Never thought I'd have to send *kids* to fight the Imperial Army."

"I actually recently met the devil in the east. I still have my doubts we'll see anything here."

The commander gave a small chuckle at Drake's words. He doesn't say it, but the tired look on his face more than conveyed his hope that Drake was right.

They exchanged salutes, and Drake received a bottle of alcohol instead of the usual cigarettes before being guided by Commander Ballmer's adjutant to meet the company he'd be flying with.

Though maybe *meet* wasn't the best way to put it, given how Drake already knew pretty much the entire company. It very well could've been that they took the time to gather up veterans from his old marine mage battalion for him.

"Boys!"

"Lieutenant Colonel."

They caught up with some idle chitchat, and Drake found out that most of them were posted to various places on a provisional basis, ready to move wherever their country needed them for missions like this.

Drake knew that once he was finished here, he'd be sent back east as a multinational volunteer. He found himself wondering if there was a way to bring some of these men back with him. While he wasn't one to count his chickens before they hatched, his job in the east would certainly be much easier with these old bags of bones at his side!

Another thought crossed his mind… Could deploying such elite soldiers be a sign that the higher-ups truly believed there was a good chance of the Devil of the Rhine making an appearance?

"Still, will that monster really show up?"

He couldn't shake the idea that the Devil of the Rhine was actually in the east, busy chasing Colonel Mikel around.

Had the intelligence community placed their full trust in their friend from the Empire—their spy—and mobilized everything in hopes of intercepting the target? It just seemed too good to be true. Drake couldn't wrap his head around the idea of the whole thing.

It seemed so surreal that a mage brigade and the Home Fleet would go so far to prepare for the so-called day of the attack.

What's worse was that in order to intercept the enemies, they were operating around the clock for maximum readiness. It was enough to make one question their sanity. Drake spent his time picturing what would happen after the whole thing flopped—how he and a couple of the boys would laugh their country's big mistake off at some pub.

Sadly, thinking about this got old around the three-day mark.

Be that as it may, sometimes fact truly could be stranger than fiction. On the last day of August…they finally received word of the guest they were expecting.

The first sign was the noisiness of the radio airwaves. Dispatch was much more active than usual; it was clear something was going on.

Chapter V

By the time Lieutenant Colonel Drake noticed it, the battle would already have begun. "Looks like the day of reckoning came at the end of the month this time, too," he grumbled to himself and gripped his weapon, and that was when command sent a transmission that explained the situation.

"Daniel 01 to all units. Our submarines have spotted an enemy! It's the Empire's forces. Their fleet is coming!"

Drake felt puzzled the moment he heard Commander's Ballmer's message... Was the spy's intel really on the mark? He even felt surprised.

Delving too deeply in information warfare made one begin to doubt everyone. Was there really a spy? Or was it all a ruse to feed the Commonwealth false information?

He decided it was better not to think about it for the sake of his mental health.

All he had to do was his job, and he would do it his way. Either way, he knew that General Habergram had made a mistake about one thing.

He still fully believed that the Devil of the Rhine was in the east. Nothing could possibly change his mind about this. That mage was in the east, terrorizing those poor, poor Federation soldiers.

Though he knew he would probably have to face the devil again once he headed back east himself... Little did he know that all his thoughts on the subject were about to fly out the window.

"Hmm?"

There was a faint mana signal. A peculiar tension filled the air.

The same kind he felt in the east.

...It was a signal he'd never forget—Rusted Silver's.

"God damn it all. And here I thought I had a guardian angel looking out for me."

Was his angel out to get him? This level of negligence was hard to forgive during a war. Lieutenant Colonel Drake wanted to arrest his guardian angel for desertion in the face of the enemy. He rubbed the back of his neck and shook his head before addressing his troops.

"Number ten, men. Get ready for a bloodbath."

This signal...there should have been a limit to how terrifying signals could be. There was no way for him to mistake it for any other. He could identify her signal even in his sleep.

As much as he didn't want to believe it, nothing in this world was guaranteed.

"Alert Commander Ballmer this second. Tell him we're going to be fighting a battalion of devils."

"He's already mobilizing the troops, sir."

So even veterans needed to see it to believe it, eh?

Drake looked out over his company. They were alert, but there was still a noticeable lack of tension in their shoulders. That wasn't necessarily a bad thing…but it certainly wouldn't be the case had the men seen the devil with their own eyes.

He needed to tell them they were going to be fighting for their lives.

"If anything, this is going to be a brutal kill-or-be-killed battle. Think of the enemies as actual demons. Don't be fooled by their looks."

"This is that little girl we're talking about, right?"

"She may look like a young girl, but heed my words. She's nothing but a conniving little monster."

Drake warned his comrades, but they somehow thought he was joking and laughed it off.

"You can't be serious. Maybe you've spent too much time in the east, Colonel?"

The apprehension had completely drained from the man. Drake could tell from his posture, and that was all well and good, but he knew their opponent was going to be tough, even for these veterans.

"Listen up, my fellow marine mages. I'm only going to say this once." Drake knew what he was about to say was as ungentlemanly as possible, but he persevered. "Don't hesitate just because you find a woman on the other end of your sights. You need to kill them if you don't want to die. If you spot a little girl, shoot her out of the sky without a second thought."

"You catch something out there in the east? Maybe sleep with the wrong gal?"

"No, I'm healthy as a horse and thinking clear as a whistle. Although I almost wish you were right."

This was war.

They were fighting in that war as marines first and foremost.

"Gentlemen… These are our seas. Become monsters if you have to out there… If you don't want to die, you need to aim to kill. Today's the day we send those bastards to their graves at the bottom of the channel."

The Commonwealth had an advantage in numbers. They were fully prepared thanks to their intel and had the support of a powerful naval force as well. The balance of power was completely in their favor. Turned out that the politicians and the higher-ups could set up some damn good fights from time to time.

"Let's do this! It's our fight to win!"

▶▶▶   AUGUST 31, UNIFIED YEAR 1927, SKIES ABOVE THE CHANNEL   ◀◀◀

This was supposed to be a surprise attack.

That's what it said in the plan at least!

I took all conceivable courses of action possible to keep this a damn secret.

So what the hell are *those*? No, I don't even need to ask. They're black battleships—a veritable fleet of capital ships.

Rulers of the deep, the kings of the ocean. It's the Commonwealth Home Fleet.

Well, more like a small *part* of their fleet. It's easy to tell this from the lack of the famed dreadnoughts they're so proud of. The fleet nearby is built around older models of fast battleships and battlecruisers.

As detestable as it may be, it's more than enough to take out our fleet. Despite being only a small part of their armada, it seems like more than enough to take out the Imperial Navy's entire fleet operating in the Northern Sea. Even our High Seas Fleet would only match this group in numbers, if at all.

Either way, the fleet we have now is like a bunch of ants about to be smashed by an elephant. It won't be much of a fight—it'll just be a massacre.

Of course, numbers aren't the real reason we're doomed.

What I'm really worried about is how the enemy will make their move.

Right when we're about to execute a surprise attack, we just so happen to run into a larger fleet that's ready to fight?

"Argh, there's no way this happened by chance."

I'd believe in Communism or Being X before believing this was the outcome of sheer luck. In other words, coincidences like this don't exist.

I'd already been suspicious about this, but…my prior knowledge from my original world tells me at a glance that this is a preplanned welcome party, and it'll be full of fun and surprises.

I had my suspicions before, but now I'm certain.

It's a magic trick.

They must've fully deciphered the Empire's encryptions. The Imperial Army encodes all their secret orders before sending them by radio, so… this isn't something as simple as a small leak. It means they're listening to everything we say.

Good grief. And to think I went through all that trouble to mask the 203rd Battalion's movements.

This is why we can't win.

As my desire to change jobs only grows stronger, I ball up my fists and grit my teeth while facing this new harsh reality. I know I'm fighting for the losing side.

Information is a matter of life or death. Regardless, this is something that could have been avoided.

It would've been possible had the rest of the Empire done the same as me and abstained from using radios to communicate. I don't know if it was the idiots from Western Army Group command or the navy…but the utter lack of operational security makes me sick.

"I'm going to let them have it when I get back. That goes for General Romel, too—I need to raise hell about this."

Actually doing so is going to be a challenge, however. As much as I want to point out the problem, I can't prove that our codes had been deciphered.

It's a case of *probatio diabolica*. I need proof I don't have. The Imperial Army has incredible confidence in the flawlessness of their codes. If they didn't…then the various departments of the military wouldn't broadcast every damn morsel of our operations.

How cruel, reckless, and absurd.

"How could something this utterly stupid ever happen?"

"Lieutenant Colonel?"

I answer my adjutant's worried expression with overflowing agitation.

Chapter **V**

"First Lieutenant Serebryakov, remember what we're seeing here today. This is the result of a slipup made by high command. Argh, this is why the outcome of the war is so uncertain!"

I'd scream, *You imbeciles!* if that was an option. If not for my place in society, I'd quit right here, right now. Not much can be done out in the field to fix management's mistakes.

I may adore effort, but I abhor pointless effort.

Effort needs to be made with an appropriate means and objective. Moreover, it needs to be done so strategically, constructively, and in the right place, or else it's meaningless. Effort is a means to an end, not the end.

Although a long-term outlook such as this serves no purpose to the situation I find myself in now.

I never knew that human beings could be so simple. The enemies before us are the problem at hand. I need to do something about them.

I can see the imperial fleet below, panicking as they quickly change course.

Though we have some battlecruisers, there's a tragically small number of them. If they pick a fight with the Commonwealth Home Fleet, all that awaits them is a watery grave.

There's no reason to waste so much life and tax money.

The commander of the navy? Well, what is there to say about him...? It seems like he's got a good head on his shoulders, seeing as the ships are already scrambling to retreat.

It's good to be quick on your feet.

Though it'd be nice if they sent their air support a message while they're at it... I guess that's just how much of a panic they're in, though. They lack experience.

"It must be nice being in the navy. The less experience they have, the more they can shelter in a friendly harbor."

Judging by the naval strike force's commander, I'd wager he hasn't seen many battles yet. It seems like there aren't many experienced imperial marines.

Though, for the sake of all that's good in the world...it would've been nice if we had a submarine or two to help us escape.

"Should we call a nearby friendly submarine on an open channel? No... It'd likely be pointless."

I grumble to myself, only to reject my own question. This feels like a bad comedy... Tanya shakes her head.

Most of the imperial submarines stationed off the Commonwealth coast are unable to be contacted by radio. They're likely lurking at the bottom of the sea where signals can't reach them. If only I had a stupidly long antenna, then maybe I could send signals strong enough. Oh well. No point in wishing for things I don't have.

Now, here's a little quiz.

We have a single battalion, and the enemies have a whole brigade. They also have an overwhelming naval fleet.

I have no plans to plunge into their ship's anti–air fire, but it's also totally unfair that the enemy air units can rely on their ship for fire support and resupply.

By unfair, I mean they'd have the advantage in a long-term battle. So should we turn tail and run alongside our friendlies? Uh-uh, no can do. If we run away with the ships we're supposed to defend...we'd have to match their pace.

And that's definitely not a pace that can outrun enemy aerial mages.

Instead of being weighed down by them, it's much more prudent to split up. I definitely don't want to escape with the fleet, only to ditch them when things get too close for comfort.

"Attacking is the best defense, he says..."

"Lieutenant Colonel? Have you made your decision?"

I give a big nod of confirmation to my adjutant.

"Alert the ships. Tell them, *Continue evasive maneuvers without us. We're going to draw the enemy mages away*, over."

"But aren't they already leaving without us?"

My adjutant gives a wry laugh as she points out the brutal truth. I feel compelled to respond as her boss.

"Visha, be more forgiving of the newer recruits."

As long as they don't make the same mistake again, this is acceptable. An organization that doesn't forgive its employees is one that will force them to lie. A company needs to weed out whoever is causing the failures and fix them if they're going to put an end to such problems. That isn't possible if the employees hide the truth from the company, though.

"The navy is still new to battles. We should commend them for making the right decision and escaping. I look forward to seeing them fight another day."

"If there is another day for them. We'd better tell *them* not to pick on the small fry."

"Which them?"

My adjutant flashes a vicious smile.

"Isn't it obvious? The Commonwealth Home Fleet. Should I go petition them to stop? I feel like the imperial ships below could at least wait for us to try that out first."

I scowl at my adjutant's childish phrasing. If she makes any mistakes, all responsibility will fall on me.

"Don't do that, First Lieutenant Serebryakov."

"Oh... Was it too indiscreet?"

That's not it—I shake my head.

"Come on now, adjutant. I need you to straighten up. The whole point of war is to *pick on the weak*."

"Right?!"

I declare this with absolute confidence.

"It would be a big problem if we were to do what we scold others for. We need to be consistent."

"By consistent, you mean...?"

"Let's do the same thing as them! You hear that, comrades? We're going in."

With a wave of a hand, I give the signal—the signal my troops have been waiting for since they came from the east.

"We're charging the Commonwealth? Wunderbar, I can still remember that day I chased around that police officer."

Major Weiss says a joke over the radio, tossing the ball into my court. It's his way of getting the troops to relax.

I take the opportunity to join in his jest and return the pass.

"There are no police officers at sea, only those ghoulish marine mages."

"Sounds like just the fun we've been waiting for."

I can hear my deputy thump his fist on his chest. How dependable... If only he had interests in anything other than war, he'd make for some superb human capital. While I detest the idea of changing how people think on the inside too much, this is one of the rare times I wished I could.

Be that as it may, we're at war, and this is a battle. My only wish is to do my work earnestly and honestly.

"Get ready, troops! Let's give them a little taste of the maneuver warfare we perfected in the east. We'll fly circles around the slow Commonwealth fleet!"

This is when I remember First Lieutenant Serebryakov's suggestion. Contacting the Commonwealth may not be such a bad idea.

It could be a chance for her to use her own assets as a human resource.

"Lieutenant Serebryakov, prepare a radio broadcast for all signals."

"Roger. What are you going to send?"

"*This is the Imperial Army. Calling all pathetic amateurs. We're here to teach you a lesson. Enjoy the maneuvers we've prepared over in the eastern front.* That's all, Lieutenant."

First Lieutenant Serebryakov motions to say something but then closes her mouth… It's a simple provocation, but such tactics have their place from time to time. The message we send needs to be understood by even the most brainless of fools.

Their logic going into battle is a valuable military asset. You see, nothing gets an idiot more riled up than being called an idiot.

This is precisely what makes them idiots, ironically enough.

My adjutant translates the message into polite Commonwealth, and from afar, we can see we are successful in provoking our enemies.

Apparently, their commander doesn't have any self-control. Oh? Their movements aren't uniform, either. Perhaps some of them are moving independently… Are they ignoring orders? If that's the case, this is going to be easier than I thought.

It seems they don't even know the basics of combined arms.

"We've got a big load to haul today, troops."

I grin.

It would be difficult to take on an entire brigade even on a good day, but a brigade's worth of unorganized soldiers isn't frightening in the slightest. Leadership and teamwork are the keys to committing violence on an industrial scale.

Hit someone with one finger? Congratulations, you've poked them. Curl five fingers into a fist? You'll send them flying. It's an incredibly simple concept.

Chapter **V**

"They're scattering before they charge us. How bold. To think they would ignore the risk of friendly fire and abandon any attempt to support one another."

"Visha, that's a sign of their fighting spirit. We should praise their effort."

When I see my adjutant giving me an unexpected look, I simply smile.

"We'll praise them, then destroy them."

"So you want to pick on the amateurs, ma'am?"

"We'll crush whoever challenges us. Should we refrain from attacking them just because they're weak? Wait, you don't actually hate picking on the weak, do you?"

"It's one of my favorite things to do, Colonel."

This is the same adjutant who just demanded that the enemy stop picking on the weak. Though I don't want to infringe on my subordinate's freedom of thought...I have no choice but to question her sense of justice.

"Adjutant, I'm going to write this down on your personnel record. Benevolence is an important thing to have. You should live your life caring for others. All humanity is a family, after all."

Of course, this is mostly a joke, and everyone knows it.

""""Ha-ha-ha-ha!""""

Now this is a workplace overflowing with laughter. Other than First Lieutenant Wüstemann's company falling slightly behind, there are no problems with our positioning.

"Now, unfortunately, this is war. Let's show these amateurs how to dance!"

I give the orders, and the entire battalion immediately shifts gears.

Against a brigade, a battalion that sticks together only stands to be surrounded.

So what are we supposed to do?

The answer's simple—charge first.

Anyone who knows their war history understands this. Weiss and Grantz know this best.

Even the replacement officers, like Wüstemann, have learned this important lesson on the battlefield.

The two-thousand-foot altitude difference isn't a minor advantage. Tanya and the rest of the 203rd Aerial Mage Battalion, however, boldly throw this advantage away.

The four companies split up into four cone formations so that they can easily support one another. They will fall like four drills and penetrate the Commonwealth's unorganized line.

It's important to always get the drop on your enemy in a battle.

Unconcentrated incoming fire can hardly be considered threatening. And taking fire from several uncoordinated sources will never penetrate a well-trained mage's defensive shell as long as they're never allowed to focus fire. Conversely, a simple charge can be made incredibly deadly when executed in tandem with an entire company. From the moment the two forces engage in combat, the 203rd enjoys the fruit of victory from the bottom of their hearts.

The other side? Oh, those poor, pathetic amateurs!

Our less experienced opponents tend to take the luxury to stop flying before aiming and firing. Don't they know that stopping for even a second to aim makes them sitting targets?

"It's like penguins trying to fly."

Their panicked flight patterns are laughable as well.

The Commonwealth computation orbs were made with an emphasis on maneuver warfare. They are light and nimble…therefore, they don't stand out much when they aren't in motion. The 203rd is more than experienced enough to crack open their defensive shells like can openers. My troops have opened more than their fair share of formidable Federation defensive shells in the east.

It's a one-sided process.

We cut open the enemy's protective film with our magic blades, then use the help of gravity to pierce their defensive shell. This results in a stunned enemy mage letting out a bloodcurdling scream—after which they're considered *neutralized* as they make a swift descent to the sea below.

The scene is enveloped in violence.

The sparkle of enchanted blades, explosion formulas, and the occasional sprays of blood light up the sky like a violent storm.

"I thought this the last time we faced off, but the Commonwealth mages are so much *softer* than the Federation's. It sure makes things easier on us, don't you think, Colonel?"

In response to my adjutant's words, I give a strong nod. They're like eggs. It only takes a single tap for their yolks to come gushing out.

Chapter V

The few odd veterans protecting the new recruits pose more of a challenge...but there aren't a lot of them.

"Their strategy is half-baked. They need to spread out the inexperienced mages more to keep them from getting swallowed up by the chaos of battle."

We may even be able to bring the whole brigade down if we can shoot down the veterans who will come rushing to protect the newer recruits. They should be a bit more professional. This ended up being a figment of my imagination that no longer matched reality.

"I feel like their mages used to be stronger."

"I agree. The Commonwealth may as well follow the same school of thought as the Federation Army and change to tougher orbs. Though... the same could probably be said for us."

The lack of battle experience for newer troops is a problem shared by all the warring states at this point. Since amateurs only have their morale to rely on when they charge, giving them an orb that creates a stronger defensive shell and letting them focus purely on defense has proven to be the superior strategy.

It's a sad reality. To think that instead of cultivating our best and brightest, we'd need to create a system to coddle the least capable. It feels like a stroke of luck that my troops don't suffer from these issues. I like to think it's a product of their daily training and my guidance.

"Major Weiss and Lieutenant Grantz are doing well."

"What about Lieutenant Wüstemann?"

"His company needs some work. They're close to getting a failing score...but I'll give them extra points for learning during wartime. Compared to the enemy, they're pulling their weight."

I begin creating my own explosions while evaluating my subordinates.

"First Officer! Be a bit more brutal with your kills!"

"Are you sure, ma'am? I thought we were prioritizing breaking up their forces so we can penetrate their perimeter."

"That's a good idea, but this time we need to have First Lieutenant Wüstemann learn a thing or two about fighting. Show them how it's done!"

"Roger!"

If on-the-job training is my only chance to teach them, then I'll have to make the most of this opportunity. They might develop some strange habits from learning through trial by fire, but this is a good learning opportunity nonetheless... Though, honestly speaking, putting troops through the wringer is the best way to whip them into shape in general anyway.

For now, I have to make do with what I've got.

"First Lieutenant Wüstemann, do you copy? We're going to lead some prey your way. Think of it as a team-building exercise for your company."

"R-roger that."

"Relax. You and your team are doing well. Not only that, look at your enemies. They're drowning in the sky."

The young first lieutenant lets out a sigh of relief when this gets pointed out to him.

"It's like looking at how we used to be."

"That's exactly right. We need to take them out today before they reach your level."

Enough experience will turn any amateur into a pro. Not only that, but this is war. Everyone is putting their life on the line, which is one of the greatest motivations for incredible personal growth.

"We must defang our enemies while we have the chance."

"This really is war..."

"That's exactly right," I say with a nod.

Though there isn't much time to indulge in such reveries. Major Weiss is moving fast and driving the enemy forward, after all. I bring my company with me to begin the hunt. First Lieutenant Wüstemann's reserve company only needs to rush the group of confused mages.

This should be a quick and effective way for them to build real experience.

I can only laugh at how weak our enemies were.

I shake my head.

"We've been at war for too long."

"Colonel?"

"The enemies are this weak, and yet the replacements are having trouble with them? What happened to our friendly army in the west? Just how bad is the current state of affairs here?"

It hurts my head just thinking about it.

Chapter V

We've fought the Commonwealth aerial mages many times, and it's always the marine mages getting in the Empire's way.

Though there's a chance I've fought them unofficially in other places as well.

…There's also a good chance the Commonwealth aerial mages have lost the bulk of their talent. The fact that they still pose a challenge for the Empire despite how weak they've become makes the Empire's weakness just as apparent.

War creates a massive deficit in human capital.

"There's something wrong with all this…"

I clear my mind with a shake of my head. It isn't my job as a field commander to take into consideration my homeland's human resources situation.

That's a job for my superiors. A superior who ranks much, much higher than me, in fact.

Someone at my pay grade should only think about how to produce the greatest results with minimal losses on the battlefield. In other words, I need to produce results as a soldier—nothing more, nothing less.

"Kill our enemies for the beloved fatherland. And kill them for the land they love as well. War should be kept simple."

I tell my subordinates to cast more explosive formulas and let out a wry laugh as I find myself growing uncharacteristically sentimental. There's a more modern, civilized part of me that shouldn't be able to accept the amount of human life we're stealing. But I'm nothing more than a cog in something much bigger. That's all.

That's why I want to end this current dogfight as quickly as possible.

"Numbers are a weapon unto themselves. It seems that it'll take quite a while to break down a full brigade."

Sadly, things just aren't going my way.

Despite dominating the battlefield, there's only so much damage and confusion we can inflict on an entire brigade. I add in my own formulas here and there to try and rout them…but the enemies are maintaining unit cohesion on the whole.

Maybe they're just trying to keep us here? At the very least, in terms of organic numbers, there are too many soldiers who are only there to fill in as a body. Though awkward and ineffective, there's still a barely working chain of command. Managing such a brigade would cause tremendous mental stress.

They probably won't last another attack or two.

"First Lieutenant Grantz, protect First Lieutenant Wüstemann and go make some friends."

"Am I to pull them away from the line? Roger!"

"Good thinking, First Lieutenant Grantz."

Grantz has learned a lot under General Zettour. He's much easier to use now. Is this all thanks to the discipline of a high-ranking officer? I'll need to ask the general about his teaching methods.

For now, I'll need to rely on my tried-and-true methods. Trial by fire is the best sort of on-the-job training I know.

"Wüstemann, no need to be afraid. Follow Grantz's lead and watch his moves!"

"R-roger!"

Tanya unleashes a rain of fire that turns an enemy mage into mincemeat before cheerfully addressing her subordinate.

"Relax, First Lieutenant. Look at yourself. You need to loosen up."

"But, Colonel…sh-shouldn't I try to keep my focus?"

It was a serious answer a greenhorn would give, and it wasn't ideal.

There are certainly times where focus is critical, but humans are like rubber. If you stretch them out as far as possible, they'll just lose their elasticity. Conserving your energy when you don't need to use it could be considered an indispensable skill for surviving battles.

"A battle isn't something you can enjoy if you're stiff and severe. It's healthier to loosen up a bit and go with the flow. This is the key to making it out alive."

My XO unexpectedly decides to chime in while blowing a group of enemies out of the sky.

"Out of curiosity, Colonel, what are you thinking about when you're fighting?"

"I'm not thinking about anything. That's another trade secret. Do with it what you want."

There's something that I can't deny when I'm watching my battalion go to work.

With the exception of the replacements, it's mostly a band of warmongers. However, they act with control. I'm going to repeat this since it's important, but these soldiers move like a well-oiled machine. Each of them is a violent cog that keeps the greater whole running smooth.

To put it in another way...I have no preference about my soldiers' convictions as long as it keeps them from panicking on the battlefield.

They can believe in flying spaghetti monsters for all I care.

"We have to be earnest and work long and hard hours. Whoever wins the battle will be the side who does this more."

I parry the swipe of a marine mage who comes charging in and shove my magic blade through his back, mumbling to myself before letting out a sigh.

Our enemies are mad as hell at this point. As if getting angry will make them better. If that were the case, I'd be more than willing to implement hate sessions for my own troops.

"Lieutenant Wüstemann, it's like the colonel said... You need to relax."

It seems the man is getting the gist of it. I can see the tense first lieutenant loosen up and begin to navigate the skies with a bit more grace.

"That's it, that's it. Now you're getting it."

Grantz and Weiss are doing a fantastic job drawing the enemies out. They skillfully toy with their catch and maneuver in a way to keep their attention away from First Lieutenant Wüstemann's company. The seemingly thin sky is incredibly vast. The enemies are too focused on whatever danger they see directly ahead of them.

This is what ends up doing them in.

In a three-dimensional battle, you're a sitting duck if you can't maintain situational awareness in all directions. After the enemies lose sight of First Lieutenant Wüstemann, they get hit from an angle they never see coming.

While their technique still needs some work, their momentum and morale are both commendable. The glimmer of their formulas violently exploding through the sky is met with the screams and anguish of our enemies. This symphony is the sound of a successfully executed flanking maneuver.

"I suppose my advice was useful."

I almost feel like a proper educator for a moment. There may be a fulfilling and rewarding aspect to teaching others.

No, I'm actually quite sure of this fact by now.

Education is extremely important, if not only for cultivating the limited human capital they had left. War is about making your army as efficient as possible. The inability to do this is met with death.

In a way, it's sort of the ultimate competition.

If you fail to raise your people right, you won't be able to win a war, or a race, or anything at all really.

The scene playing out before me speaks volumes about this point.

My clever subordinates outmaneuver the enemies, isolating them from the brigade. While there are parts of it that could still use some work, the fact that the replacements are following up with their own attack is proof that they can get the job done.

Although it isn't something I'm prepared to let them do entirely on their own just yet.

"So you've managed to take on a battalion with two companies? Your execution is by no means poor, but there's still ample room for improvement."

First Lieutenant Wüstemann's unit still isn't very good at pushing their enemies back. They lack impact as well. The enemy is getting flanked, and both Weiss and Grantz have them positioned perfectly, and yet they're unable to completely wipe them out!

The enemies have been packed into a spherical kill zone, so Wüstemann's unit needs to charge into that space and destroy the enemy. They're focusing too much on maintaining a proper formation for the sake of firepower—what a waste.

With a sigh, I swallow my complaints in the hopes that they'll improve in the future.

This is the best I have access to for now. You can't quit a card game just because you don't like the hand you were dealt.

First Lieutenant Wüstemann and his troops are giving it their best to produce results.

While still rough around the edges, the company shows the fighting spirit and initiative needed to take on a full battalion. I need to give praise when the troops deserve it. While managerial staff always have their own perspective on how work should be done...it's unfair to push those ideals onto the staff.

They haven't been trained properly yet. If something happens, the responsibility will fall on my shoulders.

"If only there was more time… Things would be different."

Their lack of skills directly correlates with their lack of training. I hate that I have to solve this problem on-site during a full-fledged dogfight.

I can hardly believe it. Both my allies and our enemies have completely forgone proper training!

Despite all the gunfire and formulas, as the battle presses on, my common sense is the greatest source of agitation.

What a waste of perfectly good industrial goods. It's a good thing that our enemy has such terrible aim…but the sheer volume of steel and gunpowder being used in this fight is deplorable. It's the worst possible use of human and fiscal capital. What's worse, they completely ignore the human component—the most important part!

What do militaries think people are?!

I can't bear to watch as the enemy forces practically drown at this altitude while repositioning my company. They've barely changed their formation at all, and their long-range magic formulas are basically accomplishing nothing. They don't even have a proper firing pattern—it's almost jarring.

They've ignored training far too much. A better world and a better environment are both born from properly cultivated human capital! Don't they know this? War is nothing but a massive, tremendous waste.

They say that people are the castles, walls, and moats of an army, but it feels like we're fighting a literal wall of flesh.

I float in midair with a daunting pose and lament the state of the world from the bottom of my heart, but alas—I'm but a civil servant. What one wants to do doesn't always coincide with what they must do.

Dodging enemy fire as it comes my way, I watch my troops make their next charge. It feels like they no longer need to surround the enemies for the newbies.

"Major Weiss, let the new guys handle it from here."

"Roger. What should we do?"

He asked the question more like it was an invitation.

The enemy brigade is in the middle of throwing us a party just a short distance away. Though we've gained a bit of wiggle room, the 203rd is chronically understaffed… That means we always have to be on the move.

"You already know the answer. It's time for work."

I answer my first officer in a lighthearted tone before reorganizing my company. There are no slipups as my soldiers skillfully return to their positions with great haste.

This is what separates the 203rd from other units.

It's our three-dimensional maneuverability born from hard-fought experience. Dogfights get hectic, and it can be hard to determine enemies from allies, so maintaining control of your unit and having them move in tandem trumps everything else.

This was considered basic knowledge before the onset of the war, but…it's something that seems to have been completely forgotten.

"Shall we?"

"Let's."

With a big wave, I send my subordinates toward the target.

"We're heading right for their center."

"Let's move."

Tanya's soldiers see her lightly clench her fist and know exactly what to do. She doesn't need to say much. It's business as usual, after all.

Aim for their commander and kill him before he realizes what's going on.

It's the only way for them to win this battle where the more well-trained imperial soldiers are at a disadvantage due to being far outnumbered. For the 203rd, which has been deployed in various capacities in different theaters, using a tactic like this is routine.

On Tanya's orders, the deputy commander and his troops begin to fly in and conduct their attack runs.

They produce an inferno of explosion formulas that blow the Commonwealth mages who pepper the skyline out of the air. With the sound of screams as their musical score, Tanya and her troops cut straight through the Commonwealth formation.

Halfway through their attack, the enemy ships below do their best to send up some supporting anti-air fire. Flak and tracers fill the air…but as the Commonwealth gunners have to worry about hitting friendlies, most of their support fire is wasted in irrelevant airspace. The imperial mages barely need to avoid it.

The elite mages, each of whom were baptized by fire, barely pay any mind to it. Our advance is like a hot knife slicing through butter.

They move deep into their line, going straight for the jugular.

Pushing their way past the enemies, the soldiers move toward their floating target.

A single, older gentleman in a sky full of young mages.

Tanya grins as she watches the man she assumes is the Commonwealth commander flail his arms and call out orders in a hoarse voice, desperately attempting to get a handle on the chaos and get his troops back under control.

"There he is! Now's our chance!"

The two ace companies are easily able to plow through the thinly spaced line of brigade mages. It's simple to behead the more panicked soldiers.

That isn't to say they've lost their chain of command.

As much as they try to stop the 203rd…their formation isn't solid enough. What really does them in is their slow reaction times, though. This is especially true for their commanding officer.

The older gentleman doesn't even try to put his subordinates between himself and his enemies and powers up his defensive shell to fight. What an incompetent fool, unable to use his men appropriately.

"Kill him!"

〉〉〉 THE SAME DAY—ON THE OTHER SIDE 〈〈〈

Why are we just sitting on the sidelines, watching idly, while our boys are getting killed out there?

Lieutenant Colonel Drake felt intense aggravation and sadness he couldn't do anything with. He watched as the youths of his nation were devoured by a group of monsters. *Why am I helpless to do anything?*

He wanted to charge forward and annihilate the Empire's fiends that consumed everything and everyone in their path.

He was there, however, as part of the backup. His company was being held as a tactical reserve. Even if he put himself between the brigade and the enemy, there wasn't anything he could do to quell the chaos.

"Damn it, I can't take this…"

Every time the enemy opened fire, another of his comrades fell from the sky.

It couldn't be more obvious that they were losing the battle.

"Shit!"

He wrestled with the idea of abandoning his post to go help—a dilemma all smaller groups of reserve units faced since time immemorial. It was important to stop troops for chasing down and attacking the enemy ships. Keeping a reserve to put out fires was also critical. This made Drake and his troops something of a trump card for Commander Ballmer should he need them.

In other words, a company was a convenient unit to hold back during battle.

The brigade would do the fighting, and the company would be called in on the commander's timing.

That was how it was supposed to work anyway…

Drake watched on in utter disbelief. It didn't seem possible that a brigade of this scale could be so easily dismantled.

"Help! The enemy! They're too strong!"

"Agh, ahh…it hurts…"

"Mama, mama, mama…"

"Calm down! Stay in formation!"

"Keep your eyes peeled for the enemy! Don't focus only on what's in front of you!"

"Commander under fire! Commander under fire!"

"Quit your crying! Stop yelling for no reason! Ready your weapons…"

Explosions, screams, and the weeping of soldiers who were still children came pouring in over the radio.

"What the fuck…?"

There was a brigade's worth of marine mages out there, but they clearly had no hope of defeating the enemy *battalion*. It was like watching a bunch of Boy Scouts running up and taking a swing at finely tuned instruments of war.

"*These men* are Commonwealth marine mages?"

Even though they had a huge advantage in numbers, most of the Commonwealth's soldiers were on the verge of having a mental breakdown. Drake couldn't believe what he was seeing.

It would be understandable if they didn't have the numbers to match the enemy or were at least giving as good as they got considering their tactical advantages. There was precedent for imperial aerial mages turn-ing into ruthless barbarians on the battlefield. Drake had seen this for himself.

But what he was seeing now… The marine mages were supposed to be the pride of the Commonwealth, but even a brigade of them wasn't putting up much of a fight. As shock and doubt gripped his heart, Drake shook his head and took a few deep breaths to collect himself.

He couldn't do anything but watch as events played out. If he ever felt the need to avert his eyes, he knew it wouldn't be long before he became the enemy's new prey. Still, it was the definition of an unbearable sight.

He watched as young soldiers were stripped of their defensive shells with optical sniping formulas before falling to their deaths. They were amateurs, too inexperienced to avoid enemy fire or make use of optical deception formulas.

They were like lambs led to the slaughter, unable to fly properly—many could barely float in place. He wouldn't have known they were soldiers had it not been for their uniforms. It was a hard sight to take in for someone who'd been an officer since before the onset of the war. He wanted to shake his head and pretend it wasn't happening.

That it was all just a bad dream. The Commonwealth marine mage troops were supposed to be the toughest of the tough. It should've been impossible for any of them to falter like this.

Nevertheless, he couldn't escape this reality. Why was that? Because he could picture the bitter face Commander Ballmer would make! He could hear him lamenting over his young soldiers and their lack of training!

"Ah, son of a bitch."

Whenever he had to work together with older officers such as Colonel Mikel and Commander Ballmer, he always ended up having to face this harsh reality. Commanders were always older, and soldiers were always younger. Anyone who fit in between was already resting in peace.

And today, yet again, Drake would watch mere children go to their graves. He could only hope that the ships below would be able to pick up as many downed mages as they could.

"Fledglings, he called them. That certainly wasn't an understatement."

Drake knew it was too late for him to be having this realization.

Despite how much he wanted to intervene, there wasn't much he could actually do. He played with the thought of casting some long-range optical formulas of his own, but it was too risky considering how tangled up the two sides had gotten.

Shaken to the core, Lieutenant Colonel Drake confirmed something with his subordinate to take his mind off the mess.

"C'mon, these must be our bottom-of-the-barrel mages, right?"

"Not at all! Look, they're able to fly."

He couldn't believe what the man, a friend of his, was saying. *He makes it sound like the newer recruits don't even know how to fly.*

"Wait, you call that flying?"

While the marine mages were regularly touted as the masters of three-dimensional warfare, the ones currently in the sky were clearly still stuck on their second dimension. Without any awareness of the space above or below them, they were being served up on a platter by the cunning imperial mage troops.

"They're practically drowning out there."

Drake said this with a sullen expression, but his subordinate half scolded him with his response.

"Ah, right. I forgot how much time you spent in the east, Lieutenant Colonel. Turnover is high in the homeland nowadays."

"So you're saying this is standard?"

To Drake's dismay, his subordinate answered with a firm yes.

"General Ballmer is one of the better commanders. The army has to rush through training as quickly as possible to get new recruits up and running. It's impressive that he's gotten them to the point where they can move like a unit."

Hold the phone—Lieutenant Colonel Drake almost started trembling, and not because of the battle that played out before him. These shoddy mages were considered some of the *better* ones?

He watched as the enemy effortlessly peeled off their protective films with explosion formulas. They call these mages *up to par*? The hard-as-nails machines that the Federation fielded could withstand anything short of a direct hit from an optical sniping formula.

Drake gave his fellow ace a depressed look, and he replied with a simple answer.

"Think of it as a pseudo-unit—they're almost like real mages."

"You can't possibly think that's a good way of putting it."

Unable to hide his shock, he was overcome with the urge to jump into the fray and help his allies as they were mercilessly mowed down by the enemy.

"Looks more like a fire that needs putting out," he suggested, to which his partner gave a nod. The ace mages knew they could stand by idly as the situation grew worse and worse.

They needed to intervene.

"We have to do something. Damn it, I wish we had a marine mage battalion from before the war!"

"On top of the brigade out there? That's asking for a lot, Colonel."

"They're still in training, so you can't count them. Who would've thought we'd be fighting a war with children on the front line. I wish someone told me this is what I was getting into beforehand."

Drake scoffed and shook his head. He knew that they didn't prepare enough for this war.

Ever since its onset, the entire war has been controlled by the imperial war machine—it decided where and when the fights happened.

Now the Commonwealth was paying for it with the blood of their young.

Thus, he could only watch as imperial mages used magic to shower the ocean below with the fresh blood of mages who were mere children.

"Fucking hell. If there really is a god, I want to clock him in the head one day!"

The injustice of the situation was absurd, and he found it harder and harder to keep looking away from it. Too many lives have been paid to the god of death; it was time to do something.

"Daniel 01, Daniel 01, this is Pirate Commander. Requesting emergency permission to join the fight. All reserve soldiers are ready for action! Make the call!"

"Pirate Commander, this is Daniel 06. Please hold!"

"Huh?"

The voice that answered him wasn't the brigade commander but his aide?

Were things too chaotic for him to personally handle requests?

It was hard to make the call to move in without Commander Ballmer's permission. Should they respect their role as reserve soldiers?

With the way things were, the battle was going to end with them doing nothing but watching helplessly.

The situation wasn't good—the brigade was slowly being broken up and crushed piecemeal. They could hear Commander Ballmer's aide trying to raise his voice on the radio in an attempt to bring some semblance of control to the line.

All this did was serve to spread more fear and panic.

Drake wondered, *Should I jump in on the radio?* He didn't want to make things tougher for the commanding officers who were already under immense pressure…

This inner conflict he found himself struggling with would be brought to an abrupt end by outside forces. It was like a battle-ax came chopping the knot that had been welling up inside of him.

Then it happened soon after the enemy company split into two groups.

"Daniel 01 down! Daniel 01 down!"

A brigade officer could be heard screaming this over the radio. The panic in his voice was palpable. The worst imaginable turn of events had happened.

"Wh—?!"

This can't be happening, Drake wanted to shout.

The Commonwealth's brigade had been completely dismantled by a single battalion. The worst part was it had ended with the death of the very leader who had been trying to bring the chaos back under control.

Ah, right…

Decapitation tactics were the Empire's forte.

It was the Devil of the Rhine they were fighting—Commander Ballmer was the obvious first choice for their surgical attacks.

Drake could see that the battle was already playing out exactly as the enemy had planned it.

What was their next goal? This was also obvious. It had to be warships that chased their allies below. He could already see them effortlessly streaking down toward the Commonwealth fleet below. This was bad.

Drake knew it from his core.

The girl out there was the Devil of the Rhine, and she was free to act as she pleased. The situation couldn't get any worse than this. They needed to do anything they could to stop her from having her way.

Lieutenant Colonel Drake decided to take matters into his own hands.

"Pirate Commander to all marine mage units! Pirate Commander to all marine mage units! I'll be taking over command for this battle!"

It didn't matter if he had to force his way onto the battlefield. In fact, it was this sort of forced momentum that often turned the tides of a battle. This was no time to remain calm. The only way to get a positive number from a negative number was to multiply it with another negative number. Drake flew off at full speed. He rapidly climbed as he entered the area of operations. He was about to show them all how a true marine mage could fight.

"Get a hold of yourselves! Look at their numbers! They're still human! You can kill them! Calm down and raise your damn weapons!"

Drake was fortunate to have had his run-in with the Devil of the Rhine in the east, where he also commanded young soldiers. Thanks to that, he knew what he needed to tell them in order to bring them back into the fray.

He counted himself lucky for the accursed experience. *Now go to hell, you bastard.*

"This is war! Shoot to kill and become a hero! Use your weapons! Don't get shot down! Look for the enemy and fire! Don't lose sight of them! Kill them all!"

He shouted over and over on the radio, telling the soldiers what they needed to do. He assured them that they could do it and that the enemy wasn't immortal.

Drake shouted like a beast, but his orders were simple enough to bring the lost soldiers to their senses. He moved to the very front of the line and charged in screaming.

Being calm on the battlefield was always the best course of action, but that wasn't something new soldiers were capable of doing.

Instead of asking for what he couldn't have, Drake made use of the next best thing that he had on hand. He rallied and emboldened his soldiers.

"Marine mage company, charge! Let's show the young mages how to kill!"

What a terrible sight to see.

The Commonwealth soldiers weren't charging in as soldiers but as killers. This was essentially the failure of the military as an organization. But it was the only way Lieutenant Colonel Drake could come up with to get his men to fight the way they needed to. He had to rally them in some way to change the flow of battle.

Any kind of momentum was good momentum, even if it was fueled by hysteria.

To really kick his units into gear, he needed to give them a taste of hope. To do this, he was going to need to ease the mounting enemy pressure on the battlefield. In other words, he was going to need to be their shield.

Hopefully, this would give them the time they need to pull themselves together. Hopefully, it would bring back their will to fight. Hopefully, friendly reinforcements would show up on the horizon.

He only had hope to rely on at this point.

Either way, the only thing he could do was endure until whatever hope decided to show up.

"Time for the adults to show the kids a thing or two!"

》》》   **THE SAME DAY, 203RD AERIAL MAGE BATTALION**   《《《

War never goes the way one hopes it will.

After dominating the enemy brigade, my plan was to hold a little get-together with the enemy fleet, where I intended on giving them a couple explosion formulas as gifts. This got canceled when my adjutant warned of a tactless new enemy.

"Lieutenant Colonel, new mage troops have joined the battle."

I look over to the area she pointed out and see enemy mages quickly approaching.

They're coming in a little too quick. At a glance, I can tell that these mages are far more skilled than the brigade we'd just taken apart.

While their numbers are nothing too concerning, I can tell this company of mages that's been kept in reserve knows how to fight. The 203rd had no choice but to hit the brigade with everything they had from the very beginning, so seeing that the Commonwealth saved the best for last makes me want to cry foul play.

A company joining the fight won't have any major effect on the outcome of the battle.

A flawless company, however, could easily change the pace of battle.

Were they using the brigade as a meat shield before sending in the real powerhouses? It reminds me of the Federation. I have to admit that I never imagined in a million years the Commonwealth would play such a card.

I scoff at that thought and give myself a self-deprecating chuckle.

"They've tricked us."

We were too fixated on our prey and completely missed the forest for the trees. I remember the day when I lost most of my troops in the Northern Sea.

The same potential for heavy losses rears its ugly head again. No, it's worse than that.

During that battle, at least we could still expect replacements. I went into this fully knowing that we aren't going to get replacements anymore... And that was after being told that I should be grateful I have a full battalion in the first place. This was said to me by a member of the General Staff Office speaking to their strongest aerial mage battalion.

In other words, this couldn't possibly get any worse.

I feel a chill run down my spine at the thought of losing any of my subordinates.

The Commonwealth always brings out their best when it comes to love and war. Damn it.

"Duck hunt over! The duck hunt is over!"

Unable to completely shake the feeling of unease, I send that warning over the radio.

"New enemies have appeared, and they know what they're doing!"

I wave my hands and point out the incoming Commonwealth mages. Thankfully, my troops know exactly what I mean. Having previously split up to divide the brigade into small pieces for defeat in detail, my companies form back up in a new formation.

The perfect way they reorganize themselves without showing even a hint of fatigue is almost beautiful. They probably wouldn't suffer too much return fire were they to attack the ships below. We're actually in a good position to set a destroyer or two ablaze. In the same vein, we could also easily beat a hasty retreat if need be.

But they are currently in the midst of a battle with a brigade. At the end of the day, mages are a product of science. They are susceptible to wear and tear, and their ammunition is not unlimited. If we're supposed to create some sort of alchemy-like miracle, I'm going to need dozens more of my Elinium Type 95 orbs.

The Type 97 Assault Computation Orb is an impressive piece of gear, but they are still within the realm of reason. How's our ammo looking? Worst-case scenario, could we somehow manage the rest with only orb formulas?

That wouldn't be a problem against an unskilled enemy. Everything changes if we're facing a logical enemy, especially the type who is willing to use their own troops as a shield.

"How scary...to think they'd use their younger soldiers as cannon fodder..."

I didn't expect this fight to devolve into an all-out war like this.

I grit my teeth as I only just barely manage to keep a *Those cheaters* comment to myself.

I can't get over how unfair the whole situation is. I also see my soldiers as a form of meat shield and an important one at that. This should be self-evident. All humans value their own lives over others. But are humans not social animals?

I can't shake off my surprise at the fact that the enemy would use such a strategy so blatantly.

No, no, no.

The fact that Commonwealth mages came flying at us the way they did is also hard to comprehend.

Are they sane? Should I take them off my list of potential employers? Either way, this is hardly the time to be thinking about this. I cram my anxiety into a deep corner of my mind and quickly focus on how to approach the new fight.

"Deputy, how do you think we should cook these new enemies?"

"...I don't like the turn this has taken. It makes me shudder to think they've played a trick like this."

"Good thinking. Damn the Commonwealth. They were hiding soldiers who know how to fight. What a loathsome tactic. Never thought they'd use their younger soldiers as cannon fodder."

What started out as picking on a weaker enemy turned out to be a calculating trap.

Keeping a fleet lying in wait for the Empire's naval squadron wasn't enough. They had to assert dominance over the sky as well.

I want to turn tail and run right this second, but...

Sadly, my position prevents me from doing so. Getting the mages out of there would be simple, but we need to buy enough time for the navy to put some distance between themselves and the Commonwealth. This is why I can't stand those sluggish ships!

"There are some real cunning bastards on the enemy's side, smart enough to use their newer soldiers as shields. I should be the last person to say this, but it feels like we've been at war for too long."

I air my grumbles out over the radio, and First Lieutenant Serebryakov interjects.

"Should we have gone easier on them, then?"

"Do you want to be the one to tell your comrades' families the bad news if they don't make it home? I prefer to limit the crying to the families of my enemies."

Keeping your stakeholders happy is a key part of working for any organization. It goes without saying that I would love to do something for a potential new employer if it were in my power to do so. I know that it's important to make a good impression *somehow*! That said, it would be a huge mistake for me to try and do such a thing under these circumstances.

It would be incredibly idiotic for a person looking for a new job to let their coworkers know that's what they're doing. You need to get your new job first, and then you can slowly ease the people around you into the idea.

It doesn't work the other way around.

The moment your coworkers see you as *someone who wants to change jobs*, no matter how valuable a human resource you may be, you're labeled as unreliable.

I can attest to this as someone with expertise as an HR representative.
A worker loses the quality known as trust the moment the employer

identifies them as *ungrateful*. Losing that trust is like getting cut off from oxygen. If they don't have a new air tank in the form of their next employer lined up beforehand, they'll choke.

This is why I know the decision I need to make and refuse to let my companions down. It'd be nice if things were easy for once, though.

"We'll knock them out of the sky. Stay close to your wingmates. We'll end this with one final blow."

I keep my eyes on the enemies while I listen to a chorus of *rogers* respond over the radio. If I had a chance...I was originally planning on hitting them with a long-range formula, but it's probably better not to get greedy.

The incoming Commonwealth mages unleash some optical sniping formulas as suppressing fire, but it's easily avoided. They also make quick work of our deception formulas as well. Their skills as mages are palpable.

At this point, I notice something peculiar about how our enemies are moving.

"Those mages are moving strangely."

"What?"

"See for yourself, First Lieutenant," I say while gesturing toward the enemy just before I pick up shouting coming over the radio.

I can hear something on the open channel. It's in Commonwealth.

What are they saying? I listen closely.

"This is war! Shoot to kill and become a hero! Use your weapons! Don't get shot down! Look for the enemy and fire! Don't lose sight of them! Kill them!"

I hear a litany of revolting phrases one after the other. I can't believe my ears.

"Disgusting..."

I wince at the sheer barbarism of our enemies. This man is inciting his troops to commit simple murder.

"So what they say is true. There's nothing gentle about Commonwealth men the moment they step away from the mainland."

I didn't expect to hear my adjutant giggling in response.

"Listen to them, Colonel. It's abhorrent, isn't it? They want to murder us."

"Indeed. I am speechless. To think things could get this barbaric."

"Maybe we should let them know who they're dealing with by show-ing them some real violence."

I should probably correct this kind of talk. I'm able to recognize my own mistake when I've made one. The Commonwealth soldiers aren't the only ones who are broken.

Now that this has been established, I realize I'm facing an existential problem.

I must be the only sane person left on the battlefield.

He knew he was the one who shocked the fear out of the young soldiers by riling them up.

Lieutenant Colonel Drake knew that he had created a conundrum for himself as he flew straight toward his enemies.

It felt like he had created an entire brigade's worth of First Lieutenant Sues.

He threw away any semblance of control that Commander—no, the now-deceased *Lieutenant General Ballmer* had instilled within them and transformed the battlefield into a version of hell on earth.

"We've picked up the Empire's radio channel. It's pretty bad."

Lieutenant Colonel Drake furrowed his brow at his subordinate's report.

"What, more taunting?"

His last encounter with an imperial mage was still fresh in his mind, but what he was about to hear would cause him to sigh.

What is with those imperial dogs? Evidently, they were urging their troops to murder the Commonwealth troops. And here he thought they would try to retreat, but it looked like they were ready to fight to the death.

"Hell…would it hurt to flinch at least a little?"

"What should we do, Colonel? Should we keep going?"

He blinked for a moment, caught off guard by his adjutant's words.

"You bet your ass we are. If we're going to die, it's going to be on a battlefield."

"Roger!"

*　　*　　*

And thus, the two crazed commanders on either side both gave their orders.

""Fire at will!""

The two sides laid into their enemies with everything they had at the very same time.

A battle of raw firepower unfolded where the elite mages on either side prioritized a quick victory over preserving their strength, and it was an endurance test for both commanders.

They gambled their victory on massive formulas, creating chains of explosions that lit up the night sky.

The air around the explosions twisted and warped, an amalgam of science and magic screeching back and forth as the veteran mages on either side poured every fiber of their being into maintaining their defensive shells to stay alive.

The atmosphere around them shook with a thick reverberation that even these skilled mages had never experienced before.

""Stay in formation!""

Both commanders knew exactly what they needed to do.

They needed their sides to stay together.

They needed to keep the outgoing violence tightly coordinated.

Each of the battalions fought as a unit.

At lung-collapsing altitudes, expert mages on either side relied on the uppermost limits of their knowledge and experience as the battle raged on. They constantly used explosion formulas for suppression—though they constantly looked for the opportunity to land the occasional kill. Lure and deception formulas laced the smoke-filled air.

Both sides closed the distance, magic blades at the ready, fully prepare for hand-to-hand combat in the air...but after multiple people demonstrated their willingness to use explosion formulas at point-blank range, an uneasy distance emerged.

They ebbed and flowed, going back and forth as they read each other's movement at the highest level.

Nevertheless, there were no signs of either side letting up.

Chapter V

Tanya flew at the center of her formation, glaring at her enemies with malicious eyes.

The Commonwealth reserve unit had brought the brigade back to its feet. That said, even if quantity has a quality all its own, a herd of sheep led by a lion will still fall prey to a pack of wolves.

For the Imperial Army, however, this turn of events happened after they'd already taken out their primary target.

It was like an utter nightmare.

The same could be said for Lieutenant Colonel Drake, who had successfully brought his troops back from the brink. The only actual authority he had here was over a lone company. All semblance of command that Commander Ballmer had strung together for the brigade had been long lost.

This left him with a panicked mob and a single company of mages.

He had commanded a group of soldiers who might charge ahead at the drop of a hat to just fire at will—there was no way for them to use their numbers effectively at this point.

The only thing he could rely on was his company of ace mages. In this regard, and to his great annoyance, the enemy battalion was under the command of the Devil of the Rhine. It wasn't just any battalion but a battalion of elite mages.

To think there were still that many skilled mages even left in the war! Their flying seemed largely unaffected by the altitude, and they were able to maintain their formation when flying through three dimensions. To put it bluntly, this was the epitome of unfairness.

Ah—a single groan escapes each of the commanders' mouths into the war-torn sky.

Both commanders told themselves that their enemy was no longer human and were fully convinced that the enemy had the advantage in numbers.

Neither of them could escape. Neither of them could show weakness in front of their soldiers. They both bore the burden of protecting friendly ships far below.

In both of their hearts, they cursed the entire battle with the worst words they could come up with.

They also both cursed their superiors who put them in this situation.

"Damn it! We're always behind in numbers!"

Tanya lamented about how her enemies were always able to make their comebacks with numbers ever since her time on the eastern front. She wanted nothing more than for her battles to be simple for once. *War shouldn't be fought unless it could be done safely and easily!*

Not that she could say any of that out loud—she needed every ounce of oxygen to stay in the air.

Lieutenant Colonel Drake, on the other side, also cursed the war he hated so very deeply.

"Damn it! It looks like I'm going to get caught up in another exorcism! Where are the damn priests when you need them?!"

Is there really a God watching over this world? If anything, Drake thought it much more likely a witch was watching over them from her accursed cauldron. He didn't care who they were—he only wanted them to hand over a marine mage battalion that had formed before the war!

With his mind full of idle complaints, Drake channeled mana into his computation orb while he endured a headache to cast his formulas. Maintaining control of his troops, he directed his subordinates to focus fire on a single point.

My damn head hurts—he cursed the heavens once more.

Coincidentally, the commanders on both sides came to the same conclusion at that very moment.

""Why does it always have to be this way?!""

They both lamented over having to pick up the pieces of somebody else's mess as they unleashed sky-warping formulas at each other.

Humans tend to want what they can't have. The grass is always greener on the other side. A battlefield, however, is not the right place to dwell on such feelings.

Both sides needed to suppress whatever perceived strength they thought the enemy had with their own firepower. Ignoring holes in their own formation, they tried to surge forward and exploit holes in the enemy formation. In order to live, both Degurechaff and Drake—two lieutenant colonels forced to fight the same war—barked their orders in angry voices.

The side that took control of the skies for a second time would be the four companies that made up the imperial mage battalion.

"Each company! Charge! Don't get boxed in by their suppression fire! Keep them pinned down with your speed! Move, move, move!"

Those four companies were like four separate heads of a Hydra.

Chapter V

After deciding to suppress her enemy with the many heads, Tanya tasked her units with forming a new formation and then cutting the throat of their new target—Lieutenant Colonel Drake.

But there wasn't a marine mage in the land who knew more about the Empire's decapitation tactics than Drake. He could analyze and react to their movements with a speed that was unlike anything Tanya had ever seen before.

His short chain of command allowed him to deploy his forces swiftly. He needed to make use of his numbers, even if it meant taking control of the entire sky by filling it with fire.

"Concentrated fire! Focus your fire! Stay calm and use our numbers against them! Keep them pinned down!"

Drake ordered what was left of the brigade to open fire as he unleashed his own formulas in an attempt to neutralize incoming enemy attacks. The newer recruits were only able to fire in a straight line, but his company of aces could use this fire to create a net capable of keeping the enemy away.

It went without saying that such suppression fire wasn't outside the realm of the 203rd's imagination.

Charging an enemy always entailed braving some amount of fire. It meant plunging directly into the enemy's formation, after all, so their success depended entirely on their ability to survive any withering fire that came their way.

The highly skilled mages maneuvered their way through enemy fire, but what happened next left Tanya awestruck.

"Dispersing randomly while advancing... Wait, they're firing back while strafing?!"

The mage brigade pulling off such a counter meant that they could see through Tanya's maneuvers. It was no mystery that the Commonwealth reserve mages were highly skilled, but them countering her evasive charging tactics so completely caught her off guard.

Tanya wasn't the only one in awe, though, as the same thing was happening to Drake on the other side.

From his perspective, the enemy had evaded his net of fire that he'd hoped would obliterate them. He scoffed to himself and shouted at the top of his lungs in an attempt to get his men to focus their fire even more. Tanya, however, wasn't the type to let something like this go unnoticed.

The enemy had made a fundamental change in how they're moving. She laughed bitterly at herself and got ready to engage with the enemy company that she believed was responsible for this dramatic change.

"Everything changed ever since that new company joined. They must be…a command section. What a pain in the ass."

A single company shouldn't have had this much impact on the tide of the battle. The issue was this company knew how to fight, and they'd successfully rekindled the broken brigade. The way the battle was panning out told Tanya this company was something they couldn't just ignore.

Tanya rubbed her temples while she dipped and dodged through a hail of enemy formulas. While still imperfect, they'd turned a useless brigade into an absolute force to be reckoned with.

Tanya still couldn't believe what she was watching. This mage company was far too dangerous to let survive beyond this battle.

"Adjutant, reorganize the troops. We're going in."

"We're going to force our way through?"

"That's right." Tanya affirms her question.

The risk was immense, but it was a risk that had to be taken. The enemy they were facing was a real threat. Forgoing this preventative surgery could lead to a disaster down the line.

She didn't have time to worry about the repercussions of surgery. Only necessity dictated what she had to do now.

"We have to do it. We need to take out their leader, and fast."

If they left him alone, he would grow into something that can't be quelled.

Tanya made her decision quickly, and First Lieutenant Serebryakov came to the same conclusion at nearly the same speed.

"Roger. Let's put out this fire while it's still small."

The imperial commander and her adjutant both agreed on the decision and instantly leaped into action.

They abandoned maneuvering around the enemy for a better position and began climbing as fast as possible.

They were followed by the rest of their battalion, with the entire imperial unit all surging upward at once. They breezed past ten thousand before settling at around fourteen thousand. This is well over two thousand feet of what should have been physically possible with their machinery. High up in the sky, the battalion began to create a new penetration formation.

It was an altitude far too high for any harassing fire from below to reach. Realizing this, Drake shouted out, "Damn it!"

For a single moment, it seemed like the enemy might have been putting distance between themselves and the Commonwealth. It was a brief moment, but for the newer troops, it was more than enough for them to lose their nerve.

Drake didn't even have to look at them to know.

The enemy had thrown off their rhythm.

"Fuck, fuck, fuck!"

Where the hell is that guardian angel of mine? Are they off in some random pub getting hammered? Fate can be such a bitch!

Why does life have to be so full of difficulties like this?!

Drake relied on his ace company to provide a base of fire…but it wasn't enough to defend against the enemy plunging into them with this great an altitude difference.

Drake had experienced the same zoom-and-boom tactic back in the Federation. He could feel his wounded shoulder crying out to him.

The enemy was going to bull-rush them. Drake recognized this as soon as he saw them start climbing. He knew exactly what they were doing, but he couldn't do anything about it other than curse this twist of fate.

"Not this again! Is it just going to be a repeat of last time?!"

He could see what direction the battle was headed in and knew that he'd only have one chance to attack. He needed to make sure that one chance would be enough for him to slay his foe.

Filled with the determination to annihilate his target once and for all, he began to cast a new formula.

Drake wasn't going to let the opportunity slip through his fingers this time. He watched and waited for his chance.

His eyes were set on Tanya. She was able to make out his face as well, and she let out a massive groan on the inside.

"Hmm?!"

She suddenly recognized his face. There was only one person who came to mind when she wondered who it could be. It was none other than the loony mage she had met out east! What in the world was he doing here?!

She questioned his presence but quickly came to terms with it.

The only sort of soldier who could ever use comrades as a barrier in battle was someone who had fought alongside the Commies. It appeared that these ruthless tactics were the result of nurture not nature.

As frightening as this was to learn, Tanya knew she needed to kill the man here and now.

Fully determined to do just that, Tanya shouted.

"You freak! I'll kill you for sure this time!"

She wasn't the only one shouting—Drake roared from below as well.

"Rusted Silver! You're going die today!"

These two hounds clashed for victory and survival.

Both hounds, though, were very intelligent.

They were creatures of the modern age; instead of fangs, they girded themselves with steel and magic.

They were both military beasts—that was exactly why Tanya and Drake both pegged the other as insane and what brought them to the logical conclusion that they had absolutely no choice but to kill each other with their very next attack.

For better or for worse, they were both at a similar level when it came to making tactical decisions. They were both expert mages—pros when it comes to the fundamentals of aerial combat.

In other words, they both chose the only reliable way to kill each other.

And that was to use explosion formulas at ultra–close range.

The plural is important here. They were both planning to use multiple formulas.

An explosion formula at such a distance would endanger the caster as much as it threatened the enemy. It was essentially just one step below suicide bombing.

Be that as it may, what would happen if the caster was able to time their attack perfectly? What if they were able to transfer all their magic into their protective film and defensive shell immediately after casting?

The decision to use explosions at this range would be suicidal for most mages. These two, however, both calculated that there was a tiny window of opportunity where they could pull off the seemingly impossible.

They both made the same conclusion. That they needed to bring their enemy within range, then throw up a strong enough shield to survive the ensuing catastrophe. Even if they were caught up in the explosion, as long as they could shield themselves, then they would have a chance to survive.

The chance was admittedly small, but if there was a way to come out of this alive, then their decision was already made. They shared similar mindsets in this regard as well.

They both knew that their best chance to defeat the enemy was to blow themselves up. Unfortunately for them both, this was far less certain if the enemy decided to try the same thing.

They both unleashed their explosion formulas at close range, but by the time they picked up on the fact that the resulting detonations were more powerful than they had anticipated, it was already too late. They were both blown away, but Lieutenant Colonel Drake still poured all his mana into his defenses.

He even abandoned his flight magic.

Maintaining only his breathing enhancements, he reflexively curled into a ball as he plummeted through the burning sky, just barely managing to keep himself alive.

Tanya, on the other hand…took more drastic measures.

She begrudgingly committed to her decision and pushed all four cores in her Type 95 to their absolute limits. Quietly humming a hymn, Tanya drew upon her well of mana to create a powerful attack.

She chose to maintain her flight formula and opted to cut off a handful of other formulas. She continued to use magic to create her own oxygen, and she still had enough left to raise a proper defensive shell thanks to the little relic known as the Type 95 Computation Orb.

The difference in their orbs would be the determining factor in the face-off.

Though they both executed the same exact move, the difference in their equipment led to entirely different results.

The loser of the battle only barely managed to survive as he was sent hurtling toward the ground while trying to get his flight formula up and working. And the victor—she flew high above him as her hymn shifted from a crescendo into a triumphant cry. Taking full advantage of this, Tanya began pelting her falling opponent with magic.

The battle was a one-on-one between the two commanding officers.

A rare sight to see in modern warfare, but its effect on their respective forces' morale was tremendous.

The winning side stole all momentum from the losing side.

And it went without saying that the winning side was perfectly aware of this.

They knew that their victory was due solely to their superior technology and not technical skill.

At the end of the day, a victory is a victory, and a loss is a loss.

Tanya was determined to let the whole battlefield know who the victor was. She shook her head to forget the damned prayer and took a deep breath.

After recomposing herself, she barked out her next orders.

"I've taken out the enemy commander! Now it's time to show them what true violence looks like!"

It was important to capitalize on opportunities whenever they presented themselves. The instincts needed to make this happen were what separated the veterans from the soldiers on the battlefield.

It came down to pure violence.

Or the right attack.

Like Kellermann during the Battle of the Marengo, the imperial mages needed to make the most of this opportunity.

"Volley fire! Use three explosion formulas!"

Three companies of mages, followed closely by a slightly disoriented fourth company, came together as the 203rd Aerial Mage Battalion and unleashed a hail of hellfire. The Commonwealth soldiers could only watch on as their allied marine mages were engulfed by the blazing flames.

"We've taken out the enemy forces! The ships below are vulnerable! We've created a path for our allies!"

First Lieutenant Grantz looked to Tanya with excited eyes; he's waiting for the command to charge in. She responds to him, though, by shaking her head and alerting him that now is their time to retreat.

"This isn't the east, First Lieutenant."

"But, Commander? Shouldn't we…?"

"Remember the basics from the Western Air Battle. The longer we dally, the more likely unexpected guests will show up. We can't afford to stay too long."

Chapter V

Were this the eastern front, where the fighting was spread out over a much wider expanse of land, they may have had the leisure to linger and thoroughly lay waste to their enemies…but these were Commonwealth waters.

The battle was taking place far too close to the enemy's base of operations.

Their mage battalion had already pulled more than their weight in seeing this operation through. They had successfully defanged the brigade of mages that had been the core of their enemy's air defense. All while keeping losses on the imperial side to a minimum.

The fact that they had just been ambushed was what truly convinced Tanya to go with the safer, more conservative course of action. She also didn't feel the need for her battalion to stick its neck out any further for this plan.

"There's no reason for us to risk our lives while our troops are retreating after a failed attempt. I'm not a fan of losing my subordinates for no reason."

"I supposed we've done enough to cover our navy's retreat."

"We have," Tanya confirmed. She was glad First Lieutenant Grantz was a sharp man. If the enemy wasn't going to chase the Imperial Navy, then it should be okay for them to leave. Tanya and her battalion had more than earned their salary for the day.

"Now that First Lieutenant Grantz agrees, it's time for us to follow suit and retreat. Please resist the urge to send the enemy any farewell presents."

"What? I assumed you'd send them another farewell letter to poke fun at them…"

Tanya's adjutant seemed surprised, but her colonel simply shook her head.

"Our plan has ended in failure. We're not in the position to ridicule anyone."

Sighs could be heard as the mages quickly withdrew from the area of operations.

It was the same as always.

They had scored another small victory.

It was a valiant victory overshadowed by a thin veil of greater defeat.

That thin veil, however, was more than enough to fully block out their achievements, no matter how brightly they shined.

After all, the Imperial Army had lost the battle. They knocked against the wooden walls of the Commonwealth, only for their fist to bounce right off.

Once all was said and done, Tanya had to think about where she would go next.

"Damn it all. I'm going to give General Romel an earful when I get back."

 THE SAME DAY, WESTERN ARMY GROUP COMMAND FOR THE IMPERIAL ARMY

At this very moment, the barking of a man could be heard coming from the corner of the Western Army Group command center, which was occupied by its owner for once. The first report he had received…was the worst news imaginable. Lieutenant General Romel was struck by the harshness of reality in his own office.

"Shit!"

He paid no mind to the blood streaming from his fist as he slammed it on his desk again.

The report informed him that their troops had encountered enemy forces. Not only that but the ones lying in wait were none other than the mighty Commonwealth fleet. Their original plan was a surprise attack to fulfill a political objective. General Romel had used what little military force he could still muster up for the operation. He knew they didn't stand a chance if they were met with any amount of serious resistance.

This meant that the plan had failed.

The failure of the plan aside, there was an even bigger question that plagued his mind.

"Why?! How did they know?!"

He looked around the room with bloodshot eyes, begging for an answer that was not forthcoming.

Failure was always a possibility from the very start. Lieutenant General Romel only hoped that the plan would go at least half as well as planned.

The fog of war, eh? What a strange and completely accurate phenomenon.
The more time he spent on the battlefield, the more he was faced with random instances of poor luck and profoundly outrageous bouts of incredible luck. The goddess who governed fate could be so utterly cruel. Her whimsy and tendency to play favorites knew no bounds.

Even so, what happened this time was impossible.

Romel never predicted that such a miscarriage of strategy would rear its ugly head.

The general did literally everything imaginable to minimalize risk and maximize his chances for success. He held back nothing in terms of resources in the name of making this plan come together.

He had played every card in hopes of winning this battle. There should've been no dead ends.

He did everything humanly possible to make sure it was conducted to a tee. These plans are carried out by people, of course. He knew this—he knew there was a limit to how careful people can be.

Nevertheless, this knowledge didn't stop him from raging at the impossibility of it all.

"Why was the Royal Navy there?!"

Was it a coincidence that the enemy would place their fleet right where the Empire least wanted them to? Any strategist worth his salt could tell they had clearly been lying in wait. He hated it, and as much as he didn't want to accept it, this was the reality of the situation... It meant that top secret information was being leaked to the Commonwealth.

The enemy had detected their plan and intercepted them... It wasn't as if they were dealing with maneuver warfare in a desert. It would've been different had they acted on false information they intercepted from enemy transmissions...if it was the Empire that had been fooled.

This attack was initiated by the Imperial Army, though. So how did this happen?

"I can't believe this. There's no explanation for it."

He cradled his head; he almost felt like drinking himself into oblivion to forget the problem for even a moment. Nicotine would have to do for now... He composed himself but only for a moment.

Romel roamed his office aimlessly like a wounded beast when he realized there was a sound coming from somewhere. A phone was ringing.

Chapter V

Just as it was starting to get on his nerves, he then came to another realization. It was the navy. It was a report from Fleet Command—the report he wanted to hear most. Or at least, that's what it should've been. The general wasn't in the correct state of mind to hope for the best.

He took a moment to catch his breath before picking up the phone.

"Hello… What are the losses?"

His furrowed brow relaxed slightly when he heard the words *successful retreat* and *minimal casualties*.

Though their plan had failed, it hadn't ended in catastrophe for their forces. It was the most minor of silver linings.

Had he been blessed by the gods? Or was it his inability to capture the Goddess of Fate that caused his failure?

The general mulled over it for a moment, but he had no idea which it might be. Nevertheless, this was a new development. Lieutenant General Romel finally had the chance to get more details on their defeat.

"I'm glad the navy came out of this largely unscathed. When can I expect a more detailed report?"

They told him that he'd have it as soon as they returned to the harbor.

He hung up the phone. He was feeling more impatient than eager… but if he needed to wait, it would give him an opportunity to catch his breath and shed his frustration.

"Wait, wait. That's it… I need to calm myself a bit. Somebody…! Get me a hot coffee!"

The poor soul who brought him his piping-hot coffee had the misfortunate of watching the general practically inhale it next to a mountain of cigarette ashes as he tried to get his bearings on the situation.

He needed it to bring himself back from the shock of the entire ordeal.

His stomach churned as the hot liquid, which burnt like hellfire, came flowing in… The pain helped anchor him to reality as it mixed with the ever-present stress of overwork.

And thus, he was able to achieve the appearance of calmness when he received the long-awaited report from the navy.

Everything was riding on this report.

It was a thin brief. This was because it was their initial after-action report. Either way, the sparse details were more than enough to quench Lieutenant General Romel's thirst for information.

What caught his eye the most was the enemy's formation. It affirmed the hunch he had when he first caught word of their force's interception.

It was already suspicious that the Commonwealth had their Home Fleet waiting for the Imperial Navy in the channel. What he saw on those pages turned his doubt into conviction.

"They aren't even trying to hide it anymore."

It was more than evident that the enemy fleet had prepared multiple fast-moving vessels to intercept the naval squadron he had put together with an emphasis on speed. Not only that but they even had the audacity to bring a mage brigade with them. Normally, Commonwealth fleets were never accompanied by mage units larger than a regiment. The notion that they'd coincidentally deploy an entire brigade was absolutely preposterous. While it was the Home Fleet he was dealing with, massing an entire brigade of mages was no easy task.

An even bigger problem presented itself in the attached report provided by Lieutenant Colonel Degurechaff.

The title alone was enough to floor him.

The emergency report was titled "Enemy Mage Movements—The Use of Soldiers as Sandbags/Similarities to Eastern Battle Tactics," and it spelled out the lieutenant colonel's awe and rage at the lengths the Commonwealth had been willing to go to during their battle.

It was much worse than a simple leak in information.

Only the insane would think this was all a coincidence. Every sign pointed to the enemy having predicted the Empire would use their prized 203rd Aerial Mage Battalion and crafting a direct counter to fight them off.

"Looks like there's a leak that needs fixing…"

Romel had learned about the importance of keeping information secret in the southern theater.

He had experienced a battle that could only be won by deceiving their enemies with false information. It was a terrible battle to fight, and one he would never forget. Ever since he almost fell for the false report sent by the François Republic in the desert, he made it a point to trust his eyes and ears while keeping his lips shut tight…

This experience was what made him very picky about the intelligence agents he worked with. The general was confident that he put more effort into his collection of information and analysis when proposing this plan compared to his colleagues.

"But I guess I'm no match for the pros."

He couldn't hold back his grimace.

"At the end of the day, I'm nothing more than a general. A senior staff officer. Intelligence is by no means my forte."

He learned how to win battles at the war college, not how to conduct espionage. The most he had ever learned about the subject was to make sure all communication was encrypted.

Quite frankly, he was in no place to speak about the subject.

The Empire had no infrastructure for waging systematic information warfare...

"Those damn Commonwealth spies. Nothing is out of their reach."

Lieutenant General Romel shook his head in frustration.

The situation couldn't get any worse. What bugged him the most was the need to be suspicious of people who were ostensibly on his side. He didn't know which stupid soldier had screwed up where, but the fact that the core of his plan had been leaked to the enemy meant that they needed to conduct an audit of the entire army.

"...Could it be our codes? Or a traitor? Perhaps a spy? Or just simple human error?"

Every question was met with suspicion.

What is this, some sort of spy novel? Romel grumbled on the inside—but oh, how much more complicated and mysterious nonfiction could be. What plagued his mind the most was the question of where the leak came from.

"Damn it, I can't be sure of anything now, can I?"

General Romel cursed himself as he—without even realizing it—reached for another cigarette. He bit down on the butt while his mind raced.

Should he mobilize every intelligence agent they had?

"That won't be enough."

It stood to reason that he would need to reorganize the entire western front.

There had yet to be any signs of the Federation Army having insight on the Empire's war efforts in the east...but either way, they needed to circumvent the leak.

But how was he going to get the word out?

He slammed his fist onto his desk again. *That's right—this is the over-arching problem.*

He reflexively brought his hand to his head to keep himself from getting dizzy.

Even the integrity of the Empire's encryption was in question. He couldn't use the radio at a time like this. If he was going to be careful, he needed to send the message directly through a fellow officer.

But who could he trust? There were many officers. But...how was he supposed to trust any of them? The fact that there may have been a leak meant that no precautions could be considered too careful.

Even more frightening was the possibility of handing critical information directly to their spy.

When it came to the mobile headquarters he used on a daily basis, it was very difficult to take counterintelligence measures comparable to when he was at his base of operations. Not to mention the possibility that the enemy could simply be taking advantage of a flaw in their system...

"Fucking hell!"

He had a bad feeling—the same feeling he had out in the desert when enemy snipers were a constant threat. He knew there were enemies lurking nearby, but he had no idea how to locate them!

It felt like there was a gun being pressed against his head.

At this rate, he was a sitting duck—the perfect catch for a hungry hunter on the prowl for dinner. It was only a matter of time before enemy hunters came, smacking their lips.

"With things as they are..."

It was no longer a matter of strategy.

It was something much simpler.

"Even Plan B may be..."

...in danger, he tried to say, but his mind was plagued by too much anxiety to get the full sentence out.

By its very nature, Plan B was meant to be kept secret at any cost. If word got out it was in the works, it could spell the end of the Empire itself.

What were the chances that word had already reached enemy ears? Could they ever get such information during a war like this?

Chapter V

"...Ah, shit, shit, fucking shit."

He almost felt like he could hear the blood draining audibly from his body. His vision blurred, and he just barely managed to hold on to a chair for support before finally falling. He found himself staring at the ceiling from the floor.

He couldn't stop sweating. It wasn't hot in his office. The sweat came from a frigid feeling inside him that ran up and down his spine. His heart wouldn't stop racing.

After two deep breaths, he managed to control his breathing, but his body wouldn't stop quivering.

He'd never felt such fear before, not even on the battlefield. Romel was more nervous than when he gave his first orders as a second lieutenant. He found himself recalling the pain he felt in his stomach the first time he went into battle. Just thinking about it made him almost smile.

His biggest fear used to be making a mistake. But now that very notion was all but laughable. Simple planning mistakes didn't matter at all anymore!

General Romel decided to try and smoke the anxiety out of himself. After failing a few times to get his cigarette lit, he just sat there with the butt wedged between his lips.

What a nightmare.

"Forget politics."

If the Empire really had been infiltrated by an enemy spy, then it could spell disaster for them.

What would happen if the enemies picked up on the General Staff Office's insight regarding the army's inability to continue the war? What would happen then?

The world would probably come together to a bring swift end to their war.

No. The buck wouldn't stop there.

The consequences would be far more decisive than a few countries simply banding together. Should their enemies realize the Empire was on its last legs, they would most definitely place oppressive restrictions on their war-torn nation. The situation was deteriorating in quantifiable terms and with incredible speed.

It also begged the question of whether Ildoa would remain neutral, an issue that had been the source of so much anguish for Lieutenant General Romel when he was down in the south.

"What if we have to fight Ildoa...?"

Even the mere thought of it was enough to make him sick to his core.

With all the fronts they were already fighting on, opening up another one would bring their war machine to a grinding halt. The Empire would surely collapse.

There was no feasible way for the Imperial Army to take on such a task.

The war was already long past a point where it was manageable for the Imperial Army to conduct any meaningful, decisive attacks. At this stage in the game, they had to put their full power into just maintaining the lines where they were.

Should they have to fight Ildoa, there was no hope they could muster up an attack.

"Could we theoretically pull off a defensive war in the mountain region?"

Even for the aggressive Lieutenant General Romel, the only plan of action he could come up with in that war-gaming scenario was to go on the defensive. This was representative of their total lack of options.

The real issue was that the army was quickly running out of soldiers.

He thought about the current state of the Western Army Group. It was already a shell of itself. Official documents showed that most of the former first-class soldiers worn down in the east had either already collapsed or were being used for security purposes in occupied territories. Even lighter-staffed divisions wouldn't amount to much in the current situation where they were too rare to be taken into account.

As a specialist, he knew they wouldn't be able to pull off an attack anytime soon. However...the specialist in him had insight for danger pointed in another direction as well.

"Ildoa is positioned against the Empire like a knife at our throats. What if the Commonwealth or Federation were to advance into the Empire via Ildoa?"

How long would the Imperial Army last against the Federation Army if they were to swing through Ildoa? He needn't even play with the idea for it to send chills down his already ice-cold spine.

At the moment, the Empire was narrowly managing to defend itself on the eastern front.

If forced to simultaneously fight Ildoa in the south, the battle would undoubtedly take place in the mountain range that separated the two countries. It wasn't an environment suited for maneuver warfare, meaning if they were able to create a defensible base there, it would at least be expected to hold for some time.

The fact that it was close to the Empire made it easier to keep supplied as well. It would certainly be much easier to manage than sending soldiers down south again. That's all it was, though. They would inevitably need to take resources earmarked for the east and move them south.

Before long, the Empire would bleed out. It was only a matter of whether it would happen in the east or south.

And again, this was bearing in mind the sheer thinness of the line between the Empire and Ildoa. The general wrestled with this same problem when he was out on the Rhine. It would be fatal for the mainland if they were to suffer a major aerial assault.

"We're barely holding out against the Commonwealth's jabs as it is…"

They wouldn't be able to maintain their air defenses, let alone ground defenses, should their fronts get split up any further. They lacked the equipment, personnel, and everything else they needed to do so.

Two fronts alone were already more than enough to cause fear for him.

While he feared for the future, a single idea crossed his mind.

It came like a flash, as if he didn't think of it himself.

Deep within the confines of Lieutenant General Romel's mind, he thought up one new possibility.

"What if we hit them with a preemptive strike…?"

There was still time to knock out Ildoa before they entered the fray.

If they acted soon, there were still enough resources for them to pull off a full-scale Zettour-style strike.

If they acted soon, before Ildoa could mobilize…it might be possible to knock them out of the war before they considered joining.

It was possible but also purely theoretical.

Though a broken man, General Romel maintained his levelheadedness as he scoffed to himself.

Impossible.

"I can't let fear convince me into committing suicide. The one thing the Empire can't endure is to create even more enemies. Especially now that we can't be sure who to trust within our organization."

At this point, the general's ceaseless tremors came to an end, and he finally managed to light the cigarette that'd been sitting patiently between his lips.

He enjoyed the military tobacco as the tar seeped into his lungs.

The radical thought he had earlier stayed with him, though, like a stain on his brain—a stain in the shape of a high-heeled boot.

From behind the stain, the idea peeked its head a second time.

"Should we take them down while we…?"

The general was interrupted before he could say anything else. His thought was cut off by a commotion coming from outside his office. A slight scowl appeared on his brow before he stood up.

His command center was known for how lively it was…but never to the extent where it completely lost any sense of order.

What's going on? He moved toward the door with an inquisitive expression, only to have it practically kicked in from the other side by an angry magic officer.

"General Romel! I'd like to request an explanation from you!"

The little officer was filled to the brim with anger and resentment.

It was Lieutenant Colonel Degurechaff, and she shouted out General Romel's deepest suspicions.

"Why were the enemies waiting for us?!"

Oh yes.

He greeted her with a grin and sharp eyes. Rusted Silver naturally responded with words of frustration.

"How the hell are we currently handling our secret information?!"

She's absolutely right to be mad. He nodded and continued to grin.

"That's an excellent question, Lieutenant Colonel Degurechaff. Would you like to know the answer?"

"Please, that's exactly what I'm here to find out!"

"I don't know."

The frank way with which the general responded left Tanya almost speechless.

"What?"

Chapter V

What's with that face? What did she expect him to say?

It didn't matter; she would have likely come to the same conclusion as he did. In fact, she probably already had. It was likely why she was visibly angry.

"Either there's a traitor among us, the enemy has deciphered our codes, or some form of human error. Which do you think is most likely?"

"If those are my three options, then I know exactly which it is."

Just as he knew she would.

"If you think you know, then let's hear your answer."

The two of them looked at each other briefly before saying in unison, "It's our codes." Of the three, their encryption deserved the most suspicion. Their agreement was a source of great exasperation for them both, but they knew this was the most likely answer.

That was why they both hoped the other would say something different. Lieutenant General Romel asked Tanya for her reasoning. The answer he received was incredibly logical.

"Would any individual traitor have access to the entire picture? The only way that would be possible is if it were you who was the traitor."

Precisely. Romel was of the same opinion. It was strange. He almost felt angry with how accurate her diagnosis was. The entire thing had him mad.

That was why he decided to lift his own mood by picking on his subordinate.

"Could it not be you as well?"

"What? You think it's me?"

"You were a part of the task force and had access to the entire plan. If you were to try and defect to the Commonwealth, it would've been the perfect bit of information to take with you."

The lieutenant colonel stared back at the general with incredible anxiety pouring from her entire being. The general could feel her beginning to question his sanity.

"I'm just joking with you. You should get a hold of yourself, Colonel."

He kept it to himself that that he was in a similar state only moments ago and flashed her an easy smile. It was times like these where he took pleasure in being able to pick on his younger officers.

Unfortunately, a laugh or two wasn't going to dig them out of this hole. The idea that there might be a traitor was asinine. The Imperial Army conducted thorough background checks on any and all personnel who came into contact with vital information. They had thick files on each and every officer—it was simply how the army operated.

In other words, it was nigh impossible for something as ridiculous as a traitor to be among their ranks.

Which meant...

"...This changes everything. There's no longer a Plan A or B with the way things are now."

Toi, toi, toi

————— Colonel Lergen knocking on the door of the General Staff Office —————

The deputy director's office being enveloped in chaos was a strange sight to see. Though maybe not so strange given a more recent perspective...

There was no shortage of chaos in the Empire as of late.

On the battlefield, experience dictated that there exists a fog of war. Politics, however, were shrouded by a different kind of haze. When stuck in a situation where nobody could make heads or tails of anything, even the cleverer strategists couldn't help but feel dull and slow-witted.

Having a vague yet smoldering irritation looming overhead wasn't anything out of the ordinary for these people.

There was something different about the general mood that day, though.

"...Should we consider this good or bad news?"

The general gazed at his map with both of the aforementioned feelings in mind. Surrounded by a curtain of dark cigarette smoke, he exhaled slowly.

"I haven't had a smoke this good in quite a while now."

The reason for this deliberation came from the east. That hound Zettour had pulled off a major win on the eastern front, greatly extending the Empire's atrophied life span in that theater.

He nursed the front back to life, pulling off an unprecedented counterattack.

The operation he dubbed *a revolving door* pushed their line back to where they needed it to be. It was a massive development, so much so that the other officers were already joking about Zettour's "forward advance" being a double entendre for his inevitable promotion.

"That con artist. It makes me remember the old days. He always acted so scholarly, despite being the most ruthless of us all."

Reminiscing about his old friend and their past brought a smile to the general's face. It had been a while since he felt good while looking down at a map. This advance proved that through good strategy, it was possible to turn the tables on the war, despite being so hopelessly outnumbered. It was like a small beacon of hope for the downtrodden General Staff Office.

Though a beacon...it didn't change the fact that the country was in a rut.

"All that being said, this is as far as his tricks can get us."

The curt comment slipped out as his shaking hand reached for some tobacco. Even Zettour's best efforts only amounted to a tactical victory on the battlefield.

Winning battles was always a good thing, but this also highlighted the pitiful condition of their war effort.

It was also a feat that no one else could have pulled off. He could leave the eastern front in Zettour's hands. This drew a great deal of pressure off the general.

Albeit...not enough to provide him with any real breathing room while he had to wheel and deal in the capital. The man was exhausted. Physically, yes, of course—but even more so mentally! He was at his wit's end with all the mental stress he had accumulated.

It didn't help that he had to deal with political affairs, something he was not well versed in.

"I can only hope those two pull through for me."

There was a tone of self-deprecation in his voice.

Bureaucrats worked for the bureaucracy, and politicians only have themselves in mind, while the members of parliament simply made demands, and the imperial family had its own ambitions and schemes.

They each abided by their own schools of thought and vernacular, making it difficult to stay on the same page with any given group at any given time. There was nothing more difficult for a strategist than working with people who operated under fundamentally different logic. It often involved too much pointless arguing.

It felt like the general was constantly walking on a tightrope.

He had a war to fight, and yet all the superfluous bureaucracy was really testing the integrity of his blood vessels.

"How much longer am I going to have to keep this up...?"

The idle complaint escaped his lips, and without even realizing it, the general was striking the core of the problem at hand.

They had won again in the east, and despite their loss in the west, their efforts there forced their enemies to stay on their toes. The Empire had managed to prove to the world that they wouldn't go down easily or without a fight...at least not for now.

Looking at it another way, that was all they'd accomplished.

The entire nation was walking on dangerously thin ice. Lieutenant General Rudersdorf shrouded a sigh in heavy cigarette smoke as he thought deeply about the situation.

They needed more time.

Sadly, the Empire's hourglass had run out of sand long ago. The only way they were going to get any more was to flip the entire hourglass over.

Though the real problem was the fact that they were stuck in an hourglass in the first place.

"...The army needs to engage in total war under one commander."

Zettour's success in the east sang this tune louder than anything else.

It proved that through well-executed strategy, the Imperial Army could remain an untouchable superpower.

General Romel's failure in the west also served as an important lesson as well.

The Imperial Army was incapable of pulling off a victory on an unfamiliar battlefield without proper coordination.

The difference in outcome between the two battles was far too great. It painted a very clear picture for Rudersdorf's inner strategist.

"We need a single chain of command."

The army needed more than its General Staff Office. The country needed a Supreme Army Command that controlled the entire war from one point. It needed to operate independently of Supreme High Command, parliament, the imperial family, and the will of the people.

"These factors are what keep us tied down."

He silently smoked a cigar after switching over from cigarettes for a change of pace but found himself more preoccupied with a new idea in the corner of his mind.

Could they win with a single chain of command in charge of

everything? It wasn't certain. Nevertheless, it was a way to speed things up—a way to end these tightrope shenanigans and allow the army to wield their limited time and resources...

The question of *necessity* flashed through Lieutenant General Rudersdorf's mind before he grimaced with an uneasy chuckle.

"I shouldn't get ahead of myself..."

He was about to carelessly make a decision on a troubling matter.

Plan B was still a contingency plan.

They still had Counselor Conrad to rely on and a possible road to peace through Ildoa. No matter how slim the odds were, Plan B would always have to take the back seat as long as there was a chance for the Empire to extract itself from all of this.

"I can't let my imagination get too out of hand. I know Zettour needs his overactive imagination to come up with those tricks of his on the battlefield. It's something I thought I'd never have to entertain, though."

He tries to shrug the notion off with a laugh, but it stubbornly lingered.

The idea has planted itself in his mind.

An idea for the worst-case scenario. A scheme for what the country would look like under martial law, should it come to that. An emergency solution. One with decent prospects for success, at that.

Though...it wasn't something any sane soldier who pledged their loyalty to the imperial family and the fatherland could follow through on without losing control of themselves.

He almost wanted to read a mystery novel, anything to take his mind off all this.

Although—that said—be that as it may...

Lieutenant General Rudersdorf mulled over the bomb sent to him from the west.

"There are too many issues to deal with, starting with General Romel's emergency report."

He received a warning from the general via a sealed message hand-delivered by an officer. Cigar in mouth, he thought about the problem long and hard, but not unlike the smoke in the air around him, it wouldn't disappear.

Though the warning was more like a hunch, the grounds for his hunch were highly concerning.

The warning stated that it was likely their encryption had been broken. A devastatingly shocking notion should it be even partially true.

The mere potential for a problem like this was more than enough to make the general tremble. He needed to audit the codes... Confirming each branch of the military, each with its own practices, would entail an immense undertaking, but it absolutely had to be done.

He didn't even want to think about the chances of there being a spy in the Empire. Simply listing all the various possibilities didn't help to single out any of the actual problems!

"I really hope there isn't a traitor among us. Though I suppose it would be a much more serious problem if they really had managed to decipher our codes. Either way, this is..."

A dispute regarding their top-secret information was a major setback.

To make matters worse, Lieutenant General Rudersdorf had no way of knowing whether his codes really could be trusted.

The Commonwealth had incredible intelligence-gathering capabilities. As much as he didn't want to admit it, the Empire was behind the rest of the world when it came to espionage.

It was the Albion chaps he was dealing with. The Empire was like a child when it came to intel compared to its contemporaries.

How frightening a concept intelligence was. It would be fatal for a sense of distrust to permeate its way through the army. For better or for worse, the Imperial Army had little to no experience when it came to holding its own in suspicions and investigating doubts.

Could they even pull off a Plan B in a situation like this...?

He considered abandoning the situation that could trigger Plan B in the first place. Either way, he needed to plan for the worst or else it was over for the Empire. As a strategist, it was his duty to have a plan for any given worst-case scenario.

And Lieutenant General Rudersdorf always carried out his duty earnestly.

"We can't be sure about the state of the army, for internal and external reasons."

He held his cigar in one hand. He knew that there was no going back.

The fatherland, the Empire, had killed too many of its young. The grief of those who lost loved ones was a tremendous weight on his shoulders—like a curse.

Chapter VI

Lieutenant General Rudersdorf had an explicit self-awareness of the obligation he owed the countless number of men and women who had given their lives believing in their country's ultimate victory.

They believed in the Empire—in the Reich.

This was why he took it upon himself to consider every possible avenue and implement a solution he thought was best. No matter what the outcome was. He would do what needed to be done when it needed to be done…even if it meant initiating Plan B.

"…We'll have to see how Ildoa moves."

As resentful as the situation was, the fate of the Empire depended on their ambiguous treaty with Ildoa. The Ildoans held the key to this war. How it ended for the Empire was entirely at their discretion.

What an unpleasant position it was to be in.

The Ildoans had maintained their neutrality since the outset of the war and were one of the few countries that continued to provide the long-embargoed Empire *limited* but still much-needed support.

Their neutrality on the global stage made them an obvious choice for brokering a peace treaty. If there was any country that could take the reins in negotiations…it was surely Ildoa and no one else.

The issue was that Ildoa was in an incredibly advantageous geographical position.

They were adjacent to the mainland of the Empire and were a global player in their own right but had yet to exchange blows with the Empire during this great war.

Although a formality, the Royal Ildoan Army was a beloved ally of the Imperial Army. And though their alliance contained offensive and defensive clauses, Ildoa remained a *bat* that flitted from side to side while only ever settling somewhere in the ambiguous middle…which was why the idea of prodding the bat with a stick and then unleashing a horde on them was a horrifying one.

Ildoa was too valuable an asset to both sides. The person in charge of the treaty wouldn't be able to hide their tears of despair if they lost access to the supplies they received from Ildoa along with the strategic buffer they provided geographically. Both the Empire and its enemies pored over every statement Ildoa put out, trying to discern their true intentions.

For the Empire, the core of the issue laid less in their intent and more in their ability to carry out decisive action.

"Ildoa is…too dangerous a country for the Empire."

The two-front war was already a nightmare. They wouldn't be able to handle yet another front while they were bogged down in the bloody trenches of the east. Such a task would surely be beyond any miracle the great, soon-to-be General Zettour could pull out of his proverbial hat.

Not to speak like the man, but should this war continue for much longer, the Empire wouldn't have any more bullets, supplies, or people left. This was something Zettour said often, and he was right. The Empire needed to avoid the unavoidable and impending bankruptcy at all costs.

The problem was, the right decision wasn't always the best one during times of war.

"I'd like to keep them as an ally if at all possible. But…are they foolish enough to share our fate in this terrible war?"

The Ildoans were far too clever to abandon their own interests to fight on the front lines in the name of neighborly love.

Their military was in control, and they were far more logical than they were friendly.

Their highest priority was to avoid getting caught up in a war in the first place by maintaining their neutrality. This meant that the Empire theoretically shouldn't have to worry about the country throwing their mutual treaty into the garbage and advancing north. The Ildoans weren't altruistic enough to hurl themselves into the war for either side.

"And that's exactly why they can't be ignored."

The simple truth was that the Ildoans were loyal to themselves first and foremost. They would maintain their neutrality for as long as the Empire had a fighting chance in this war.

Their dedication to remaining neutral was unparalleled.

For the Empire, they couldn't do any more but hope this was the case. For the Empire's enemies, however, it was very possible for them to bring the Ildoans to their side. Even if the Empire figured out a way to solve the persistent issue of Ildoan territorial disputes, the final results would likely remain the same.

Ildoa would lose a reason to stay neutral the moment the Empire showed obvious weakness. Therefore, in order to keep them at their current state of vague neutrality, it was imperative for the Empire to maintain its *unbeatable image*, continuing to fortify its borders and keep the Ildoans believing that war against the Empire was too risky.

"It won't be possible. Things are going to fall apart."

The Empire was still in the fight for another few months.

They could manage another half year, maybe even a full year if they did absolutely everything possible.

But there was no way for them to win.

If there were no signs Counselor Conrad could pull through with the negotiations, preventative measures may have to be taken.

"As backward as it may seem, there's still time."

They could hit Ildoa before they could tell what was coming. It would involve pulling firepower from the east and occupying the Ildoan peninsula. It was a way to acquire defense in depth and fortify their southern border.

He knew bringing Ildoa into the war was a terrible idea and that it was only a way to prolong the inevitable collapse their country faced. But if such an attack truly could prolong said collapse…then surely it was worth consideration. In that light, it suddenly started to seem more than worth it.

"It must be done… I must carry out my duty."

If it was time he was after, he was going to have to get his hands dirty… And he had at most a year to get moving.

In the east, there was a victor. A victor who had pulled off a multitude of incredible military feats.

A victor with a cynical grin on his face—Lieutenant General Zettour—laughed at the likelihood that his medal and general insignia would arrive at any minute while he scanned a large map spread across his desk.

The map, filled to the brim with details and notes, now reached much farther east than before. Foreign news outlets weren't subtle about hiding their shock with what they considered the Empire going back on the offensive, but…reality proved much less magical and heartening than the newspapers.

"We've won this battle. But our front line is about as solid as a house of cards."

The map told the whole story. The truth was that the Imperial Army was barely holding on, and it had only just managed to create a new foothold for itself.

The Federation Army had lost this position, but it was more or less akin to pruning a massive tree. It wouldn't take long for a thick tree trunk to force its way back into this territory. After all, the massive tree that was the Federation still held on to its ground quite firmly.

The Empire's tree, on the other hand, only showed further signs of its wilting and steady decline.

It was a problem, and the entire Empire was racking their brain to think of every solution they could to fill this gap. Ingenuity was no longer enough to win this war. This was why they were faced with a pressing need to prune the land around them and why they created the Council for Self-Government. Zettour had used all his intelligence and ability to get that up and running.

He even had the council prepare a volunteer division for him, a testament to his diligent, hard work. They needed to create something out of nothing. The general thought about how much of a con artist he had become.

In terms of manpower, however, the most he would receive were two or three divisions. That was the absolute limit. He didn't even dare dream for the number of divisions to reach the double digits.

The Federation, on the other hand, was mobilizing fresh divisions by the dozens.

"This difference in manpower is enough to make me sick... Strategy can only get us so far against such an overwhelming difference in numbers."

Lieutenant General Zettour reached for his cheap military tobacco while he reviewed the telegram that contained details for his promotion to general. He always thought the reluctance to recklessly use high-ranking officers on the front lines was a sign of a healthy military. Now he was a general, which ignored all protocols about the front lines. The stars seem to carry much less weight to them now.

He'd heard before somewhere that losing armies produce high-ranking officers en masse... He never imagined he'd experience such a trend in the Empire.

Keeping this ironic anecdote to himself, he begrudgingly turned his attention to something he wished he could ignore.

It was the map, and it showed how many reinforcements the Federation Army had been able to bring up from the rear juxtaposed against his own sparsely populated front line. The glaring lack of soldiers was more than evident along his entire line.

And to make things worse...there was evidence that the enemy was bolstering their forces wherever his line seemed weakest.

"Are those Communists better than an old bag like me?"

Zettour rubbed his chin. All he could do was give a sardonic laugh at this unforgiving reality. No matter how many times he won individual battles, there wasn't a single sign that they could win the war.

How many more times did he have to annihilate his enemies and drive them from before him?

At the start of the war, the Empire had to deal with about two hundred Federation divisions. The general knew that he had eradicated most, if not all, of them.

Despite this, there was a very solid wall of yet another two hundred Federation divisions facing off against the Imperial Army. It was impossible to keep up the ruse that the Empire had the troops to match.

In order to level out the playing field, he waged battles against enemy divisions in groups of ten, even twenty at a time, and came away victorious every time.

Despite his best efforts, the Federation showed no sign of suffering personnel shortages.

To top it all off, their tactics were steadily getting better, too. It was a slow, grinding battle of attrition at this point, and the Imperial Army was no longer able to keep up with the rate of losses. They currently had one hundred and fifty divisions manning their line in the east. Most of these divisions were already worryingly understrength.

The war had gone on for too long. Far too long. The Empire was coming apart at the seams and would soon tear beyond the point where repair was still possible.

Total war was nothing more than the foolish act of using your own home as tinder to keep a flame going. An illogical act demanded by a necessity that was dictated by military rationale and a little devil known as his country's raison d'état. From the front line, it almost seemed to Lieutenant General Zettour like he was in an hourglass full of sand, which was made out of the future his ancestors had left behind—sand that was steadily funneling to the bottom.

He needed to put a stop to this.

"I know what I must do, but…"

He rubbed his temples as he privately grieved on the inside.

I'm well aware that something needs to change! This was exactly why he remained silent while the military's Plan B slowly materialized behind the scenes.

He knew what he could and should do, and he was prepared to carry out his duty if push came to shove.

"I know this for a fact."

He knew that it was all in the name of necessity. It wasn't only he who knew this; it was everyone in the military.

They had to pay for whatever future they had with the blood of the young. It was an immense burden to carry.

Anyone stationed on the eastern front was overcome with a pervasive sense of unease. They all searched for a silver bullet, craving a way out of this like addicts craving opium. Nevertheless, the general couldn't help but laugh at a life worth of training spent to become a senior staff officer.

His training forced him to recognize how pointless it was to think in the short term.

It was still possible to continue piling the lives of their young into this war. If this was what they were going to do, then he would pile on as many as he needed to—even make a fortress out of bodies if that was what the situation called for—so long as it would buy him time. This was the mindset of a senior staff officer… He knew that his country had gone too far.

"I used to think I was a good person, but look at me now."

He could hardly consider himself good in any sense of the word.

Realizing this was the first step in making the heady decision. He said, "Even a well-meaning senior staff officer is still a part of an evil organization… My desire to be good is overshadowed by the fact that

Chapter VI

I'm an officer. I see that now. It is we who are the chimera the Empire has given birth to."

Necessity.

This word was all it took for an officer to make his move without even a moment's hesitation. They were no longer people but cogs in the war machine.

"…I can't fool myself any longer."

He took a moment to think about how he always thought of himself as a good person. On the eastern front, he has framed himself as an officer who knew what to do and how to get the job done.

He didn't know when, but at some point, he found himself recognizing a handful of other officers, who had been willing to dirty their hands alongside him on the eastern front, as superior to their peers. The first person who came to mind was Lieutenant Colonel Degurechaff.

He always recognized her military prowess, but he realized that this may have been because she wasn't a run-of-the-mill soldier.

Lieutenant General Zettour gave a small but very clear chuckle.

Oh, I see, he thought.

So it's that simple.

He laughed at how ridiculous it all was.

"A regular soldier would have hit their limits on the eastern front long ago…"

The officers who had gone through nothing more than standard training retained their path back to humanity.

What if, though, it took a rational machine—not a human—to reliably fight in this all-out war? It more than explained why an overly theoretical person such as himself would get promoted to general this easily.

"This is why they're throwing these stars around."

This meant that his wicked logic and rationale was valued more than the *good nature* of his peers. This wickedness of his was a sort of emergency measure, but he had to accept that it was becoming the norm for him.

The reason for this was simple as well.

"We can't win in the east. We need more of…everything."

The animals known as senior staff officers were monsters—monsters that had the heart and soul of the Empire poured into them. They were absurdities brought to life for the purpose of making the impossible possible. Give this creature a lever, and they shall move the world.

There existed, however, far too few of these monsters.

To make more of them…they needed an ideal vessel that had the potential to become one. The officers were chosen after being filtered out by a rigorous series of trials at the war college—there was no hope for them to pump out more anytime soon.

All said and done, it was a serious conundrum. It would be impossible to turn the entire army into monsters. But their inability to do exactly that would bring the war to a screeching halt. They could no longer hope for an all-out victory in a war like this.

"At this point, I take it we have only politics to rely on."

They could continue to fight. They may be able to pull off a win here and there. While they did this, though, what they really needed was victories *off* the battlefield.

But…was this feasible?

It could have meant they would have to eventually accept their defeat. This was the world of politics.

Even if they lost, if they could keep their defeat at a figurative score of fifty-one to forty-nine… If they had only lost by a margin of two points on a scale of a hundred, could he convince his inner strategist that it was a technical victory?

Zettour had spent most of his career as a strategist fixated on victory and defeat.

"…That idiot Rudersdorf probably wouldn't accept these terms. I'd wager it's a fifty-fifty chance he does."

He was a soldier who was quick to seize an opportunity. The man had thorough and extensive knowledge of how to fight and win a war. Zettour was no stranger to this—it was what he and the other officers had obsessed over at the war college.

When it came to military operations, Zettour doubted he could outmaneuver Rudersdorf. This was why he wasn't worried about the war itself.

He would happily let Rudersdorf fight it.

The waters got murkier, however, when politics became a part of the equation. In this regard, while there were grounds to be hopeful… Zettour's primary concern with Rudersdorf was his *career*.

It was a fine difference but a difference Zettour had some experience in navigating.

"He does have a habit of always giving orders with the worst possible timing."

The terrible truth was that the general had spent too much time in the General Staff Office focusing purely on strategy. While Zettour knew he was no exception to this, generals who were forged as senior staff officers were a unique bunch.

Needless to say, he never let this fact go to his head. But he was only human, and sadly for him, he was constrained by his personal experiences and the environment he grew up in.

The biggest factor was how outstanding the man was as a strategist. He wasn't going to stand for failure.

Zettour knew full well he was a second-rate general and that Rudersdorf's style of command was the genuine product. In other words, even though he himself knew there was room for cooperation…he questioned whether his friend knew how to achieve objectives with anything besides force.

He shook his head, which was starting to hurt.

Zettour could only hope that his concern would turn out to be all for nothing and that one day the two could joke about it over drinks someday.

"I'll have to send him a letter… I'll need a political officer to send it as well."

It'd be better if I could talk to him face-to-face.

Unfortunately, the distance and their respective positions presented a logistical hurdle that prevented them from doing this. It was easy for him to send messages about sharing his expert opinion on military affairs pertaining to each other's positions…but they couldn't converse about the deadly toxin that manifested itself in Plan B through official channels.

Ah.

The general realized something for the first time.

"I could never really guess what that man was thinking."

Though Zettour always thought of Rudersdorf as a friend, he truly was unpredictable. Whatever he was planning, it was beyond the imagination of the future general stationed in the east.

Lieutenant Colonel Tanya von Degurechaff had simple desires. She only wished for things that most humans probably desired as well.

To speak in concrete terms, she sought out the maximization of utility and the freedom of the pursuit of happiness.

Her recent encounters included a dogfight with some insane Commonwealth marine mage in the east. Then, when she made it to the west, General Romel hit her with a nasty mission. Though this annoyed her, she carried out her duty—only to find that same crazy mage was waiting for her there as well.

"What is he? Some kind of creepy stalker?"

As disturbing as the thought was, there was some rationale behind it.

The truth was that the enemy had been following them around the continent. There was something off about that multinational volunteer unit. It made Tanya dizzy just thinking about it.

She felt like her clear, healthy mind was being put through an industrial-grade milling machine.

"...I need a vacation."

Tanya grumbled to herself out loud, but her own remark became fuel for a new realization.

For better or for worse, there was a strong underlying François element to the part of the western territory where they were currently stationed—and it still retained a semblance of civilization. Save for the occasional bombings that could be heard in the distance here and there...it was like heaven compared to the east.

There was plumbing, electricity, and even a bed. Not to mention the food, which was to die for. The point being, it was the perfect place to enjoy the bare minimum civilization had to offer.

Above all, the most important detail was that General Romel's plan to storm the Commonwealth had hit a roadblock, leaving Tanya with absolutely nothing to do.

Chapter VI

"Maybe, just maybe…"

I could take a moment for myself. As soon as that thought passed through her mind, the young, battle-hardened aerial magic officer moved like the wind without a moment's hesitation. Tanya was already well versed in writing up and processing government documents. She didn't even require the help of her adjutant as she whipped up the requisite forms and used her own authority to give herself the final stamp of approval, officially going on a vacation.

All that was left to do was quietly submit the documents. Tanya found her adjutant at her battalion's camp, which also acted as their Kampfgruppe's command center.

"First Lieutenant Serebryakov! I will be taking the day off today!"

"Um…" Her adjutant cocked her head with a confused look about her. "Taking the day off?"

"That's right—I'm not working today!"

Her adjutant clapped her hands and smiled in a way that suggested she'd forgotten about the concept of *time off*.

"…That's unusual of you, Colonel."

"What is?"

"No, I just figured that you haven't taken a day for yourself in so long."

Having this pointed out to her made Tanya laugh out loud. Her aide was right, of course. Tanya couldn't even remember the last time she had taken out the vacation stamp to authorize her own time off.

There weren't many opportunities to take time off in the first place, given the circumstances.

She had been sent from the east to the west to the capital…and excluding her little excursion to the south in Ildoa, she hadn't had a real vacation in so, so long.

"There is a problem within our battalion of people not using their paid time off. This isn't limited to only me."

"We've been managing to make enough time for ourselves to sleep, but we haven't been able to get any rest beyond that for a while now."

Tanya gave a firm nod.

She looked at all the faces in the command tent. They all resembled her own. Why wouldn't they? The mage battalion wasn't normally given enough time to rest properly in the first place.

On top of this, they were only the Lergen Kampfgruppe in name. The reality was that the Kampfgruppe revolved around the 203rd Aerial Mage Battalion, which was used in whichever theater they happened to be needed. Even the most loyal soldier would want to apply for leave at some point.

Of course, Tanya was too concerned with self-preservation to ever admit this aloud. That wasn't to say she'd stop herself from affirming the notion with an exaggerated nod should the topic present itself.

"Behold, Visha. Now is the time for me, your commanding officer, to set an example for the rest of the battalion. If I don't take time off, there's no way my subordinates ever will."

Pretending to be a manager who cared could really take a toll on a girl... She needed to play the part, though.

As far as she could judge by her aide's response, her statement was received fairly well.

"...Our battalion does tend to skip out on vacation time."

Were her subordinates overly serious by nature, or had they given up on the idea of taking time off after being at war for so long? They were always on point about taking a turn on the watch rotation, but when it came to taking time off, the mage battalion was incredibly lackadaisical.

If Tanya didn't take the initiative to take time off, then her subordinates never would, either... The fact that Tanya was wrestling with this notion at all was a clear sign that she and her battalion were terminal workaholics. As far as Tanya could tell, though, it could simply be that their collective concept of *paid time off* had been pounded out of them by artillery fire on the battlefield.

Well, you know why... She let out another sharp laugh.

The entire command center's ears perked up at Tanya's mention of taking a day off, and suddenly each and every one of them had glimmering eyes.

"If I take a day off, will the entire Kampfgruppe follow suit all at once?"

She glared back at her subordinates, and the collective glimmer quickly vanished. *Oh my*, it looked like her subordinates were still humans after all. This was a good sign.

"It appears everyone has been holding back."

Tanya's adjutant interjected with a vague expression after her superior's assertion.

"If we can take time off, we would like to as well. If now is our chance, then I…don't mind processing any applications as well. Do you think it would be a problem, ma'am?"

"There's no problem at all. Though I suspect you all were able to rest a bit back at the capital… You have a right to your vacation time. If you can use it, feel free to do so."

Each and every member of her battalion did far more work than their salaries justified. While it was a bit late in the game for this, it was Tanya and the 203rd Aerial Mage Battalion's right to apply for their earned time off.

Rights are important, after all. If there was such a thing as an inviolable sanctuary, Tanya knew that it could be nothing other than an individual's rights. This was a given throughout history. A country that couldn't respect an individual's rights…naturally didn't respect their rights to own property, either. In other words, they would become Commies.

Her subordinates were hesitant. No one was getting up and saying, *I'll take my day off, too!* That was somewhat concerning to see. It was strange for someone who worked at command to suppress their desire for vacation.

Unlike an exploitative corporation…Tanya intended to respect the rights of her workers.

"Troops, you don't need to feel guilty. Rather than workers who hide their discomfort as they work, I'd prefer workers who get their job done after taking an appropriate amount of time off for themselves. Does anyone disagree?"

Tanya's words encouraged her subordinates in just the right way.

One after the other, the applications for time off begin to pile up on her desk. Some of the more intuitive soldiers even gave her their application without the date filled in. And so Tanya, together with her adjutant, began the task of processing the mountain of applications.

To her surprise, applications had poured in from the entire Kampfgruppe.

She figured at least Major Weiss would stick around… Every application spelled out exactly how they intended to spend their time off, whether it be going home or taking a short personal trip. It appeared Tanya's soldiers were aware of her strong relationship with the General

Staff Office and figured she could squeeze them for all sorts of travel subsidies. It shouldn't be too difficult considering she could make the necessary arrangements with the Railroad Department. She'd be able to make the best arrangements for the applications that involved long-distance travel through the benevolence of Lieutenant Colonel Uger.

That said, if they didn't have any seats available for military use, it was going to cost them money. With a sigh, Tanya commanded her adjutant to use the battalion's secret funds to fill in the gaps.

Is it okay for us to do this? It was clear what Tanya's adjutant was trying to communicate to her with her eyes.

"Mages are the military's greatest asset, so we can't neglect to do what-ever we can to keep them rested and in good spirits. Therefore, mark the classified funds as maintenance and repair expenses."

"I'll take care of it, ma'am."

Tanya nodded before standing up from her chair. Now that her subor-dinates' applications were taken care of, it was time for her to enjoy her own time off.

"Finally, I can get some time to relax."

"That's for sure, but…as a lieutenant colonel, isn't the most you can do just lounging around in the barracks?"

That much was true. For a commanding officer to leave their post, they needed authorization from a much higher place… Tanya would just have to get that later. It wasn't as if she didn't have access to Colonel Lergen's stamp, but were she to use it here, it could lead to problems down the line.

"While I take a small break here, I'll send my actual application for real time off to the Western Army Group. For now, I'm going to leave the command center and spend some time in the barrack's lounge. Does that sound uncivilized to you? I feel the ability to use what little freedom I have is a decent way to lift my mood."

Tanya rejoiced on the inside at the idea of not having to worry about work for a day.

"In fact, what do you think about me treating you to some coffee?"

"I'd love to join you, ma'am."

"Adjutant, this is a special occasion. Why not take the day for yourself as well?"

In response to Tanya's invitation, however, Visha said something that showed just how deeply she'd been influenced by the Imperial Army's work culture.

"Accompanying you makes this a part of my official duties, no?"

"Your point being?"

"I'll abandon my post and join you."

That's what I thought, Tanya thinks as she bursts into laughter. To think, this is the same adjutant who once openly cried before her on the Rhine front. Tanya never imagined that she'd say something like this.

"I guess it's a soldier's duty is to always be on point. You've become quite the dependable adjutant."

"Um, are you sure it's okay for me to leave my post...?"

"Of course it's not. I'll authorize it for you."

A person who uses their rights appropriately deserves recognition and praise. Tanya adored the harm principle from the bottom of her heart. Almost as much she believed in the sanctity of private property.

As they made their way to the lounge, First Lieutenant Serebryakov clapped her hands as if she's remembered something crucial.

"Oh, that's right. Captain Meybert prepared a gift for us when we arranged that meeting with him before the battle! Let's enjoy it with our coffee! I'll go get it!"

Tanya's adjutant ran off but soon returned with a few cans labeled *Imperial Navy Pineapples.*

"These are...canned navy rations?"

"He said to think of it as a form of hush money from the submarine Fleet Command. He wants us to keep quiet about the mistake the commanders at that harbor made."

Oh, that incident. Tanya knew what the captain wanted her to keep her mouth shut about. It was that time that amateur navy personnel failed to defend his own port. Colonel Lergen was livid when he tried to shirk responsibility for it.

"A bribe? How shameful."

She picked up a can and ascertained that the pineapples were soaked in delicious syrup.

"We'd better dispose of all evidence before anyone finds out."

"Affirmative!"

And that was how the two of them gathered whatever treats they could find before convening in the lounge, where Tanya and First Lieutenant Serebryakov had a small coffee break.

They spread out their collections of edibles on the lounge table. It was a collection of cultural goods.

Tanya slowly picked up the finest coffee beans she had to offer and hand roasted them in a frying pan. First Lieutenant Serebryakov skillfully prepared them with a grinder. They then steamed the ground beans with boiled water before Tanya's adjutant expertly poured the enchanting black liquid into their cups.

The now-uncanned Imperial Navy pineapples tasted unbelievably delicious as well.

Tanya wore a big smile on her face, thoroughly enjoying this moment. Her adjutant, who sat comfortably next to her, showed a slightly serious expression before raising a question.

"Is it okay if I ask you something?"

"What's that?"

"Well...I wanted to ask where this war is going."

The question caught Tanya off guard. She flashed a scowl as if the sweet pineapple wedge in her mouth suddenly turned sour.

The war was the last thing she wanted to talk about during her precious time off.

"That's a peculiar question to ask."

"Well, there aren't many opportunities to ask you these sorts of questions one-to-one, so..."

Tanya couldn't reprimand the young woman for politely asking her opinion. It was a chance for two officers to share what they thought without the rank and file watching.

She felt it was probably better to be frank with her, at least to a certain extent.

"I wouldn't dwell too much on it... Right now, our highest priority is making sure we all make it out alive."

"Is that how you feel, Colonel?"

"A war can only be ended through victory. As far as I can tell, there isn't anyone fighting right now intending to lose. However..."

Tanya took a breath, and then a sip of her scrumptious Ildoan coffee, before saying what had to be said.

Chapter **VI**

"We are soldiers. Well, in your case, you were supposed to be a conscript before you eventually joined up of your own accord... And of course there were certain circumstances that went into your decision to do so..."

"I'm an officer, ma'am. I joined for the same reasons as everybody else."

First Lieutenant Serebryakov nodded to Tanya. They were both the same in this regard. As civil servants, they were the instruments of their nation's sovereignty. It would've been nice if they could receive their pay for little to no work like run-of-the-mill civil servants, but they had to earn their pay in full unfortunately. Despite Tanya being against slavery, considering the sheer volume of unpaid overtime hours she and Visha had put into their jobs, they were effectively a pair of quintessential public servants.

Tanya shook her head and focused back on the topic at hand.

"For soldiers who are conscripted, they have a place to go home when the war ends. For a soldier who enlists, however, they're seen as throwing their lot in with the military. Being an officer is much tougher than you may think."

"Um, what do you mean by this?"

"We aren't privileged with the option of death, however sweet a release it may be. We're here on our own accord, so we need to fight until the very end. That is why we need to survive through this war."

There was nothing more important than their lives. For Tanya, the idea of escaping one's fate through suicide was something she'd never be able to understand no matter how much time passed.

"Are you saying that we can't win?"

"I'm not one to partake in wishful thinking. I highly doubt that we'll lose, though."

"...What?"

"What's that, Lieutenant? Are you a defeatist?"

"N-n-no, but..."

Her adjutant looked completely bewildered. Tanya pegged her for a dualist—the type that felt naturally inclined to define everything in terms of black and white. It was a suitable personality for a 203rd mage. Tanya's soldiers were always facing the two extremes in the form of life and death. She decided to take this opportunity to teach her adjutant a small lesson.

"This is a good chance for us to figure this out, then." Tanya placed her coffee onto the desk with a soft *tap* and then pointed at Visha before continuing, "You ask if we can win this war? The answer to that is, we won't know until we try. But I can assure you that we won't lose."

"...Is there some secret way for us to turn the war around in the works?"

Come on now, Lieutenant, Tanya almost blurts out at her adjutant. *Turn the war around? You're killing me, Visha!*

Tanya could feel her brow furrowing on the inside at her adjutant's remark. It wasn't something she should reprimand the young woman for, but the idea that they needed to *turn the war around* was already a clear sign of her doubt in the military.

In other words, even First Lieutenant Serebryakov recognized that the odds were stacked against the Imperial Army.

"Lieutenant, there's no big secret. You just have to use your head."

"Um... Could it be that there's some groundbreaking new technology? You know, just like last time. When the Elinium Arms Factory pulled through for us!"

Tanya could feel a headache coming on just hearing mention of the damned place. She furrowed her actual brow this time.

If left to his own devices, the mad scientist Schugel creating some odd invention wasn't entirely out of the question. Tanya only hoped she would be entirely uninvolved if that ever came to pass.

Of course, that was neither here nor there... The real issue at hand was what the war stemmed from in the first place.

"There's no secret weapon or plan or even a magic staff involved in this. Do you have any idea what I'm getting at?"

"P-please enlighten me, Colonel!"

Tanya didn't intend on her remark to sound reprimanding, but it came off that way evidently, judging by the response she received. To think, this is supposed to be a private conversation between two off-duty soldiers.

"It's simple. The answer is politics."

War was just an extension of politics, after all. Though it was conducted through force of arms and open warfare, the fact that it was humans who were doing the fighting meant that politics would always be a part of the fundamental equation. Whether or not they won or lost, the greater battle would still be decided purely through political means. Tanya reiterates this point to First Lieutenant Serebryakov so that she won't forget it.

"At the company level, victory and defeat is a simple thing to discern."

"Right!"

Tanya lightly held her finger to her brow as she realized there was a pressing need to educate her soldiers a bit more. She needed to teach them more fundamental knowledge about things that *weren't* directly related to war.

"Let's look at battalions or regiments or even brigades and divisions. Victory is as clear-cut as the law of physics for any of these. But what happens when we look at a whole country? Pure military strength doesn't dictate the victor when we get to this level."

"So we have to think about how we execute our attack?"

"Yes, that is correct. Even animals use knowledge when they go on a hunt. Look no further than a pack of wolves."

Her adjutant gave an eager nod of understanding when Tanya used this example. She happily popped another pineapple wedge into her mouth as she quickly came up with her conclusion.

"Oh, well, that's simple, then." First Lieutenant Serebryakov eagerly continued, "So whoever throws the strongest punch wins."

"…First Lieutenant, it seems you are in dire need of reeducation. Let's review. Look back at what you learned before you became an officer."

"Um, uh… Oh, wait, Colonel. We're on break, so let's save this for later."

"*You're* still on duty."

Ugh, her adjutant looked as if she was about to cry. Her tears weren't something worth considering, though. One must pay for the mistakes one makes.

"I'm a commanding officer—I can't let my soldiers slink off with insufficient knowledge. First Lieutenant, take some time to review your studies and come back to me with a report on the answer. That's an order."

Recognizing she was the one who brought this problem onto herself, Tanya's adjutant's eyes begged her for mercy… Unfortunately, Tanya used up all the mercy in her small body to grant her subordinates time off en masse.

Visha wouldn't be working overtime on this—she was in luck.

Since it was an order…First Lieutenant Serebryakov returned to her post where she could spend her time on duty doing the homework she created for herself.

Although this left the person who bestowed the homework unto her in a very bad mood. For you see…the sad, fatal deficiency in the Empire had manifested itself in her adjutant's lack of awareness.

The Empire relied far too much on the instrument of violence it has created.

"Visha's ridiculous remark is a sign that the Empire thinks they can't beat their way out of any problem."

The Empire relied too much on its strength.

The fact that they have pretty much gotten by on that alone until now had set that paradigm into stone for the country.

If this nation had its Bismarck, there may have been another path for them to go down.

Oh, Bismarck.

You were truly a great man.

However did you manage to get the reins on your country during the unprecedented times of imperialism you lived in?! If only there was a diplomat half as capable as you in the Empire of today!

Tanya shook her head to clear her mind.

There likely was a Bismarck in the Empire. The saddest part was that she predicted the Empire would never be able to properly utilize such a person.

Tanya was almost certain of this prediction.

Her nation put jingoism on a pedestal and looked down on pessimism and cautiousness as cowardice.

The Empire subscribed to the school of thought that, as a victor, victory was the overarching imperative. Those who even considered defeat a possibility wouldn't make it anywhere in the Empire.

In other words…for Tanya to maintain her career, she needed to channel everything toward achieving victory and nothing else.

Something that would prove to be an all but impossible challenge.

Chapter **VI**

She still had her sights set on a job change and knew that she would probably have to start sooner rather than later. Nevertheless, she was a part of the military, and they were at war. The same way a company would fire an idiot who filled out a job application in their office chair, she knew she'd end up in front of a firing squad should the army catch wind of her ambitions.

She'd end up a literal stain on the execution grounds. Tanya wanted to end her life peacefully, singing the song of civil rights. The worst outcome for her would be one that would humor Being X.

Due to his stern military mannerisms and incredible gravitas as a leader, Lieutenant General Rudersdorf was often taken for an intrepid man. Most people outside of the military, who only worked with him superficially, thought of him this way.

From the perspective of a subordinate of his, such as Colonel Lergen, however…it wasn't his intrepidness but his competence that made him a difficult man to work for.

He was ruthless with those he considered incompetent, and he was practically merciless in the way he brought out the best of what each of his subordinates had to offer—always asking for *more* than their best efforts.

He was definitely one of the most difficult high-ranking officers to serve under.

However, a portion of the blame should also be shouldered by the sheer importance of the weighty tasks entrusted to the General Staff Office. This deep-seated hatred for incompetence was a common trait shared among all the senior staff officers and wasn't something unreasonable in itself. The general was even magnanimous enough to entertain the opinions of his subordinates. Though an abused direct subordinate himself, Colonel Lergen had to admit that while his superior had high standards, he could also be reasoned with.

The deputy director of the General Staff always needed to think with as clear a mind as humanly possible when it came to strategic planning. It was a given for anyone who worked under him in the Imperial Army.

This was why Lergen couldn't shake the tremendous shock he felt when…he doubted the orders given to him by his superior.

That day, he'd find himself shell-shocked in the deputy director's office where he was called.

"You wish for me to oversee the creation of a *counter-insurrection plan* for…the Empire?"

The title of the proposal used the word *pacification*, but Lergen knew how these things worked in real life and what it actually meant.

Regulations during times of war were growing increasingly strict, especially at this late stage. There was only one faculty that could move troops through the imperial capital at will.

"It is a contingency plan. We need to be prepared should a situation ever arise."

It took Lergen all his might not to arch an eyebrow with each word that came out of his superior's mouth. Despite this, Colonel Lergen took it upon himself as a career soldier to play the part of an expert and extended his opinion.

"General, with all due respect, I think this may be a bit overboard. It's too early to be considering precautions such as these. I believe they are unnecessary where we currently stand."

"Oh?"

His superior—the deputy director of the Imperial Army General Staff Office, *Lieutenant General Rudersdorf*—glared back at him…but Colonel Lergen held fast, concealing the cold sweat he felt pouring down his spine and keeping up his brazen appearance as he continued.

"Considering the political, civilian, and security conditions in the imperial capital as of this moment, I am confident there is no impending concrete threat. The most I can come up with is the potential for soldiers to revolt… But seeing as there's virtually no chance of this happening, I'm left wondering why a plan such as this would be necessary."

The colonel continued with grandiose terms, all a part of his act.

"As a strategist, my suggestion would be to send any troops used for law-and-order operations in the capital to the east or west as much-needed reinforcements."

It was nothing short of a miracle that he was able to get all this out without tripping over his words. Or maybe the devil was watching him from somewhere with a grin.

Colonel Lergen suddenly felt overcome by a strange sensation the moment he finished his sentence. Why on earth was he being forced to engage in such sophistry in the Imperial Army General Staff Office in the first place?

"You have a point, Colonel."

"Sir?"

Without a moment of thought, his superior nonchalantly nodded to Lergen before continuing.

"Very well, I won't have you work on this plan."

Lergen couldn't hide the tension draining from his shoulders as his superior surprisingly agreed with him. Just as Colonel Lergen let down his guard, however, a second arrow came flying toward him in the shape of a cigar box.

A simple glance was enough to know the cigars were of the highest quality.

To be given this at a time when the General Staff Office was currently trying to figure out how to deal with the overseas embargo the Empire had been being hit with... The box was terrifying. What was his superior going to ask of him in return for a product of this caliber?

"Have a cigar."

"I shall abstain, if you'll allow me to."

"Why so reluctant, Colonel Lergen? Let's have a little chat since I have you here anyway."

A little chat? Judging from his superior's daily tendency to hate all things unnecessary, Lergen was overcome with an incredible sense of discomfort. While he respected his boss as a man of the military, Colonel Lergen was a senior staff officer.

There was a limit to how much he could pretend not to see, hear, and say.

"If it has to do with the military affairs, I'm at your service."

Lieutenant General Rudersdorf silently listened to this formal response as he smoked his cigar. He lowered his head and fixed his eyes squarely on Lergen...until he eventually continued with a quiet voice.

"You should humor your superiors. Or are you unable to speak frankly?"

"I can exchange in banter with you as a soldier. But…I'm not the type who could ever be a yes-man."

"That's how every man should be." The tension from the general's lips loosened with a grin. "But there are merits and demerits to acting the right way."

"…Sir?"

"Have a cigar. And pull up a chair while you're at it."

Lergen knew this meant he should prepare for the worst. He detested the audible gulp that escaped his throat. Forcing the stiff joints in his legs to move, Colonel Lergen slowly lowered himself into one of the chairs in the office.

Now that he was in this situation, he figured he'd make the most of it.

He opened the box and enjoyed the rich fragrance of a proper cigar for the first time in a long while.

It was much better than anything he was used to smoking, even more so than the cigars Counselor Conrad had procured for him during their meeting. So much for the Foreign Office being the epitome of the Empire's sophistication. Colonel Lergen had no choice but to think about the irony that metaphor represented.

The army was more precious to the Empire than its Foreign Office. The country prioritized the military over diplomacy. If there was a direct correlation between this mindset and the caliber of cigars they could get their hands on…then how much poison was hidden away in the cigar he smoked that very moment?

"What would you like to talk about, sir?"

"What do you think of the current situation?"

"That we are still in the fight. And that there likely isn't a way out of this beyond active and persistent diplomacy. Though it goes without saying that while we will require the help of Ildoa, the Empire needs to be the one to initiate the negotiations."

His superior nodded in agreement, causing Colonel Lergen even more discomfort. Though he couldn't quite describe it, he knew there was something hidden behind his superior's assent.

His superior would continue speaking before he could figure out what that hidden meaning was, though.

"Our biggest problem is time."

Chapter **VI**

With an exasperated scowl, the general mentioned their greatest challenge.

"Our country is slowly but surely bleeding out. We'll be dead before long. That is the situation we're currently facing. If we don't close this wound soon, a prolonged death is all that awaits us."

"I feel that if you force an exhausted patient to do fruitless labor, chances are the shock will simply kill them sooner."

"Your point being? What, does that mean you'd give up on the patient?"

"I feel like it'd be best for such a surgery to only be considered after a period of reduced activity if their wounds are critical. Even if the surgery were to succeed, what's the point if the patient dies?"

The lieutenant general folded his arms thoughtfully before giving his brief retort.

"...Colonel Lergen, you're a fool."

"Please enlighten me on your opinion of the matter, sir."

"I wouldn't want to hurt my hand—" he said as he literally raised a fist.

Knowing where this was heading, Lergen interrupted him before the general got too caught up in a *different* performance.

"Sir! I ask you to refrain from fooling yourself."

"Oh?"

"What can you do with a fist?! Anyone can hit someone once! They may even get away with it a second time. But where does it all lead?"

Those who lived by the sword, died by the sword—and the Imperial Army was effectively one great big sword. Too much swinging and it would be the Empire that wound up down in a puddle of its own blood.

Colonel Lergen knew full well that this was only a theory on his part.

"So you want me to rely on the bureaucrats? You want to place your hope on Counselor Conrad and pray that he'll pull through for us without a hitch?"

"The military isn't anything more than precisely that—a military."

Lergen remembered the day diplomatic negotiations in Ildoa went south, leading to the end of their hopes for a quick armistice. If a simple soldier could've made a difference then, he wished they had been there that day...

He felt the same now given the situation at hand.

Colonel Lergen's rationale, on the other hand, strongly denied his feelings of *shock*.

"We're senior staff officers. Standard training dictates what we should do."

"Standard training teaches you nothing more than a single standard. It's our prerogative to reevaluate what our standards should be."

He said this nonchalantly, but the meaning it carried was something heavy enough to make the senior staff officer's expression stiffen.

"General, are you insinuating that you could redefine the standards in the middle of a war like this?"

"...Nothing is possible if you never try. How many things do you think are chalked up as impossible without ever being tested?"

"We are a fist, sir. We're nothing more than an injured fist."

"Let's say that you're correct, for argument's sake. Then let me ask you this. Do you really believe that we could never be anything more than a fist?"

It's more basic than that... Cigar in hand, Lergen continued in a hoarse voice.

"We fight the wars, and the politicians run the country. We have the bureaucrats to bring us together. This is the foundation on which our country is based."

It was frustrating. It was difficult to tolerate. Lergen almost wanted to lash out when he thought about it. He knew it was the forbidden fruit, and yet...there was something utterly captivating about General Rudersdorf's plan!

But these were just his own personal feelings.

It was nothing more than a knee-jerk reaction born of how he felt on the inside.

"Sir, as an individual, there is something about your plan that I do find tempting. As a colonel, however, it's not something I could ever get behind."

Lergen could share a recognition of the dire circumstances their country faced—they both shared an awareness of the issue. As a military expert, however, he couldn't prescribe the general's plan as a solution.

Chapter VI

Contingency plans were akin to life insurance. They weren't something that should be forced into action!

Colonel Lergen sat and waited to be reprimanded by his superior.

"Excellent. That is the right mindset to have."

Lergen never dreamed the man would agree with him.

It actually threw him off a great deal. Despite knowing it was impossible to avoid getting ambushed, he walked right into it like a fool. In a sense, this could be considered a rare tactical experience.

"Therefore, you need to throw all common sense out the window."

"What?"

The ability to bargain was something that was drilled into senior staff officers.

Though a commander in name only, Lergen had done more than his fair share of studying the conditions on the eastern front and made sure to learn whatever important lessons there were to be gleaned from the war front. But this full-frontal assault, a classic example of deep battle executed by Rudersdorf, pierced through the crevasses of his scattered mind.

"They talk about the three branches, but it really all comes down to Supreme Command."

Lergen didn't even need to ask what the general was referring to.

"It pains me to say this…but the imperial family can no longer keep up with the times. Meanwhile, the bureaucrats have created an echo chamber for themselves. Where they should act as a bridge between the government, the military, and the imperial family, they've become a bunch of indolent loafers. Colonel, our country is…long overdue for a revolution."

The conversation was getting far too specific. The statement was something a serving soldier should never say about the system their country was founded on, let alone the imperial family.

Lergen reflexively shook his head before interrupting his superior by blurting out, "Sir!"

"Colonel, you're a straight arrow. Straight as they come… All right, I think we have a good sense of where we both stand on the issue. I don't plan on doing anything outrageous."

"Then surely the outrageousness of your statement isn't lost on you?!"

Lieutenant General Rudersdorf nodded with an expression that looked like it had been carved from a boulder.

"Keep in mind that this is merely a contingency plan. It's just something to have ready. There's no need to get up in arms about it. There's no better path out of this than, as you say, through legitimate channels. There are no grounds for me to disagree with you there." He continued in a terribly exasperated voice, "I believe you fully understand what your duty is as an officer. Therefore, we should both stick to what we know best."

"I've never forgotten my duty."

"…Good. You're free to go. Take those cigars with you. They're a gift."

Lergen knew there was no refusing this offer. It felt very much like the cigars were being pushed on to him more than freely given as a gift.

He graciously gathered the box up before giving a salute and taking his leave from the deputy director's office. After a few deep breaths, he got the oxygen he desperately needed after that intense back-and-forth.

It felt like he couldn't think straight.

Without much thought, he took out one of the cigars and placed it in his mouth, only to shake his head and change back to his usual cheap smokes. He was too used to smoking military-issue tobacco at this point.

So what was he to do with the rest of these cigars?

"I feel like these aren't something I should keep for myself…"

He felt hesitant about smoking them alone, almost guilty. It wasn't as if they were a bribe or anything, but he didn't really know what to do with them.

He figured he'd better give them to somebody else entirely.

Taking a moment to ponder who the busiest person in the General Staff Office was…he quickly realized he didn't even need to think about it. Though it would be something of a trip, there was only one department that deserved these. With the cigars in hand, he made his way to the labyrinth that was the Railroad Department.

With the occasional salute given to the random acquaintance or soldier he met on the way, Lergen walked through the cold halls of the General Staff building.

During this short trip, he found himself thinking about the plainness of his workplace. There were sparse decorations here or there, but it was nothing compared to the Foreign Office. It made sense to him why Lieu-tenant Colonel Degurechaff would scoff at their building.

The General Staff Office was a home for those who did real work.

Colonel Lergen approached the door of one of its civilians and called out as he knocked.

"Lieutenant Colonel Uger, are you there?"

There was no response.

Was that too quiet? Lergen knocked harder, but nothing came in return.

"He must be out. Strange, he's usually in around this time…"

Urged on by his suspicion, Lergen poked his head into the office, where he saw a sight he somewhat expected. There was a railway offi-cial, out cold on top of his desk. Sleeping on the job was a fairly serious problem, but considering how much work Lieutenant Colonel Uger was inundated with, Lergen could only feel for the man.

He'd just finished organizing the massive train schedule that enabled General Zettour's mobile warfare in the east. It was extremely doubtful the Empire had arranged any time off… Lergen couldn't bring himself to reprimand the man.

Should I just leave the cigars with a note?

No, Colonel Lergen figured it would be better to wake the man up and order him to get some rest. He approached the desk when a series of documents sprawled across it caught his eye.

"This is…the train schedule for shifting the theater…?"

Uger finished this days ago, and it was already being passed around. What other explanation would there be for him to be sleeping on his desk?

"But…this is…"

He did a double take. Was this a train schedule for the south? The only theater to the south would be…

"Ildoa?"

Now it had completely captured his interest. He looked over the doc-uments and found a list of intricate numbers. They were statistics on different trains and stations, but they were oddly detailed.

He was about to run his eyes over a few more of the documents when the owner of the office groggily emerged from his slumber finally.

"Hmm? What? Oh, when did you get here, Colonel?"

Colonel Lergen kindheartedly waved his hand at the man as he gave a few long blinks.

"At ease. You must be exhausted."

And no wonder, considering how arranging the train schedule was one of the most difficult jobs in the entire General Staff Office. There was a limited supply of train cars but an endless amount of demand for them. Just maintaining the rails alone was of critical importance during the war. The demands included provisioning new railroads that had to be laid—and to make matters worse, strategists always required a two-way railroad, which included converting Federation tracks to a gauge usable for Empire trains.

It was complicated to the point of being beyond human comprehension, but the army found a way to make things work. They were hated by the Reichsbahn, feared by the Railroad Department, and complained about by the frontline troops for the lack of provisions they received, but they did their job no matter what.

They worked in the shadows to ensure the nation's logistics never failed. There was no one more deserving of these cigars.

"Maybe these will help take your mind off things. I got them as an apology from General Rudersdorf for physically threatening me earlier today."

Lieutenant Colonel Uger accepted the cigars without really thinking about it.

"Thank you. Oh, uh, sorry about earlier. You saw me at my worst, Colonel Lergen."

"If it was anybody other than me, this would've been considered a leak."

"…There aren't many people who have full access to all General Staff information."

He wasn't wrong.

Colonel Lergen easily had more authority than even the lieutenant generals at the beginning of the war. He was authorized to access almost as much information as General Zettour when the war first broke out.

He could feel the tremendous responsibility building alongside said growing authority. After all, it wasn't as if he was in possession of a magical cauldron. Having authority over others didn't give him the power to create something out of nothing.

Not to mention the exceedingly large amount of stress that came with the territory.

"I guess access is really the only benefit this job entails. And, well, the occasional fancy cigar. I could do without the pressure I have to put up with from above, though…"

"Ha-ha-ha, capable people are destined to work themselves to the bone until the day they die."

"Lieutenant Colonel, don't pretend you're not in the same boat. I know what you've been up to lately. It's easy for me to picture you being sent around the office and having people pile their odd jobs onto you."

"I appreciate the gift. Ah, I know. Were you interested in these?"

Uger organized the papers before placing them in front of Colonel Lergen. It was the same schedule for shifting the theater from before. The colonel flashed an overt grimace.

"…I'll be honest—I'm having a hard time making sense of the plans."

"What? You must be joking."

The comment caught Lieutenant Colonel Uger off guard. To him, it was no different from any other regular old schedule. For a man of the railway, it was nothing more than that. However, for a strategist in charge of various aspects of the war, Lergen had an entirely different perspective.

"These documents are for Ildoa, are they not?"

Lieutenant Colonel Uger simply said, "That's right," with a sigh. "It's a train schedule and one that has a railroad expert…falling asleep on top of a map of Ildoa. I must say, it's a very ominous plan, if nothing else."

Why was the General Staff Office making railway arrangements going *toward* Ildoa at a time like this? The idea of there being such a map in the building was borderline preposterous. Ildoa was their ally, for goodness' sake. While the country was without a doubt taking a very opportunist approach to the war…they still sent the Empire much-needed supplies.

Though it was important to remain vigilant, their neighbor was hardly a credible threat worth planning around. There wasn't much more to Ildoa than this. So why were there large-scale preparations being made to send trains to Ildoa? Lergen assumed it was a part of the nebulous Plan B.

"Lieutenant Colonel Uger, is it fair to assume you have an idea of what this could be related to?"

"I think I have an idea. Do you think so, too?"

"I bet these are preliminary preparations for something. The problem is…whether or not they'll remain preliminary."

Was this new schedule preparation in case their primary plan didn't work? That was what Lergen wanted to think, but there was something awfully tangible about the documents and the numbers. Obviously, it was yet another form of insurance.

Insurance was necessary at all stages of the game. And yet, there was this strange feeling the colonel couldn't shake about the entire thing.

"As a railway official, I can say that we regularly station troops on the Ildoa border. I'm struggling this time, though. I'm having a hard time getting enough mountain cars and maintenance cars over there."

Oh? Lergen halfway nodded, but then he felt his strange feeling grow even stronger.

"You're sending cars to Ildoa?"

"Well, just as a test."

"Wait, Lieutenant Colonel."

"What's wrong?"

Lieutenant Colonel Uger sounded oblivious, which caused Colonel Lergen to question him immediately.

"You were asked to send actual train cars there? Are you certain this isn't some sort of misunderstanding?"

"Yes, the railroad isn't at its best at the moment, so in order to plan for the future, we have to send locomotives to the site first."

"Lieutenant Colonel, I haven't heard anything about this."

"Do you need me to explain the technical reasons why we run these tests? Since we'd never fight with Ildoa for political reasons, I'm only able to send my subordinates there to research a route through the mountains."

That's not it— Colonel Lergen shook his head.

Thinking up plans for all conceivable situations was a fundamental part of nearly all military procedures. There were already multiple plans thought out regarding this very issue. There was also likely conclusive research already done regarding what Lieutenant Colonel Uger was currently tasked with doing.

Actually mobilizing machinery on the scene was entirely different from pure theory. They were using what limited resources they had for it. That was something Lergen had to be aware of, considering his position in the office.

So why wasn't he informed of any of this?

"For the trains heading to Ildoa…do you know why you were ordered to make these schedules? Actually, no— Tell me *who* gave you the orders."

"It was General Rudersdorf. He said he wanted a contingency plan in the worst-case scenario that Ildoa joins the enemy forces."

"That sounds legitimate, but…Lieutenant Colonel, we already have a plan for when that happens. The only plans that are authorized are all defensive."

"I'm sorry—I'm not sure I follow you…"

It was evident that the railway operator didn't have a grasp of the full picture, so Lergen decided to let him know the ugly truth—what this all meant from a strategist's perspective.

"For a defensive battle, we planned on destroying all railways between the two countries. We'd station forces in the mountains and focus purely on fortifying our defenses. There isn't a single plan that involves going *into* Ildoa."

They'd had these train schedules worked out since before the war. All trains would remain within the Empire's border. Though these plans lacked the power to take out an enemy army in one fell swoop, the country could use what troops it had within its borders to buy itself time, possibly indefinitely.

Lieutenant Colonel Uger was beginning to pick up on the strangeness of the schedule he had been tasked with creating, and his expression soon twisted with anxiety as he scanned the documents again.

"So then…what kind of scenario is the general envisioning that would require me to prepare these?"

"Probably something more than just theory. Something that an officer with the authorization I have doesn't even know about yet."

It was known far and wide that the army loved their plans. That said, they also abhorred waste, and they certainly didn't have any time to spare given the current state of the war. In effect, no activities would be approved unless they had a clear goal in mind.

Which begged the question…what was the goal in mind when it came to Ildoa?

And why didn't Lergen know about it? Lergen, who was in charge of studying military topography in critical locations.

"…This is probably a top-secret operation."

Lergen let this slip out with a defeated laugh.

The best way to fool your enemies was to fool your allies, after all.

This so-called preliminary schedule was nothing more than routine work for the General Staff Office. Working on it would likely never draw the attention of a fellow officer.

This wasn't the case, though, if they had already begun moving actual machinery.

The meaning behind this was something very, very—and this couldn't be emphasized enough—*very serious.*

Though the mere hint of the so-called pacification plan from before suggested the same meaning, this did even more. It was evident…that General Rudersdorf had a lot more on his mind than even Lergen was aware of.

Plan B may very well have been nothing more than a contingency.

It was, however, a contingency prepared for extremely real circumstances.

"C-Colonel…"

"Let's grab a drink, Lieutenant Colonel. I think we may need to speak more frankly about this."

"And maybe we should have the drinks at one of our houses," Colonel Lergen suggested in a quiet voice, almost a whisper—a small hint at the precariousness of what he wished to talk about.

Though it definitely wasn't the best way to conduct things, relationships between individuals filled the gaps in an organization.

"There are one too many factors set in motion for this to be considered preliminary. I think we should…"

Work together behind the scenes, Lergen was midway through this thought when it hit him. A realization cropped up in Colonel Lergen's mind.

"Oh, I see."

He was under a timer.

"So we're in an hourglass."

They were operating under a time limit! If the army couldn't achieve their goal within the limit…would that trigger those contingency plans?

If a battle was to be fought, it would happen in the spring. They certainly weren't going to attempt major maneuvers in the mountains during the winter. The lack of snowplow trains in the schedule suggested this as well. That meant they had a year, maybe less.

The Empire had *perhaps* a year to figure something out…

Time was a big concern of General Rudersdorf's. Despite this, he'd taken an interest in Lergen's efforts to reach out to the world through diplomacy… His efforts were placed on a scale with their Plan B.

It made sense to Lergen why he was given time to push for reconciliation with Counselor Conrad—that time came with a clear limit.

This explained why Lieutenant General Rudersdorf had placed such high hopes in him!

He trusted Lergen but also gave him a time limit. A limit the general would likely never share directly with Lergen…

The plan was more than likely a surprise attack.

The more he thought about it, the more Lergen was convinced that if they were going to pull it off with any real chance of success, it would have to be in the spring. Or perhaps February or March at the earliest.

Lergen knew he'd be asked to negotiate like his life depended on it. For the general, it served to either lower their enemy's guard or to actually pull through with successful diplomacy.

Either way…he was now a part of an inconceivable framework.

He didn't need to look any further than the concrete plans the general had the railway staff working on. There was a good chance that the trigger was a literal trigger.

He hated politics. He hated them with his entire being. It was why, up until that point, Lergen felt a distance from them and those who actively engaged with them. He only wished whoever controlled politics did it well.

Now those politics had forced their way into his domain—military planning—and he needed to face reality.

"Colonel Lergen? Are you all right?"

Lergen looked at the lieutenant colonel. He could see the obvious worry in his eyes. This man was a railway specialist. He was in charge of making the trains run on time. Maybe, just maybe he…

"Hey, Lieutenant Colonel. I feel bad to ask you this, but I need you to do something for me…" The colonel apologetically lowered his head. "I know you can't do much more than you already are. And I know you may think it's inhumane of me to ask for more. You'd be right to think so."

Even so, he needed to make the request.

The devil called *necessity* required more time. To get this time, Lergen needed the Railroad Department to devote itself to the Reich. As incredibly stupid as it seemed, it was necessary.

"I need more time before the battle shifts to an Ildoan front. Can you stretch out preparations for this schedule as long as possible until then?"

"Colonel, with all due respect…us railway operators are barely scraping by as it is."

Lergen knew this. It was self-evident. But he needed whatever amount of time he could get, no matter how little.

He didn't know if the attack was planned for mid-spring, or if it was an *early spring blitzkrieg*. If he could get even an extra month or two, there was a chance that things could turn out differently…

There was still hope.

It would be up to Counselor Conrad and the diplomats. If they screwed up, who knew what might befall the Empire. There was also a chance of things slowing down on the Ildoan side in terms of negotiations.

He could tell that the chances would be slim going into this.

But even a slim chance was still a chance. He wasn't going to let his only chance to potentially save the Empire, the Heimat, pass him by.

Would his struggle end in vain? Was it nothing but a pathetic last-ditch effort?

Colonel Lergen was fine with that. He knew what he needed to do.

He didn't know where this path would lead him. It didn't really matter to him. It may only slightly differ from Lieutenant General Rudersdorf's path. What mattered was that he felt it was a way to help the fatherland, and he'd do anything for the nation's sake.

That's what it meant to be a senior staff officer.

He could no longer afford to stand idly by as the time he no longer had slipped through his fingers.

"I need more time to save the Reich. To save our country. Please. Do whatever you can to buy me some."

No longer concerned with appearances, Lergen was practically begging Uger at this point. The train operator let his shoulders fall and slumped over before letting out an exhausted, sad laugh.

"Looks like I'll be putting in much more overtime from here on. I doubt I'll be able to head home at all. I can already see my daughter crying."

The man was a good husband and father. Lergen knew this but gave the man his tall order nevertheless. It was his job, and he was going to do it, but this didn't mean he didn't feel bad about it.

"I'm sorry. Feel free to hate me for this, Lieutenant Colonel."

"I will, but either way…let's do this, together."

They would struggle.

They would fight.

Tooth and nail, with everything they had.

""For the Reich!""

(The Saga of Tanya the Evil, Volume 10: Viribus Unitis, fin)

Appendixes

State of the War in Maps

State of the War in Maps

①

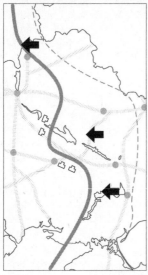

②

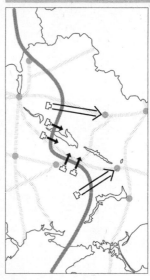

Part 1

1 General Zettour pulls back from the eastern front due to lack of manpower.

2 Questions arise pertaining to the mass reduction of eastbound trains and retreat from key railroad tracks.

3 The Federation Army pushes forward.

Part 2

1 Based on General Zettour's usual tactics, the Federation Army prepares for an assault at the base of their salient.

2 The Imperial Army creates the illusion that they will attack the salient with a feint operation. They effectively lure the enemy with carefully placed artillery assaults.

3 The main forces of the Imperial Army circle around the salient to execute a brazen full-scale assault.

③

④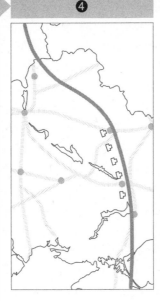

General Commentary

The con artist tips the scale in his favor.

Using the enemy's plans against them, General Zettour takes a high risk gamble by concentrating his forces to a dangerous extent and comes out victorious in a series of key battles.

By annihilating the Federation's ability to mount a major offensive in the near future, he brings stability to the eastern front.

Part 3

1 General Zettour attacks, using enemy railways to reclaim lost territory.

2 Successfully launches a sneak attack against the Federation Army while breaking their supply chain.

Part 4

1 The Imperial Army succeeds in driving into the east.

2 Learning from past experience, the Federation Army makes a quick escape but leaves their heavy artillery and tanks behind.

Afterword

Thank you for waiting for Volume 10 of *The Saga of Tanya the Evil*.

It's a cool, early spring right now... Well, maybe not while you're reading this, but let's just pretend it is for the sake of afterwords!

For those brave heroes out there who bought all ten volumes at once and read up until the afterword—it's a pleasure to meet you. Despite it being potentially out of season, I like to pretend it's the spring because that when I feel Pacific saury (or *sanma*, as we call them in Japanese) taste the best.

Enough with the casual formalities, though. Let's get back on topic; I owe you all an apology. I'm very sorry that you had to wait extra long for the tenth volume to come out...and that my delay caused Chika Tojo's tenth volume to become delayed as well.

For personal, non-health-related reasons, I needed more time to work on this one.

Please let me reiterate that the issues were not health related. Other than the impact on my mental health after getting an earful from *Tanya* readers about spending time on my other series like *Yakitori* and *Treason Agency* on social media, I'm as healthy as a horse.

I feel bad about subjugating my readers to my own personal trifles, so let's leave it that there were hardships happening behind the scenes.

Now, to get on topic.

Volume 10 is meant to focus on representing the Empire entering its death throes as a nation. I wanted to depict a feeling of there being nowhere to go, a sense of being trapped and helpless. An impulsive thirst for a way out to escape where the country is heading.

I may have spent a wee bit too much time going into detail regarding these depictions... Part of me thinks I made this buildup slightly too long.

That buildup, though, is about to explode from the next volume and onward.

Here's a different, totally unrelated topic about something I enjoy.

I think it's so cool when the serious middle management types such as Lieutenant Colonel Drake, Colonel Calandro, and Colonel Lergen endure the many occasions a pain churns their stomachs!

Keep this and the subtitle for Volume 11 (*Alea Iacta Est*) in mind, and well, this is kind of a spoiler, but look forward to the bright light emitted by the Empire in the next volume.

I'll finish with something I imagine is already slowly getting out there: Tanya's up-and-coming movie.

There are a lot of factors that go into these things, but with the help of my friends at NUT studios, I'm thinking the movie, which will depict its own original story, should be out around the time we're pushing to release Volume 11.

Well, it's less than I'm thinking and more like my editor in chief is dreaming this will happen.

And for those authors out there who were picked up by an editor and managed to make their debut... When we give predictions for when our next book is set to release, sometimes things like printer mishaps and spelling errors cause setbacks...

Well, this time, my editor saw me through with a brilliant, beautiful smile on his face, so you other writers out there needn't worry about me.

I'll finish by saying thanks where it's due.

The only reason I've managed to get this far is thanks to so many people who have supported me. A lot of people collaborated to make this volume happen as well.

I want to thank my designer Next Door Design, the people in charge of the printing press in Tokyo, my editors Fujita and Tamai, as well as my illustrator Shinotsuki.

I'm sorry to always cause you all so much trouble.

And while this may be a bit too much information, and I know it will make my two editors laugh at me, I'll continue to do my best to give you guys some good news on the marriage front before I hit the grave.

I feel bad that I can never meet the deadlines and have the utmost appreciation for my readers who are willing to wait for me. The movie should be ready at any moment now.

I'll see you next time.

End of September 2018, *Carlo Zen*